Praise for Dead and Not So Buried

"Conway is to the ego-crazy world of Hollywood what Carl Hiaasen is to Florida's wacky underbelly. The exploits of Gideon Kincaid explode into an action-packed page-turner that is nothing short of hilarious."

— Rick Berman, writer and executive producer of *Star Trek*

"*Dead and Not So Buried* is good and goofy, comfortable as an old shoe and fresh as a daisy…I raced right through it, never quite knowing where Conway would take me next, laughing all the way."

— David Jacobs, creator of *Dallas* and *Knotts Landing*

"A fabulous read! If you loved *L.A. Confidential* or are a fan of Hammett, Chandler and Spillane, you are going to love this thriller—a page-turning tour de force that combines mystery, murder and mayhem with razor-sharp humor. Conway's ingenious plot with its show business milieu has more twists and turns than a bent corkscrew and his shocking dénouement will leave you begging for a sequel."

— E. Duke Vincent, author of *Mafia Summer, The Camelot Conspiracy*

"Conway knows his genre and he knows Hollywood. A fast, breezy caper that will keep you guessing and laughing."

— Mark Frost, author of *The List of Seven* and *The Second Objective*

"James L. Conway has fashioned a page-turning, surprising, and very funny thriller and he's created a gloriously messed-up hero, P.I. Gideon Kincaid. I look forward to encountering a lot more of Kincaid in the pages of Conway's future novels."

— Stephen Collins, actor and author of *Eye Contact*

DEAD
AND NOT SO
BURIED

DEAD
AND NOT SO
BURIED

A Gideon Kincaid Hollywood Thriller

James L. Conway

Seattle, WA

CAMEL
PRESS

Camel Press
PO Box 70515
Seattle, WA 98127

For more information go to: www.camelpress.com

Cover design by Sabrina Sun

DEAD AND NOT SO BURIED

www.jameslconway.com

ISBN: 978-1-60381-866-7 (Trade Paper)
ISBN: 978-1-60381-867-4 (eBook)
Library of Congress Control Number: 2011941570
10 9 8 7 6 5 4 3 2 1

Printed in the United States of America

For Rebecca

Contents

Prologue

Lightning ripped the sky like a knife through flesh.

Okay, that's a little much. Fact is, there was no lightning. Hell, there wasn't a cloud in the sky. But kidnapping is a heinous crime, heinous enough for a little atmosphere. So even if there was no lightning, there should have been.

The Kidnapper broke in through the rear gate. A crowbar snapped the rusted chain. His size eleven boots left a clear path across the dew-sodden grass, past the flowers, through the statues, to her chamber.

Having long since vacated her body, she couldn't hear the scratching and scraping as he broke into her sanctuary. Couldn't see him as he entered her cold, white room. Never felt him sweep her into his arms.

The Kidnapper shuddered. She looked terrible, much worse than expected. Her white gown was streaked with dirt and mildew. That shock of blond hair was reduced to just a few sparse, wispy patches. And her face was a mess. At least she didn't smell.

She fit easily inside the oversized burlap bag. He pulled the cord. Outside once more, he scanned the grounds with his sharp green eyes. Nothing. He cocked an ear. Just a solitary siren destroying someone's peace a few miles away.

He placed the ransom note in the doorway then tossed the bag over his shoulder and retraced his steps toward the rear gate. Except for stealing Marvel comic books from Harmon's Drug

Store when he was a kid and doing a little coke when he first got to Hollywood, this was the first time he'd ever broken the law. He'd expected the anxiety buzz, but the hard-on was a complete surprise.

His car was parked a block away. The top was down on his black SL 550. He placed her carefully on the back seat. He didn't bother buckling her in, though; after all, his victim had been dead for almost forty years.

He slipped behind the wheel of the convertible. Once he got the ransom he'd pay off the leasing company. He was getting sick of their repo threats. Everybody's repo threats.

The car purred to life. The kidnapper smiled as he put the car into gear and drove away from the cemetery. Unbelievable. He'd actually pulled it off. He'd kidnapped one of Hollywood's greatest icons.

And now everyone would have to pay.

The Beginning

I was in my office when the call came. Sitting at my desk admiring the front cover of a paperback novel. My paperback novel. *Rear Entry,* by Gideon Kincaid. That's me. Ex L.A. cop turned private detective turned novelist. The Joe Wambaugh of the PI set.

I should be so lucky. The book had only been out for two weeks. Too soon to tell if anyone would buy it. Dreams of fancy cars and private planes were on hold as I continued to earn a living poking through other peoples' lives.

Hillary came in from the outer office. "I'm sorry, Gideon," she said, her features twisted in compassion.

My own features were twisted in confusion. "Sorry about what?"

"I understand if you don't want to talk about it."

Hillary's my secretary, a smart twenty-five-year-old with all the good stuff—blond hair, blue eyes, great body. But there's a sweetness to Hillary, an endearing naivety that makes me look upon her as a little sister. All my thoughts about Hillary are pure. Well, almost all of them.

"I'll be happy to talk about it," I said. "If I had any idea what we were talking about."

"Death."

"If you're asking me to take a stand, I'm definitely against it."

I've known Hillary since she was ten years old. Her father, Jerry, was my partner for a couple of years when I was driving a black and white out of the West Valley Division. A couple of years ago she showed up looking for a job. I'd just lost my secretary, and Hillary needed the job, so I said sure. She didn't just want to be a secretary, she told me, she wanted to be a PI like me. I told her I'd show her the ropes but never really got around to it. Truth is, she's so good in the office I'd hate to lose her.

"Okay," she said. "I didn't think you'd want to talk about it. But it won't do you any good to, like, keep all that grief inside. It'll fester and feed on itself. Eat away at your insides until your soul dies and you become one of the walking dead. A spiritless zombie going through life like a blind man in a garden." She did that from time to time—rattled on in New Age nonsense. Something to do with her being a native Californian. "Anyway," she said. "Alex Snyder's on line two."

"Alex Snyder?"

"From the mortuary ..." She said it like only an idiot wouldn't know what she was talking about.

"Of course, the mortuary ..." I said, as if I knew what the hell she was talking about. It's never a good idea to let your secretary think you're an idiot. I picked up the phone. "Gideon Kincaid."

"This is Alex Snyder, from Westside Cemetery. I wonder if we could meet."

"Look, if this is some kind of sales call, I—"

"No, Mr. Kincaid. This is business. Important business. Please, I need to see you right away."

Somebody must've stolen a headstone, I thought. Or maybe his teenage daughter had run away. It didn't really matter. He needed help, and that's what I did for a living. "All right, Mr. Snyder. I'm on my way."

My office is in Sherman Oaks, in a strip mall on Ventura Boulevard. Above a pet store called The Bunny Hop. My romantic soul felt I should have an office in one of the funky old buildings on Hollywood Boulevard—much more Chandleresque. But I get the creeps in Hollywood. Frankly it scares the shit out of me. Not the weirdos, the gangs, or the homeless. But the decay. If society can let the Boulevard of Dreams turn into an urban nightmare, what chance does the rest of the city have?

Westside Cemetery is in Brentwood, about twenty minutes from Sherman Oaks, so I used the time in my car to catch up on my literary career.

"Bad news."

"Sales are slow?"

"Slow would be good. They're nonexistent. The publisher's decided the title's the problem. *Rear Entry* sounds like a sex manual for gay men."

I was talking to my agent, Elliot. He's got a boutique agency for writers on their way up. Or down. I wasn't sure which category I belonged in. "Elliot, the title was their idea."

"Everybody makes mistakes."

"Let them make mistakes with Grisham's next book."

"Almost nobody writes a bestseller their first time up. Not even Grisham."

"It took me three years to write *Rear Entry*, and now you're saying I have to write another book?"

"You told me you wrote for the pure joy of it."

"I was lying."

"I warned you writing was a tough way to get rich."

"I thought *you* were lying."

"Never fear, Bubele. It's not over until the buyer for Barnes and Noble sings. If they give us a doorway display, hell, who knows ..."

"Anything I can do to help? Interviews? Book signings?"

"Reality check, Gidman. You're nobody. James Patterson does interviews because he's famous. People will watch a show to see him. Ratings go up, he sells more books. It's a help you/help me kind of simpatico. Stephen King does a book signing because he's famous. People come to a bookstore just to see him. More people in the store mean sales go up. We've got that help you/help me thing going again."

"But they got famous writing books."

"Correctamundo, but they wrote bestsellers. Writing bestsellers made them famous. And fame is the ultimate passkey. Before you can hit the interview/book signing trail, *Rear Entry* needs to become a bestseller."

"But how will it become a bestseller if I can't do any interviews or book signings?"

"Welcome to Catch 22 Land—chicken and the egg and all that."

"So that's it? There's nothing I can do?"

"You could get famous first. Break a big murder case. Solve a million dollar diamond heist. Marry Lindsey Lohan. You need something to single you out, something to make people sit up and take notice."

Yeah, right, I thought. *Who's going to notice a two bit PI?* "All right, Elliot," I said. "Thanks for the advice."

"Wait, I've got one more piece of bread to throw upon the waters."

"What?"

"Don't give up your day job."

Dead and Not So Buried

There's something very soothing about cemeteries—all that grass, the flowers, the fountains, the birds. It's a shame they're wasted on the dead.

The Westside Cemetery is in the heart of Brentwood. It's small—only about two acres—but some of Hollywood's biggest stars are buried there.

I was shown into Alex Snyder's office by his secretary—a middle-aged woman who oozed warmth and compassion. Alex Snyder also oozed warmth and compassion. He was the kindly grandfather type—late sixties, thick gray hair, natty moustache, reassuringly plump. He smiled as I entered, shook my hand. "Mr. Kincaid, a pleasure to meet you."

"Please, call me Gideon."

"Gideon," he said, smiling.

"Will there be anything else?" the secretary asked.

"No, Bernice, thank you."

She closed the door. Snyder pulled a .45 Smith and Wesson out of his desk and shoved it in my face. "Where is she?"

"Get that gun out of my face before I make you eat it," I said. It's tough to talk tough with a gun an inch from your nose, but I didn't think he'd really pull the trigger.

He pulled the trigger. The bullet blew a hole in the wall a micro millimeter from my left ear.

There was a scream from outside the door then a fearful

Bernice asked, "Alex, are you okay?"

"Just dandy, Bernice," he said, his eyes never leaving mine. To me he said, "The next one is between your eyes. Now, where is she?!"

"Who?"

"Christine."

"Christine who?"

His eyes nearly bored holes in mine before he said, "You don't know, do you?"

"No."

A little more cornea drilling, then: "I believe you." He lowered the gun, backed away and sagged into his desk chair. "I'm sorry, Mr. Kincaid. I hate violence, but this kidnapping's got me a little crazy."

"Maybe you should start at the beginning."

"I got a call this morning at five-fifteen. One of the gardeners found Christine Cole's crypt open and her body missing."

Holy shit. "Christine Cole?"

Christine Cole was one of the biggest movie stars of the sixties. A model turned actress, she vaulted to fame the year after Marilyn Monroe died and took her place as Hollywood's "it" girl. A sultry blonde with a killer body, Christine oozed sex. And she used it. To the gossip columnists' delight, Christine unabashedly slept her way through the rich and famous. And she battled some personal demons with drugs and alcohol. But Christine also had talent, and she made a string of hit movies. Four, to be exact, and only four. Because, on a foggy April morning, a drunk Christine lost control of her silver Jaguar XKE on the Pacific Coast Highway and plunged to her death. She was thirty-three years old.

Her death had shocked the world. And, like that of Bogart and Monroe, Christine's fame had only increased since her passing. Her image was on everything from tee shirts and coffee mugs to perfume and push-up bras. A true Hollywood icon.

Someone had robbed her grave. Stolen her corpse.

Who steals a corpse?

I said, "There can't be much of her left after forty years. Just bones, right?"

"Bones. The gown she was buried in. And some jewelry. She was buried wearing a bracelet, necklace and diamond ring."

"Valuable?"

"On another body, no. But these were on Christine Cole."

"How much is the kidnapper asking?"

"Two million dollars."

It suddenly hit me. "Wait a minute … why'd you think I knew where the body was?"

"Your business card was attached to the ransom note."

"What?"

"The kidnapper says you have to deliver the money." He handed me the note. The words looked like they were cut out of a variety of magazine articles.

> IF YOU WANT TO SEE CHRISTINE AGAIN, HAVE GIDEON BRING $2,000,000 IN USED $100 BILLS TO THE NORTHWEST CORNER OF HOLLYWOOD AND VINE AT 3 P.M. TODAY, OR I'LL SELL THE BODY, BONE BY BONE.

My business card was paper-clipped to the top of the page. In the six years I'd been a PI, I must've given out hundreds of business cards. Was this guy an ex-client? Someone I'd interviewed? Someone who'd picked up my card from a desk? No way of knowing. "I'll be happy to deliver this ransom free of charge." I wanted to find out who this son of a bitch was.

"I appreciate that, but I'll pay for your time—as long as you promise me you won't do anything to jeopardize the safe return of Ms. Cole's remains."

In other words, don't let it get too personal. "I won't." Something was nagging at the back of my brain. There was a familiar aspect about all this, but I couldn't get it to bubble to the surface. "I'd like to see her crypt."

"The funeral itself was small, only thirty-five guests. But

outside the gates stood hundreds of reporters, photographers, police officers and fans."

We were standing in front of the open crypt. The marble facing had been pried off, the bronze casket slid open. The only thing inside was the dried remains of a few roses.

"I played the organ," Alex Snyder said. "You know what they requested? 'Yesterday.' Christine loved the Beatles."

A set of footprints in the still-wet grass led to a rear gate. The chain had been broken, snapped by a crowbar, from the looks of it. Probably used the same crowbar on the crypt. "I could talk to a few neighbors," I said. "See if anyone saw anything last night."

"Absolutely not! Don't talk to the neighbors. Or the police. Anyone. We'll be ruined if the tabloids find out we lost Christine Cole's body. I just want to pay the money and get her back."

"You realize the kidnapper might take the money and not return the body."

"I'll take that chance. Will you help me?"

I fingered the ransom note and my business card. "I don't think I have a choice."

Another Day, Another Couple Million

At two forty-five I got off the 101 at Vine and started south. In my trunk was a large black duffle bag filled with two million bucks in cash.

I didn't know what the kidnapper had planned for me, but I did know he—or she—was smart. I'd checked the ransom note and my business card for fingerprints. Nothing on the card, nothing on the notepaper or the magazine letters. But I didn't expect to find prints in obvious places. Any idiot would know to wear gloves when assembling a ransom note. But fingerprints are sometimes left in not so obvious places—embedded in the adhesive tape or on the back of cut-out letters. No such luck. Our kidnapper had been careful.

On the four corners of Hollywood and Vine there's a tattoo parlor, a pizza place, a rundown office building and a cut-rate drug store. Kind of underwhelming for Moviedom's most famous address. I found a spot on Vine just south of Hollywood and parked.

Another famous L.A. landmark is the Hollywood Walk of Fame. The bronze stars embedded in the sidewalks line both sides of Hollywood Boulevard from Gower to La Brea, and both sides of Vine from Yucca to Sunset. Over 2,400 stars are walked on by millions of people every year. I tell you this because, as I fed the meter, I happened to look down and notice that I was standing on Eddie Bracken's star.

I looked at the northwest corner of Hollywood and Vine. No one stood there. I looked around and saw no one who seemed to be looking at me, but I knew that somewhere, someone was watching every move I made.

I left the ransom in the trunk of the car, crossed the street and leaned against a building to wait.

Funny what goes through your mind at times like this. Christine Cole had died in 1967. If she'd lived she'd be almost eighty years old. Playing grandmothers. Great grandmothers. A wrinkled, gray-haired woman.

And that would be the way the world pictured her.

Not as the sumptuous blond who sizzled on the screen while making love to Warren Beatty in *Deadly Ransom*. Not the alluring young widow who'd seduced Paul Newman in *Never Again*.

She would be just another aging actress.

But Fate had something else in mind for Christine Cole. Forever young. Forever beautiful.

And I couldn't help but wonder, given the choice, which legacy would she have wanted?

A car alarm went off. The simple kind: HONK HONK HONK. These days nobody looks twice when a car alarm goes off. They are so easily activated. Someone bumps a car. Someone accidently triggers it while locking or unlocking a car. An alarm almost never means that a car's being stolen.

Except this time.

The HONK HONK HONK sounded familiar. I looked down the street just as my Ford Taurus squealed out of the parking space and roared down Vine. I bolted across Hollywood Boulevard—just missing a bus—and down Vine in pursuit of the car. I ran over Rex Ingram's star, Blanche Thebom's, Alistair Cooke's, Bronco Billy Anderson's, Greer Garson's and Red Buttons' … but it was too late. The car wove in and out of traffic, then turned a corner and disappeared. My Taurus and the two million dollars were gone.

Now I'll be the first to admit that not all my cases turned out the way I'd hoped. There were a couple of missing person cases where I'd struck out. A few blown surveillances. Hey, nobody's perfect. But having your car stolen with a two million dollar ransom inside is pretty fucking embarrassing.

Before I had too much time to feel sorry for myself I heard a cell phone ring. My cell phone. I answered. "Hello."

"Missing something?" A deep voice, cocky.

"Who is this?"

"You don't really expect me to tell you, do you? I like your car, Gideon. It's got a lot of get up and go. Too bad it got up and went." He laughed. Then I heard a HONK, the screech of brakes and the crash of broken glass. "Oops. You do have insurance, don't you Gideon? I'm afraid I've had a little fender bender." I could hear the engine roar and the receding sound of honking horns. "The engine still runs fine, so don't worry."

"Who is this?"

"You're the detective. You tell me."

I racked my brain trying to recognize the voice. I couldn't. "Am I going to get my car back, or is that part of the ransom, too?"

"That depends. The ransom in the trunk?"

"In used hundred dollar bills."

"Good man. I always thought you looked dependable."

"So we've never actually met?"

"Oh, we've met."

"When?"

"That's for me to know and you to figure out."

"What about Christine's body?"

"She'll be in the trunk of your car. I'll call your office in an hour and tell you where to find it."

"Wait. Why me?"

"Because you owe me, pal. You owe me big time." And with that, he hung up.

Number One on the Call Sheet

"You owe me, pal. You owe me big time."

Christ, what a lame line, the Kidnapper thought as he dropped the cell phone into his pocket. Right out of a bad TV show. Which is where it had come from. That guest shot on *Shadowchaser* a couple seasons ago.

The director had loved his performance. "Brilliant, Roy. You gave me the fucking chills."

Roy Cooper, by the way. Our Kidnapper.

Roy had modestly accepted the compliment while privately thinking he should get an Emmy for making such a bullshit line sound real, much less chilling. *Nobody talks like that in real life*, he thought.

Well, he'd been wrong. This was real life and he'd just laid the line on that private dick. Was it life imitating art or art imitating life? Who gave a shit, as long as Gideon Kincaid was now the one with fucking chills?

Roy took the entrance ramp onto the Westbound Santa Monica Freeway. Traffic was light; it wouldn't take long to reach LAX.

Roy had enjoyed making *Shadowchaser*. It had been shot on location in Vancouver, a beautiful city. They'd had that cute little redheaded production assistant, Kimberly, who he'd banged in his trailer on the last day of shooting. The *Shadowchaser* performance had helped get him the role in *Jailbait*. The movie that was supposed to make him a star. *Yeah, right.*

Well, now he was the one writing the script. He was the one controlling his own destiny. No more casting offices filled with the same collection of hunky unemployed actors. No more five-line roles as bad guy of the week. No more being listed number twelve or thirteen on the call sheet. He was the star of this production. And this time he would get Hollywood's attention, once and for all.

For the second time that day Roy pulled into the LAX long-term parking lot 3. A few hours earlier he'd parked his SL550 in an isolated corner, then taken the shuttle to the terminal and a bus back to Hollywood for his three o'clock 'appointment' with Gideon.

There was so much to remember, Roy thought as drove through the lot. So many details to get right. The plan would only work if the cops couldn't find you. And they had so many ways to turn a fingerprint, a cotton fiber, a footprint or a speck of dust into an ID. He'd worn surgical gloves to make the ransom notes. But he couldn't very well wear surgical gloves driving Kincaid's car. Talk about looking suspicious. He'd thought about leather driving gloves, but no one wears driving gloves in a boring piece of six-cylinder crap like this Taurus. He'd have to wipe down the car.

He'd worn gloves last night, so fingerprints weren't a problem. But footprints could be. And there was always the possibility that dirt from the cemetery had clung to his clothes. So he ditched the gloves, crowbar, pants, jacket and boots in five different dumpsters, in five different parts of town. He'd also worn size-eleven boots even though he actually wore size-ten shoes. Never hurts to confuse the enemy.

Roy reached the Mercedes, parked next to it. One of his first acting jobs had been on *Criminal Minds*. He'd played a cop-hating, tobacco-chewing redneck, who ran a chop shop. In one scene he'd had to show someone how to steal a car in thirty seconds. The producers had hired a technical consultant—a reformed thief named Fingers—to teach him. Roy had learned well. During the scene, he jimmied the car, used a dent puller to disable the steering wheel lock and stuck a screwdriver into the column to jump-start the car. Elapsed time: twenty-eight seconds.

And now, once again, art was imitating life, or life imitating art or whatever. In Hollywood, Roy had jimmied open Kincaid's Taurus, setting off the alarm. A quick tap with a dent puller had disabled the steering wheel lock; a little jabbing and twisting with a screwdriver had started the engine, shutting off the alarm.

Now he pulled the screwdriver out of the steering column, killing the engine. Fingers had also shown Roy how to break into a trunk using a screwdriver and a hammer. So, with a quick glance to make sure no one was watching, Roy popped open the trunk, found a black duffle bag, and unzipped it. Inside were stacks and stacks of hundred dollar bills.

Two million dollars. More money than Roy had ever seen. Ever dreamed about. His fantasies were always about fame. Being recognized. Being idolized. Being asked for autographs. Oh, mansions, cars, yachts and private jets were in there somewhere. But they were the icing on the cake. It was the head-turning, people-whispering, finger-pointing kind of fame he relished.

Still, two million bucks was nice. Especially since it was just the beginning.

Roy opened the Mercedes' trunk. Inside was a burlap bag full of bones. Roy swapped the bag of money for the bag of bones, just like he promised. Well, *almost* like he promised.

He hoped that shitbag Gideon Kincaid liked surprises. This was going to be the first of many.

Who Hates You, Baby?

As far as I knew there was only one person who really hated me. My ex-wife. And the feeling was mutual. Oh, I've pissed a lot of people off during my thirteen years as a cop and six as a PI. Nobody likes getting arrested, and as a private eye I've nailed people for everything from insurance fraud to adultery. But usually when you catch someone doing something wrong, they know it's wrong. They don't hate you for catching them; they hate getting caught. It's not personal.

Well, with our Kidnapper it sounded personal. "You owe me, pal. You owe me big time." Who the hell was it?

I called Hillary, asked her to pick me up, then paced along Hollywood and Vine making a possible enemies list.

Robbie Lipman. I accidently hit him in the face with a BB gun when we were twelve and knocked out all his teeth. Boy was he mad. But that was twenty-eight years ago, and now he's a dentist making half a mil a year. Hell, he should be grateful. I'm the one who got him interested in dentistry in the first place.

Sister Margaret Russo. She tried to run me over in the parish bus after I arrested her for playing Pull the Pokey with boys in her second grade class. But she's still locked up in the Sybil Brand Institute, teaching bull dykes how to conjugate Latin verbs.

Hillary drove up in her blue Prius. "This wouldn't have

happened if you let me work in the field with you," she said.

"If you'd been here you would have done something stupid like chase him."

"And caught and, like, captured him. Case closed."

"Or he might've gotten away, kept the money and the body."

"He might anyway."

"Too true." I told Hillary about the phone call and the cryptic, 'You owe me, pal.' "So," I asked. "Who hates me?"

"Stacy."

"Besides my ex-wife."

"I've been ticked off at you a couple of times."

"You don't count."

"What'd his voice sound like?"

"Male. Deep. No real accent."

"Maybe he, like, disguised it."

"That's hard to do without it sounding phony. This guy sounded natural."

Hillary sucked on her lower lip as she thought about it. God she was cute when she did that. "Eli Cochran?"

Eli Cochran. He was an artist. He painted feet, mostly, but he was very good. And successful. His toes were hanging all over the country. One day his wife woke up and he was gone. Along with the bank accounts and a gorgeous USC co-ed. His wife wanted me to find him. I did. Living on a houseboat near Seattle. I dutifully told the wife, expecting her to send a divorce lawyer. She sent a hood with a hammer, who crushed Eli's hands. Eli didn't blame the hood or the wife. He blamed me. He blamed me so much he threw a Molotov cocktail through my office window. Hillary grabbed the fire extinguisher while I chased him down in the parking lot. He pleaded temporary insanity and was sentenced to the State Mental Facility at Camarillo.

"No, Eli's still locked up." Suddenly something caught my eye. I couldn't believe it! "Stop the car," I shouted.

Hillary swerved to the curb and slammed on the brakes. "What? You see your car?"

"No." I pointed. "Look." She followed my gaze to a bus stop. Sitting on the bench was a middle-aged woman reading a paperback book. *My* paperback book, *Rear Entry*.

Hillary smiled. "Cool ..."

The woman was about halfway through. Probably at the part when the detective, Digby Magee, discovers his beautiful client is actually a porn star. "Think she likes it?"

"She looks positively riveted."

I had this fantasy: I'd see someone reading my book and sit down next to them. I'd look over and ask if they liked the book. The answer, of course, was that they loved it. Then the reader would look at me, flip to the back cover, see the author's picture and realize I wrote the book. I would sign the book and leave, basking in their praise.

Dare I? What the hell. I opened the door. "I'll be right back."

As I sat next to the woman I noticed she was on page 156. Digby has just slept with his beautiful client for the first time. I've been with a few women in my time, and I'm far from a prude, but I've got to tell you, writing a sex scene is weird. You feel like you're making love with the whole world watching. But I went for it and got pretty specific.

Anyway, as she turned the page, I asked, "I've seen that book around. Any good?"

The bus came. The woman stood, looked at me. She cocked her head, recognizing me, unable to figure out from where. Then it hit her. She turned the book over, looked at the picture, then at me. "You wrote this?"

I was smiling from ear to ear. "Yes, ma'am."

"Pervert!" She threw the book at me and got onto the bus.

That's why they call them fantasies.

Puzzle Pieces

As promised, the kidnapper/car thief called my office an hour after he stole my car. "Your car's at LAX. Long term parking lot 3."

"Are the bones in the trunk?"

"Open it and find out." He sounded final, like he was going to hang up. I eyed the Sony tape recorder I'd hooked up to the phone, hoping to record enough of his voice to jar my memory.

"Wait. Don't hang up yet. At least give me a clue who you are."

"I am anyone." The line went dead.

"I am anyone," I repeated, rewinding the tape. "What the fuck does that mean?"

"It means he's, like, very metaphysical," Hillary said. "Or very confused."

I replayed the tape so Hillary could hear his voice.

> "Your car's at LAX. Long term parking lot 3."
>
> "Are the bones in the trunk?"
>
> "Open it and find out."
>
> "Wait. Don't hang up yet. At least give me a clue who you are."
>
> "I am anyone."

"Recognize the voice?"

"No."

"Me neither," Hillary said. "But he sounds all full of himself. Superior, like."

I rewound the tape to the end of the call.

"I am anyone."

"Listen to that," I said. "Hear the conviction in his voice? The pride? It's not an idle statement. It definitely means something. I just don't know what ..."

I found my Taurus parked in lot 3. The front bumper was crushed, both headlights broken. A 757 roared above us as Hillary asked, "You think this means he got on a plane?"

"I think it means he's a lousy driver."

There were scratches on the driver's side door where he'd obviously used a jimmy to get in. The steering column was pried open and the trunk lock had been punched out. The car was dusty; I hadn't washed it in a few weeks, so I could clearly see the areas where he'd wiped away his prints. This guy wasn't making any mistakes.

I opened the trunk. The duffle bag was gone, replaced with a smaller burlap bag. I unzipped it enough to see what was inside—bones.

"The knee bone's connected to the thigh bone. The thigh bone's connected to the hip bone ..."

Alex Snyder stood over Christine Cole's bones, now spread out on a worktable in his mortuary lab. In another corner of the lab, a mortician was working on the naked body of an old man.

"I know the song," I said. "Want me to sing along?"

"No. But the song is anatomically correct. Unlike these bones."

"What?"

"We've got three femurs. Only one scapula and no humerus. These aren't Christine's bones. Some of them aren't even human. Dog or monkey, I think. And the jewelry's missing."

That son of a bitch, I thought. "That son of a bitch," I said.

"Why'd he switch the bones?"

"To blackmail you again," I said. "Or the Cole estate. Or he may just plan to sell the bones on the Internet to the highest bidder. A lot of movie nuts would pay a fortune for one of Christine Cole's bones."

Something was working in the back of my mind. Why did all this sound so familiar to me?

"A lifetime spent in the eternal care business and I'm going to be remembered as the moron who lost Christine Cole." In the seven hours I'd known Alex Snyder, I'd seen him go from a grandfather oozing warmth and compassion to a gun-wielding maniac to his current incarnation—a hopeless man on the brink of despair. He crossed to a desk, picked up a phone. "Do you happen to know the number of the police?"

Then it hit me. "Wait," I said. "Give me a couple more days. There may be a way to get the body back."

"Really. How?"

"Find the kidnapper."

"You know who it is?"

"No. But I think I just figured out where to start looking."

The Plot Thickens

I love bookstores. Picking up a new book fires my imagination. Inside could be adventure, suspense, humor, passion—or the key to catching a kidnapper.

I read a lot of books. Mostly mysteries. And I read even more book jackets, trying to decide what to buy. Somewhere, sometime, in the last few months, I vaguely remembered reading a book jacket that had something to do with Christine Cole and kidnapping.

So I drove to the Barnes and Noble just a few miles away in Westwood and parked myself in front of the mystery section. There was a whole wall of mysteries, hundreds of them. I'd decided to start my search in the A's and work my way toward Z. A little predicable, I know, but also logical. But first I had to make a little detour, to the K's. Kemelman, Kemprecos, Kijewski ... Kincaid. By God, there it was, *Rear Entry*. Two copies. I took one off the shelf and looked at it. The cover art was very cool. There was a close-up of a terrified beautiful woman, and in her eyes you could see the reflection of a man standing in a doorway, a .38 in his hand.

On the back cover was a drawing of a chisel-faced detective kissing a nearly naked blonde. The blurb:

> When starlets start dying in tinsel town, there's only one man for the job: Hollywood's toughest PI, Dempsey Magee.

There followed a few quotes by popular thriller writers:

> Written by a PI who knows what he's talking about.
>
> A rough and tumble ride through the mean streets of L.A.
>
> Dashiell Hammett would've loved this guy.

I knew the publisher had solicited quotes from some of their other writers to help sell the book, but I still enjoyed reading them.

Inside the back cover was a black and white photo of me and short bio. It would've been nice if I looked anything like the drawing of the hunk on the cover of the book, but I don't. My hair is light brown, on the long side, a bit unkempt. My eyes are hazel, my nose a little too small and my chin, a little too big. A sly smile tugged at my lips. You know that kid in class who was always making wisecracks? That's me.

The bio mentions my years as a cop and PI and says I'm currently sleuthing away in L.A. while I work on my next book. I would be working on my next book if I could decide what to write. I knew it would be another Dempsey Magee mystery, but I hadn't decided on the plot. A crooked charity. Jury tampering. Or maybe illegal shenanigans at Santa Anita racetrack. I had a few ideas but none that really turned me on. Based on my agent's less than glowing assessment of *Rear Entry's* prospects, I'd better decide quick.

I put the book back, moved to the A's, pulled down a copy of Edward S. Aarons' *The Sinners,* and went to work.

Two hours later I found eleven books I wanted to buy and the book I was looking for, *Eternal Love*, by Barry Winslow. On the cover was a drawing of Christine Cole's open, empty crypt. Sound familiar? The blurb on back:

> Panic strikes Hollywood when a madman kidnaps the corpse of Moviedom's sexiest leading lady, Christine Cole.

Barry Winslow's picture was inside the back cover. A handsome guy, maybe fifty, with a long face, bushy eyebrows and impossibly green eyes that looked out at you with fierce intelligence. But he was trying a little too hard to look hip in his luau shirt, jeans, and snakeskin cowboy boots.

His bio said:

> Winslow is the author of three books and creator and executive producer of the hit TV series, *Payback.*

I'd seen *Payback* a few times. The hero was a world-weary ex-boxer turned detective. Good stories with lots of action. I liked it.

I wondered for a moment whether I could turn my hero, world-weary PI Dempsey Magee, into the main character in a TV series. Maybe I'd ask Barry Winslow about it—right after I asked him if he knew who kidnapped Christine Cole.

Then it hit me. Those three words: *I am anyone.* What better way to describe a writer? He becomes all his characters. All his characters are part of him. He is, in fact, *anyone.* Promising, very promising.

My collection of eleven books in hand, I was heading for the cashier when a thought stopped me in my tracks. What if word spread through a big chain like Barnes and Noble that an obscure new mystery was starting to sell like hot cakes? Would they order more copies and move it to the front display? I grabbed the two copies of *Rear Entry*, and, balancing the pile of books like a street juggler, made my way to the front counter.

The cashier, Emily—if you could believe her nametag—smiled. "Looks like someone's going to open their own bookstore." Emily had UCLA co-ed written all over her. She was cute, if bookish, nineteen or twenty at the most. Brown hair tied in a bun, big brown eyes hiding behind retro glasses. Freckles everywhere.

"Just doing a little catching up." I showed her the two copies of *Rear Entry*. "And buying a treat for a couple of my friends. This is the best mystery I've read in years. A real rough and tumble ride through the streets of L.A." A stupid thing to say, I know. But I'd just read the quote and, you know how it is.

"Really," she said, looking at the cover. "With that title I thought it was about, well, an alternative lifestyle." She turned the book over. "Isn't that funny. Amos Parker thought it was a rough and tumble ride, too."

Oops. "He's a great writer. He should know."

"Maybe I'll give it a try."

"I bought your only two copies, but tell you what ... why don't you keep that one and I'll buy another when you order more."

"Actually, I was just being nice. I'm majoring in eighteenth-century English literature and I think pulp trash like this has poisoned the minds of the masses and slowed the mental evolution of the species." She smiled sweetly and handed me back the book. "Now, will that be cash or charge?"

Poisoning the minds of the masses, indeed! I tried to think of a witty comeback for Emily. Some intelligent defense of the literary form I love. An example of how mystery fiction has bettered the lot of the common man. How the hours of entertainment enjoyed by reading "pulp trash" has inspired ordinary men to extraordinary acts of courage or great leaps in science or even little leaps. But I couldn't think of any.

Okay, mysteries haven't added a lot to the collective knowledge of our planet. But is there anything wrong with giving the masses a little pleasure? Eighteenth-century English literature, indeed. You need a dictionary to read that shit.

Anyway, I looked into those freckle-framed eyes and said, "Cash."

Take that, college girl.

Beam Me Up

I drove through the Paramount gates at a few minutes after six p.m. I spent a lot of time here a few years ago when they hired me to find out who was stealing props from the set of *Star Trek*. Things like phasers and tricorders kept disappearing from Paramount and showing up at *Star Trek* conventions held all over the country. Authentic props from the show, whether stolen or not, were worth thousands of dollars. I hid a video camera in the prop room and caught the thief poaching two bars of Ferengi latinum and a Klingon disrupter—the perpetrator was one of the studio medics.

Paramount was thrilled and spread the word about my reliability to the other studios. Since then Warner Brothers had asked me to find out who was leaking script secrets from *Gossip Girl* to the *National Enquirer* (one of the hairdressers) and Fox had asked me find out who stole the President's chair from the *24* set (the key grip).

Getting in to see a hot producer like Barry Winslow wasn't easy. But Hollywood is a town of well-scratched backs. Everyone is always doing a favor for everyone else. So I called Paramount's head of security and he called Barry Winslow, who agreed to give me a few minutes.

In the *Payback* production office I was told Barry had been called to the set. They were shooting on the New York street, an amazingly lifelike collection of storefronts and shops. They even have a subway entrance.

I arrived to find Rick "Tornado" Marshall—the world weary ex-boxer—standing in the middle of the street talking to Barry Winslow. Winslow's outfit matched the one on the book cover—luau shirt, jeans and snakeskin cowboy boots.

Tornado, a former heavyweight boxer, stood six foot three, a buzz cut framing his battered face. His dialogue on the show was usually limited to a few grunts and lines like his patented, "Big mistake." He wasn't a great actor, but he oozed charisma, and that's what TV stars are made of.

Tornado and Barry were surrounded by five guys dressed in black Ninja outfits, an impatient director and a bored crew. Tornado didn't look happy. "Why can't my shirt be ripped?"

"Tornado," Winslow said, "your shirt's ripped in every episode. It's becoming a joke. The audience knows we're coming to the final action scene because your shirt always gets ripped."

"How else they going to see my muscles?"

"They don't have to see your muscles every week. The audience tunes in to watch you kick ass, not flex your lats."

"I look good in a ripped shirt."

"You look good in anything, babe. Now, come on, this week let's just try it with our clothes on."

Tornado draped a muscle-bound arm around Barry's shoulder. "I spend two hours a day in the gym, Barry. Two hours of lifting, pressing, curling, sculpting. Two hours of aching and sweating. Jumping. Jogging. Rowing. Light bag. Heavy bag. Two hours every day. And I don't do it to be hidden under a fucking shirt." The friendly arm around Barry's neck was now a headlock and the producer's face was turning bright crimson.

"I see what you mean, Tornado," Barry croaked. "You've got a great body, be a shame not to show it off."

"Exactly." Tornado released his grip. "That's what I love about television," Tornado said. "It's a collaborative art."

"I don't know why I put up with this shit." Winslow and

I were walking back to his office. His color had returned to normal, but his ego was still sucking oxygen. "I got the idea for *Payback* watching the Tornado's last fight. Remember how Jacobson had Tornado on the ropes; landing punch after punch to his head, and the dumb, crazy, son of a bitch just wouldn't go down? There was no quit in that man. I said, 'Now there's a *real* hero. What he lacks in talent, he makes up for in courage and stubbornness.' Americans love that. Clint Eastwood in *Dirty Harry*. Bruce Willis in *Die Hard*. Harrison Ford as Indiana Jones. John Wayne in just about anything. Tornado was a natural.

"So I go to see him the next day in the hospital. He's just found out that after he pays his trainer, corner men, sparring partner, publicist, training camp, ex-wife, and taxes, all he's going to have left from his three million dollar purse is eight grand. Not a lot to show for having your jaw shattered, your nose broken and your brains scrambled. And he was depressed as hell. So when I told him I was going to make him a star he did everything but kiss me. Talk about grateful, hell, during the first season he called me 'Mr. Winslow.' Always respectful, never changed a line of dialogue. Used to begin every interview with, 'I owe it all to Mr. Winslow.'

"Then *Payback* makes the top ten. Tornado is on the cover of *Entertainment Weekly* and *Time*. He gets a big time agent and falls in love with a money-sucking bitch who fills his head with buckets of shit. Suddenly all the scripts stink and he wants to choreograph all the fights. He's got to have more money. Bigger trailer. Full-time masseuse. Chef. And now it's ripped shirts in every show ... Christ, I hate television."

"Why don't you stick to writing books?"

"Money. I produce twenty-two episodes of *Payback* a year. I make more money producing just one episode than I've made writing my three books combined."

We entered the Cooper Building. As we walked into Winslow's office he was descended upon by his assistant—an officious black woman who must've outweighed Tornado by twenty-five pounds—and with her dreadlocks, pierced ears, nose and eyebrows, she looked meaner.

"Mission accomplished," she said. "The rough cut's been changed to three o'clock. Music spotting at five. I moved the story meeting to eight-thirty Friday morning and casting's been set for eleven. At one-fifteen the limo will take you to LAX and Air France will whisk you away to Paris." She handed him an envelope. "Tickets for you and the lucky lady. Don't forget your passports."

"Thanks, Maggie." Maggie went back to her desk and Winslow turned to me with a sly smile. "Another perk that comes with producing a television show. I can afford to fly to Paris and impress the shit out of hot young actresses. Not to mention my two million dollar condo in Century City or my Porsche." He slapped the plane ticket into the palm of his hand with a grim satisfaction. "When I was writing books I lived in a one bedroom dump in North Hollywood and drove a Volkswagen Rabbit. Believe me, rich is better." He settled into a leather chair behind a mahogany desk filled with piles of scripts and DVDs. He gestured for me to sit as he asked, "So, what can I do for you?"

I thought about telling him that I, too, wrote novels. Well, a novel. That I thought Dempsey would make a great character for a TV series and maybe we could develop it together. After all, I'd like to fly to Paris whenever I got horny. And a condo in Century City sounded great. But I was here on business. Somebody had desecrated Christine Cole's grave. Blackmailed the cemetery. Switched the bones. And my only lead was Winslow. In spite of my earlier musing on the *I am anyone* connection to other writers, I didn't think Winslow had done it. He didn't sound like he needed the money, and I'd never met him before so I don't think I *owed him big time*. But his voice did sound a little like the guy on the phone, so, watching him carefully for any reaction, I said, "Somebody's kidnapped Christine Cole's remains."

"You're kidding."

"Nope. Just like in your book. Someone broke into the crypt, blackmailed the cemetery for two million bucks."

Winslow barked out a laugh. "You know I've always worried about some bozo reading something I've written then doing it for real. A really rockin' bank robbery. A cool murder. But I never figured anyone'd actually try and kidnap Christine!"

Winslow's surprise seemed genuine. If he was lying, he was damn good at it. I said, "The kidnapper also switched the bones when we made the ransom exchange."

"Just like my book. Hey, I hope the real life case has a happier ending."

So did I. In Winslow's book the villain went on to steal the bodies of Jean Harlow and Marilyn Monroe before finally being killed in a bloody shootout.

"Just out of curiosity, Mr. Winslow, where were you last night?"

"What? Am I a suspect?"

"No. But you did write the book, and while anyone could have read *Eternal Love* and gotten the idea, well, you did get the idea first. So, I have to ask."

"You're not going to like the answer. I was home. Alone."

"See any of the neighbors? Talk to anyone on the phone?"

"Nope."

"Then you don't have an alibi."

Winslow's impossibly green eyes flared. "You're starting to sound more like a cop than a PI."

"Sorry. I used to be a cop. Old habits die hard."

"Cop, huh? LAPD?"

I nodded. "Thirteen years."

"Why'd you quit?"

Hell of a question. I could have told him the real reason—that if I hadn't resigned I would have gone to jail. Instead I gave him my stock answer: "I got tired of all the bullshit."

"Yeah," he said, interested. "Like what?" Writers love talking to cops. Cops are the living, breathing, three-dimensional versions of what writers just imagine. And an endless source of story ideas.

"Like suspects who kept trying to change the subject when I was interviewing them."

He bristled. "Look, Gideon, I've got nothing to hide." Then he laughed self-consciously. "It's just that I don't have an alibi for last night."

"What about for three o'clock this afternoon?"

He started to look nervous, uncomfortable. "Why three o'clock?"

"That's when the kidnapper picked up the ransom."

"This is spooky, man. At three o'clock I was standing in front of the Cinerama Dome waiting for my agent."

"Then you do have an alibi."

"No. I waited half an hour but he never showed up."

"You call his office?"

"Yeah. But he was out."

"But you talked to him when you made the appointment."

"No. Maggie gave me the message." He called out, "Maggie!" She stuck her dreadlock-drenched head in the door. "Did you talk to Glen personally about that three o'clock meeting?"

She seemed confused for an instant, and then brightened. "No. A message was left on voicemail during lunch."

"See if you can get him now." She ducked back out.

"Anybody see you at the Dome?"

"Sure, plenty of people walked by. Nobody who'd remember me."

"So you don't have an alibi."

"No." He laughed again, but this one was humorless. "If I didn't know better I'd say someone was trying to set me up."

Maggie yelled from her desk: "Glen's still out."

Winslow shook his head. "Shit. Well, as soon as I talk to him I'll find out if he called or not, but in the meantime, you'll just have to take my word that I didn't steal the body."

One thing you learn in my business is that everybody lies. Not all the time and not always on purpose. But they lie. And if you're good at your job you learn to tell when someone's lying. Sometimes it's obvious: sweat on the upper lip, halting answers as their mind races. Sometimes it's subtle: a contraction of the pupil, the picking of a cuticle. Sometimes it's invisible and you have to go on instinct. Nothing Winslow did gave him away, but deep down I knew he was lying. So was Maggie. That momentary hesitation when Winslow asked her about the agent gave her away. She didn't know what the hell he was talking about, but—ever the loyal assistant—she'd cover his back until he could explain.

Winslow suddenly stood up. "So if you don't have any more questions I've got a TV show to run ..."

I had two choices. Turn up the heat on the interview, and risk getting thrown off the lot by studio security. Or withdraw gracefully and do a little more checking into the world of the increasingly enigmatic Barry Winslow. I stood up, took out one of my business cards and handed it to him. "Thanks for your time, Barry. If you think of anything else, please call me."

"Will do. And let me know how it turns out. After all, I've got a vested interest."

At the very least ...

Shadow Boxing

Everyone knows the traffic in L.A. sucks so I won't bore you with all the details about the jackknifed semi on the Hollywood Freeway, or the hour and ten minutes it took me to drive the seven lousy miles back to my office.

Okay, I've got to say this much. The goddamn truck wasn't even on my side of the freeway; still, traffic snarled as everyone stopped to look. I mean, come on. Is life really that boring?

When I walked into the office at five after eight Hillary was still there, stacks of files piled on her desk.

"I've got it," she said.

"Well, keep away from me until you're not contagious anymore."

"No, Gideon. I've got the answer."

"Great. What was the question?"

"Who hates you? Who do you owe big time?"

"That's two questions."

"But the same answer." She held up one of the files. "Yasif Begorian."

Yasif Begorian, a former client and owner of New Horizon Loan Company—really just a fancy name for his pawnshop in Van Nuys. It was right across from the Criminal Courts Building, sandwiched between two bond bailsmen, and a favorite stop for relatives of the recently arrested as they sell whatever they can to finance a handcuff-free homecoming.

New Horizon was a twenty-four-hour operation, since crime tends to flourish while the planet's back is to the sun. Yasif was convinced that his brother-in-law, Reza, who worked the late shift, was stealing him blind. So I installed a hidden camera inside one of the guitars hanging on the wall. I should have known this job had bad juju when Reza sold the guitar the first night and my camera disappeared out the door.

The next day I planted a new camera inside a moose head over the door. Who the hell would buy a moose head, right? Unfortunately, the camera had a short. The moose head must've been cured in some kind of combustible material because as soon as the spark hit it, the damn thing burst into flames. The fire spread to a fake Persian rug on sale for two hundred and sixty-eight dollars. The fully engulfed rug fell onto a rack of cheap pink and yellow chiffon dresses stolen off the docks in San Pedro and sold to Yasif for twenty-five cents on the dollar. Highly flammable chiffon dresses. The fireball spread to a display of cheap stuffed animals bought from a bankrupt Taiwanese businessman for twenty cents on the dollar. The panda bear display was next to the storeroom where Yasif kept five cases of fireworks bought for fifteen cents on the dollar from a Mexican importer who was being deported. The flames crawled across the floor and gleefully leaped into the storeroom.

The explosion blew out windows for two blocks.

As luck would have it, Yasif's fire insurance had run out only two days earlier. The envelope containing the payment was in a dead letter bin in the post office because Yasif had used counterfeit stamps bought for ten cents on the dollar.

Yasif's shop was a total loss. And he was sued for $832,000 by the surrounding businesses.

Yasif, of course, blamed me. He swore that one day he'd eat my heart while jackals ripped the skin from my bones and buzzards fought over my eyeballs.

But before Yasif could even spell retaliation, his brother-in-law Reza stabbed him in the back. Literally. Reza went ballistic when he found out Yasif had hired me to spy on him. The stabbing severed Yasif's spinal cord. Reza's in Lompoc doing five to fifteen, and Yasif, now a quadriplegic, has found religion. I'm told he wheels himself back and forth in his house—the Koran in his lap—in an electric wheelchair bought at a medical supply house fire sale for fifteen cents on the dollar.

"I thought of Yasif," I told Hillary. "But he's found God. Besides, Yasif's got a big time accent. Our kidnapper's voice is strictly American born and bred."

She turned back to the pile of files. "I'll keep looking."

"Yes, you will. But not tonight." I picked up her car keys, dangled them in front of her. "Go home."

"Are you going home?"

"No. I've got work to do." I was planning to hit the computer, run a few checks on Barry Winslow.

She sat back down. "Then so do I."

"Go home, Hillary. I'll be fine."

"I'm sure you will, but I won't." She tried to sound angry, but mostly she came off as nervous. Standing up to your boss is tough. Saying something heartfelt, something that really matters to you, is even harder. "You may think of me as, like, just a secretary, Gideon. But I want more. You promised I could become a detective. Well, I've taken every criminology class UCLA Extension has to offer. Studied karate and Tai Kwon Do. I've taken Handgun Safety classes, Advanced Targeting Techniques and Street Combat Training. I've contacted the Bureau of Security and Investigative Services. All I need now is three years investigative experience, six thousand verifiable hours with a licensed firm. Investigative experience doesn't mean answering phones and making coffee. It doesn't mean picking you up when your car's stolen. It means actually working cases. Surveillance. Background checks. Interviews." Hillary's words sounded rehearsed but sincere. She took a ragged breath then delivered her ultimatum. "I'm sorry, Gideon, but if you don't give me the opportunity I'll find someone who will."

God, I was proud of her. We don't often put ourselves on the line. Expose what we really want. Set ourselves up for a rejection that can have life-changing consequences. Maybe if we did, we'd have a better world. Maybe if people actually stood for something in their everyday lives, we'd see happier, prouder people walking down the street. Maybe they'd have enough pride that they wouldn't have to stop and stare at every goddamn truck that flips over.

Anyway, I looked into Hillary's hopeful eyes. So blue. So beautiful. I said, "There's a lot about this job that really sucks. The hours are lousy and so's the money."

"I know. I keep your books, remember?"

"We're garbage collectors, digging through the trash looking for emotional maggots and cockroaches. We photograph infidelity. Chronicle felony. Find the liars. Expose the frauds. And when we do our job right, hearts are broken and lives are ruined."

"You're not scaring me."

"I'm not trying to, it's just that ... I want more for you. A better life than this. You should be married. Living in a big house with kids, a husband who drives a Lexus and a collie that looks like Lassie."

"I always wanted an Irish setter."

"Whatever. Don't you see? You're too ... sweet for this kind of work."

"Sweet? Yuk. That's as bad as saying I'm, like, cute."

"You are cute."

"Okay, that's it. I'm out of here." She started for the door.

"Hillary, wait!" She stopped. "All right. Call a couple personnel services in the morning. As soon as we find a secretary to replace you, I'll put you to work as an investigator."

Hillary's smile was incandescent as she rushed across the room and threw her arms around me. "Oh, Gideon, thank you." It was a platonic hug, no fig leaf-required parts were touching. But she felt great in my arms.

This was one of those times when my thoughts about Hillary

lurched from pure to passionate. Luckily, the phone rang. I grabbed it. "Gideon Kincaid."

"It's Barry Winslow. I need to see you. Right away."

He sounded scared. Terrified, in fact. "Sure, Barry. Where do you want to meet?"

"My condo: 2222 Century Towers. And hurry."

View from the Top

Roy Cooper watched as Barry Winslow hung up the phone. "Very good," Roy said. "Maybe you should've been an actor instead of a writer."

Winslow's eyes drifted from Roy's face to the Sig Sauer .9mm in Roy's left hand. "I'm too self-conscious to be an actor," Winslow said. "I can't stand people looking at me."

"Really? Then why do you drive a Porsche? Why do you wear kaleidoscopic luau shirts, thousand dollar cowboy boots and those idiotic green contact lens? Of course you want people to look at you. You're desperate for attention. We all are. But it takes a brave man to admit it. It takes a courageous man to take the ultimate step, to shed his skin and slip into a suit of imagination. To be an actor, a meat puppet ready to sacrifice one's own identity to become a mirror for the heart and soul."

He's crazy, Barry Winslow thought. I'm going to be killed by a crazy fucking actor and I've got no one to blame but myself.

Barry Winslow had been in his bedroom packing when the doorbell rang fifteen minutes earlier. Annoyed that security hadn't called to announce a visitor, Winslow hurried to the door, looked through the peephole.

He didn't recognize Roy at first. And why should he? He hadn't seen the actor in five or six years. But once the features fell into place—the dusty-blond hair, thick eyebrows above sleepy hazel eyes, strong cheekbones and chin—the name wasn't far behind. Roy Cooper. And the project, *Ramrod.* And the result—disaster.

Winslow's first thoughts were paranoid. What's he doing here? What's he want from me?

Then a more reasonable part of his brain went to work. Wait a minute, Roy Cooper doesn't know where I live. And why would he come looking for me after all these years? This must be some kind of coincidence. He just happens to be in the building, got lost, and is just looking for directions. Or he just moved in and is introducing himself to the neighbors.

Then a guilt-ridden part of the brain took over. Maybe this was fate giving him a chance to make it up to Roy. He could give him a guest shot on the show, or a small character arc. Something big enough to jumpstart his career.

Roy rang the bell again and Winslow, with hope in his heart, opened the door. Barry feigned confusion at first, then recognition. "Roy? Roy Cooper?" Winslow asked, all smiles, sticking out his hand. "What're you doing here?"

Roy's answer was to stick an automatic into Winslow's chest and shove him back into the room. Winslow's heartbeat became a deafening timpani of thuds. Adrenaline drenched his brain, transforming reality into slow motion. Anomalies caught his eye—the plastic gloves on Roy's hands, the surgical booties over his shoes, the canvas duffle bag over his shoulder. "What do you want?" Winslow stammered, damning himself as fear squeezed his voice into a high-pitched whine.

"Justice," Roy said. And that's when Winslow knew he was dead.

Jesus, Roy thought. He looks fucking terrified. I've never seen that in real life. Cool. Then he made an acting note to himself: Remember the way his eyes bug out, incorporate that into mirror exercises.

"Please don't kill me," Winslow begged.

Pitiful, Roy thought. Guy writes for a living and that's the best he can come up with when his life's on the line. "Don't worry, Barry. Do as I tell you and you'll live to hack another day."

He's confused, too, Roy realized. *Can't imagine how I got past the security desk.* Simple really, Roy had avoided the front door altogether. He staked out the building and then followed a sweet-looking grandmother type as she drove her five-year old Cadillac out of the underground parking garage to the Century City shopping mall. As soon as grandma walked inside Roy broke into the car and stole her parking garage opener. Then he used it to drive into Winslow's building undetected.

Roy's eyes took in the condo. Fabulous. A total fuck palace. Winslow had told him about it while they were shooting *Ramrod* but had never invited him up. Book-lined walls to impress, cushy leather couch for comfort, antique side chairs for class, fully stocked wet bar to bait the trap and a million dollar view to reel them in.

An object on the coffee table caught Roy's eye, a sculpture of a nude woman standing spread-eagled over a martini glass. Weird concept, but the girl was so lifelike, bare feet curled over the glass, leg muscles tensed, thighs spread to reveal a triangular patch of pubic hair, flat stomach and perfectly rounded breasts. "This must be a real conversation starter."

"It is," Winslow said tentatively, starting to feel a little better, a little less doomed, but measuring his words carefully. "And the conversation's always about sex."

"And talking about it usually leads to doing it. You dog, you. Wait a minute. You told me about this when we were shooting the pilot. I think you called it your bronze aphrodisiac."

"That's right."

"Man, you've got it all. Is it everything you always wanted?"

Winslow wondered if this was a trick question. "Yes," he ventured.

"I bet it is. Me, I've got to bring the broads back to my one bedroom dump in Westwood. Let me tell you, it takes a real cocksman to get laid in that place. Oh, talking about pussy reminds me: I've got something for you." Roy reached into the duffle bag. "Thought you might like to see this." Roy pulled out a skull and tossed it to Winslow."

Barry juggled it, then gripped it tight. His panic-addled brain was having a hard time processing. “What’s this?”

“Don’t you mean, *who* is it? Don’t you recognize her? It’s your idol, Barry. Christine Cole.”

Revelation registered on Winslow’s face. *Of course, the kidnapping that PI had told him about.* Winslow stared at the skull, unknowingly assuming a Hamlet-like pose. “Is this really her?”

“Yes.”

Winslow’s gaze turned reverential. “Amazing.” He stroked the skull, brushing the few wisps of blond hair that still clung there.

Roy watched Winslow, a little creeped out. “You two want to be alone?”

Winslow ignored the dig. “What’re you going to do with her?”

“Put her on display.”

“Really? Where?”

“Here. I was thinking of your bedroom.” Roy pointed the gun down the hallway. “Lead the way.”

Winslow did. Roy noticed old movie posters lining the wall: *Double Indemnity. The Maltese Falcon. The Thin Man.* “These real?”

“Originals, yeah. Bought them at auction at Christie’s.”

“Expensive?”

“Thousands.”

“For old movie posters? Who would’ve thunk it? Wait …” Roy stopped, looking through a doorway into a room filled with more posters. “What’s this?”

“My office.”

Roy walked in, eyeballed the posters. *Deadly Ransom. Femme Fatale. Never Again. Blue Moon.* “Don’t you mean your shrine? These are all Christine Cole posters.”

“What can I say? I’m a fan. I was fourteen when she made *Deadly Ransom,* and I fell in love. “

A desk sat in the middle of the room, a twenty-six-inch iMac sat on the middle of the desk. "This is where you do it? Create, I mean."

"Yeah."

So will I, thought Roy, *but not until later*. "Okay, back to business. Let's see the bedroom."

It looked like it was designed at the House of Letch. A sixty-inch plasma screen TV faced a king-size bed. A cat slept on one of the pillows, and the bedspread looked like it was ... No, it couldn't be. "Is that mink?"

"Absolutely."

"And let me guess. The next question the girls always ask is, 'Can I touch it?' "

"And that's when I gently stroke the fur and say: 'Of course, come, sit down.' "

"And when they do it's the beginning of the end."

"Or the beginning of the beginning."

Roy had to smile. This guy was good.

The cat woke up, blinked sleepily at Winslow, and then noticed Roy. Instant panic. In a flash of fur, the cat catapulted off the bed, skittered across the floor and out the door.

"I know just how she feels," Winslow said.

Roy noticed a half-packed suitcase on the bureau.

"Going somewhere?"

"Paris."

"Must be nice."

Roy's eyes drifted to ceiling. There was a mirror above the bed. Unfuckingbelievable. The guy had everything.

Next Roy checked out the walls. A bookcase lined one, filled with DVDs—everything from *Citizen Kane* to *Avatar*. Another wall was lined with framed 8x10 photos of Winslow with people who were supposed to impress you—movie stars, politicians.

Roy's eyes went back to the DVDs. "You have any of your own shows?"

"All of them." Winslow pointed to the third shelf. "I keep copies of all the *Payback* episodes and my three unsold pilots."

Roy noticed three DVDs at the end of the row. *Dead Run, Ramrod, Shadow Chaser.* "You know, I never got to see *Ramrod.*"

"You were really great, Roy. Believe me. A shame it didn't get on. I'll get you a copy—if you let me live through this."

"I told you, Barry. I'm not here to kill you as long as you do as you're told. And yes, I'd love a copy." Roy peaked into the master bath. Marble everywhere ... tub, shower, counter, toilet. Even one of those ... "What do you call that?"

"Bidet."

"Shoots water up your ass."

"Something like that."

"You ever use it?"

"No."

A shadow crossed Roy's face. "But we both know someone who would've loved it."

Winslow knew what Roy was talking about but didn't dare go there. Better to change the subject. "So, where should we put Christine? The bed?"

"No," Roy said. "I have a better idea ..."

They arranged the bones, head to toe, as best they could. But there were a lot of bones and they couldn't be sure where they all went. So they piled the extras in the ribcage. Then Roy led Winslow back to the living room and they made the call to Gideon Kincaid.

"What happens when he gets here?" Barry asked.

"All sorts of fun stuff."

The vagueness of Roy's answer bothered Barry, but he didn't have the guts to press it further.

"You sure have a killer view," Roy said, sliding open the balcony door. "Come on, let's wait outside."

Barry loved this view, too. Sometimes he'd sit out there with his MacBook, working. Other times just sit staring off, letting his mind wander. But he'd never been out there with someone toting a .9mm Sig Sauer before. At that moment Roy swung the gun in Winslow's direction. "I said: come out here."

Barry stepped outside. It was a clear night so you could see from Santa Monica to the downtown L.A. skyline. And thanks to an onshore breeze, you could even smell a touch of the ocean.

Roy leaned over the balcony. “Hey, we’re right above the lobby. And you’ve got a great view up Avenue of the Stars. I know, let’s watch for Kincaid’s car. He drives a light blue Taurus. Come on over here.” Winslow hesitated. “What?” Roy asked. “You worried I’ll push you off the balcony?”

“It is a long way down.”

“Hey, if I wanted you dead I would have shot you by now. Right?”

“I guess so.”

“So don’t worry. I have no intention of killing you. You’ve got my word on that. Now come on, get over here.”

Not liking it, but knowing he didn’t have a choice, Winslow joined Roy at the rail.

They waited.

Free Fall

Once a castle stood here, battlements reaching into the California sky. Next to a London train station. And a French farmhouse. And an African village.

Twentieth Century Fox's back lot was home to a thousand movie sets and a million dreams. Bad times forced the studio to sell most of its back lot in the sixties, and now it's home to office buildings, hotels, shopping centers and condominiums.

I couldn't drive into Century City without remembering the sword fights, barroom brawls, pratfalls and ankle-raised kisses that were Hollywood. Not without wishing I could turn back the clock.

Winslow's building was thirty-eight stories of expensive glass and steel. On a clear day I'm sure you could see from the ocean to the downtown skyline. From my one-bedroom unit you could see a Taco Bell and Phil's Office Furniture.

I had pulled into the circular drive, rolled down my window, and was hoping to talk the doorman into letting me park my car in front when I heard it.

The scream. Shocked. Desperate. Final.

I saw a blur out of the corner of my eye, followed by a pulpy thud.

The body landed only a few feet from my car. I leaped out and rushed to the broken, bloody mess. The jumper landed face down. But I knew who it was. I recognized the snakeskin cowboy boots and luau shirt.

The doorman, a young redheaded kid, muttered "Jesus fucking Christ," and threw up in a bed of roses. A moment later the security guard—early twenties, officious, cop wannabe—came running out to see what happened. He didn't puke, but he turned ghost white and leaned against a tree for support.

I scanned the building; saw nothing suspicious on any of the balconies. Not that I expected to. The only way to know if it was suicide or murder would be to get into that condo. I slipped past the still reeling doorman and security guard and into the lobby.

There's no directory in these high-class buildings, but a list of the occupants could usually be found on the security desk. I found it beneath a well-thumbed *Hustler* magazine. Winslow was in 2808. I pressed the up button and waited. There were three elevators. Above each elevator was an indicator telling you what floor it was on. Elevator one was on nine, going up. Elevator two was stopped on thirty-one. Elevator three was on six, headed down.

As I waited I saw Elevator two start to move. Thirty, twenty-nine, twenty-eight, twenty-eight …

It was stopped on twenty-eight. Was someone getting on? Someone from Winslow's apartment? It started moving again. Twenty-seven, twenty-six, twenty-five …

DING. Elevator three arrived. The door slid open. It was empty.

Twenty-four, twenty-three, twenty-two …

Winslow's high dive could have been a simple suicide. Especially if he realized I was on to him and he was afraid of going to jail. Or it could have been a murder, in which case, time was of the essence. Someone could still be in Winslow's apartment. I should get on the waiting elevator and get my ass up there.

Twenty-one, twenty, nineteen …

Besides, the cops could show up any second. If I had any chance to check out the condo before the boys in blue slapped up the yellow police tape, it was now or never.

Eighteen, seventeen, sixteen …

Or someone could be on Elevator two. The one who pushed Winslow out that window.

Fifteen, fourteen, thirteen …

The one who kidnapped Christine's bones, stole my car and owed me big time.

Twelve, eleven, ten …

I let the door to Elevator two close.

Nine, eight, seven …

I pulled my Glock out its holster, took up a position beside the elevator.

Six, five, four …

I never shot anyone on an elevator before, but there was a first time for everything.

Three, two, one ...

The door opened. I spun into the doorway, gun ready. It was empty.

I hate when that happens. All that wasted adrenaline. All those extra heartbeats. I punched the button for twenty-eight and began the ride up.

Why had it stopped at twenty-eight? Had someone gotten on at thirty-one and off at twenty-eight? Had they called the elevator at twenty-eight and changed their minds? Had it really stopped at twenty-eight at all? Maybe I just thought it had stopped because I was so focused on Floor twenty-eight.

DING. The door opened. I stepped into the corridor. It was empty. I hurried to 2808, tried the door. Locked. The lock was a Schlage—a simple pin tumbler type—and I picked it in about twenty seconds. Pulling my gun again, I stepped into the dead man's condo and listened.

I heard the ticking of a clock. But no footfalls. No clothes rustling. No voices. Nothing suspicious. I closed the door and stepped into a large living room.

There was a leather couch that looked comfortable and two Art Deco chairs that didn't. In the center of the coffee table was a sculpture of a naked woman spread-eagled over a martini glass. Two of my favorite things, I'll admit. But this thing was way too in your face for me.

A bookcase covered the far wall. A cursory glance revealed everything from Molière to the latest Lee Child. And multiple copies of Winslow's three books.

The centerpiece of the room, though, was a truly spectacular view. I could see from the ocean to Orange County. The sliding glass door was open. I stepped out on the patio and looked down to see Winslow's splayed body directly below. This was his launching pad. I looked around and saw nothing out of place, no sign of a struggle. In the distance I heard the whine of an approaching police car. I didn't have much time.

I did a quick search of the dining room and kitchen. I wasn't exactly sure what I was looking for. But if Winslow had killed himself, he might have left a suicide note—or so I hoped. Or Christine's bones. Or the two million bucks.

Winslow must've had a great cleaning lady or was totally anal. Maybe both. The place was spotless. I followed a hallway past very cool movie posters of some of my favorite mystery classics: The Maltese Falcon, The Thin Man, Double Indemnity. And then I heard it. A THUNK. Like something being knocked over. The sound came from an open doorway ahead. Then another noise, a CREAK. Someone was in there.

Maybe someone with a gun, like me. I decided to go in low. I took a deep breath to steady myself then I dove into the room, rolled, came up Glock first and found myself face to face with a pair of eyes. Yellow eyes. Set in a gray face. A cat's face. Sitting on a desk in the middle of the room. But he didn't sit for long. All four of his feet started spinning, his claws skating over the desk's polished mahogany; then he was airborne, flying over my head and out the door.

Feeling foolish, I rose to my feet and surveyed the room. The desk was flanked by two filing cabinets, and the walls were hung with more movie posters. Christine Cole posters: Deadly Ransom. Femme Fatale. Never Again. Blue Moon.

There was a computer on the desk. It was on. Words glowed on the monitor, begging to be read.

I'm sorry. Forgive me.

Not much of a suicide note from a man who made his living writing. If he had written it. Anyone could have typed in those words.

I wanted to search the desk and filing cabinets, but first I wanted to make sure no one else was in the condo. I left the office and followed the hallway to Winslow's bedroom.

This guy must've been a real lounge lizard. He had a mirrored ceiling, king-sized bed and emperor-sized TV. A bureau sat next to the big screen. On it was an alarm clock, nothing more. Across from the bureau was another bookcase holding a vast collection of DVDs. It looked like Winslow also owned copies of all his shows. There were a ton of *Payback* tapes and two other DVDs, *Dead Run* and *Shadow Chaser,* which I assumed were pilots or Movies of the Week he wrote.

Like so many Hollywood types, he had a wall lined with eight-by-tens of him and every famous person he could round up.

I hit pay dirt in the master bath. A huge marble tub dominated the room, and the tub was filled. Not with water, but bones. The bones were arranged to form a skeleton. There was a necklace around the neck, a bracelet around a wrist and a diamond ring on a finger. Nice to finally meet you, Christine.

Okay. Bones, suicide note ... If I could find the money we'd have a pretty strong case for suicide. But before I had the chance to look farther, I heard the sound of the front door opening and a voice saying, "No, he lived alone."

The doorman or security guard. *Shit.*

A second voice, tired and male, said, "He have any visitors tonight?" A cop's question. That was actually good news. The first cop to arrive is only supposed to secure the scene and then tape the door until the detectives arrive.

I stepped back into the bedroom as the doorman or security guard answered, "Not that I saw. But I only came on duty half an hour ago. You want, I'll call Ned. He had the security desk before me. Maybe he saw someone." Okay, it was the security guard.

I slipped into the walk-in closet, silently slid the door shut as the cop said, "Just give me his number. One of the detectives will call him."

Great! It *was* a uniform. He and the doorman or security guard should be out of here in no time.

The security guard's voice faded as he said, "Mr. Winslow sure didn't seem like the kind of dude who'd off himself." I couldn't hear what the cop answered. They must've gone out on the patio. So I waited in the dark, surrounded by a dead man's clothes, and considered my situation.

I knew that hiding in the closet was pretty stupid. I should have walked up to the cop and explained who I was—a licensed private investigator—and that I was here because Winslow might have been blackmailing my client. But I had broken in and, technically, that's against the law. If the cop wanted to give me a hard time I'd end up on the wrong end of a Miranda warning. So hiding in the closet made sense. Sort of.

"If I owned a crib like this I wouldn't be jumping out of no windows." The security guard's voice. Close. Very close.

"That's some TV." The cop's voice. Through a crack in the door I could see them enter the bedroom.

"Check out the bed," the security guard said. "Mink bedspread. This guy had all the moves."

Mink bedspread? I hadn't noticed that. I didn't even know they made them.

"Don't touch anything," the cop said.

"I won't." The cop pushed open the bathroom door. "Holy shit," he said. He'd found the bones.

"Jesus fucking Christ," the security guard muttered; then I heard an unmistakable gagging sound.

"God damn it," the cop bellowed. "You puked on my shoes.

Get out of here. Go wait in the hall!" I saw the security guard run into the hall then heard his retreating footsteps and the slamming of a door.

"Fucking asshole," the cop hissed under his breath. I heard him turn on the faucet, probably to wet a towel and wipe off his shoes.

Then I heard another sound. Breathing. Very close. Too close. That's when I realized I wasn't the only one hiding in the closet.

Someone was behind me. Taking rapid, nervous breaths. Had to have been there the entire time I'd been in the bedroom. I looked behind me and saw two glowing eyes.

Yellow eyes.

Yeah, our friend the cat. He must've dashed to the dark, cramped safety of the closet after our little altercation in the office. He was crouched on a shelf, between a pair of black Bally loafers and blue Sperry Topsiders.

I'm sure he hated the idea that I had invaded his hiding place, but as long as I wasn't looking at him, he concluded I didn't know he was here. And he could live with that. But now our eyes had danced the dance. The jig was up and when it comes to the genetic fight or flight crossroads, cats only have one way to go.

With a guttural cry he threw himself against the closet door. It sprung open and the cat was gone in a blur of fur.

The cop exploded out of the bathroom, a wet towel in one hand and his automatic in the other. He swept the room, looking for the source of the sound, and found me standing behind a cashmere jacket. "Freeze, fuckhead."

My thought exactly.

You Have the Right to Remain Stupid

"You are one dumb son of a bitch."

"I must be to have married you."

"Insult me all you want, Gideon. I'm sending your ass to jail."

"I won't be able to pay any alimony if I'm in jail."

"You don't pay me alimony now."

"I've been thinking about starting."

"Start thinking about how to take a shower without bending over. First degree murder carries a mandatory life term."

Having an ex-wife is bad enough. Having an ex-wife that's a cop totally sucks.

I sat in Winslow's living room, my hands cuffed behind me. Once the uniformed cop had pulled me out of the closet he'd snapped the handcuffs two clicks past painful, pinching my skin and cutting off my circulation. "Hey" I'd said, "I'm not the one who puked on your shoes."

"Shut up, shit heel." He searched me, found my Glock, my picks, and my PI license. I tried to explain what I was doing in Winslow's closet but he didn't want to hear it. He just dragged me to the living room, threw me into one of the Art Deco chairs and told me to shut up until the detectives got there.

I guess I shouldn't have been surprised when my ex-wife and her partner, a tall geek who looked like Ichabod Crane, walked through the door. I mean, it had been one of those days. I'd been shot at, had my car and two million dollars stolen, watched Winslow recycle himself on the sidewalk and been caught hiding in a closet at the scene of a crime. Sure, bring on my ex-wife. Why the hell not?

"You going to tell me why you threw him off the balcony now," Stacy asked, "or will I have to beat it out of you downtown?"

"Let's beat it out of him here," the geek said.

"Shut up, Ichabod," I said.

"My name's Piccolo."

I waggled my ass at him. "Pick this."

Stacy shook her head at me like a frustrated seventh grade teacher. "Grow up, Gideon."

The first time I saw Stacy she was breaking a man's kneecap with her nightstick. He was an armed robber, fleeing a Ralph's grocery store. Stacy intercepted him in the parking lot as he tried to get on his motorcycle. She had the move down perfectly—a sweeping arc finishing with a punishing snap of the wrist.

She looked great. Tall—a tad over five nine—with lustrous brown hair tied in an unruly bun. She had high cheekbones, a full, sensual mouth, and brown eyes that bore holes in whatever they looked at. And what a body. An LAPD uniform never looked so good.

I had introduced myself as I got out of my black and white with what I thought was a hip, clever line. "Do you look as good naked as it looks like you'll look naked?"

"Put a sock in it, Romeo, and read him his rights." It was love at first insult.

Back in Winslow's condo I'd said, "Tell me something, Stacy. How do you suppose I threw him off the balcony when I was standing in the driveway, next to the doorman, when he landed?"

Stacy turned to the doorman. "That true?"

"Yes, Ma'am."

"Shit," Piccolo said.

Stacy turned those hard brown eyes on me. "Then why the hell were you hiding in the closet?"

"Looking for one of my contacts?"

"You don't wear glasses."

"Looking for one of Winslow's contacts?"

"He won't be needing them anymore."

"Hiding from the cops?"

"I think we're getting warm."

Stacy and I made love the night we met. Unfortunately, it wasn't to each other. She was living with a second-string forward for the L.A. Kings Hockey team. I was dating a public defender with a thing for cops and banana-flavored love oil. But it was Stacy's face in my mind's eye that night and I tracked her down the next day.

"Look," I said as she stood on the firing range, pumping a clip of hollow points into a neat circle on the paper target, "I sort of stuck my foot in my mouth yesterday. I'd like another chance."

"Another chance at what?"

"An opening line. I want to try something charming, maybe a little quirky. Something irresistible enough for you to agree to have dinner with me."

Almost against her will, she smiled. "Go for it."

"When I look into your eyes I believe anything is possible."

She laughed. "Charming, but not irresistible."

"Maybe not," I said, suddenly serious, "but it's true." I did mean it. I didn't realize how much until I actually said the words out loud.

Stacy heard the honesty in my voice and I could see her shift gears, reassessing me. "Promise you won't break my heart?"

"I promise."

We had Chinese.

Back in Winslow's condo Stacy said, "You lying sack of shit."

"It's the truth. I was just trying to find Christine Cole's bones." I had shown Stacy and Piccolo the bones in the bathroom and the computer suicide message. We now stood in Winslow's office, surrounded by Christine Cole posters. My hands were still cuffed behind my back as I filled them in on Christine's kidnapping, the ransom demand, and the switching of the bones.

Stacy shook her head skeptically. "Wait a minute. I don't get your connection to all this."

"I don't either. As far as I know, the first time I ever met Winslow was this afternoon."

Piccolo smirked. "Yeah, right. Then why'd he say he owed you 'big time?' "

"I don't know."

Stacy said, "Obviously you have met him before. You just don't remember."

"I checked my files. Nothing."

"Was it his voice on the phone?"

"It could have been. I'm not sure."

"Well, it must've been," Piccolo said. "There's no sign of a struggle. Building security said Winslow had no visitors today. The suicide note is here. The bones are here. The only thing unaccounted for is the money. That is," he added derisively, "if Winslow ever got it."

"What's that supposed to mean?"

"I don't think Winslow ever got the ransom. I think you've got the two million bucks stashed away as your own little retirement fund."

I looked at Stacy. "Is he always this stupid?"

She looked at Piccolo. "Gideon may be a lot of things. Arrogant. Selfish. Stubborn. But he's not a thief."

"Thank you. I think."

"I forgot spiteful, insolent, and heartless."

"I think he's got the idea."

Piccolo crossed to the computer screen, read the suicide note and furrowed his brow. "It doesn't make sense. Winslow masterminds the Hollywood crime of the century and finagles two million dollars. But instead of taking the money and running, he kills himself."

"He must've panicked when he realized Gideon was on to him," Stacy said.

"No. He baited Gideon. Stuck his name on the ransom note. Called him. He was asking Gideon to find him. Something's wrong."

He was right. It had been bothering me, too. "I'll tell you something else," I said. "As far as I can tell, Winslow didn't need the two million bucks. He makes a fortune producing *Payback*, plus royalties on his books. He lives in a gorgeous condo. Dates beautiful starlets. If it was me, the only way you'd get me off the balcony would be to give me a push."

"Exactly," Stacy said.

"Unless he spent every penny he made," Piccolo said. "Gorgeous condos and beautiful starlets get expensive. He could've had a drug problem. Or gambling."

The cuffs were killing me. "You know, Stacy, I could think a lot better if the circulation wasn't cut off to my hands."

Piccolo piped up. "Nobody asked you to think."

I really hated this guy.

"Uncuff him," Stacy said.

"No way. He may not have killed Winslow, but we've got him on breaking and entering."

"Not to mention hiding behind a cashmere jacket."

"Shut up, Gideon," Stacy snapped. She took a more gentle tone with Piccolo. "Come on, give the guy a break."

There was a tense moment as Piccolo debated his options then reluctantly released me.

"You'll have to forgive Piccolo," Stacy said. "He's a little jealous."

"Jealous?" Then it hit me. "Wait a minute. You're dating this asshole?"

Piccolo smiled. "Ain't love grand?"

Talk about blindsided. I felt sucker-punched. My head buzzed. I couldn't breathe. I didn't know what to say, and when that happens what usually comes out of my big mouth is something stupid and juvenile. True to form, I said to Piccolo, "Hope you like used pussy."

"I like it fine once I get past the 'used' part."

That did it. I threw a quick combination, right cross followed by a left hook. Both shots smashed into Piccolo's jaw and he dropped to the carpet, unconscious.

"Ouch," I said shaking my hands. "That hurt."

Stacy just sighed. "I'd say you have a few unresolved issues about our relationship."

"The only thing unresolved is how you could date this prick."

"He's not a bad guy once you get to know him."

"I have no intention of getting to know him."

"Yeah, well, all things considered, this might be a good time for you to leave."

"What about Winslow?"

"He's not your problem anymore. We'll figure out if it was suicide or murder and proceed accordingly."

"My client would like his bones back."

"I'm sure he would, but they're evidence in an ongoing investigation."

"And the two million dollars?"

"If we find it, the money will be returned, too." Piccolo started to stir. "I'd leave while you have a chance, Gideon. He's going to be pissed." She handed me my wallet, my gun and my picks. "Go home."

I didn't like it, but I headed for the door.

"By the way, Gideon," Stacy said. "I'm reading your book."

Uh oh. There's a character in the book. I describe her as 'tall, a tad over five nine, with lustrous brown hair tied in an unruly bun. She had high cheekbones, a full sensual mouth and brown eyes that bore holes in whatever they looked at.' I also wrote that she was a total bitch. At the end of the third chapter her ex-husband stabs her thirty-eight times.

"How far are you?"

"Almost to the end of Chapter Two."

"Just remember that any resemblance the characters have to real persons living or dead is strictly coincidence."

Party Time

Hollywood's most beautiful actresses were there. Angelina, Charlize, Keira, Sandra, Zooey, Katie, Cameron, Nicole and Julia. And the guys weren't so bad either. George, Brad, Leonardo, Taylor, Denzel, Keanu, Jude and Shia.

Lady Gaga blared from the speakers. Not her latest CD, but the real live Lady Gaga, doing her friend, producer David Hunter, a favor. It was his birthday and Hollywood's royalty had turned out in force.

Roy enjoyed the view but he'd seen enough. He wasn't there to stargaze. His reason was much more diabolical. He circled around the outside of the Holmby Hills mansion. Roy always loved Tudor houses. Had hoped to own one if his acting career had ever taken off. Well, now he'd have the money from the ransoms.

As he passed the living room Roy saw Quentin and Steven in a heated discussion by the fireplace. Reese and Jake were flirting. Demi and Ashton were dancing.

As Roy reached the patio he took a glass of champagne from a passing waiter and sipped it while thinking about his afternoon at Winslow's condo.

It had gone perfectly. The look on Winslow's face when he shoved him over the balcony was priceless. Surprise mixed with reproach. His shocked expression practically screamed, "But you promised!"

You lied to me, you son of a bitch. Led me like a lamb to slaughter. Well, now I've fucked you. Big time.

What had Winslow done to Roy? What did the scribe do that condemned him to that terrifyingly definitive belly flop? The memories were all too fresh for Roy ...

Thunderous applause. Clapping. Stomping. Chanting his name. "ROY! ROY! ROY!"

Not just when he scored touchdowns. Not just when he won basketball games. Even when he acted. Even when he did that dumb role in *Oklahoma*.

ROY! ROY! ROY!

High school had been a glorious time for Roy Cooper. Hell, his whole childhood was blessed. Cute as a baby, adorable as a little boy, handsome as a teenager. He had it all. President of the student body. Prom King. Voted Most Likely to Succeed. A full football scholarship at Georgia State.

He blew his knee out sophomore year, but by then he was already a BMOC. The teachers loved his brains. The women loved his looks. The men loved his charm. And although his athletic career was over, the acting thing was going great. He was cast as the lead in every major university production, and it was simply understood that one day he would be a big star.

The week after graduation Roy borrowed five grand from his dad and made the move to Hollywood. The dean of the drama department had a friend working at one of the smaller talent agencies, who after a quick meeting agreed to take him on. The meeting was a real ego trip for Roy. The agent oohed and aahed over him, telling Roy he was the next Tom Cruise. Roy didn't know then that all agents are full of shit and his was more full of shit than most.

Next, the agent sent Roy to get pictures. Another head trip. The photographer oohed and aahed, telling him he had George Clooney's chin, Mel Gibson's ass and Brad Pitt's eyes. The photographer also charged Roy 600 bucks for an hour's work, but Roy's head was so full of butterscotch he gladly paid.

Two days later Roy walked into his first audition—a guest

shot on a new TV drama, *Street Life*—and got the shock of his life. The room was filled with guys just as good-looking. For the first time in his life, Roy wasn't the handsomest man in the room.

No problem, he told himself. He'd ace the audition. In college, auditions were a formality. He'd walk in, chat it up with the faculty and the director for twenty minutes, then breeze through the reading and get the role. So, dripping with confidence, Roy walked into the conference room.

There were four people sitting around a table. Two were women, both heavy, both the wrong side of fifty, dressed like they shopped at Slobs 'R Us. Next to them was a fat, bald forty-something-year-old dude with a pockmarked face. He was eating a Snickers bar.

They were listening to the guy sitting at the middle of the table. He was younger, early thirties or so, and intense. Skinny, with bushy black hair stuffed into a Panavision baseball cap, he had big black eyes, a bigger nose and a beard. He was clearly a Spielberg wannabe, but a nerd through and through.

People like these had followed Roy around his whole life. Hoping they could touch a little of the magic, hoping they could somehow become part of Roy's crowd. Losers. Roy knew he had it made.

The Spielberg clone, who Roy assumed was the director, finished talking and took his first look at Roy. "Ah, shit, another pretty boy! Claudia, don't you know any actors that look like real people?"

"This *is* how real people look in Hollywood."

The director stuck out his hand. "Got a résumé, handsome?"

A flustered Roy handed him his résumé and managed a smile identical to the one in the photo.

The director looked at the picture, flipped over the résumé, and scanned the credits. "What the fuck is this?" The director ignored Roy, staring at Claudia. "Nothing but a bunch of college plays. What, am I supposed to give acting lessons?"

"Barney Magnuson at TPA recommended him."

"Oh, in that case, don't even bother reading. You got the part."

Roy's heart leapt for an instant, actually believing his agent had that kind of clout. Then …

"Come on, Claudia, Barney Magnuson wouldn't know an actor if he bit his dick off." He tossed the résumé back to Roy. "Here you go, stud. Come back when you know what the front of a camera looks like."

Nobody had ever talked to Roy like that. Especially not a geek! Bewildered, Roy just stood there a moment. And in that moment Claudia rose to his defense. "Everyone's got to start somewhere, Justin. He starred in a ton of college productions; he must have talent. And he's got a great look. Give the kid a chance."

Justin turned from Claudia to Roy, raked him with those black eyes. "You know something, kid. Claudia may be right. Hell, folks, we may be about to see an audition that will become part of Hollywood lore. Okay, Olivier, action!"

Roy launched into the scene. He was self-conscious at first, but gained confidence with every line. Soon he was in the flow and by the time he finished he felt he'd nailed it. He looked up to find the director smiling at him. "That was very good."

"Thank you."

"But 'very good' gets you a bus ride to Nowheresville in this town. You've got to be 'unfuckingbelievably good' to even have a shot. And even then you need to nurture that talent—take classes, workshops, get on stage. It takes talent, hard work and dedication. And even that's not enough without a shitload of luck. Look, Ray—"

"Roy."

"Ray, Roy, who gives a fuck. Let me ask you something, Ray. You've always had it pretty easy, haven't you? Captain of the high school football team? Prom King? BMOC? All that shit?"

"It's Roy."

"Right, sorry. Well, those chiseled looks of yours gave you a pass through high school and college, Ray, but not here, not now. This town is full of guys who look just like you. Genetically fortunate beefcakes who've had smoke blown up their asses their whole lives and figure they're the next Matt Damon. There are thousands of you out there. And you know what most of them end up doing for a living? Working in restaurants, waiting on guys like me. Or in dealerships, selling cars to guys like me. Or in real estate, selling homes to guys like me. Guys like me who had nothing going for them in high school and college but brains. Guys like me who guys like you would dis as geeks. Guys like me who now decide whether you'll eat steak or chicken. So if you're smart, Ray, you'll put your perfect ass on the next seat back to Bumfuck, because guys like me love to get even with guys like you." Justin's eyes went from Roy, to Claudia. "Next!"

Roy's reaction to Justin's humiliation surprised even Roy; he wasn't angry. He wasn't defensive. He was relieved.

Roy knew he'd been given a lot of breaks because of his looks. And he knew he couldn't take any credit; that was just the way he was born. Now, he wasn't about to turn down a blowjob or two, but at the same time, a sense of insecurity had been sneaking up on him, a longing to be appreciated for something concrete. Something he'd actually accomplished.

So after the casting fiasco, Roy dedicated himself to becoming a real actor. He enrolled in classes with Howard Fine and Brian Reise. Took acting workshops at the Odyssey and Matrix theaters. Rented DVDs of great performances by hunky leading men who could also act. Russell Crowe in *Gladiator*, Clint Eastwood in *Unforgiven*, Harrison Ford in *Air Force One*, Mel Gibson in *Braveheart*—and watched them over and over again.

Roy did get a few acting jobs to pay the bills, guest shots on *Nip/Tuck, CSI: Miami, Lost*. He even worked as a waiter—six months at Morton's, four months at The Palm. Restaurants haunted by agents, producers, writers and directors. Restaurants where serving the right customer might lead to an important break.

Then, on a hot August night, Roy served sea bass with garlic-mashed potatoes to this guy wearing a silk luau shirt and earring. The guy was reading a script as he ate, making notes in the margins. Roy started up a conversation and found out that the guy's name was Barry Winslow. He was a writer-producer, and he'd just sold a pilot script called *Ramrod*, a PI show set in Honolulu about an ex-Navy SEAL turned detective.

"I was a Navy SEAL before I became an actor," Roy lied, an accepted practice in Hollywood.

"Really ..." Winslow took a good, long look at Roy, and said, "You're certainly the right type. Have your agent call my office in the a.m. and we'll set up an interview."

Three days later, Roy auditioned. He'd worked for hours on his performance. He thought he'd really gotten *inside* the character. But what he thought didn't matter; he had to impress the people in the room.

Roy took a deep breath and began.

RAMROD

> Don't talk to me about sacrifice. I've watched the woman I love bleed to death on a scorched desert floor. I've stuck a bayonet in the heart of my best friend to protect our country's secrets. I sent my mother on a doomed flight to Paris—a plane I knew had a bomb on board—for the good of the nation. So don't talk to me about sacrifice. Sacrifice is my middle name!

Roy's voice echoed in the conference room as he finished his audition, and after a dramatic pause he looked up from his script at the five people sitting on the couch: Winslow—the director—two casting people and a network executive, Jerry Marshall.

Jerry was about thirty-five, impeccably dressed in a blue Brooks Brothers suit, white shirt and Nicole Miller tie. Jerry was plump, with bright red hair, pale blue eyes and a cocksure smile on his lips, implying that he—and only he—knew the secret of life. And in a way he did. The network had the final say in all pilot casting decisions and that made Jerry the 500 pound gorilla.

Every eye in the room was on Jerry, trying to gauge his reaction. God forbid someone would say it was great if Jerry hated it. Therefore, in another Hollywood tradition, no one said anything until the gorilla grunted.

Jerry twirled a pencil between his fingers and said, "Excellent."

"Great."

"I loved it."

"Fabulous."

"Brilliant."

Jerry pointed his pencil at Roy. "Barry tells me you really were a Navy SEAL."

Okay, there's lying and there's lying. If someone asks an actor if he can ride a horse, the answer is always yes, even if they've never seen a horse. The answer to the questions, 'can you swim (drive a stick shift, play guitar, dance)?' is always yes. If the actor gets the part, he goes out and learns how. This Navy SEAL charade was pressing the envelope a bit, but Roy didn't think it was a good time to announce that he was a fraud. He said, "Yes, sir."

"Ever kill a man?"

From Jerry's bloodthirsty tone, Roy knew the answer Jerry wanted to hear and gave it to him. "Yes, sir."

"Gun, knife, bare hands, how?"

Roy's mind fast-forwarded through scenes from war movies he'd seen and plucked one out. "I cut the throat of an Iraqi trying to sneak through our lines."

"Cut his throat," Jerry said. "Was there a lot of blood?"

Enough already with the blow-by-blow, Roy thought. "It's not like in the movies," Roy vamped. "Cutting a man's throat is like opening a faucet. Blood spurts everywhere. And there's this horrible gurgling sound."

"How long did it take for him to die?"

How the fuck should I know? "Thirty-eight seconds."

"He the only man you killed?"

"No. I dropped a hand grenade into a tank, taking out the four-man crew."

Jerry smiled. "I remember when John Wayne did that in *Sands of Iwo Jima*."

Join the club.

Jerry stood, walked over to Roy. "Are you wearing underwear?"

"Excuse me?"

"Underwear. Do you have on underwear?"

"Uh, yeah."

"Boxer or brief?"

"Boxer."

"Good. Would you mind taking off your clothes but leaving on your boxers?"

"What?"

"Roy, Ramrod spends a lot of time in the ocean. In a swimsuit. So it's important for the actor we cast to have a great body."

Roy did have a great body. He spent hours every other day at the gym to keep it that way. So, feeling a little foolish, he stripped.

Jerry circled him like a new car he was considering buying. "You're in excellent shape."

The others chimed in. "Fabulous."

"Tip top."

"Great definition."

"Brilliant."

Jerry turned to Winslow. "I think Ramrod should have a tattoo."

"Absolutely," the writer-producer said. "In fact, I'm surprised you don't, Roy. I thought all SEALS had tattoos."

"It's ... a religious thing."

"What religion bans tattoos?"

"Jews," the casting director said. "Funny, you don't look Jewish."

Fuck. Now Roy wasn't only lying about being a Seal, he just turned himself into a goddamn Jew. "I converted."

"But you don't have a problem with Ramrod having a tattoo, do you?" Jerry asked.

"Not at all."

"It wouldn't be a real tattoo, of course, just something the makeup people would draw on and take off."

"Great."

Jerry did another circle around Roy. "Now the question becomes, where do we put it? Here ..." he said, wrapping his hand around Roy's bicep. "Or here ..." Jerry traced his fingers across the other bicep. "Or here ..." He placed his hand on Roy's chest. Jerry now stood face to face with Roy. Very close. Too close. "What do you think?" he asked.

Roy desperately wanted to take a step back, put some space between himself and this network creep, but he was afraid of insulting him. He stood his ground. "I think my right bicep would be best. I'm right-handed; we'd get to see it more."

Jerry wrapped his hand around the bicep, squeezed it gently. "Good choice."

"Excellent."

"That's what I was going to say."

"The left would never work."

"Brilliant."

Jerry stared deeply into Roy's eyes. "Jerry Bruckheimer taught me that the eyes are the windows to the soul. And to be a TV star, you've got to have great windows. Well, Roy, you've got great windows." Then Jerry turned to the room and announced: "And we've got our star!"

"We've got a problem, Roy."

"Problem? But my agent said the deal was almost closed."

Winslow was in his office using the speakerphone "Jerry wants another meeting first."

A worried Roy leaned back on his apartment's red plaid couch. "Why?"

"He's got a few concerns he wants to discuss with you."

"Okay ..."

"At his house."

Roy's gaydar went off. "His house? No offense, Barry, but I got some weird vibes off Jerry. You know, the way he stared at me. The way he touched me."

"You afraid he's going to make a pass at you?"

"Well, yeah, I am. Don't get me wrong, I got nothing against gays, but Jerry's just … creepy.

"That's just Jerry's style, Roy. I think he was trying to see how you'd handle the pressure. I don't even think he's gay."

"I don't know …"

"No meeting, no role."

"Why do I have to meet him at his house?"

"He's twisted his ankle or something. He's doing all his business from home this week."

"I don't know ..."

"Tell you what, Roy. I'm so sure that this is on the up and up I'll meet you there. He certainly won't try any funny stuff with me in the room."

That's true, Roy thought. Besides, he told himself, there was no way Jerry could physically force him to do anything. Roy outweighed him by seventy-five pounds. "Okay, I'll do it."

"Great. Six-thirty tonight, 356 Sunset Plaza."

"You'll be there the whole time?"

"Absolutely."

"See you there."

"I'm afraid you've been less than honest with us, Roy." Jerry sat in an overstuffed leather recliner looking at Roy, who stood at a picture window, the sensational view of the Sunset Strip wasted on his back. Winslow was busy at the bar, mixing drinks.

Roy looked down, embarrassed. "You found out I wasn't a SEAL."

Jerry's left ankle was wrapped in gauze, and the rest of his plump body was wrapped in a royal blue Armani robe. "We were getting ready to issue a press release announcing you'd been cast as Ramrod, and leading with the delicious morsel that you'd actually been a Navy SEAL. Luckily our legal department checks every press release, and a quick call to the Defense Department revealed your little ruse."

"I didn't mean anything by it. "

"We know that, Roy," Winslow said, handing him his gin and tonic. "Besides, we didn't cast you because you were a SEAL, we cast you because you're the perfect actor for the role."

"But I still looked like a complete idiot to Frank," Jerry said, referring to the president of the network. He sipped the martini Winslow handed him, smacked his lips in satisfaction. "Perfect, Barry. Thanks."

Roy took a nervous gulp of his drink. "So what happens now?"

"Now I decide whether you keep the role or we recast."

"But you just said I'm perfect for the role." Roy took another nervous pull of the drink.

"I lost face, Roy. That's Commodity Number One in this town. A price must be paid."

"What kind of price?"

"I haven't decided yet. Maybe a renegotiation of your deal. Or ..."

With a long swig Roy finished his drink. "Or ...?"

"A personal favor." Jerry leaned back in his recliner, his robe dropped open a bit, revealing the dark tangle of his pubic hair and the accompanying paraphernalia.

Roy tore his eyes away from Jerry's balls and gave Winslow a look that said, I told you so.

Winslow forced a smile. "What say we all have another drink?" Winslow started for the bar; Roy started to go after him, to tell him he had to get out of here when he suddenly reeled, overcome with vertigo. He grabbed the back of a couch then slumped into it.

Winslow asked, "You okay, Roy?"

"I don't know. Feel funny. Dizzy ..."

"Don't worry, Roy," Jerry said, standing. "You'll be fine in the morning. And the star of your own show."

Roy shook his head, realizing numbly that he'd been drugged. It was like being in an Oliver Stone movie, bombarded with bizarre images. The city lights buzzed like a swarm of fireflies. Winslow, his face melting like an image in a Dali painting, backed out of the room, closing the door behind him. Jerry, his face grotesquely elongated, whispered something in Roy's ear. But Roy didn't hear anything. Another wave of vertigo engulfed him and he passed out.

Daylight blasted through the picture window. Roy opened his eyes, winced as the bright light burned a hole in his brain. He groaned. A sledgehammer was doing overtime on his brain. He could feel every hair on his body, and they all hurt. And he was thirsty. God almighty, his tongue felt like a giant tampon in his mouth.

He sat up and looked around, surprised. He expected to be in his own bed, but he was on a couch in someone's living room. Naked. His clothes were piled on the floor next to him, and a Navajo rug hung about his shoulders.

Oh, shit, he thought as a jumble of fragmented images from last night sliced through his memory like shattered glass. *What the fuck had happened?*

"Oh, good, you're up," Winslow said, walking in with two cups of steaming coffee. "I was beginning to think you'd drunk yourself into a coma."

"Where are we?"

"Jerry's house."

Jerry's house? What the fuck was he doing at Jerry's house? Roy took the offered cup of coffee. "How'd I get here?"

"You drove yourself, as far as I know. Don't you remember coming over last night?"

"No."

"What is the last thing you remember?"

Roy's memory was broken and scattered like a spilled jigsaw puzzle. "Fuck if I know. What day is it?"

"Thursday."

"Wednesday ... Wednesday ... I got to the gym early, hit the weights. But kept my cell phone close in case my agent called to say our deal was closed."

"But he never did, because I called you and said there was a problem."

"I don't remember that. There was? Is?"

"Was. Jerry found out you weren't a SEAL, but you two talked about it last night and now everything's copacetic."

"Why am I still here, naked?"

"We started drinking to celebrate. After about ten G&Ts, you passed out, so Jerry and I took your clothes off and put you to bed on the couch. I was too drunk to drive so I bunked in the guest room."

The pieces weren't quite fitting together, but Roy was in too much agony to worry about it. "Where's Jerry now?"

"At the network. I'm late; it's almost ten-thirty and I've got to get to the studio. Stay here at long as you want, and I'll see you tomorrow, eleven-thirty sharp."

"Eleven-thirty? Where? Why?"

"For the press conference, Roy. We're going to introduce the world to Ramrod. Congratulations, you're a TV star!"

It took a few days, but Roy finally fit all the pieces together. Not that there weren't hints. Freaky flashes of a man's hands on his shoulders, hot breath in his ear.

He'd been raped. Drugged and raped. Rohypnol, probably, the date rape drug. But what the hell was he supposed to do about it? He'd been announced as the star of the upcoming pilot, been to the press conference, and wallowed in the attention. He'd worked hard for this moment, and confronting Winslow or Jerry would only get him fired. Besides, he rationalized, he couldn't be sure that's what happened. So Roy kept his mouth shut.

Three weeks later, while in Hawaii shooting the pilot, Roy got drunk at the wrap party at the Honolulu Hilton and pulled Winslow aside. "You drugged me, didn't you?"

"What're you talking about? This is the first time I've seen you all night."

"Not tonight. At Jerry's. My blackout. You drugged me."

"That's crazy, Roy."

"What'd he do, threaten to pull the plug on the pilot unless you cooperated?"

"You're drunk, Roy. Look, you did a great job on the pilot, you deserve to let it out a little, but—"

"He raped me, and you helped him! Hey, for all I know, you took a poke at me, too."

"I'm not gay."

"But he is, isn't he?"

Roy's voice was beginning to pierce the music and conversation, Winslow pulled him farther away from the festivities and said in a fervent whisper, "Yeah, he's gay."

"And he fucked me, didn't he?"

"Don't go there, Roy. Just believe that you drank too much, passed out, and nothing happened."

"But something did happen!"

"And now you're a TV star."

"Yeah, but at what price?"

"There's always a price, kid. Everyone in Hollywood's made his or her deal with the devil. But unlike in *Faust*, this town is full of devils and we're forced to deal again and again."

Unfortunately for Roy, his deal with the devil was a bust. When the pilot was finished and screened for a test audience they hated it.

Roy's agent gave him the news. Told him the test screening was so bad, Roy would be considered damaged goods by the networks for a while. Suggested he get back that waiter's job. Roy left messages for Winslow, messages that were ignored. Tried to call Jerry, silence.

Roy knew he'd been fucked. Emotionally by Winslow. Literally by Jerry. He wanted to get even but didn't know how. Violence didn't even occur to him. He was young and still had his whole career ahead of him. So he decided to wait until he was famous then use his power to destroy them.

But a couple of things went wrong. First, Jerry was murdered. Found stabbed to death in his apartment. Police suspected robbery; Roy suspected an actor who'd also been 'roofed' and had the guts to do what Roy had not. Second, Roy didn't get famous. And he now realized he never would.

Winslow and Jerry weren't the only ones to fuck him, just the first. So it was time to balance the books. If he couldn't be famous, at least he'd be rich. And get even in the process.

Lady Gaga finished "Poker Face" as Roy remembered getting even with Barry Winslow—those delicious last few moments on the balcony. Roy relished the look on Winslow's face as he pitched back over the rail. Savored the scream. But he didn't watch him land. No time. He had too much to do before Kincaid made his way up.

First stop, the office. Roy typed a suicide note into the computer:

> I'm sorry. Forgive me.

Not the most literary of efforts, he knew, but all someone who'd blurted out a clichéd, "Please, don't kill me," deserved.

Next stop, the bedroom. Roy wanted Gideon and the cops to suspect suicide, at least for a little while, so he had to get rid of the suitcase. Suicide victims don't pack for vacations before offing themselves. Roy threw the clothes into the valise and stuffed it in the back of the closet.

Just outside the bedroom door, Roy stopped. His eyes went to the bookcase, to the shelf of DVDs. To the copy of *Ramrod*. Winslow would never be able to send him a copy now, so Roy took the tape, leaving a spot between the other two pilots, *Dead Run* and *Shadow Chaser*. He pushed the two DVDs together. No one would suspect anything was missing.

Not bad, Roy thought as he rushed out the condo's door, less than a minute after Winslow's "suicide." He mashed the elevator call button. Moments later there was a DING and the door opened. Roy didn't get on the elevator; he was planning to take the stairs. He hoped Kincaid was standing in the lobby waiting for an elevator and would notice the car stopped at twenty-eight. That ought to confuse the shit out of him.

Roy took to the fire stairs to freedom. After dumping the gloves and surgical boots in a couple of dumpsters, he congratulated himself on a job well done.

Roy picked his way through David Hunter's rose bushes to a stand of magnolias planted outside the kitchen. Through the mullioned windows, he saw a handful of servants preparing hors d'oeuvres as Meg and Mila dropped frozen strawberries into glasses of champagne. Francis, Marty, and Clint stood on the patio smoking Cuban cigars.

As Roy rounded the house, he found most of the guests gathered in the backyard watching Lady Gaga rock out.

Roy stepped from the shadows into the crowd. He was dressed like he belonged. Hell, he looked like he belonged. He was Hollywood handsome with a thousand watt smile.

Now, where was she?

His eyes picked through the crowd. Movie stars. Directors. Producers. Writers. Studio executives. Agents. Managers. Personal trainers. The food chain in all its glory.

Finally he spotted her. Jennifer. Sitting alone, poolside. She looked jealous. Staring at birthday boy David, probably wondering why he was sitting next to Kristen instead of her. Roy was surprised, too. David had been quoted many times saying he loved Jennifer more than anything in the world.

Roy drifted toward the pool. Jennifer flicked her brown eyes in his direction, figured he looked harmless enough, and then turned back to David. She looked so sad.

Roy stood behind Jennifer. She stayed focused on David.

Roy reached into his sports coat and opened the sealed plastic bag holding the chloroform-soaked handkerchief. In one quick move he sat down on Jennifer's chaise lounge while covering her nose and mouth with the handkerchief.

She only struggled for an instant before her body went limp. Roy scooped her up and slipped her beneath his coat. She fit easily; after all, Jennifer only weighed four pounds. Four pounds of purebred miniature poodle.

Roy dropped the envelope containing the ransom note on the chaise lounge and casually worked his way around the side of the house, through the hedge, into the neighbor's yard and down the mansion-lined street to his SL550.

He'd done it again. Another perfect kidnapping. And, with any luck, another perfect murder.

Wake Up Call

I slept like shit. Barry Winslow kept invading my dreams, jolting me awake. I saw him flying through the air, screaming.

And that was the problem. He was screaming. Most people who commit suicide jumping off buildings don't scream. They want to die. But when Winslow jumped he sounded like Pavarotti digging for an encore. Maybe somebody had pushed him.

I finally climbed out of bed at about four o'clock and fired up the computer. I raided a few data banks and discovered that Winslow had three accounts at Chase, but they totaled a little more than twelve hundred dollars. I also found records for his personal services corporation, Barwin. He had a pension plan once worth over 1.3 million. But he had been taking early withdrawals over the past year and its current value was less than fifty thousand dollars. Winslow had serious money troubles.

And that spells motive. So maybe somebody hadn't pushed him.

He did lie to me, I thought. He said he was outside the Cinerama Dome when the kidnapper stole my car. I could tell he was lying, and his assistant, Maggie, lied too. He had no alibi at the time the body was stolen. He has to be guilty, right?

I needed to talk to Maggie. So I woke up my pal with Paramount Studio Security, got Maggie's address, and,

Starbucks drink in hand, knocked on her apartment door at seven-fifteen.

She was wearing a muumuu and eating a bagel when she opened the door. Her dreadlocks were piled on top of her head. "You," she said, in a tone somewhere between surprise and disgust. "I'm not supposed to talk to you."

I handed her the coffee. "Hope you like caramel macchiato."

"I prefer mocha, but this will do." She took the coffee and walked inside. I followed her, closing the door behind me.

"Who says you're not supposed to talk to me?"

"Police. They told me you were practically a criminal." We reached the kitchen. Small, but organized. You could tell she liked to cook. She smeared her bagel with a thick gob of cream cheese.

"Two cops? An attractive dark haired woman with a deep-seated hatred of men, and a tall, geeky-looking guy with a bruised chin?"

"That's them."

"So they told you about Barry. I'm sorry."

She shrugged. "Yeah, me too. Want a bagel?"

"No, thanks." She didn't seem too upset, so I said, "You don't seem too upset."

"Barry was an okay boss, but we weren't friends or anything. He treated me like an employee. Kept his distance, if you know what I mean. Never even asked if I was married. If my folks were alive. If I had kids. Nothing. So, I'm sorry that's he's dead. But I'm not about to shed any tears."

"Did the cops tell you how he died?"

"Suspected suicide. They're still investigating."

"Did they ask if Winslow was having money troubles?"

"Sure. And he was. Lord, that man could spend money. He was always flying the bimbo of the week to some exotic place. Buying her clothing and jewels. And he loved to gamble. Blackjack was his game but loser was his name. I don't care how much money Paramount paid him, Barry found a way to spend it. I'll bet I've got more money in the bank than he does. Er, *did*."

A Siamese cat poked its head into the room, took one look at me, and beat a hasty retreat. "Winslow had a cat, too," I said.

She nodded. "Christy."

"As in Christine Cole."

"Yeah. He had a thing for the actress. Cute little cat. Wonder what's going to happen to it?"

"Winslow have any relatives?"

"No. *I* did ask. Parents dead, only child. "

"Then I guess the pound will get the cat."

She grimaced. "I might not have been crazy about Barry, but I did love that cat. Maybe I'll adopt her."

"Did the police tell you about the bones?"

"What bones?"

"Christine Cole's grave was robbed yesterday. Her bones were found in Barry's bathtub."

"No shit?"

"No shit."

"Didn't he write a book about that?"

"Eternal Love."

"Right. That why you came to see him yesterday?"

"Yeah."

"Barry and I may not have been close, and it doesn't take a blood relative to tell you Barry Winslow was no angel, but he wasn't the type of man to go poking around in someone's grave."

"That's why I wanted to talk to you. See, I got the definite impression Barry lied to me yesterday. And that you covered for him."

She nodded. "All that Cinerama Dome shit. Yeah, total lie. His agent never called."

"Then he was picking up the ransom at three o'clock?"

She laughed. "The only thing Barry was picking up at three o'clock was Tornado Wallace's wife's butt. Barry was banging her in Screening Room 5."

"You're sure?"

"I was there, sweetheart, guarding the door. They met once

or twice every week, supposedly to go over her script notes. But if they were dotting i's and crossing t's, they were doing it between orgasms."

Almost to myself I said, "So Barry couldn't have picked up the ransom."

"Nope. That means he didn't kidnap the bones either, doesn't it?"

"Yeah."

"Then who did?"

"Probably the same guy who killed him."

"And that is ..."

"A good question."

Heaven Sent

I got to the office a little after nine. Just in time for the first job interview.

"Do you type?"

"Eighty words a minute."

"Take dictation?"

"In three languages."

"Any of them English?"

She laughed. "Of course, Mr. Kincaid."

Hillary asked, "What are the other two languages?"

"Spanish and French. I also know Latin, but not too many people dictate in it anymore."

Her name was Bridgette O'Reilly. She looked like her name—pretty, with fiery red hair, green eyes, pale skin and rosy cheeks. She was rail thin and had the closed body language of the timid. According to her job application, she was twenty-two and fresh out of college.

I asked, "What was your major?"

"Religion." She blushed. "I'm afraid there wasn't much choice at the convent."

Hillary's mouth dropped open. "You're a nun?"

"Sadly, no. When I was still a novice I realized I was too flawed to follow in the way of the Lord."

I had to ask. "Flawed? How?"

She dropped her eyes, embarrassed. "I have needs, Mr.

Kincaid. Needs that prayer and meditation alone will not satisfy."

Hillary looked confused. "Are you talking about financial needs?"

Bridgette shook her head, her voice almost a whisper. "Sexual needs." She raised her head and stared me down. "There's a fire burning inside me that can only be extinguished by the bodily fluids of a man who is righteous in the eyes of our Lord."

The color drained from Hillary's face. "Well," she said, "I think that's all we need to know." She grabbed Bridgette's job application and stood up. "Thank you very much, Ms. O'Reilly. We have a few more people to interview, but we'll inform you as soon as we've made a decision."

Bridgette's eyes remained locked on mine. "I do hope we can work together." She got up, looked at Hillary, smiled sweetly. "Thanks for your time."

"Don't mention it." As soon as Bridgette stepped into the hall Hillary slammed the door. "That girl is one bead short of a rosary."

"Too bad. I always wanted to dictate in Latin. Investigate, investigatis, investigatum." The phone rang. I was closest, so I answered in my best Latin: "Ave, Imperial Investigations."

The voice was female and officious. "I have David Hunter calling Gideon Kincaid."

My heart leapt. "David Hunter, the producer, David Hunter?"

"That's right. Is Mr. Kincaid available?"

Holy shit! This was it. My big break. David Hunter must've read my book. He wants to buy the movie rights! "You bet I'm available. I mean, I'm him. Gideon Kincaid. And yes, I'm available."

"One moment, please." A click, a brief pause, and he came on the line. "Mr. Kincaid, I need to see you as soon as possible."

"Of course, Mr. Hunter. Just tell me when and where."

"My office. Warner Brothers, one hour."

Yes!

Guilty Pleasures

It only took me twelve minutes to get from Sherman Oaks to Burbank. There was a pass waiting for me at the Warner Brothers gate, so after I parked I spent forty-five minutes walking around the lot, fantasizing.

I graciously accepted the Academy Award for best Screenplay and thanked my seventh-grade English teacher, Mrs. Applegate. Then Universal Studios hired me to write and direct a film that became the highest grossing movie in history. Every man, woman and child in America saw it. Twice. I won my second Oscar, this time for directing.

"Can I help you?" It was David Hunter's receptionist, a beautiful young Eurasian.

"My name's Gideon Kincaid. I'm expected."

"Of course." She indicated a couch. "If you'll take a seat, Mr. Hunter will be right with you."

As she picked up the phone to let David Hunter know I was here, I crossed to the plush leather couch and sat down. A copy of *Daily Variety* lay on the coffee table. Beneath a headline WINSLOW TAKES DIVE, it had a brief story about the suspected suicide of Barry Winslow. Since *Variety* goes to press before midnight, it hadn't had time to do anything more than print the official police line. I suspected that by tomorrow the paper's front pages would be filled with interviews and related stories.

An object beneath the *Variety* caught my eye—the edge of a paperback book. I pulled the paperback free and smiled to see that it was a copy of *Rear Entry*. Hell, if David Hunter was going to make a movie of my book, he'd naturally spread copies around to help hype it. I picked up the paperback, held it up to the receptionist. "I see you've got a copy of my book."

"Oh, that's not ours. It was left here by someone."

That surprised me. "Really. Who?"

Before she could answer, David Hunter's office door opened. Hunter stepped into the reception area, followed by Stacy and Piccolo. "Her," the receptionist said, pointing at Stacy.

Stacy glared at me as Hunter stepped forward, hand extended. "Mr. Kincaid, David Hunter." We shook. David Hunter was short, no more than five seven or eight, about thirty pounds overweight. He was bald, with a pudgy face, and long, flat ears. His deep-set brown eyes sat beneath bushy black eyebrows. The individual parts might not sound all that appealing but somehow Hunter made it work. He radiated confidence. Intelligence. And his personality filled the room. Talk about charisma.

"I think you know Detectives Wilson and Piccolo," he said. Wilson was Stacy's last name. She had never taken mine. She said it diminished a woman to change her name just because she married a pair of balls. I should have known then I was headed for trouble. "Come in, please," Hunter said, leading the way into his office.

As I followed him, Stacy and Piccolo fell in step next to me. "I finished Chapter Three," Stacy hissed in a whisper.

"Asshole," Piccolo added needlessly.

Hunter, hearing none of this, said, "Thanks for coming over on such short notice, Mr. Kincaid." His voice was somber.

"Please, call me Gideon." I glanced at Stacy and Piccolo. "I get the feeling you didn't ask me here to option my book."

"I didn't know you wrote a book," Hunter said.

"Paperback trash," Stacy sniped.

"That's a matter of opinion," I sniped back.

"Well, I'll be sure to read it," Hunter said, "as soon as you get Jennifer back."

Then I realized: "Another kidnapping."

Piccolo said, "Mr. Hunter's poodle. She was kidnapped from his house during a party last night."

David Hunter's poodle was almost as famous as he was. Whenever Hunter had his picture taken for an article or was videotaped for an interview, Jennifer was invariably sitting on his lap or curled up in his arms. So, Hunter was a little eccentric. His movies had grossed over a billion dollars. He was allowed.

"A ransom note was left," Stacy said, "demanding that *you* deliver the money."

Déjà vu all over again.

Stacy handed me the note. My business card was paper-clipped to the top.

> IF YOU WANT TO SEE JENNIFER AGAIN, HAVE GIDEON BRING $2,000,000 IN USED $100 BILLS TO THE DRAGON FLIGHT RIDE AT MAGIC LAND. TODAY, 3:55 P.M. NO TRICKS. NO COPS. OR I'LL COOK AND EAT HER.

"Mr. Hunter," I said. "The note says 'no cops.' Just out of curiosity, why'd you ignore the warning?"

"I didn't. I made the mistake of showing the ransom demand to studio security, and they called the police."

"Professional courtesy," Piccolo said.

"Professional insubordination," snapped Hunter. "I told them not to. And if anything happens to Jennifer, it will be professional unemployment."

I glanced at the note again, at the time for the ransom drop. "Three fifty-five. That's a funny time. Why three fifty-five and not four o'clock?"

"What difference does it make?" Piccolo said. "Three forty-five. Three fifty-five. He's just trying to jerk our chains."

I looked at Stacy. "I guess this officially makes Barry Winslow's high fall a murder investigation."

Stacy nodded, "Yep."

An angry Hunter started to pace. "First he steals a corpse, now a dog. What kind of sick bastard are we dealing with?"

"No way of knowing," Stacy said. "But we'll be following Gideon. When the kidnapper picks up the ransom, we'll arrest him."

"No way," I said. "You saw the note. No tricks. No cops. If he spots you on my tail he'll kill the dog."

Piccolo sneered. "He won't spot us."

"That's right," David said, "because you won't be there. I want Jennifer back and I won't authorize any action that could jeopardize her safety."

"We're the police, not studio security," Piccolo said, trying to sound tough, but coming off more like Mayberry's Barney Fife. "You don't tell us what we can and can't do."

Hunter looked at Stacy. "Is he always this stupid?"

"Yes," I said.

Piccolo took a step toward me, but Stacy moved between us. "Mr. Hunter," she said in her most conciliatory tone, "if you don't want us to follow Mr. Kincaid, we won't. But I'd like to emphasize that the kidnapper is a dangerous man. He killed Barry Winslow yesterday. Threw him off a twenty-eighth story balcony. And he's obviously got an agenda. He's not just after Jennifer, or your two million dollars. I'm afraid he might be after you. The best way to make sure he doesn't hurt you is to catch him. And the best way to catch him is to follow Gideon."

Hunter looked at me. "What do you think?"

"Let me answer by asking a few questions. Did you know Barry Winslow?"

"No."

"Did he ever work for you?"

"Not that I remember. I've used a lot of writers over the years, and I'll have one of my assistants check the files, but I don't think Winslow and I ever worked together."

"And we've never worked together before?"

"No."

"Or met before?"

"I don't think so."

I shook my head. "Somehow we're all related in this thing. Winslow. You. Me. This feels like a vendetta. Someone is getting even with us for perceived wrongs we've committed against him."

Hunter grunted. "Everybody in this town's got a grudge against someone."

"But this guy's gone postal," I said. "Even though none of us knew each other, there has to be a common denominator that can lead us to the killer."

"I'm sure there is," Hunter said. "But we've got a three fifty-five deadline. It's already eleven o'clock. I've got to get two million bucks in cash and you've got a ninety minute drive to Magic Land, so if you don't mind, I'd like to postpone the *Murder She Wrote* crap until after you've recovered Jennifer."

"Fine," I said.

"Now," he said. "Back to my first question. Do we allow the police to follow you?"

"No," I said. "Our only chance to get Jennifer back is to follow the ransom note's instructions. No tricks. No cops."

Stacy drilled me with her eyes. If looks could kill, I was bagged and tagged.

I'M GOING TO MAGIC LAND!

Even hardboiled detectives have parents. And when I was ten, mine took me on a vacation to Southern California. We lived in Milwaukee. I was an only child and my parents ran a corner grocery store. Not much profit in comic books and Cokes so it took Dad three years to save for the trip.

We flew to L.A. on United. A smiling stewardess pinned a shiny pair of wings to my shirt. Dad spent the flight trying to figure out how to use the super 8 movie camera borrowed from our next door neighbor. Mom got drunk on screwdrivers. Funny what you remember.

We went to the beach, took a tour of a Hollywood studio then spent three glorious days in amusement park central, Anaheim, California. Day one was Disneyland. We went on the Teacups, Peter Pan's Flight, Mr. Toad's Wild Ride, and the Matterhorn. I climbed trees on Tom Sawyer's Island, explored Atlantis on the Submarine, and drove my first car at Autopia. Day two was Knotts Berry Farm. I loved the Ghost Town and Jungle Island, but my favorite the Corkscrew. A rollercoaster with two 360-degree flips. Day three was Magic Land. My favorite. We rode the Gargoyle Maze, Dragon Flight and Tooth Fairy Ride. Watched the Big Foot Vs. The Abominable Snowman show. And the Magical Zoo was awesome. The animatronic Cyclops, Centaurs, Dragons, Unicorns and Winged Lions were so lifelike you'd swear they were real.

It was the greatest vacation of my life and I flew home with a suitcase full of souvenirs and a lifetime's worth of memories.

Two weeks later, my parents were murdered. Shot to death during a robbery at the store. The killer was never caught. I was shipped out to live with my Uncle Phil in Glendale.

If I'm hardboiled, that's when I was first dropped into the bubbling water.

"The whole thing's confusing," Hillary said. "I mean, how'd the killer get Winslow to call you?"

"We'll never be sure," I said. "But I'd guess he put a gun to his head and said, 'Call me or die.' "

Hillary and I were in my car, driving east on the 10, about two miles from the Magic Land exit. It was three o'clock, and we were flying along at sixty miles an hour.

"So the killer forces Winslow to call you and then watches from the balcony for your car to arrive?"

"When he sees me pull up, he throws Winslow off the balcony."

"Wow. Talk about your cold-blooded murderers."

Suddenly all the cars ahead of me slammed on their brakes. I did, too, skidding to a stop millimeters from the Dodge Grand Caravan in front of me. "Jesus Christ, now what?"

"I see police lights flashing up ahead."

"Probably another fucking accident." I was a little more uptight than usual. After all, I had two million dollars in a backpack in the back seat and only forty-five minutes to deliver the ransom.

The guy behind me honked. I hate that. What do these people think honking's going to accomplish? He honked again. Goddamn it! I turned around and gave him a dirty look, at the same time spotting a car stuck in the traffic jam about three rows back. It was a plain wrap Ford favored by the police department. The driver and passenger tried to duck out of sight when they saw me. Stacy was behind the wheel, Piccolo rode shotgun. I opened the car door. "I'll be right back."

I walked through the sea of frozen cars. Stacy and Piccolo exchanged a chagrined look, and then Stacy rolled down her window. “Don’t start, Gideon.”

“I thought we had an agreement.”

“You and Hunter had an agreement,” Piccolo said. “We never agreed to anything.”

I turned to Stacy. “If you want to catch this son of a bitch, let me work alone.”

Stacy laughed. “Yeah, right. Last time he stole your car.”

“This time’ll be different.”

“I know,” she said. “This time we’ll handle it.”

Traffic started moving again. But I didn’t. A chorus of horns bleated as pissed off drivers inched around us. “You saw the note,” I said. “If he spots you he’ll kill the dog.”

“Get a grip, Gideon. We’re talking about a goddamn dog! We’re in a no-lose situation here. If he doesn’t see us, we grab him as he leaves the park. If he does see us, all we lose is a dog.”

“Or he could get pissed off and shoot me.”

Stacy smiled. “Like I said, it’s no-lose.”

A guy in a pickup truck drove by, giving me the finger. I flipped him back as I thought it over. I had my own plan to catch the kidnapper, which I wasn’t about to share with them. However, I knew that no matter what I said they were going to follow me. So, I figured, I might as well include them.

“Okay,” I said. “What’s the plan?”

“You meet him at Dragon Flight,” Stacy said. “And we handle the rest.” Stacy dropped her car in gear and roared off, leaving me in the middle of the 10 Freeway, surrounded by a cacophony of curses and car horns.

Abracadabra

The microchip has become the PI's best friend. From night scopes to lipstick cameras, bugs to homing devices.

I had a SpyZone GPS AJ-1800 sewed into the lining of the backpack. It sent out a signal strong enough to be detected within a five-mile radius.

The plan was simple. I'd go into Magic Land and make the exchange while Hillary waited in the car with the AJ-1800's tracking unit. If I got back to the car before the kidnapper left the park, great. We'd use the GPS device to follow at a safe distance. If he left the park before I got back to the car, Hillary would follow him and keep me posted by phone.

The only fly in the ointment was Stacy. I didn't know her plan. But I figured that was okay. If Stacy and Piccolo caught the kidnapper, great. If not, I still had my AJ-1800. So, I decided not to worry.

Big mistake.

Walking into Magic Land was like stepping into a time machine. Brothers Grimm Boulevard looked the same to me as it had thirty years ago. As I walked past Neptune's Workshop I was flooded with memories. I saw the Magic Emporium where I'd bought my magic wand. Cupid's Corner where Dad had bought super 8mm film.

As I crossed that cobblestone street toward The Snow Queen ride it was hard to believe I was that same ten-year-old boy.

Ten-year-old Gideon had been full of dreams. I'd wanted to be a baseball player. Or an astronaut. Or run a corner grocery. Because Mom and Dad worked so much, I was often left alone, so my dream included marriage and a big family. Eight or nine kids like the O'Malleys on the corner. I wanted to coach Little League and be an Elk, like Dad. I wanted a house with a swing set and a big lawn I'd mow every Saturday. Simple dreams from a boy filled with hope.

God, I miss that kid.

There were lines in front of the Hansel and Gretel, Rapunzel and Rumpelstiltskin rides. But the longest was in front of Dragon Flight. I loved the part where you flew over medieval London and battled other dragons. It seemed so real. Judging from the line, it hadn't lost its appeal.

It was three-fifty. I had five minutes to wonder which of the thousands of people was the kidnapper, wonder where Stacy and Piccolo were, wonder why I was supposed to be here at such a weird time, wonder what happened to the dreams of that freckled-faced kid from Milwaukee.

BRRRING.

It sounded like an old-fashioned telephone ring. A cell phone ringtone, no doubt. BRRRING.

Loud, too. I looked around, but nobody seemed to be reacting to it.

BRRRING.

The sound seemed to be coming from a trash container. Why would someone throw away a cell phone?

BRRRING.

Of course ... Ask not for whom the cell phone BRRRINGS. It BRRRINGS for thee. I dug through the empty popcorn bags, ice cream sticks and churros wrappers until I found a cheap Motorola. I pulled it out and flipped it open. "Hello."

"You're not as dumb as you look."

"Yes, I am," I said before realizing what I said. "I mean ... Fuck what I mean! Where's the dog?"

"Where's the money?"

"In the backpack."

"Good. See the bench to your left?"

"Yes."

"Take off the backpack. Put it on the bench and sit down next to it."

I did.

"Good," the kidnapper said. "Now chill. I'll be by in a bit to pick it up."

"What about the dog?"

"All good things come to he who waits. Oh, and I'll want the cell phone back. Put it in the pack with the money." Click, he hung up.

Smart request. Cell phones contain a treasure trove of information. From fingerprints to call records, cops love cell phones. Hell, they can even use them to triangulate your location. But I had my AJ-1800, so I dropped the Motorola into the backpack.

I did a quick scan. Still no sign of Stacy or Piccolo. No hint of where the kidnapper/car thief/ murderer could be hiding.

Then I heard the sound of an approaching brass band. Kids jumped up and down in glee. Parents focused their video cameras as they lined the street. A parade! *Son of a bitch*, I thought. That's why I had to be here at 3:55. The killer was going to use the parade as cover.

The Pied Piper led the procession of Magic World costumed characters. The classics like Cupid, Merlin, Rapunzel and those creepy Goblins. Then came some of the new stars, Piper the Pixie, Elvis the Elf and Tommy Troll. It's not that I keep up, but you can't buy a Big Mac anymore without seeing some damn promotion for the latest Magic Land 3-D movie.

Suddenly Merlin danced out of the parade and toward me. Merlin is, of course, a man completely enclosed in a costume. He's got a huge head with busy eyebrows and the trademark long flowing beard. He swept the backpack off the bench with his left arm, and then danced through the crowd of squealing kids and back into the parade.

Shit, I thought. This guy's good.

Then I heard it. Piccolo's whiny voice: "Freeze, police!" I spun to see Piccolo burst through the crowd, weapon drawn. Stacy was a step or two behind him.

Suddenly Merlin's left hand exploded, blown out by the bullets fired from the gun hidden beneath the costume. Stacy and Piccolo dove for cover as the shots zinged harmlessly off the pavement. Stacy rolled, came up, gun ready. But Merlin was standing in front of the Jack and the Beanstalk float. Stacy was too smart to shoot in a theme park full of kids.

Piccolo wasn't. He leveled his automatic and fired. Merlin lurched left, the bullet missed him and hit Rapunzel. The impact of the blast lifted her off her feet and into the arms of a stunned Rumpelstiltskin.

Merlin was a better shot. He fired twice, both shots hitting Piccolo. One bullet tore into the bulletproof vest, the second was buried in his left shoulder.

Stacy worked her way past Tom Thumb and Thumbelina, trying to flank Merlin. As she raised her weapon, a 315-pound plumber from South Bend, Indiana—on vacation with his wife and three kids—saw what he must've thought was a crazed woman trying to shoot the beloved Merlin and decided to be a hero. He dove, wrapping his huge arms around Stacy, and drove her into the ground. Stacy let out a cry as the wind was knocked out of her.

That left me. Now I could've been smart, let Merlin leave the park and just use my tracking device to follow him. But bullets were flying, my ex-wife was watching, and the testosterone kicked in, making me stupid. So I pulled the Glock out of my shoulder holster, jumped off the bench, and leapt into the fray.

Meanwhile, Merlin grabbed Ali Baba by the arm and yanked him off his black stallion. Merlin tried to put his feet in the stirrup, but the costumed boots were too big. He tried to pull himself up by the horn, but the costume was too heavy.

By then I'd reached him. I threw a punch, catching Merlin squarely on the jaw. Unfortunately, the thick costume cushioned the blow. Merlin swung the backpack at me, hitting me in the face. Dazed, I dropped to my knees. He whacked me in the head again, and I went down, double-dazed.

Merlin leapt onto the Jack and the Beanstalk float and from there jumped onto the horse. By now, people were beginning to figure out Merlin was a bad guy. Elvis the Elf and Tommy Troll tried to rush him. Merlin fired twice—dropping both of them—kicked the flanks of the horse and rode off.

I got to my feet and stumbled after him, watching helplessly as he galloped into the Deep Dark Forest.

"Do something," Stacy wheezed as she joined me, still fighting for breath.

"All right," I said, and ran. Not after Merlin, but in the opposite direction. I ran past the charging security people, past the siren-blaring ambulances. I ran through the panicked crowd, and charged toward the exit.

I jigged around a terrified little girl, clinging to her equally terrified mother. I leaped over a sixty-something women clutching a twisted ankle.

I burst through the main entrance into the parking lot. Police cars and ambulances screamed through the sea of cars toward me. My Taurus was parked about a half mile away, wedged between a Lexus and a Ford Aerostar. I had to get to my SpyZone AJ-1800, but I was pooped. I'd run about as far as I could without cramping up or throwing up. Luckily I saw one of the parking lot trams at the curb, the driver standing next to it, staring at the incoming procession of cops and paramedics. I slid into the front seat and floored it!

Now a souped-up golf cart pulling eight twenty-four-foot tramcars doesn't exactly burn rubber, but I was pleasantly surprised when it accelerated rapidly.

The tram driver spun as he heard his tram driving off and yelled at me, "Stop!"

I didn't.

The tram driver ran after me but the tram was really starting to roll now—twenty, twenty-five, thirty miles an hour. In a last ditch effort, the tram driver dove and grabbed onto the bumper of the last tramcar. Hanging on by his fingernails, his legs dragging across the asphalt, he slowly tried to pull himself into the last car.

What was wrong with this guy? We're talking about a tram here, not the prototype of the stealth fighter, and he was doing an Indiana Jones, risking his life to stop me.

Suddenly a motor home pulled out ahead of me, blocking the road. I yanked the wheel hard left, ducking into the nearest row. But as I skidded past a Mercedes, just missing its bumper, I knew the law of physics was about to wreak havoc.

Force, mass, and inertia combined to send the train of tramcars behind me into an ever-widening arc, whipsawing the trams toward a line of parked cars. I glanced back to see the tram driver's eyes saucer open in horror as he slid helplessly toward a Cadillac Eldorado. He let go and was slingshot past the Caddy, under a battered Ford pickup and into a Lexus LS400 with the personalized plate: HPYFCE. The tram driver hit with a sickening thud and slid to the ground, unconscious.

Behind me, the caravan reached the end of its arc. The coupling snapped on the last tram and it flipped over, tumbled once head over heels, and smashed into an old Volkswagen bug.

The second-to-last tram also broke free. It hit a Honda Accord first, crushed the hood and shattered the windshield. The tram then bounced into a Chevy Lumina, crunched a Toyota Celica and mashed a Jaguar XJS before it came to rest, upside down, on top of three Harleys with New Mexico license plates.

I thought to myself, *Thank God this isn't a movie.* In a movie, the motorcycles would've blown up. Things always blow up in movies, but almost never do in real life.

KABOOM! One of the motorcycles blew up. KABOOM! The other two blew.

I just kept going, faster now that I was pulling fewer cars. I zoomed past more incoming black and whites, squealed a right turn into Row Q34—my train of tram cars snaking obediently and safely behind me—and skidded to a stop next to a surprised Hillary. She was standing outside the car, staring incredulously at the fireball.

"What happened?"

"The expression, 'It's a long story,' comes to mind," I said, jumping into the car and starting the engine.

Hillary climbed in next to me. "Where we going?"

"After the kidnapper." I picked the AJ-1800 off the seat and handed it to her. "He could be half way to L.A. by now. Which way's he moving?"

She studied it for a confused moment and said, "He's not."

"What?"

"He's not moving. Unless this thing is, like, broken, he's still in the park."

Abracadabra Already

Thousands of people spilled out the Magic Land exits as Hillary and I fought our way back into the park. We could hear snippets of conversation from the fleeing masses.

"Merlin had a machine gun and opened fire on ..."

"No, *sixty* hostages, in the Gargoyle Maze . . ."

"Arab terrorists, who else would bomb ..."

"Two hundred dead so far and they're still ..."

The rumors were flying. Judging by the armada of news helicopters circling above us, I knew that every TV station in L.A. had interrupted regular programming to report that murder and mayhem had visited Magic Land. The news media loves this kind of shit. The bigger the disaster, the better. Live remotes. Expert interviews. Useless speculation. If corpses could spin in their graves, Edward R. Murrow's would look like a tornado hit it.

Cops and paramedics swarmed over the scene of the shooting. Yellow police tape had already been strung as shocked Magic Land security people kept back the morbidly curious.

I spotted Stacy, radio in hand, standing by her wounded partner. When she saw me she rushed over. "Are you nuts, Gideon? You watch that murdering SOB ride off one way and you run off the other? I always knew you were a fucking asshole, but I didn't realize you were a chickenshit fucking asshole."

She did have a way with words. "You find him?" I asked.

"No, he's vanished."

I held up the AJ-1800. "Maybe this'll help." We were getting a signal, strong and steady, to the north-northwest, about half a mile away. I headed at a quick trot in that direction, Stacy and Hillary beside me.

Stacy barked into her radio. "This is Wilson. I may have a 20 on the perp. I'm mobile, moving from Brothers Grimm Land to the Deep Dark Forest. Request backup."

We got it. With every step we took, it seemed like another cop joined us. By the time we passed the Cave of the Cyclops, we were twenty-five strong.

The AJ-1800 led us to the bathrooms across from Mermaid Lagoon. "In there," I pointed.

The cops formed a semi-circle surrounding the double doors, and then looked at Stacy for instructions.

"Don't go in there," I told her.

"You think he's got a gun aimed at the door?"

"No. It's a men's room."

Stacy withered me with a look, and then turned to the cops. "Gonzales, Pederson, Jacobs, back me up ..."

"I'm going in, too," I said, pulling my gun.

"Forget it, Gideon. This is police business."

"Only because you and your nitwit partner fucked up the drop. If you'd let me do it my way ..."

"Can it, Sinatra. You're waiting out here." She turned to her cops. "On three. One, two ..."

I've never been good at taking orders and wasn't about to start now. I handed Hillary the AJ-1800, shouldered past Stacy and burst into the bathroom.

Merlin was standing against the back wall, his arm up, gun aimed at my heart. Swinging my gun into position, I dove for the floor.

I fired three times. My shots sounded like hand grenades in the tile room, and I kept waiting for the echo of his shot. It never came.

I looked up to see three ragged holes in Merlin's chest. He didn't move for a moment; then he tipped over and fell.

The costume was empty. As Merlin landed, his head popped off and rolled across the floor, coming to rest in front of me. We were nose to nose.

The door banged open as Stacy and the cops ran in, guns ready. Hillary came through the door next, a panicked look on her face. "Gideon?!"

"I'm fine," I said picking up Merlin's head and looking at the empty costume. "But we're too late. He's gone."

Hillary aimed the AJ-1800 at one of the stalls and pushed open the door. My backpack lay crumpled on the ground, empty. "He switched the money into another bag," I said. "Damn it."

Hillary reached into the backpack. "There's something in here." She pulled out a key with a Magic Land logo stamped on it. A locker key.

Locker 257 was one of the small lockers—you know, the one you rent to store a breadbox. I slipped in the key as Hillary, Stacy and all twenty-five cops gathered round. They'd followed me back to Brothers Grimm Boulevard, all the way from the Deep Dark Forest. I felt like the Pied Piper. I was also starting to feel a little smothered, so I said, "I wouldn't be surprised if the SOB planted a bomb in here."

They all took a giant step back. Much better.

Ever so slowly I turned the key. When it clicked open, there was a collective flinch. I glanced back nervously, milking the suspense, and then swung the door open.

I screamed and jumped back. The crowd scattered, running for cover.

Everyone but Stacy. She knew my sense of humor too well. She just stood there, glowering. "Not funny, Gideon."

"Maybe not 'guffaw, laugh till you cry' funny, but it was definitely 'Ha Ha' funny."

"Four people have been shot, twenty-seven more injured in the panic, and you're making jokes. Grow up, Gideon."

"Don't start with that Peter Pan complex shit again, Stacy. Even if it's true." As Hillary and the cops reassembled, I reached into the locker and brought out Jennifer, the poodle. She had a glitzy rhinestone collar around her neck, but no leash. The tiny dog flopped over the edges of my hands, lifeless.

"Is she dead?" Hillary asked.

"No, I feel a heartbeat. Probably drugged."

Hillary gently petted the dog. "Poor baby ..."

"My poor baby ..." A grateful David Hunter said, hugging the dog to his chest. "What has he done to you?"

Stacy and I were poolside at Hunter's Holmby Hills home. I'd sent Hillary back to the office.

I looked at the huge pool, manicured gardens, humongous mansion, collection of servants, and wondered what it must be like to live in this kind of luxury. Being rich has never been one of my ambitions. If so, I never would've become a cop. But when you see how the wealthy really live, you begin to realize that being rich is a pretty good deal. Whenever I leave Beverly Hills after spending time on someone's rambling estate, I find myself stopping on the way home to buy a lottery ticket.

"Mallory," Hunter said to his butler. "See if Dr. Crawford can come right over."

"Vet?" I asked.

"Dean of the UCLA School of Veterinary Medicine." The dog was awake now, but groggy. She tried to focus on Hunter as he nuzzled her. "Nothing but the best for my itty bitty baby ..."

Amazing. Even the rich and powerful are reduced to blithering idiots when talking to a fuzzy ball of fur.

Hunter turned his attention back to us. "I understand that people were hurt."

"But no one was killed," Stacy said.

"How's your partner?"

"Shot twice. His vest stopped the first, but he took one in the shoulder. Luckily, it's not serious. He'll be back to work tomorrow."

"Thank God." Hunter's voice hardened a bit. "What I don't understand, Detective, is how he came to be shot at all. I thought we had an agreement."

Stacy met his eyes, defiantly. "We did, but Detective Piccolo and I decided that we had too good a chance to apprehend the kidnapper so we—"

"Fucked everything up," Hunter interrupted, taking the words out of my mouth.

Stacy's gaze faltered for a nanosecond. She refocused and said, "I made a judgment call. I'll stand by it."

"You'll do just that after I talk to the mayor." He turned to me. "Did you know Wilson and her partner were at Magic Land?"

"Yes."

"We gave him no choice," Stacy added quickly. "I told Gideon that we were staking out the drop whether he liked it or not."

I looked at Stacy, surprised. She'd always been honest, but I never expected her to stick up for me.

Hunter seemed impressed, too. "Good. I thought you were a man I could trust, Gideon. Thank you. And now that Jennifer's back, I'd be happy to read your book."

Read my book? My heart started doing the Samba as the fantasies swirled. He'd read the book. Buy the rights. Make the movie. Then a sequel. Before you know it, *Rear Entry 6* is playing at theaters everywhere. I'd be rich. Famous. Better looking. I'd buy the mansion next door. Maybe even get a poodle.

"Well, that's great. I'm mean, thank you very much, Mr. Hunter. Very much. I'll have my agent send one right over."

But Hunter's attention was already back on Jennifer. "Let's get the baby something to eat ..." He started across the patio toward his house, scratching behind the dog's ears, then stopped. "Oh," he said, "You can have this back."

"What?" I asked.

"The dog collar."

Stacy shook her head. "That's not our dog collar."

Hunter frowned. "It's not mine, either. Oh, well ..." He started to take it off.

I looked at Stacy, trying to make sense of the collar. "If Hunter didn't put it on Jennifer ..."

"And we didn't put it on Jennifer ..."

"That means the kidnapper put it on Jennifer."

"Why would the kidnapper put a collar on ..." It hit us both at the same instant.

The same instant Hunter unbuckled the collar and started to take it off.

I took a step toward Hunter and started to call out a warning.

Too late. The collar exploded.

Puppy Chow

Blackness. And a sound: BEEP. BEEP. BEEP. That's all I heard. But I'd heard those BEEPS before. On TV. In movies. In Intensive Care, where my mother struggled with two bullets in her before the BEEP BEEP BEEP turned into a BEEEEEEEP and she died.

I was in a hospital. I slowly opened my eyes and found myself staring into the concerned but still beautiful face of Hillary. "Did you touch the face of God?"

"Excuse me?"

"When you had your near-death experience. Did you see, like, a bright light, a long tunnel and God standing there in glowing robes?"

Near-death experience? What the hell was she talking about? My brain felt waterlogged. I tried to sit up but none of my muscles would respond. "Where am I?"

"Cedars Sinai. Did you know parking here costs four dollars and fifty cents for every fifteen minutes? Don't you think that's, like, way too much? I mean people feel bad enough coming to a hospital to visit sick family and friends. And then to charge them millions of dollars to park their cars is, like, adding insult to injury."

"Why am I at Cedars?"

"You were blown up. Well, almost blown up."

It started coming back. "The collar."

"The paramedic said your heart actually stopped. That is so cool. I mean, you're the first dead person I ever met. Well, *almost* dead person. There's so much I want to ask you. Like, did your life pass before your eyes? Did you have an anxiety wash and feel like totally liberated? Did you want to stay in the white light when God said 'Go back ... Go back ...' Did God speak English?"

"God didn't speak at all."

"Oh, well, sure, God wouldn't have to speak. He could just think it. Telepathy, right?"

"There was no tunnel. No light. No glowing robes."

"No God?"

"No God."

"Hmmm. He was probably too busy with Mr. Hunter."

"How is he?"

"Dead."

"And the dog?"

"Really dead."

"Stacy?"

"Alive and complaining. She's down the hall."

"Badly hurt?"

"A few lacerations on her left arm and a bruised hip."

"The explosion bruised her hip?"

"No, *you* did when you fell on her."

"When did I fall on her?"

"When you were blown up. Almost blown up. The concussion, like, knocked you off your feet."

"Do I still have ten fingers and toes?"

"And two arms and legs and one very cute nose."

"I didn't know you thought my nose was cute."

"A lot of you is cute. And black and blue."

"The concussion."

"It mashed your skin into your bones, the doctor said. But aside from almost dying, you're in pretty good shape."

"If my heart stopped who restarted it."

"Stacy. She gave you CPR."

"Shit. Now I owe her my life."

"Would you rather be dead?"

"Can I get back to you on that?"

"You can go back to sleep. The doctor says you need rest."

"I'm not tired."

"Yes, you are. You're exhausted."

"I feel like I'm drugged up."

"That, too."

"Why?"

"So you won't scream out in agony." She stroked my forehead with her fingers. "Now sleep."

I did.

"Wake up, asshole."

I opened my eyes. Stacy stood there, Hillary hovered protectively behind her.

"They're releasing me," Stacy said, "so I thought I'd stop by and let you thank me for saving your life."

"Thank you."

"And tell you I did it instinctively. If I'd thought about it at all, I probably would've let you die."

"I have no doubt."

Then her expression softened. "How do you feel?"

"I killed my client. How do you think I feel?"

"Self pity. That's a new character flaw."

"Admit it, Stacy. If I had been smart enough to realize what the killer was up to, I could've saved Hunter's life."

"Hey, I was standing next to you. I didn't think of it, either. But I'm not going to take responsibility for the murder. It's not our fault this guy's a fucking maniac."

"Listen to her," Hillary said from the doorway. "You can't blame yourself."

They were right. When a cop or a PI tries to take responsibility for all the evil in the world they usually end up eating their gun. I asked, "What'd forensics find out about the bomb?"

"The collar was made of C-4. Detonated when it was unbuckled."

"So our killer's had training in handling explosives."

"By the way, the press has dubbed him, The Gravesnatcher."

"Wait, they know about Christine's kidnapping? I thought we'd agree to keep that a secret."

"Somebody must've leaked it," Stacy said.

"Shit, Alex Snyder's going to kill me," I said, remembering the look in the funeral director's eyes when he pointed the .45 at my face. "Can we at least return Christine's remains to him?"

"No, not yet."

"I called him," Hillary said. "Told him that Christine was in police custody and being cared for with the utmost respect. I gave him my guarantee that you would personally return her to him as soon as the case was closed."

I looked at Hillary, impressed with her initiative. "Great, thanks."

"By the way," Stacy said. "The Chief is putting together a task force."

"I want in."

"You'll be the guest of honor."

I looked at Hillary. "When am I getting out of here?"

"Tomorrow morning, unless your heart stops again, you go into convulsions, or die."

I smiled, looked at Stacy. "Florence Nightingale, she's not."

"But she cares about you. Which is nice, and also a complete mystery to me. Anyway, the task force meets at nine tomorrow. Be there or be square." Stacy started for the door, then stopped. "I should warn you that a *few* cops are worried about you being in on this. They think you're working with the killer."

"By a *few* cops, you mean your partner, don't you? Piccolo."

"Yeah."

"Well, he's worried about the wrong thing."

"Really. And what should he be worried about?"

"Who's next."

He's Back

Lisa Montgomery was the most beautiful woman in the world. At least, that's what the November issue of *People* magazine said. Roy had to agree. Especially as he watched her undress through the bedroom window. She was wearing a red dress. Single-strand pearl necklace. Fuck-me pumps.

She was sitting on the edge of the bed, reaching down to unfasten the shoes. Roy glimpsed her nipples through the top of her dress as she bent over. Hard and pink. She kicked the left foot free. Then the right. An ankle bracelet caught the candlelight, winked playfully.

Roy was in a good mood, even though things had gotten a little out of hand at Magic Land. No one was supposed to get shot. Rapunzel, for Christ's sake. But, then again, nothing ever goes *exactly* according to plan.

Mayhem at Magic Land! Disaster at Magic Land! Merlin in Mourning! Each TV station had their own corny name for the afternoon's adventure, but none of them mentioned Jennifer's kidnapping. Or the two million dollar ransom. Or the David Hunter connection. Oh, they mentioned his murder. But they didn't mention the PI and the cop who were also caught in the blast. And they didn't tie David Hunter to Barry Winslow or Christine Cole.

Roy had been warned that the cops would try to keep a lid on it. He couldn't let that happen. Getting the publicity was part of the plan. So he'd made a few anonymous phone calls, filling in a few blanks. And he knew someone else who would be making a few calls, too, unofficially confirming everything Roy said.

Roy's attention returned to the bedroom window. Slowly, languidly, Lisa stood up and stretched, her arms behind her, her breasts pressing against the dress. Again, her nipples teased him, clearly visible beneath the flimsy fabric.

It was almost like she knew Roy was there. Like she was putting on a show.

Roy's breath quickened. She was even more spectacular than he remembered. Her blond hair fell nonchalantly to her shoulders as she took a sip of champagne, her tongue darting out of her mouth to catch a recalcitrant drop. Oh, those sweet, sensuous lips!

Lisa glided into the bathroom, disappearing from view, although Roy could still see her shadow sharply etched into the wall. She reached back and unfastened the dress with long, delicate fingers. A shrug of her shoulders, and the dress dropped to the floor.

Roy heard a cough. Then a sneeze. Goddamn it! He spun around in his seat and glared at the guy sitting behind him, who ignored Roy and blew his nose. This is why Roy hated movie theaters. Too many people, eating popcorn, unwrapping candy, blowing their fucking noses.

Roy turned back to the screen. Lisa was stepping into a shower. The water cascaded over her perfect body, but again, all the nudity was implied. The director showed you her thighs, stomach, neck, calves but no clean shot of her tits.

Roy wasn't surprised; after all, Lisa Montgomery had been crowned Hollywood's latest Girl-Next-Door, and America's Sweetheart could never do a nude scene.

But Roy had seen her nude. Touched those breasts, buried his face in her golden bush. Roy remembered what it was like to actually make love to her.

The taste of her lips.

The feel of those nipples between his fingers.

The way she gasped as he entered her.

Locked her legs around his waist.

Dug her nails into his back.

In fact, Roy had been the first to ever sleep with Lisa. He took her cherry his junior year, while rehearsing Georgia State's fall production of *Othello*.

Lisa had been in love, but Roy had only been sport-fucking and dumped her after their one night together. She'd been broken-hearted, but hey, it wasn't his fault when a chick was stupid enough to buy his line.

How was he to know she'd end up a big Hollywood star?

How was he to know he'd bump into her again?

How was he to know she'd finally get even, keep him from getting that movie?

The movie that could've made him a star.

Well, it was time to fuck her again.

A Tisket a Task Force

"We are dealing with one smart motherfucker." Captain Mary Rocket looked out at the thirty cops crammed into the conference room and shook her head. "We've had four crime scenes: Westwood Memorial Cemetery, Winslow's apartment, Hunter's mansion, and Magic Land. And so far, not one solid piece of evidence."

As she paced around her office, Mary Rocket favored her right leg; her left was withered as the result of a birth defect. Although nearing sixty, she looked closer to forty. She wore her hair in an Afro and dressed in traditional African clothes that complemented her skin, so black it appeared almost purple. She might have passed for a U.N. ambassador from Zimbabwe.

"Not that the crime lab doesn't have stuff to work on; there were tons of prints in Winslow's condo. Thousands of prints in the Magic Land locker and bathrooms. They found so many prints in David Hunter's mansion that his three full-time maids ought to vamoose their fat butts back to Guatemala. *However,* I got a funny feeling that not one of these prints belongs to our Gravesnatcher."

Mary Rocket sizzled with energy. She worked fast. She talked fast. She limped fast. All that zipping around was infectious. Spending a few minutes with Mary Rocket was like having a jolt of adrenaline injected directly into the cerebral cortex.

"He must be wearing gloves. We've searched the neighboring

environs of all four scenes and found no discarded surgical gloves."

Occasionally, a crook's stupid enough to take the gloves off and throw them away right outside a crime scene. Fingerprints can be found *inside* the gloves.

"We've collected fibers and trace evidence from all the scenes," she went on, "cross-checked and catalogued them. But we've got no common denominators yet. The Gravesnatcher fired five times at Magic Land. We checked the five 9mm shell casings we picked up. Nada."

Sometimes a perp loads his gun long before he plans to use it and often forgets to wear gloves. It's easy to leave thumbprints when you're shoving a bullet into a magazine or cylinder.

"You missed a crime scene," I called out from the back of the room.

"What's that, Gideon?"

"My car. The Gravesnatcher stole it when I tried to deliver the Cole ransom."

"Why haven't you brought it by the crime lab?"

"Because the Gravesnatcher wiped it down. Perfectly. Even got the spot most perps miss—the rear view mirror."

Mary Rocket nodded. "Like I said, one smart motherfucker."

I looked at the other cops squeezed into the room. I knew most of them. Detectives now, they'd worn uniforms when I'd been a cop, six years ago. Now they were members of the LAPD's most important task force. There was a buzz in the room, a palpable vibe. This was a life or death hunt for a serial killer. The men and women gathered in this conference room were filled with a sense of purpose, of duty.

I'd loved that feeling when I was a cop. And sitting there, I realized how much I missed it.

Captain Mary Rocket turned to Stacy. "Tell them about your interview with Merlin." Eddie Glover, that afternoon's Merlin, had been found bound and gagged in a gardening shed near the employee walkway behind the Ugly Ducking ride.

"Well," Stacy said. "He said President Obama did it." This

earned her a mixture of groans and laughs. "He'd just finished his shift and was heading in to take a break when someone grabbed him from behind, pulled him into the bushes, ripped off his Merlin head, and shoved a wet, smelly rag over his face."

"Chloroform," Hector Ruiz said. He was the criminologist assigned to the task force. Only five six, with thick glasses and a bushy moustache, Hector looked like a bookworm. But looks are often deceiving. Hector was an adrenaline freak. Anything for a thrill. Bungie jumping. Sky diving. He'd even done Niagara falls in a barrel. The guy was fearless. "We found the rag buried in the bushes."

"That's when he got a look at his attacker. Just a glimpse. But he swears it was President Obama."

I couldn't resist. "Maybe we should check the President's alibi."

"I already did," Mary Rocket said. "He was in Bangor, Maine, speaking at a Save the Whales rally. So I figure the Gravesnatcher was wearing a mask. You know, one of those Halloween things. Stacy, did he get any feel for the man's height? Weight? Did he speak? Any other indicators?"

"No. He said it all happened too fast. The last thing Merlin remembered was wishing he'd voted for McCain."

Mary Rocket let the laughter ripple through the room. She was a big believer in morale, and now was a good time for the cops to bond. She knew they were going to need the unity.

"Okay, kids," she finally said as the room settled down. "On to the grunt work. Landsbury, Ruiz, McDonald: you've got the mask. Find out who makes Obama masks. Who sells them locally. Who's bought them in the last sixty days.

"Semel, Whitmore, Miller, Fleck: check the explosives angle. He made or paid someone to make that collar. Track the C-4. The FBI may be able to help. And rattle the cages of all the paroled boom boom felons. These guys talk to each other. Someone may have heard something.

"Chang, Inch, Lang: you've got videos. Neither the cemetery or Hunter mansion had surveillance cameras, but Winslow's building and Magic Land did. Unfortunately, Magic Land's got 267 of them. Pull all the tapes, narrow your time line to two hours either side of the crimes and start looking."

Chang raised his hand. "Looking for what?"

"Matches. Take a look at all the men who entered Winslow's building up to two hours before his murder and see if you can find a face that matches on the Magic Land tapes."

A sense of gloom descended on Chang. "There must've been 20,000 people at Magic Land that day."

"Twenty-eight thousand, four hundred sixty-seven. I already checked."

The gloom turned to despair as Mary Rocket moved on. "Since this feels like a revenge thing, Walburg, Laidman, Correll: you're going to connect the dots. Start interviewing people. Check files and records. I want a list of everybody who ever had associations with Winslow and Hunter. Then cross-check the lists. There have to be some names on both lists, and one of them could be our killer."

"What about me?" I asked. "I seem to be connected to the Gravesnatcher, too."

"You do, indeed. Hell, boy, he seems to have a downright crush on you. Including your business card on all his ransom notes. Calling you. You may be the key to the whole damn case. I'm going to put a Tap and Trace on your office and apartment phones, while you do two things. First, put together your own list. Write down every name you can think of—everyone in Hollywood you've ever socialized with or worked with. We'll compare it to Winslow and Hunter's."

"And second?"

"Don't get killed. Remember, this guy's smart."

"Too smart," a voice said from the back of the room. A whiny voice I recognized. Piccolo. He looked a little worse for wear. He was pale and his left arm was in a sling, but his mouth was in overdrive. Until he was fit enough to return to active duty, he'd been reassigned to a desk. "Almost," Piccolo went on, "like he's being advised by someone who knows police procedure."

I knew what this son of a bitch was implying, but Mary Rocket didn't. "You think he's working with a cop?"

"No Ma'am. Someone who *used* to be a cop. Maybe someone who was kicked off the force and has a grudge to settle." He was looking right at me. His words were pointed enough to draw blood. "Maybe someone who put himself into the middle of the case so he'll know what the authorities are doing every minute of every day."

Mary Rocket was flabbergasted. "You actually think Gideon's in on it? You got any proof?"

"Just my gut, and it's never wrong." That got a few titters from the back of the room. Piccolo spun to the dissenters. "Well, it's not!" He turned back to the Mary Rocket. "Incarcerate him, Captain. We've already got Kincaid for breaking and entering Winslow's condo. I guarantee it's just a matter of time before we deduce he's the mastermind behind the Gravesnatcher."

"I hear things, Detective," Mary Rocket said, "lots of things. Sometimes I think I hear too many things and I wish I could have a specially designed high-tech filter that only let the important, police-related facts in and kept the more mundane gossip and innuendo out. But science hasn't caught up to my needs, yet. So I'm stuck hearing all this shit. And some of the shit is about you and a certain female police officer. One who used to be married to somebody in this very room. Somebody who may be stirring up emotions in you that are clouding your usually impartial judgment. So I'm going to take what you and others have said under advisement, and I recommend you do the same."

Chastised but unbowed, Piccolo mumbled, "Yes, Ma'am," and sneered at me.

My cell phone vibrated. I glanced at it. I had a text message from Hillary. Three numbers that sent a chill down my spine. It was the code Hillary and I had worked out, the code to use if another Gravesnatcher call came in. 666.

"Imperial Investigations." Hillary sounded just as cute on the phone.

"Hi, it's me."

"666."

"I know. I know. I know. I got your message. Now give me the details." I was on my cell phone, and since no one in the conference room could hear Hillary's side of the conversation, sixty pairs of curious eyes stared at me.

"There's another ransom note with your card attached."

"Who got the note?"

"Lisa Montgomery." Instinctively, I looked at Stacy. She caught the look and returned it curiously. She had no way of knowing Hillary had just mentioned the movie star, Lisa Montgomery. My former client, Lisa Montgomery.

The woman who had broken up our marriage, Lisa Montgomery.

Things were about to get really ugly.

"I hope the Gravesnatcher kills the bitch!"

"And you said *I* had unresolved issues about our relationship."

"Oh, no. I have totally clarity about our relationship. It sucked. You sucked. Every hour, minute and second of our relationship sucked."

Stacy and I were arguing in Mary Rocket's office. The Captain watched from her desk chair, a bemused smile on her lips. "I seem to recall a period of time when you two were googly-eyed love birds. Staring at each other across the bullpen. All those endless liplocks in the parking lot. Hell, I even walked in on you two doing the wild thing in a storage closet."

"He may have been fucking me," Stacy said, "but he was probably thinking about Lisa Montgomery."

"I didn't even know Lisa Montgomery then."

"Then you were thinking about some other half-wit actress."

"Lisa Montgomery happens to be quite smart."

"Now I'm stupid."

"No, I just said Lisa's smart."

"Fine. She's got better cheekbones, bigger tits, a nicer ass, *and* she's smarter than me."

"I never said that. I've always admired your brain."

"So I'm ugly."

"I didn't say that, either." I turned to Mary Rocket. "Help."

"I'm not getting in the middle of this."

"You fucked that slut in *our* house! In *my* bed!"

"It was *my* bed. When we moved in together we combined furniture. *I* had the bed. You had the bureau, couch and end tables."

"But they were *my* sheets! You fucked her on *my* sheets!"

She had me there. Lisa and I also screwed on Stacy's couch, but I didn't think this was a good time to bring it up. So I said, "Look, I'm sorry for what I did. I've told you that. Hundreds of times. Sorry and ashamed. And I paid for it with a divorce. But the fact is," I went on, "this all happened five years ago. We're divorced. Leading separate lives. Our marriage and my affair are history."

Rage still contorted Stacy's face. "Just tell me one thing. When you heard Lisa Montgomery's name today, when you realized you'd be seeing her, did you think, 'Hey, maybe I'll get to sleep with her again?' "

Yes, I thought. "No way," I said.

The Captain stood up. "What difference does it make? Unless we get our act together, in a few days Lisa Montgomery and Gideon will probably both be dead." Mary Rocket always did have a way of cutting through the bullshit. She turned to Stacy. "I'm going to reassign you. You're clearly too invested in the personalities of the case to continue."

"No, Captain, you *can't* take me off the case."

"I just did."

"The press will think I've been reassigned because of the Magic Land fiasco."

"I'll admit a sacrificial lamb spin is certainly possible. Let's be honest: you fucked up big time at Magic Land."

"But—"

"No 'buts.' You fucked up the surveillance then got David Hunter killed. Mistakes I'd expect from a lot of cops, but not you. You're too good. So there's only one way to explain your clouded judgment. Gideon. Unfortunately, your ex-husband is now at the center of this investigation and you continue to demonstrate an inability to handle your emotional baggage. So, you're reassigned. Report to Hernandez at the Vice desk. Now."

Stacy was furious. There was so much she wanted to say, but knew that saying anything to Mary Rocket would only get her into deeper trouble. She turned from the Captain to me. "Good luck," she said through tight lips and exited.

Mary Rocket shook her head. "What a waste."

"Because she's such a good cop?"

"No, because you two made such a good couple."

We did, I thought, wistfully. "No way," I said, angrily. "That relationship had 'train wreck' scrawled all over it. Anyway, Lisa Montgomery getting a ransom note may actually be good news."

"How do you figure?"

"Another ransom note means another ransom drop. And this time we're going to catch him."

Ten-Percenters Are a Dime a Dozen

"This could be your big chance."

"Forget it, Elliot."

"But they're all calling. *The Enquirer. Extra. Star.* I asked and you answered. Single yourself out from the crowd, I said, and you've done it! You know that thing about fifteen minutes of fame? Well, someone just punched your stopwatch."

I was driving west on Sunset Boulevard, just passing the Beverly Hills Hotel, on my way to Lisa Montgomery' house in Brentwood. Mary Rocket had wanted to come with me. But I said the Gravesnatcher has insisted on no cops, and he might be watching the house. So she'd reluctantly agreed to let me go solo.

Meanwhile, my agent Elliot was figuring out a way to capitalize on the Gravesnatcher's murder spree. "I've already talked to the publisher. I asked them to pull all copies of *Rear Entry*, then reissue it with a new title and cover art."

"What new title and cover art?"

"That depends. See, I've got two ideas. If you catch the Gravesnatcher, there will be a picture of you and the murderer, with a caption that reads: 'From the man who buried the Gravesnatcher, a startling look into the mind of a murderer.' Then the title: *Death of the Gravesnatcher*."

"But *Rear Entry's* about a grizzled old PI, his young, naïve nephew and the porno star the kid falls in love with."

"I admit the cover might confuse a few people, but the book's good, so fuck 'em."

"What is the second idea?"

"This one'll sell more books, but you won't really get to enjoy the success."

"Why not?"

"It'll be published posthumously."

"After the Gravesnatcher kills me."

"Exactamente. The cover will be a picture of your grave. And this is my favorite part, the new title's on your headstone! Great, huh?"

"Inspired. What's the new title?"

"*Ultimate Sacrifice.* Dig the caption: 'Read the tragic story of Gideon Kincaid's brutal murder at the hands of the bloodthirsty Gravesnatcher.' "

"I'd point out again that neither the title or slug line have anything to do with *Rear Entry.* Still, if I'm into your flow, your response would be something like, 'Fuck 'em.' "

"And the horse they rode in on. Opportunity is knocking and we've got a revolving door."

"You're mixing your metaphors."

"Stir-fry 'em for all I care. Listen to me, Gideon, KA-CHING! We're rich! We cash in now with *People*—they'll be good for at least a hundred grand. Then we refuse to talk to the press until this monster is caught. *Silencio.* But once the Gravesnatcher's behind bars—or, better yet, shot to death in a desperate, bloody gun battle, where you, though seriously wounded, heroically fight back, and finally kill him—once the Gravesnatcher is history, we open negotiations. Book rights. Movie rights. Action figures. Tee shirts. Coffee mugs. Lunch boxes. The whole ball of wax. You'll be a household name and I'll be recognized as the marketing genius who made it all happen."

"It doesn't feel right."

"Why not?"

"I don't want to trick people into buying my book. *Rear*

Entry is good. But if people buy it thinking it's about the Gravesnatcher they're going to be pissed off. They'll hate a book I'm proud of. A book they might've liked under normal circumstances."

"Nobody's buying your damn book."

"But if I get a little publicity from the Gravesnatcher case I'll mention I'm also a writer and the curiosity factor should sell a few books."

"Listen to yourself. Sell a *few* books. *Bubele,* I'm talking *New York Times* bestseller list. Amazon Top Ten. Book of the Month Club."

"I won't lie about *Rear Entry,*" I snapped. "It is what it is. If you've got a problem with that, then I've got the wrong agent."

You could almost hear him shifting gears. "Lie? I'd never ask you to lie. I was just testing your integrity, Gid-baby, and I'm proud to say you passed with flying colors."

"Bullshit."

"All right, I'm sorry. I'm trying to make you rich and famous. Shoot me."

He was trying to lay a guilt trip on me, and it had worked. Frankly, Elliott was only saying out loud the same things I'd been thinking. Everybody else cashes in when fate points a finger at them. Why not me? Everybody else does the talk show circuit, sells movie rights, writes books. Why not me? I'd make enough money never to have to peek, pry or probe again. I could buy a big house with a fabulous, book-lined den and write any book I wanted on a polished mahogany desk, in front of a warm, crackling fire.

So what was bothering me? I didn't quite know. Couldn't put it into words. It was a feeling. No, more than that: a conviction. Call it instinct. Or integrity. Deep down I knew what was right and wrong.

"Look, Elliott, I appreciate all the thought you've put into this. And I do think the Gravesnatcher may end up being a great, if morbid, opportunity. But I want to come through it with my life *and* my dignity."

"Say no more, Gid-man, we are in perfect sync. I will simply collect the barrage of offers, telling your adoring suitors we will have no comment until your selfless role of Hollywood hero has come to an end. Or some such shit."

Ain't Hollywood grand?

Déjà Vu

Lisa had come up in the world. The last time I saw her she lived in a funky Laurel Canyon two bedroom; now she had a Brentwood zip code and a sprawling Mexican-style ranch house with stucco walls, tile roof, pool and tennis court—all hidden behind a white stucco wall and protected by a large electric gate.

There was a buzzer at the gate. A video camera, too. I punched the button. A voice I didn't recognize asked, "Who is it?"

I looked into the camera. "Gideon Kincaid."

"Come in." With a metallic squeak, the gate swung open.

Two cars were already parked in the circular driveway. A classic Mercedes 280, ivory, in immaculate condition. Lisa's car, I remembered. And a dark blue Lexus LS. I was about to ring the bell when the front door swung open. Expecting to see Lisa, I had my most charming smile in place. It died on my lips as I found myself staring at a short, skinny woman with stringy black hair, a disapproving look in her eyes and a scowl on her face. At once imperious and condescending, she looked at me with contempt. "Let's see some identification."

I flashed my ID while I asked, "Who are you?"

"Joan Hagler. Lisa's manager."

Joan handed my ID back. "Come in." She led me inside. Over the travertine tiles, down a lithograph-lined hallway to Lisa's living room. The room was all white. Walls, couch, chairs. Even the piano was white. The room had high ceilings and a massive white marble fireplace.

Sliding glass doors looked out on the backyard. Someone was swimming laps in the black bottom pool. I could only see the top of a blond head and graceful arms cutting through the water, but I knew it was Lisa.

"Lisa will join us in a minute," Joan said. "In the meantime, I'd like to ask a few questions."

"There is only so much I can reveal about the case," I said. "I'm afraid details about ongoing investigations are kept confidential."

"I wasn't talking about the Gravesnatcher. I was talking about you."

"Me?"

"Yes. Why is Lisa so afraid of you?"

Oh, that ...

Let's flash back five years. I was sitting at my desk, nursing a hangover, when I heard a frightened voice with just a trace of a southern accent: "Will you be my hero?"

I looked up and was impaled by a pair of green eyes. Lisa's blond hair was shorter then, styled a little like the early Beatles', and she wore a pink sundress tight enough to make me think that was *all* she was wearing. She looked young—twenty-two or twenty-three at the most.

I wondered for an instant if she was some sort of gin-induced hallucination. Surely she couldn't be real. I mean, scenes like this only happened in bad noir films.

"Lieutenant Rocket said you might be able to help me," she said urgently. "Please, I'm desperate."

Now, I probably would've still helped her if she'd been fat and seventy-five, but the prospect of rescuing *this* damsel in distress was irresistible. "You have a name?"

"Lisa. Lisa Ann Montgomery. My agent wants me to drop the Ann. 'Too southern,' he says. So you can just call me Lisa."

"And I'm Gideon. Your knight in shining armor."

She thought she was being stalked. She'd never exactly seen a stalker. But she *felt* him. When she was driving. Shopping. Even at home. And things were missing from her house. A bracelet, hairbrush, a pair of pink panties.

Since no threats had been made and Lisa had no suspects, there was nothing the police could do. So Mary Rocket told her she needed a private investigator and recommended me.

I followed Lisa to her rented Laurel Canyon bungalow. Simple but homey, it was filled with thrift shop furniture, fake Tiffany lamps, needlepoint pillows, and framed photos of her on stage in various college productions.

She'd told me she was an actress and had just been in her first movie, a romantic comedy called *Moonbeams and Magic*. It was a huge hit, and the green-eyed actress with the short blond hair was getting all the attention. But there was a price to her newfound fame. The stalking started two days after the picture opened.

Lisa wanted to know how the stalker was getting in. I checked the doors and windows, which she claimed were always locked, and found the problem. The lock on the sliding glass living room door was loose. A couple of tugs and it slid right open.

Leaving Lisa in the house, I searched outside for signs of a stalker. The centerpiece of the backyard was a hot tub. I think everyone in Laurel Canyon got one during the fad-crazed '80s. There was a tiny patch of grass, a couple of scraggily fruit trees, and a small brick wall where the yard met the hillside. No clues here. The front yard yielded just as little.

Then I noticed an abandoned house across the street. No doubt a victim of the housing market collapse, the house had a 'For Sale' sign stuck in its overgrown lawn and a hastily erected cyclone fence surrounding the property.

While examining the perimeter of the fence, I found a section that had been cut and peeled away then reattached with garbage ties, creating a temporary gate. I slipped inside the fence, reached through a broken window and opened the back door.

I did a quick search of the house and struck gold in the master bedroom. A sagging, drained waterbed dominated the room, no doubt a leftover from the '70s—just as fad-crazed as the '80s. In front of a corner window, directly across from Lisa's bedroom window, I found the detritus of a stalker—overflowing ashtray, empty beer cans, crumpled fast food wrappers. I also found something else. The bottom of the window facing Lisa's bedroom was stained with a crusty, milky film—dried semen.

I told Lisa what I'd found, not bothering to mention the fact that her stalker would stand in front of the window, watching her walk around her bedroom, and masturbate. I told her to stay put tonight. I was going to stake out the house across the street and wait for her stalker to arrive.

I made myself a nest across the hall from the master bedroom in what—judging from the Barbie doll wallpaper, pink carpet and drapes—must have been a little girl's room decorated amidst the fad-crazed '60s. There was no way of knowing if the stalker showed up every night, at what time, or how long he stayed. So I checked my watch—8:17—and settled in for a long wait.

As I sat there, I realized I was living a cliché, a PI with a beautiful woman as a client. I couldn't help but wonder if this case would follow the rules of pulp fiction, which would require me to end up in bed with her.

Not an entirely unpleasant thought, I had to admit, especially at this point in my life. My marriage to Stacy was falling apart. She was ready to leave me.

Incredibly ambitious, Stacy was desperate to outdo her old man, a thirty-seven-year veteran of the LAPD who'd died at his desk, a Captain. Now that I'd been forced off the force, Stacy was worried *her* career would be damaged, a guilt by association thing. This possibility made her even more critical, impatient, demanding, sarcastic, and bitchy than usual.

It didn't help that my self-esteem was at an all time low. At the risk of sounding too much like a Jonathan Kellerman psycho thriller, my ego had been betrayed by my superego, so my id was paying the price. I'd lost the only thing I'd ever really wanted—to be a cop—and I had no one but myself to blame. Having a beautiful young starlet confuse gratitude with desire and show her thanks by ripping my clothes off might provide a little compensation.

My reveries were interrupted by the squeak of a floorboard, the crinkling of paper and the familiar smell of McDonald's French fries. A glance at my watch told me it was 9:02.

I slipped out my gun as I heard the intruder climb the stairs. A man crossed the hall and entered the bedroom, a McDonald's bag in one hand, a bottle of wine in the other. He had his back to me, so I couldn't see his face, only his long, dishwater-blond hair tied in a ponytail. He was about five eight or nine and wore a black leather jacket, jeans, and work boots.

I crept to the bedroom doorway. His back was still to me as he stared out the window. He took a swig from the bottle then muttered to himself, "Come on, baby, daddy's here."

"So am I, asshole," I said in my best hard-ass cop voice. "Freeze."

He didn't. He spun instead, hurling the bottle of wine at my head. I ducked, but his throw was low, and I ending up ducking right into the goddamn thing. I dropped to my knees, dazed. He charged right past me, plunged down the stairs and out the front door. I would have chased after him, but that's when I blacked out.

"Gideon?"

I opened my eyes to find two beautiful emeralds staring at me. A fogbank encircled my brain. *Such beautiful eyes*, I thought. Then my nose twitched as I smelled wine and my skin crawled. I realized I was soaking wet.

The eyes settled into a face—Lisa's face—and she looked worried. "Gideon, are you all right?"

I struggled to my knees as an excruciating headache finally burned through the fog. I patted the side of my skull and felt a lump the size of an egg. Grade A jumbo. The big ones. The really big ones.

I looked down. I'd been lying next to my gun in a puddle of wine. I picked up the Glock and, embarrassed, stuck it back in my holster.

"When you didn't come back I got worried. Thought something dreadful might've happened."

"What time is it?"

"Just after midnight."

Christ, I'd been out for three hours. "Something did happen. Your stalker is real."

"I knew it!" she said, relieved she wasn't crazy and fearful of what that entailed. Then my present circumstances hit home. "Where is he? What happened?"

You hired a pathetic loser, I thought. "Let's just say, he got away," I said. "I do have a general description of him, so don't worry; next time he shows up, I'll catch him." I didn't have the guts to tell her he'd have to *back* into the room wearing the same jacket, jeans and work boots for me to identify him, since I was too busy staring at the incoming bottle to look at his face.

"Just to be safe, I don't think you should stay here tonight. My wife and I have an extra bedroom. You can bunk with us."

"So how long were you a cop?"

"Thirteen years."

"Wow, I didn't know you could retire after only thirteen years."

"You can't. I quit."

"Oh. Why?"

We were driving from Laurel Canyon toward Stacy's and my three-bedroom house in Van Nuys. I had one hand on the wheel while the other held an ice pack to my throbbing head. Lisa had just asked the million-dollar question: why had I quit the force? What the hell should I tell her? The standard, I got sick of all the bullshit, or the truth? I'd never told anyone the whole truth, but something about the trusting way Lisa looked at me made me want her to know what had really happened.

"You have to put up with a lot of bullshit being a cop. The courts make it almost impossible to arrest anyone, then the D.A.'s won't prosecute unless it's an ironclad case. Even if you get to court, L.A. juries let everybody off anyway."

"O.J. and all that."

"Yeah. But once in a while, when the evidence is *just so*, a jury *has* to come back with a guilty verdict. However, you need incontrovertible evidence."

"Fibers, DNA, stuff like that?"

"No. Fibers and DNA can be argued. The science can be questioned, the chain of evidence. *Incontrovertible evidence* means things like fingerprints, security camera tape, unimpeachable eyewitnesses, confessions. Nothing circumstantial. Nothing debatable. Nothing a weak-kneed judge or half-brained jurist could throw out. That's the only way you can get justice in this crazy town. So that's what I arranged for Ernie Wagner."

"Who?"

"Ernie Wagner, a subhuman cretin who beat and raped old women. He'd hang around the Fairfax district, pick out a victim shopping alone and follow her home. He must have been locked in some weird Oedipal fantasy, because they all looked alike—in their mid-to-late seventies, always short, usually under five feet, with their hair dyed red."

"He actually raped old women?"

"Seven we knew about. He'd knock on the door, identify himself as a cop, flash a store-bought badge, and talk his way in. He'd beat them, often breaking the jaw and nose, then tie their hands and feet and gag them with duct tape. He'd light a cigarette and touch the burning embers to the left breast, again and again—twenty-three times, always twenty-three times, forming the shape of a heart. Finally he'd sodomize them."

"My God—"

"We caught him with a decoy. One of our dispatchers matched the body type and a Hollywood make-up man turned a thirty-four-year-old Valley girl named Crystal into a red-haired septuagenarian. We trolled for three days before he took the bait, followed her to our rented apartment and talked his way in with the tin badge. After he threw his first punch we came out of the bedroom and took the freak down.

"That's when the headshrinkers moved in. Told the court that he'd been abused by his mother, convinced the jury that society had failed poor Ernie. He was sentenced to ten years in the Camarillo State Psychiatric Hospital. After only three years Ernie convinced his keepers that they were geniuses and had cured him. Congratulating themselves, they returned Ernie Wagner to society."

"No!"

"Oh, yeah. I only found out about it because some irate reporter for the *L.A. Times* picked up on Ernie's release and wrote a scathing article. Two days later my partner and I were called to a Fairfax apartment, where a seventy-six-year-old woman named Ida Glass lay, bound head and foot, mouth duck taped shut, a heart burned into her left breast."

"Ernie—"

"No question. Only this time he'd made a mistake. Her neck was broken; she was dead. Looking down at that poor, pitiful woman, I realized that no matter how hard I worked to avenge the dead, between the prosecutors, judges, juries and shrinks, scumbags like Ernie would always get away. *Not this time,* I promised myself. No matter what, Ernie was going down.

"But Ernie was smart. In the seven earlier rapes he'd worn a condom. He never left any sperm, no pubic hair, no fingerprints, no trace evidence whatsoever, so tying him to this murder wasn't going to be easy. I decided to increase the odds. But my new partner, Victor Chu, was a real straight arrow, so I'd have to go rogue. Since Victor hadn't worked the earlier rapes, he hadn't made the connection to Ernie, and I didn't say anything. While he searched the living room, I drifted into the kitchen. On the counter I found a matched set of knives sticking out of a wooden block. Five knives, each knife in its custom-sized slot. I slipped one of the knives out of the block and into my pocket.

"Later, after my partner and I'd left the crime scene and split up for the night, I made a call to the Camarillo facility, got an address on Ernie, and made a quick stop at a 7-Eleven to buy some duct tape."

"Duct tape?"

"I was going to plant the knife in Ernie's apartment to tie him to the murder, and since I knew the brand of duct tape Ernie used from our earlier lab analysis, I wanted to leave traces of the adhesive on the knife."

"Icing on the cake sort of thing?"

"Exactly. So I cut a piece of duct tape with the knife, then threw away the tape, wiped my fingerprints off the knife and dropped it back in my pocket. Next I called my partner Victor, said I'd made the connection to Ernie and told him to meet me outside Ernie's apartment in Silverlake. It was three a.m. by the time we banged on Ernie's door. While Victor questioned him I searched his apartment. Ernie denied everything, but of course had no alibi. Said he'd been home alone watching TV all night. Then I 'found' the knife on the floor of his closet and we busted him."

"So you had your incontrovertible evidence."

"We never needed it. Three days later Ernie's throat was slashed in a jailhouse brawl over cigarettes, and he bled to death on the floor of the rec room."

Lisa digested this as we crested Mulholland and began our descent down Coldwater Canyon into the Valley. "Wait," she said, confused. "I don't get it. If Ernie was killed anyway, and you never used the fake evidence to convict him, why'd you have to leave the police department?"

"Ernie was innocent."

"What?!"

"Four days later Mort Stein, the guilt-ridden son of our

seventy-six-year-old victim, confessed to killing his mother."

"But the duct tape, the burned heart ...?"

"They were printed in that *L.A. Times* article. Mort pulled a copycat number and would've gotten away with a perfect crime if he'd been able to handle the guilt."

"And if Mort had killed his mother, the cops wanted to know how Ida's knife got into Ernie Wagner's closet."

"Yep. I played dumb and never confessed, but everybody knew. A few anal types in the D.A.'s office wanted to press charges, but the Chief was afraid of what would happen if the press found out the city's finest were framing suspects. He let me resign."

What I didn't tell her was the thing that had hurt me most. I expected the wrath I got from the brass and the D.A. What I didn't expect was the cold shoulder I got from all my friends on the force. I was suddenly a pariah. Nobody wanted to be seen with me. Nobody wanted to talk to me. I was not only cut out of the force, I was cut out of their lives.

Lisa studied me in silence as I turned into my driveway. She must've felt my vibe, because she asked, "You lost a lot more than your job, didn't you?"

"You smell like shit."

"Actually, it's Robert Mondavi Reserve Chardonnay, and it goes for almost twenty bucks a bottle."

"But I think Mr. Mondavi manufactures it for people to drink, not bathe in."

"Nothing ventured, nothing gained."

Stacy and I were standing in our bedroom; a suitcase was open on the bed, filled with Stacy's clothes. She'd been packing when I got home and had barely looked up when I'd walked in. I'd told Lisa to wait in the living room while I explained to Stacy why she was here—something I hadn't had a chance to do yet.

The repartee that Stacy and I exchanged was actually our sorry excuse for not talking about what was really bothering us. We could dodge the issues by dueling pithy one-liners. The sniping provided emotional armor, protecting us from talking about the day-to-day un-pleasantries. The horror of work, our front row seats to humanity's underbelly, and our deteriorating marriage. A marriage that had been great for a while—all hand-holding, long, hot unmotivated kisses, sex three or four times a week. A marriage that had been stressed by work and then ruptured by my evidence planting. Divorce seemed inevitable, but neither one of us was willing to mention the D word. Funny thing was, I still loved Stacy. In my suddenly topsy-turvy life, she was the only remaining constant. Problem was, she thought of me as a pariah, an embarrassment to the police department, and a detriment to her career.

I'd fucked everything up.

Stacy pointed at the lump on my head. "Is that a softball growing out of your brain or are you just glad to see me?"

"Actually, it's the answer to the question: why doesn't the human skull make an effective bottle opener?"

"The Mondavi connection, no doubt. Why am I thinking today didn't go so well?"

"Looking at your half-packed suitcase, I'm wondering if today is also my last day as a husband."

"No," she said, with a rare smile. "I've got a three-day FBI seminar at Quantico. I hit the friendly skies first thing in the morning."

"FBI seminar? Guess I didn't fuck up your career as much as you feared."

"No? I wasn't on the first manifest. But every other homicide detective in the division was. So I raised holy hell until they added me." She stopped packing and looked at me, started to say something, stopped herself.

"Go ahead, say it," I said.

"Okay, Gideon, you asked for it: you not only fucked up your career and my career, you totally fucked up your life. Somehow you've gone from a good cop to a careless vigilante to a wine soaked PI. What's the next floor on your descent into hell—

standing at freeway entry ramps holding a cardboard sign that says, 'Will snoop for food?' "

So much for dodging the issues. Then Stacy's eyes went from me to the door. "Who the hell're you?"

I turned to find an embarrassed Lisa. I wasn't sure how long she'd been standing there, but from her look of pity, I knew it had been long enough to hear Stacy's attack.

"That's Lisa," I said, "my client."

"He wasn't drinking," Lisa said, coming to my defense. "He got hit with a wine bottle trying to help me."

"Help you what, survive a wine-tasting party gone bad?"

"She's being stalked."

Stacy looked at Lisa but pointed at me. "And *he's* the best protection you could find?"

Lisa was intimidated by Stacy, but still managed to say, "Gideon's doing a wonderful job."

"Of course he is," Stacy said, condescendingly.

"I don't think Lisa should go home until I've caught her stalker. I told her she could stay here tonight."

Stacy looked at Lisa, softened her tone. "You really being stalked?"

A scared nod of the head.

Stacy did an emotional one-eighty. Her face suddenly softened as she put a comforting arm around a surprised Lisa. "Well, don't worry, you're safe here. Gideon, bring her things into the guest room."

You see, Stacy wasn't always a heartless bitch. But as they walked down the hallway, I heard Stacy tell her, "Gideon wasn't always a total loser. He was a great cop until he lost his mind."

"You have an interesting wife."

"I might use a different adjective to describe her—a lot of adjectives, now that I think about it—but 'interesting' isn't one of them."

"She's the first woman I ever met with a tattoo of a hand grenade on her ankle."

Lisa and I were walking across the Universal Studios lot, just passing the commissary on our way to the Rock Hudson building. Lisa had already been hired for her next movie, *Heaven Sent*, a romantic comedy about a statue of the goddess Athena coming to life and falling in love with a recently widowed NFL Quarterback. We'd spent the day doing movie related stuff—wardrobe fittings, make-up tests, and publicity shots. I'd been by her side through it all, keeping a wary eye out for our stalker. So far, so good. The casting session was our last stop. There were five actors auditioning for the role of the Quarterback. Lisa was going to read with them for the producer and director.

"She showed you her tattoo? You guys must've really bonded."

"Not really. She's a little cynical for me."

"She gave you her 'mankind is spiraling toward oblivion' speech."

"Right after she told me the only lasting solution to crime in the streets is summary execution by the arresting officer. She was kidding, right?"

No way, I thought. "Of course," I said.

As we neared the stucco bungalow, I saw a handful of hunky actors pacing back and forth, script pages in hand, silently rehearsing. "I usually hate auditions," Lisa mused. "I get so stressed out my hands shake like that poor Katie Hepburn's."

"But not this time."

"This time I've already got the job, so I'm actually looking forward to it."

That's when it happened. One of the actors suddenly lunged toward Lisa. She screamed. I spun, stepped in front of the man. He was big, bigger than I remembered the stalker being. But I'd only seen him for an instant. And his hair was short. But he could've cut his hair after our little run-in. Better safe than sorry.

I put my hands on his well-developed shoulders and said: "That's close enough."

"Fuck you, bozo," he growled, trying to shove me out of the way.

Not smart. First of all, my head still hurt from the wine bottle last night. And you already know about my well-documented funk, so I was looking forward to releasing a little aggression.

I threw a right cross, but he surprised me, easily slipping the punch, ducking to his left. I wondered how he'd done that, until he set his hands—right hand lead, his left hand cocked. He was a southpaw.

No problem, I thought, remembering what Thumbs Nickerson, my Golden Gloves coach, taught me as a kid. *Fight the mirror. Right hand, left hook. One, two.* I stepped inside, throwing a right jab. As the guy instinctively raised his right hand to block it he exposed the right side of his face. I drove a thundering left hook into jaw. He staggered, stunned, and I moved in for the kill. A quick shot to the kidney bent him over, an uppercut mashed his nose, a right hook loosened his teeth, and a left cross sent him on his ass.

I was moving in for a little more therapy when Lisa grabbed me by the arm and howled, "Gideon, stop!"

I barely heard her. Blood was pounding in my ears, adrenaline coursing through my veins. That primordial bloodlust simmering just below the surface of every man had been unleashed, and it was going to take more than a few puny 'Gideon stops' to slow me down. I grabbed the son of a bitch by the shirt, hauled him to his feet and cocked my right for another punch. Suddenly two sets of arms wrapped themselves around me, pulling me off the actor. I turned to find that the arms belonged to two security guards.

"What's going on here?" the one with sergeant stripes asked.

I pulled free from their grip and pointed a finger in the actor's face. "He's been stalking my client!"

"I haven't been stalking anybody. Lisa's my friend!"

Me, to Lisa: "He is?"

Lisa, to him: "You are?"

Security guard, to him: "Well, are you?"

Him, to us: "Yes!" Now, to Lisa: "Roy Cooper. Remember, Lisa, Georgia State, your freshman year ..."

The confused cloud across Lisa's face suddenly cleared. Recognition, then something else flitted, across those green eyes; it was quick, and you had to be looking to catch it, but it was unmistakable: humiliation. Then that beautiful face seemed to regain control. Surprise took center stage and introduced embarrassment. "My God, Roy Cooper, of course." To me: "Gideon, this is Roy. We studied theater together in college. Even went out once or twice. Isn't that right, Roy?"

"If I knew you'd turn out this beautiful, we'd still be going out."

"Aren't you sweet? You see, Gideon? Roy's no stalker."

Just because they'd studied Shakespeare and painted scenery as undergraduates didn't mean Roy hadn't grown up to be a nut case, so I asked him, "Where were you last night between nine and midnight?"

"None of your fucking business."

"Now, Roy," Lisa purred in that sweet southern drawl of hers, "let's not get all cave man. Once you convince Gideon you're as innocent as a baby lamb these nice security guards will let you both go, and we can get on with the audition. You are here to audition for *Heaven Sent*, aren't you?"

"Yeah," he said, sourly. He hated to back down, give me anything, but he realized it couldn't hurt to get on Lisa's good side before the audition. "I was in Vancouver yesterday, working on *Fringe*. We shot until just after midnight. I flew back on the United Shuttle this morning."

Lisa looked at me. "Sounds innocent enough."

It did. I'd been a cop long enough to know the truth when I heard it. And now that I'd had a good, long look at him, Roy Cooper was much taller than the Stalker—at least six foot two or three. Still, I wasn't ready to give him anything. "I'll check it out."

Lisa turned to the security guards. "There, you see? We're all friends again. So if you gentlemen don't have an objection, I'd love to get back to work and find out which one of these deliciously handsome men is going to be my leading man."

Breaking up the fight was probably the high point of the year for these rent-a-cops, so I think they would've liked to milk the moment a little longer, but the horse was dead and not worth beating. "All right," Sergeant stripes said, "as long as nobody wants to file a report."

We both shook our heads.

"Excellent," Lisa said, thrilled. "Let the auditions begin!"

"He nailed it," the director said. "It's like the part was written for him."

"Ditto," the producer said, "I knew it the minute he walked in the door."

"Home run," the writer said, "Roy Cooper *is* the Quarterback."

I sat in the back of the conference room. The five hopefuls had read with Lisa, and I had to admit it, even though Roy was a bit battered and bruised from our fight, he had done the best job. There was a certain arrogance to the guy, a cockiness that came through every line. It gave him the kind of blind self-confidence endemic to so many jocks.

The producer turned to Lisa. "And you know the guy. It couldn't be more perfect! Think of the PR opportunities: 'College sweethearts reunited on the silver screen!' If you two actually hooked up again, we're talking cover-story heaven." He clasped his hands in front of him in prayer. "It's moments like this that convince me there really is a God."

"Me, too," Lisa said. "So let me make myself absolutely clear. I will not work with Mr. Roy Cooper. If you want to cast him, that's okay with me. Just release me from my contract and I'll be on my way."

"Wait, hold on," a panicked director said. "We'd much rather have you than Roy Cooper, or any actor for that matter. *You* are the star of this picture. We won't cast anybody you don't want to work with."

"None of the other guys had the chops," the producer said.

"Then we'll keep looking," the director said. "Right, Lisa?"

"As rain." Lisa started for the door. I followed.

"Just one question," the producer said. "Why? What do you have against Roy?"

She tossed him a coy smile. "A girl's got to have her secrets ..."

She started crying over her beer—her third Amstel Light. We were in my living room, watching the NBC Nightly News, when a sob wracked her body. A sob so full of suffering it broke my heart. In fact, I was surprised by the intensity of my own distress. I wanted more than anything to make her feel better. I wanted to take her in my arms, put her head on my shoulder, and tell her that I'd protect her. Tell her that nobody or nothing would ever hurt her again.

What a sap! I've heard thousands of women cry over the years. It comes with the territory, if you know what I mean, and your soul kind of crusts over when it comes to the weeping part of a case.

But the sight of Lisa crying tore at my guts. I knew why. I was falling for her.

It didn't take Freud or Jung or Jonathan Kellerman, for that matter, to figure out what was happening here. My wife, Stacy, represented everything I'd been, all the bullshit that had finally driven me over the edge.

My client, Lisa, represented all the innocence and good that the future might hold. Not to mention irresistible looks and a killer body. Although I wasn't ready to make a pass at her, I did want to do something to ease her pain. I zapped off the TV, grabbed a handful of Kleenex and sat next to her on the couch. Handing them over, I asked, "Want to talk about it?"

"No."

A respectful beat, then, "It happened in college, right? Whatever he did to you."

A nod of the head.

"You thought screwing him out of the job would make you feel better?"

"Yes."

"It didn't, did it?"

She laughed through her tears. "No, it did make me feel

better. But it also brought up a lot of old feelings I thought I'd put behind me a long time ago. "

"Pain never goes away, it just hides. I lost both my parents when I was a kid. Cried for months, then slowly got over it. Years later, I was driving my black and white past Griffith Park and I saw this family—father, mother, and ten-year-old son. The father had a picnic basket, the mother carried a blanket, and the kid had a Frisbee. They were all laughing, having a great time. Right out of Norman Rockwell. Well, it rang a wake-up bell somewhere in my subconscious, and suddenly I was crying. My partner thought I was nuts, but something about that tableau awakened the beast, and grief came crawling out of the cave."

"How did they die, your parents?"

"They were shot in a robbery."

"You poor baby." She sobbed again.

I took her in my arms, put her head on my shoulder and stroked the back of her head. "It's okay. Let it out. Let it all out."

And she did. She cried for five full minutes—a deep, soul rattling expulsion of emotion and tears. All I could think of was how good she felt in my arms.

Finally the tears stopped, her breathing slowed, steadied; then: "He swept me off my feet my freshman year. He was a junior, and I was this naïve little virgin from itty bitty Braswell, Georgia. We met at the first rehearsal for Othello. He was Iago. I had one of those slave labor jobs freshmen get—a wardrobe mistress or some such thing.

"I was in the back of the theater watching the run-through, when he suddenly saw me sitting there. He stared at me for a few seconds then stopped the performance, jumped off the stage, and ran up to me. 'What's your name?' Lisa Ann Montgomery,' I said. 'Well, Lisa Ann, you are the most beautiful woman I've ever seen and I'm going to marry you.' I practically swooned right then and there. He took me to dinner, filled me with white wine and compliments, took me dancing at the Starlight, kissed me while Nora Jones sang some sweet song, and walked me across campus, hand in hand, under a full moon. He told me I was his soul mate, that fate had steered our destinies so that we would find ourselves in the same place at the same time.

"Back to his frat house, more wine, more slow dancing. I could feel his breath on my neck, his tongue in my ear, his thing rubbing against my thing. I was hot. I felt dizzy, drunk, disoriented. Suddenly I was convinced he *was* my soul mate, that fate had been working overtime and it would be rude at the very least not to consummate this monumental event. Next thing I knew I was in his bedroom, he was pulling off my clothes and ... that, as they say, was that.

"The next morning I called Mama to tell her I'd met the most wonderful man and was going to marry him. Then I called Susie McConnell, my best friend who got sent to Smith by her rich banker daddy, and told her. Then I called my sister Lizzy. I was so happy I felt like calling complete strangers and telling them. Only one problem, Roy didn't call me.

"When I went to rehearsal that night he didn't even look at me. I tried to find him afterwards; he was gone. I called the frat house, and they said he wasn't there. The next day he didn't call me, either, and ignored me at rehearsal again. He tried to slip out a back door afterwards but I grabbed him. I was so upset, I started crying right off. 'Roy, I'm sorry,' I say, 'what's the matter? What've I done?' God, can you believe it, I actually thought *I'd* done something wrong! Well, he said, 'Look, babe, it was just a fling. A night of fun. Don't go reading anything more into it.' 'But you said we were soul mates,' I blubbered like a fool. 'You wanted to marry me!' He was so stupefied by my naïveté that he was speechless; then I guess the only thing he could think to say was the cold, hard truth. 'Look, Lisa, I just wanted to get laid, so I said whatever it took. Nothing personal.' "

Her eyes were spurting tears again. "He fucked with my mind, stuck his cock in me, broke my heart and told me it's nothing personal!" I handed her the last tissue in the box and she stemmed the tide. "Anyway, I was so humiliated I couldn't tell Mama, Suzie or Lizzy the truth. So I carried out this imaginary romance with Roy, giving them all the loving details by phone. After three months I told them we were having trouble, and a week later I told them we'd broken up. To this day they don't know what really happened."

"Maybe you can tell them now that you've gotten your revenge."

"No. I'm more ashamed of lying to them for so long than I am about that scum bucket dumping me. I think I'll just let sleeping lies lay. Okay," she said, finishing her beer. "Now it's your turn."

"For what?"

"True confessions. How'd you lose your virginity?"

"I can't tell you that."

"You've already told me you planted evidence in a murder investigation. That's a felony, if I've got my John Grisham right, so what harm could a little sexual tell-all do?"

"My first time wasn't pretty."

"And mine was?"

She had me there, so ... "Her name was Della Lovett. I'd had a crush on her since the seventh grade but she'd always had a boyfriend. The one time she was free I was dating this girl, and we didn't hook up.

"The summer before senior year in high school she was dating a friend of mine, Bobby Wolper. And lo and behold, she got pregnant. Bobby did the 'proper' thing and married her. Della stayed in school, but Bobby dropped out and got a job working at the Texaco. They moved into a tiny studio apartment and tried to act like husband and wife. Only they weren't in love, and by this time Bobby was so pissed at Della for ruining his life that he'd started to hate her. He stayed out late and ignored her when he finally did get home.

"Della, meanwhile, was starved for affection. She wasn't getting it at home, so she started to flirt with me in school. Remember, I'd always had a thing for this girl. And even though she was wearing a gold band on one hand and was four months pregnant, my heart did the rumba whenever I saw her.

She passed me a note, asking if I'd meet her at the lake after school."

I looked up to find Lisa watching me, fascinated. I was suddenly afraid she'd judge me by this story. I got self-conscious—not an emotion I was familiar with. "So," I said, finishing quickly. "I met her, and we did it. End of story."

"You fucked your friend's wife while she was pregnant and you expect to get off that easy? No way, Gideon. I want all the gory details."

"But—"

"No 'buts.' I prostrated myself naked before you. I expect nothing less. Now, bare your soul."

Reluctantly, I did. "It was the end of September, but still hot. Humid, too. She was the only one at the lake, sitting on the hood of the '74 Chevy wagon her parents got them for a wedding present, her back against the windshield, looking at the water."

"I want details, Gideon."

"She was barefoot, wearing a yellow cotton sun dress. But all I saw was skin. Legs, thighs, arms, neck. The sun was setting behind her and she practically glowed."

"What'd she look like?"

"Long brown hair, brown eyes, too. Bedroom eyes. And these fabulous bee-stung lips. She knew how to manipulate a guy. She'd tilt her head just so, and do this pout thing ... That's what she gave me, right off. She told me how unhappy she was, how Bobby had been ignoring her, how having a baby inside her made her horny all the time. But Bobby was my friend, and even though I was dying to get laid, I'd promised myself Della wouldn't be the one. Then she asked if I wanted to feel the baby, and before I could answer she took my hand and put it on her stomach."

"Show me," Lisa said, taking my hand. "Where did she put it?"

Had she just said what I thought she said? I looked at her, my face a question mark.

"Please, Gideon. Show me."

I took my hand and placed it on Lisa's stomach. "Right there."

"Then what?" Lisa's voice was softer now, throaty.

"Della took my hand and moved it between her legs."

Lisa took my hand and put it between her legs. "Like this?"

"Exactly."

"And then?"

"She started rubbing herself against my hand." Lisa started grinding beneath my fingers. "I just let her at first, not wanting to start something I couldn't finish. But before I knew it my middle finger had gone to work, poking into her yellow sun dress, rubbing back."

"Do it," Lisa said, her voice downright husky.

I looked into her eyes; the emeralds were on fire. My finger dug into the fabric and went to work. She moaned, closed her eyes, "Then what?"

"Della said I was making her wet."

"Tell me about it."

"Said she wanted to kiss me."

"And?"

"We did."

"Thank God." Lisa's lips found mine, and our tongues introduced themselves. "More," she said when we finally came up for air. "Tell me more."

"Her hand started rubbing my crotch."

Lisa's hand was on my crotch, her fingers stroking me. "Like this?"

"Oh, yes."

"And ...?"

"She told me to take off her panties."

"Take off mine."

I reached under her dress. She raised her hips to help and slipped off a pair of light pink underwear. "I hope she kissed you about now, because I have to kiss you." She almost inhaled my tongue. "And then—"

"She undid my pants."

Lisa went to work—first the belt, then the pants. Her hands dug inside, freeing my erect penis.

"And then we made love."

"Thank God," Lisa said as she climbed into my lap and gently guided me into her. God, she felt good. I put my hands on her waist but let her control the speed and depth of my thrusts with her hips. Slow and steady at first, but soon I felt myself cresting, ready to come. She felt it, too, and slowed our dance until she caught up with me. As soon as I sensed the first rumbling of her orgasm I raised my hips to meet hers, driving deeper and deeper until she screamed, "Yes!"

With an exultant groan, I came, too.

"You want another beer?" Lisa called from the kitchen.

"Yeah, sure," I said, not really sure why what had just happened, happened. Not that I was complaining.

"So let me ask you this," she said, padding unabashedly naked back into the living room, tossing me my beer and popping open hers, "How many more times did you diddle dear Della?"

"Oh, a few ..."

She leaned against the couch. "Details, please."

And each detail led to another erotic adventure. My giving Della head in the back of the Chevy led to a romp on the dining room table. After I described taking Della from behind in her tiny studio apartment, Lisa and I ended up on the bed, doggy style. It was like that, just moments from another orgasm, when a voice from the doorway changed my life forever.

"You slimy, cock-sucking bastard!"

Lisa and I flew apart like lightning had hit us. Lisa dived for cover beneath the sheets. I sat up in bed, looked at Stacy standing in the bedroom doorway and said the first thing that came to mind: "It's not what it looks like."

"It looks like you're fucking little miss helpless stalking victim."

"Okay, it is what it looks like."

From beneath the sheets a terrified Lisa mumbled, "She's not going to shoot us, is she?"

Stacy ripped the sheet off the bed. Lisa curled into a fetal ball. "I *should* shoot you, you little bitch. And to think I actually felt sorry for you."

"It was an accident."

"Backing into a mailbox is an accident. Backing into my husband's cock isn't."

"What are you doing home, anyway?" I asked, instinctively trying to mount a defense.

"There was another embassy bombing and the FBI had to cancel ..." She trailed off as she realized she didn't have to justify her presence. "Oh, that's right. This is all my fault. If I'd stayed in D.C. you two could have finished your little screwfest without me ever finding out."

"Now that you mention it."

"Well, how about I mention this ..." Stacy pulled her Glock out of her purse, started waving it in front of Lisa and me. "If you two shitbags aren't out of my house in thirty seconds, I'll turn this sorry little soap opera into the lead story on the eleven o'clock news."

We scrambled into our clothes, out of the house and into my car. There was an uncomfortable silence as I drove us to Lisa's house. Finally she said: "You never told me what happened to her."

"Stacy?"

"Della."

"Oh. Well, one day she passed me a note to meet her at the lake. What she didn't tell me was that she'd also left a note for her husband, Bobby. Telling him to meet her at the lake a half hour later."

"So he would catch you two together? The bitch."

"She'd probably concocted the whole thing as a way to save her marriage. You know, get Bobby jealous, make him realize how much he loved her … It didn't work out that way. Instead of beating the shit out of me and falling into her ever-loving arms, Bobby pulled out a .45 automatic and put three shots into her chest."

"Oh, my God."

"Then he fired two shots at me. I screamed and rolled over. Somehow they both missed, but my scream and body language must've convinced him I was hit, too. He turned the gun on himself, stuck it in his mouth and pulled the trigger."

"Get out of here!"

"Blood and brains everywhere."

"What'd you do?"

"Ran like hell back to my uncle's house and hid out in my room, waiting for the cops to come knocking. They never came. On the morning news I heard reports about a murder suicide at the lake, with no mention of a missing third party. Then I realized no one knew I was there. No one knew Della and I had had a relationship. No one was or ever would be looking for me."

"You lug a whole suitcase full of guilt around, don't you?"

"Tonight just stuffed another shirt inside it. But let's look at the bright side. I may have lost Stacy, but I've found you."

"About that ... Look, Gideon, don't take this wrong, but what happened tonight was just sex, nothing more."

My heart sank. I don't know what I really expected to come out of our relationship—if that's what it was—but I also hadn't expected her to dump me quite so quickly.

"My shrink calls it sublimation. I substitute sex for love, sex for gratitude, sex for boredom. He says sex lost all emotional context for me after that bastard Roy Cooper stole my virginity. Besides, you and I could never have a serious relationship. I mean, you're a cop slash detective. I'm an actress. Think about it. We've got nothing in common. What would we talk about? Plus there's the age thing. You're so much older."

Ouch. My life sucked enough at that moment without throwing a midlife crisis into the mix. But I knew Lisa hadn't said it to hurt me, and we'd had a couple hours of fabulous sex, so I said, "You're absolutely right. From now on we're back to a strictly professional relationship."

"I am sorry about your marriage, though."

"Yeah, well, it was taking on water anyway."

I pulled into Lisa's driveway. She started to get out, when I grabbed her arm, stopping her. "Wait."

She followed my gaze to the living room window. We could see the shadow of a man on the back wall. I took out my gun, asked for her house keys, told her to stay put, and got out of the car.

I unlocked the door as quietly as I could and slipped inside. It was dead quiet, and I was afraid the intruder had heard me and was waiting for me to make the first move. But then I heard the rustle of clothes and a drawer slide open. It sounded like it came from Lisa's bedroom, so I slowly made my way down the hall. The best way to walk silently is toe first, then heel. Toe, heel. Toe, heel.

I reached the bedroom door, pressed my back against the hallway wall and listened. More rustling of clothes, a muttered "Oh, yeah..." then the squeak of springs as he sat on the bed. I decided, now or never.

I spun into the doorway, pistol leveled.

He sat on the bed, the same ponytailed guy from last night wearing the same work boots, jeans and leather jacket. He had a pair of Lisa's panties in one hand, his cock in the other. I'd caught this freak mid-stroke.

"Freeze," I said.

This guy had a real problem with authority, because instead of freezing he rolled off the back of the bed, onto the floor, and out of sight.

Shit, I thought. "Stand up," I said. "With your dick in your pants and your hands on your head."

"You know how stupid that sounds," he said from behind the bed.

Yes, I thought. "No," I said. "Now come out before I shoot."

"You're not going to shoot an unarmed man."

He was right, but I wasn't about to admit it.

"But I have good news for you," he said. Suddenly his hand

appeared over the side of the bed, wrapped around a snub nose .38. He fired twice.

I heard the first shot whiz past my ear and I was airborne—diving back out the doorway into the hall—as the second bullet buried itself in the wall next to me. I landed on my shoulder, rolled, and slammed my already tender head into the wall.

CRASH. I heard the sound of breaking glass. I had a mental picture of Lisa's bedroom and the large window leading to the street. A mental picture of the stalker throwing a chair through the window and then fleeing.

I did a combat roll into the bedroom, came up pistol ready, but he was gone. No doubt escaped through the gaping hole in the shattered window.

My head hurt, my pride ached, and I wanted revenge. I plunged through the window, slashing my forehead on the jagged glass. The stalker was scampering around a hedge and into the street. Propelled by rage, I hurtled across the lawn, leaped over the hedge and tackled the son of a bitch. He tried to pistol whip me. I blocked the blow, ripping the .38 out of his hand.

His defiance disappeared as he looked into my face. Blood poured from the cut on my forehead, hatred sizzled in my eyes. "All right," he said, breathless. "I give up."

"Not yet you don't."

I hit him in the face with his pistol. Blood erupted from his pulped nose. Then I stood up and kicked him in the stomach. Again and again. Toe, heel. Toe, heel.

It was wrong, okay. I know it. But I was half crazy. I'd been thrown off the police department, been dumped by my wife and dismissed as too old by Lisa. There was a lump on my skull and a gash on my face. Right now it was *all* this fucker's fault.

I kicked him again as Lisa came running up, screaming for me to stop. But I didn't, I couldn't. Lisa grabbed me by the back of the shirt, pulled me back. I spun around, my arm cocked, ready to punch her, when the plea in those emerald eyes finally burned through my mania. I dropped my arm, slowly returning to my senses.

"I'm sorry," I said. "I'm sorry ..."

The stalker was an unemployed actor named Jason Tucker. He wasn't a first time wacko. The year before he'd stalked an old girlfriend. He was sentenced to twelve years, most of it for shooting at me.

He tried to sue me for beating him up, but that was thrown out of court by a judge who decided Tucker was a bigger scumbag than I was. But not by much.

Lisa was grateful, sort of. She paid the bill immediately but asked me not to call her again. She'd seen the look in my eye when I almost hit her. She'd witnessed the merciless beating I gave Tucker, the beating I'd tried to give that actor at Universal. She was afraid a monster was crawling around under my skin somewhere and she didn't want to be anywhere near him if he managed to sneak out again.

Simply put, I had scared the shit out of her.

Back to Now

"Gideon, hi! So nice to see you." Lisa glided across the tile floor in flip-flops and a bathing suit covered by a short, terry cloth robe. Her hair, still wet from her swim, was swept back from her forehead. Her voice still had a hint of the South; her emerald eyes twinkled at me above an open, friendly smile. A professional smile, though. One she might give Jay Leno or David Letterman. She took my hand, gave it a firm, confident shake. "Can it really be five years?"

"Five years, a Golden Globe and two Oscar nominations, if I'm not mistaken."

A coy dip of the head. "I've been lucky."

"Luck had nothing to do with it," the manager, Ms. Hagler, said. "I read hundreds of scripts to find the right vehicles to shape your career."

Lisa ignored her, gesturing toward the couch. "Please, Gideon, sit. Can I get you anything—coffee, soda, ransom note?"

I was glad to see she hadn't lost her sense of humor. "A ransom note would be nice."

She took a plastic bag containing the note out of a pocket of her robe and handed it over. Almost apologetically, she added, "I put it in the baggie, like on TV. Figured you'd want to dust for fingerprints and stuff."

"You're right, thanks." Then I looked at the note:

> IF YOU WANT TO SEE YOUR LITTLE DARLINGS AGAIN, YOU AND GIDEON BRING $2,000,000 IN USED $100 BILLS TO THE HOLLYWOOD BOWL AT NOON TOMORROW OR YOUR LITTLE DARLINGS WILL BE SWIMMING WITH THE FISHES.

As usual, my business card was paper-clipped to the paper.

"It's him," Lisa said, the first hint of fear creeping into her voice. "The Gravesnatcher, isn't it?"

"I'm afraid so."

"Shit," Joan Hagler said.

"Do you know who he is?" Lisa asked.

"Someone with a grudge against a writer, a producer, a movie star and a private detective."

"Jason Tucker?"

"Your stalker. He was my first thought, too. Last I heard he was still in jail, so we're checking to see if he's still behind bars. As a failed actor, he fits. Especially if he worked or tried to work with Winslow and David Hunter."

"But if he's still in jail?"

"Then it's someone else who hates us all."

Hagler squared her shoulders. "No one hates Lisa; she's a beloved American icon."

"How about another actress Lisa beat out for a movie role? A director she turned down? A grip she snapped at for talking during a take? A reporter she wouldn't make time for? A freak in the audience who thinks all Lisa's smoldering looks are meant just for him? You never know who you piss off in this business, and you never know who's going to go postal on you."

"I guess we all have enemies," Lisa conceded.

"This is all your fault," Hagler snapped at me. "If you hadn't beat up that stalker this wouldn't be happening."

"We don't even know if the Gravesnatcher is Jason Tucker," I snapped back. "And what would my pounding that piece of garbage have to do with Winslow and Hunter?"

"I don't know and I don't care." Hagler turned to Lisa. "It's not too late to call the police."

"But the note said no cops."

"Blackmail notes always say that, it doesn't mean anything. I know, let's call the FBI."

"The FBI would probably fall under the Gravesnatcher's definition of cops," I said.

"I didn't ask you. Lisa, I met the Deputy Director of the FBI at a party and—"

Lisa interrupted. "Joan, no offense, but shut up. Gideon helped me before. He can help me again."

"Thank you, Lisa. And just so you know, the police do know I got a call from you. I plan to keep them apprised of the situation without letting them jeopardize the ransom exchange. So, what did the Gravesnatcher take from you? What does 'little darlings' refer to? Jewelry?"

"Sperm."

"Sperm?"

"Sperm."

"Okay, I'm confused."

"Unless you've been living under a rock," Hagler said, "you must remember Lisa's tragic marriage to Hudson King."

Hudson King, a movie star in the James Dean mode, had met and married Lisa in a much-publicized whirlwind romance about four years ago, while they were making *Night Train to Nowhere* together. He died less than a year later.

"Of course. I'm sorry, Lisa." A nod accepted my condolences, and I went on: "And the sperm is his?"

Another nod. "Hudson and I wanted children, but not right away. Then he got diagnosed with colon cancer. The doctors thought he could beat it, but he was going to need chemo and that can make you sterile."

I got it. "So he made a few deposits just in case."

"The chemo didn't work. Nothing worked. And even though I lost Hudson, I still have a chance to have his baby."

"Someday," Hagler hastily added. "Maybe in a couple of

years, when a maternity leave wouldn't be so catastrophic to your career."

Or your commissions, I thought.

Lisa said, "I got a call from the sperm bank, CryoZy Laboratories in Beverly Hills, about an hour before the note arrived. They told me they'd been broken into last night and Hudson's sperm had been stolen."

I made a mental note to make sure Mary Rocket sent Ruiz and his dust collectors to the sperm bank, and to take a look at their surveillance cameras.

Then Lisa asked the million-dollar question. "But this really isn't about blackmail, is it? I know what happened to Winslow and dear David. I'm next on the Gravesnatcher's list, aren't I? He wants to kill me."

"Let me put it this way. The first ransom was paid, but Winslow was thrown off his balcony. The second ransom was paid, but Hunter was still blown up. There's every reason to believe the Gravesnatcher wants your money *and* your life."

"In that case, let me be perfectly clear," Hagler puffed. "Lisa's not going to die. So fuck the sperm. Fuck the Gravesnatcher. And fuck you. Lisa, darling, this'll blow over eventually and you can make a triumphant, and well-publicized, return to Hollywood. In the meantime, you're out of here."

"Is Lisa going to run or disappear?" I asked.

Hagler was confused. "What do you mean?"

"If she runs—moves to Hawaii or Hong Kong, for that matter—the Gravesnatcher can just get on a plane and go after her. Now if she plans on disappearing—giving up the business, changing her name, surgically altering her face—she's got a better chance, but no guarantees. Remember, the Gravesnatcher's now got at least four million dollars in cash at his disposal. And he's motivated. Lisa's on his list. I got a feeling he's not going to give up just because she changes area codes."

Hagler started to speak, but Lisa laid a firm hand on her shoulder. "What're you saying, Gideon?"

"Your best chance is for me to catch him. I can't do that unless you and I deliver the ransom."

Hagler laughed. “You mean like that Keystone Cops act at Magic Land yesterday?”

I stiffened. “That wasn’t my fault. The police insisted on following me. This time we’ll do it my way and catch him.”

Lisa stared out the sliding glass doors at her magnificent backyard. “It’s funny, this is one of those crossroads we encounter once or twice in a lifetime. Pick the right path or suffer ever after.” She sighed. “I’ve often envied the characters I’ve played because they get to make this kind of momentous decision once or twice a movie. But when my characters make a decision it’s dictated by the writer, and the writer knows how the story will end. Who knows how this will end? Who tells me which path to pick?”

“Me,” I said. “I’m in this, too. My card’s clipped to every one of these ransom notes and, until we’ve caught the Gravesnatcher, I’m not safe either. Say yes and you help both of us. Hell, you may still be able to have Hudson’s baby ...”

“You have a plan?”

“Not yet, but I will by tonight.”

Lisa looked at me, considering, and then made a decision. “Okay, Gideon. I’ll get the money; you get a plan.”

Plan? Plan? I Don't Need No Stinking Plan

I'd lied to Lisa. I already had a plan. The problem was, it was illegal. Sort of. Okay, totally, but I was desperate. Instead of fucking around with a police stakeout, a transmitter hidden in the lining of a backpack, or dye-tainted money, I'd decided to end it once and for all. I was going to plant a little surprise with the ransom. A letter bomb.

I didn't want to kill him, just incapacitate him long enough to capture him. So as I drove from Brentwood to Sherman Oaks I reviewed how to make a letter bomb—a skill I learned from Stacy when we were married, one that she had learned from the Army while spending three years in green.

What I didn't do was call Mary Rocket. I knew the Captain was waiting for the details of Lisa's ransom demand, but I wasn't ready to talk to the cops yet. Not when visions of letter bombs were still dancing in my brain.

I reached my strip mall and pulled into my parking lot. Or tried to. The lot was full—mobbed with TV vans, reporters, and photographers all waiting for some news to show up.

Me. I was the news. The PI at the center of the Gravesnatcher case. You can't have your fifteen minutes of fame without a press conference. And mine was waiting for me.

But I didn't have time for it. I had to try and figure out who the hell the Gravesnatcher was. Barring that, I had an illegal explosive device to manufacture so I could blow the bastard's hands off.

I thought about turning around and heading for my apartment. Too bad everything I needed was in the office. Besides, once the press gets your scent, there's no escape. So I parked in the JACK IN THE BOX lot across the street, and walked into the lion's den.

I heard a "There he is ..." when I was halfway across Ventura Boulevard. They swarmed me.

The up-and-coming cute blond from Channel 4: "What can you tell us about the Gravesnatcher?"

The gone-to-seed comb-over from 9: "Who's next on his list?"

The bounced-from-one-station-to-the-other silver-haired old pro, now on 7: "Why you, Gideon? What's he got against you?"

The ambitious I'll-do-anything-to-get-to-the-network red-head from 2: "Isn't it true you're actually working *with* the Gravesnatcher?"

I bulled through them all, climbed the first two steps of the stairway, then turned back to make a statement. "Look, I'd love to help you all, but I can't. This is an ongoing police investigation and I'm not permitted to comment."

"Don't you have anything to say to the families of those people you shot at Magic Land?" The bitch from Channel 2 again.

"I didn't shoot anyone, and if you were doing your job, you'd know that."

She smiled, happy. I'd risen to her bait and she had her sound bite for the six o'clock news.

They shouted more questions at me, but I ignored them, trotted up the stairs and into my office.

"Vultures," I said slamming the door.

"Tell me about it," Hillary said. She was sitting in front of the file cabinet, a thick pile of folders on her lap, a yellow pad filled with handwritten names next to her. "I've been, like, besieged all day. Makes you wonder how the rock stars do it—paparazzi, rabid, clawing fans, naked pictures in the mail. I mean, really, what ever happened to the right of privacy?"

"Have I gotten any naked pictures?"

"No. You've only been famous for about six minutes. However, fame isn't without its rewards. It's given us knowledge. And knowledge is power."

"What knowledge is that?"

"The answering machine can take fifty-three messages before it gets all exhausted and frizzes out."

"Fifty-three messages?!"

"Might have been a hundred and fifty-three if the machine hadn't crashed and burned." She flipped through her notes. "Let's see, most of the messages are from media types wanting interviews. Could be good for *Rear Entry* sales ..."

"Not until the case is over. Then I'll talk to everyone."

"Eighteen people called applying for the secretary job. I figure we better wait to see if the Gravesnatcher kills you first."

"Depressing but prudent."

"Eleven producers called wanting to buy the rights to your life. I referred them to Elliot. Oh, and some cops were here. They've tapped our phones and set up a trace to a substation in North Hollywood. If the Gravesnatcher calls, and we keep him on the line for, like, thirty seconds, they'll have a location."

I didn't think the Gravesnatcher was stupid enough to stay on the phone for that long, but hey, you've got to try everything.

"And Captain Rocket's called. Five times. Want me to get her?"

I needed more time to think before I brought the cops back in. "No, we'll call her later." I picked up her yellow pad. Page after page of names. "How you coming on our list of potential suspects?"

"Well, including everyone in the Rolodex, and about half your files, so far, I'm up to, like, a zillion names. Private investigation is a very people-intensive endeavor."

BRRRING.

The phone rang. Hillary reached for it, then stopped, a funny expression on her face. "That doesn't sound like our phone."

BRRRING.

Hillary leaned her head toward the phone, listening. "Nope." She picked it up. "Dial tone."

BRRRING. It was that same old-fashioned ringtone I'd heard at Magic Land.

Hillary and I followed the sound to my desk, to my upper left hand drawer. I opened it and found a cheap Motorola cell phone.

"When you'd buy that?" Hillary asked.

"I didn't." But I knew who did. I picked up the phone. "The Gravesnatcher, I presume."

"I hate that name," he said in that familiar, condescending voice. "So fucking Hollywood."

"You don't like Hollywood?"

"Hollywood is a town populated with temporary people making permanent decisions."

"Do I sense a little frustration there?"

"No, my time has come. Now I'm number one on the call sheet."

Number one on the call sheet? I wonder if he realized he'd just made his first mistake. Just given me the first real clue as to his identity.

He switched subjects, asked: "The cops tap your phone yet?"

I thought about lying but realized that if I was ever going to catch this guy, he had to trust me. "Yeah. Tap and trace. You stay on my phone long enough, they'll have your location."

"I'm not that stupid."

I eyed the Motorola. "Apparently not. When did you plant the phone?"

"Last night. Last month. Last year. What difference does it make? The news said you had nothing to do with the cops being at Magic Land."

"That's right. The cops and I had a deal I'd go in alone, like you wanted. They broke their word."

"Assholes."

"And they probably won't let me go to the Hollywood Bowl without an 'escort,' either."

"So don't tell them."

"Have to. They know I went to see Lisa. They'll want to see the ransom note."

"Fine, give it to them. Let them think we're meeting at the Bowl, but you go somewhere else."

"Where?"

"The L.A. Zoo. Gorilla cages. Same time. And Lisa better be with you."

"Why? Let's leave Lisa out of this. Just you and me, okay?"

"No." The line went dead.

Breadcrumbs upon the Water

Roy hung up and smiled. He'd surprised the PI with the hidden cell phone. Kincaid hadn't liked that, Roy could tell. Well, tough shit. Kincaid had a lot more surprises coming before this was over.

Roy looked around his one-bedroom Westwood apartment. It was cookie cutter common, one of fifty-eight units in the twenty-five-year-old building. Each with the same tan and white walls, fake fireplace with an electric glowing log, ten by ten bedroom with mirrors on the closet doors to make the room look bigger, tiny kitchen, minuscule bathroom and a view of one of the complex's brick walls. The walls and countertops were covered with memorabilia. Pictures, mostly, but a few plaques and ribbons. The flotsam and jetsam of his glory years. There were photos of his high school and college productions, as well as photos from most of his TV roles.

It was the first apartment Roy had looked at when he hit town seven years ago, and he took it instantly. Not because he liked it, because that didn't matter. He wasn't going to be here long, just until he landed his first movie or TV series.

Roy looked at the red plaid living room set he'd bought on sale at Sears the same day he'd rented the apartment. Again, Roy figured he'd only need it for a few weeks and then he'd just leave it when he moved to new digs at the beach. That was seven years ago. He was still stuck in this dump on Kelton

Avenue with a red plaid couch and matching love seat. Red plaid, what was he thinking?

He'd been so sure he would become a star. Never considered any alternative.

Never dreamed he'd be fucked over by a writer, a producer, a starlet and a private dick.

A headline from the *L.A. Times* screamed at him from the kitchen counter. "Gravesnatcher stalks Hollywood." The press was making him out to be the bad guy. Hell, he was the good guy. He was the one whose career had been ruined. He was the one that Winslow, Hunter, Lisa, Kincaid and that bastard Jerry Marshall had destroyed. He was the one that deserved retribution.

And he was getting it. He'd be out of this rattrap in no time with millions of dollars.

But Kincaid had to keep following the breadcrumbs.

This part of the plan made Roy nervous. It seemed reckless. Too in your face. Why taunt the son of a bitch? But Roy had a partner, and his partner insisted. And hey, his partner hadn't been wrong yet.

Elementary, My Dear Hillary

"He's an actor."

"Who?"

"The Gravesnatcher. He just slipped, told me he was number one on the call sheet."

"Number one on the what?"

"Call sheet. A call sheet is used on movie sets every day to announce what time the crew will start filming, which scenes will be shot in what order and what actors are scheduled to work at what times. The star of the show is always listed first."

"Ergo, number one on the call sheet. Cool."

"Also, an actor pretends to be different people. Which explains his phone statement, 'I am anyone.'"

"You are brilliant! Another mystery solved. So I'll narrow my file search to actors. Have you worked for that many actors?"

"As clients, no. But I've come across hundreds while investigating cases. L.A. may have gotten a handle on the smog, but actors are an epidemic."

Hillary sighed. "Hope shattered, she returns to the Everest of files."

"Don't despair just yet. The Gravesnatcher's left us another clue." I held up the cell phone.

"Fingerprints?"

"Not the arches, loops and whorls kind. He's too smart for that. But maybe the electronic kind. The phone was on when he planted it. Had to be for it to ring. If he made a call on the phone before sticking it in the drawer, we might get a lead to follow."

All I had to do is hit the SEND button. If he hadn't made a call, nothing would happen. If he had, the number would flash on the small, LED screen as the number was automatically dialed. I pressed SEND.

A number appeared.

A number I recognized.

485-2129. 485 is the LAPD prefix. And I'd worked at the 2129 extension.

An operator answered and told me what I already knew: "Robbery Homicide, can I help you?"

"Sorry, wrong number." I hung up.

Hillary said, "You have a really funny look on your face. Like you just saw a ghost or something."

"The Gravesnatcher called the LAPD."

"That makes, like, no sense." Then it hit her. "Unless he ... no that's not possible. He can't be working with a cop, can he?"

"The Gravesnatcher hasn't left a single clue at any crime scene. Makes you wonder, is he really that good or is he working with someone?"

"I'm not wondering. Why else would he call the cops?"

Why else indeed. Piccolo was right. Well, partly right. The Gravesnatcher had a partner; it just wasn't me.

Then something hit me. "This isn't a throw-away phone with pre-paid minutes. This is a Motorola phone with a Verizon logo. Somebody's paying the bill."

We had a contact at Verizon who always needed money to feed a gambling addiction; I scrolled through the menu and found the number. "Hillary, give Robin a call at Verizon, see if he can get a name to go with this number." I read it to her.

Hillary didn't say anything so I looked up. She was standing in my office doorway, staring into the reception room. "Hillary?"

"He's out."

"Who's out?"

"The Gravesnatcher."

"Out where? The reception area?"

"Out in the world."

Just once I'd like to have a normal conversation with Hillary. "We already know this, don't we?"

"Yes and no."

"Yes and no?"

"Yes, we know he's out in the world, but, like, until right now we didn't know for sure who he was."

"You know who he is?"

"Everyone knows who he is. Everyone watching TV, I mean."

"There's something on TV about the Gravesnatcher?"

"That's what I've been trying to tell you."

I followed her into the reception room where the TV showed the up-and-coming cute blond from Channel 4 doing a live remote from the front of our building. "To recap: Moments ago the police department released this picture of Jason Tucker ..." A mug shot of Jason Tucker appeared on the screen.

Jason Tucker, Lisa's stalker. Jason Tucker, the guy I almost beat to death in front of Lisa's house.

"Five years ago Jason Tucker was convicted of attempted murder and stalking starlet Lisa Montgomery," the reporter continued. "He was sentenced to twelve years and has been serving his time at Folsom State Prison. Somehow—and the authorities haven't told us yet, but somehow—he was released by mistake three weeks ago."

"By mistake!" I howled. "How the hell did that happen?"

A close-up of the up-and-coming cute blond came back on the TV. "Jason Tucker was an unsuccessful actor, with a history of stalking, and our sources inside the police department tell us they are convinced he's the Gravesnatcher."

Hillary put down her yellow pad full of names of potential suspects. "I guess that's that."

"I guess so."

Suddenly the front door burst open. I spun, expecting to

see an overeager member of the press corps, instead I found Detective Piccolo and two uniformed cops.

"Freeze," Piccolo said. "Up against the wall and spread 'em."

"I can't freeze and get up against the wall at the same time."

"Then let me clarify." He grabbed me, threw me against the wall. "Now spread 'em."

"You can't do that," Hillary said.

"It's all right, Hillary. Detective Piccolo is still obviously under the effects of drugs from his injuries."

"The only drug I'm on is dopamine. The body produces it when the brain is happy. And my brain is ecstatic because I've got you."

"So I haven't called the Captain back. Don't make a federal case out of it."

"Oh, I've got you for a lot more than losing at phone tag. I've got you for the big one. Kidnapping and murder."

Hillary said, "That sounds more like the big two."

I said, "It sounds like horse shit to me."

Piccolo said, "You're working with the Gravesnatcher, and I can prove it!" Piccolo started reading me my rights.

"Hillary," I said, as Piccolo droned on. "Call Victor and tell him what happened." Victor was my attorney.

"He's on vacation. Israel, I think, or Istanbul. 'Is' something."

"Then call his brother, Joel."

"Joel went with him. Islamabad, maybe."

"Just call somebody."

Piccolo: "Do you understand these rights as I've read them?"

"I wasn't really listening," Hillary said.

"He was talking to me, Hillary, and yes, I understand them," I said. He cuffed me. "You know, Detective, I've got a back door so we can avoid the electronic vultures outside."

A malevolent smirk warped his face. "Why would I want to do that?"

Piccolo dragged me out the door and down the stairs toward the phalanx of reporters. It took the press a beat or two to realize what was happening; then they were the maggots and I was the corpse.

The up-and-coming cute blond from Channel 4: "Officer, why are you arresting Gideon Kincaid?"

Piccolo gave the cameras a stern, authoritarian look. "We believe Mr. Kincaid is in cahoots with the Gravesnatcher."

Cahoots?

The gone-to-seed comb-over from 9: "And your name, officer?"

"Detective Irving Piccolo."

Stacy was going out with a guy named Irving?

The bounced-from-one-station-to-another silver-haired old pro, now on 7: "The same Detective Piccolo that was wounded at Magic Land?"

"Brutally shot, thanks to the nefarious scheming of Gideon Kincaid and his cohort, the Gravesnatcher."

Nefarious? Cohort? Where did he get these words?

The ambitious I'll-do-anything-to-get-to-the-network redhead from 2: "Have you found any of the ransom money?"

"Not yet, but we will. And I promise you all one thing: Gideon Kincaid will pay for his malfeasance."

"Pay for it?" I finally said, fed up. "I can't even spell it."

I've logged hundreds of hours sitting in interrogation rooms, but this was the first time I was the guy handcuffed to the chair. I didn't like it.

Piccolo paced back and forth as he lobbed questions at me. "When did you first meet the Gravesnatcher?"

"I'm not going to answer any questions until I see a lawyer."

"So you admit you're guilty."

"Fuck you."

"There's no use denying it. We've got proof."

"You can't have proof."

"How about your Visa card number? It was given to the operator at the mail order house to buy the dog collar that killed David Hunter."

"What?"

"And it was delivered to your P.O. Box in Santa Monica."

"I don't have a P.O. Box in Santa Monica."

"And you don't know the Gravesnatcher. Come on, Gideon, confess now and it'll go a lot easier on you."

"Do you know how easy it is to get someone's credit card number? How easy it is to open a P.O. Box in someone else's name? The Gravesnatcher's framing me, any idiot can see that."

"I'm not any idiot."

"You're telling me."

Mary Rocket limped through the door.

"Hey, Cap," Piccolo said, "I think he's about ready to crack."

"I think you're the one that's cracked," she said. "Uncuff him."

"But he's a kidnapper and a murderer."

"I told you to check out the P.O. Box lead before you brought him in. I told you any idiot knows how easy it is to open a box in someone else's name. But did you?"

"Er, no."

"So I did. The box was opened two weeks ago. The only piece of mail that ever came in was the package from Doggieworld."

"That doesn't prove Gideon didn't open the box."

"Maybe not. But why open a P.O. Box just to receive an item you're afraid the cops may be able to trace and use your real name?"

"Well ..."

"And I called Doggieworld. Luckily they record all phone orders in case of discrepancy, and they're based in L.A, so we got a copy of the conversation." She took a small tape recorder out of her jacket pocket, snapped it on.

> "Thanks for calling Doggieworld. This is Chandra. How may I help you?"
>
> "I'd like to order a collar. From your catalog."
>
> "Name please?"
>
> "Gideon Kincaid."

"Bullshit," I squawked. "That's him, the Gravesnatcher, I recognize his voice." Indeed, it was the deep, slightly condescending voice I was getting more and more used to hearing. A voice that sounded nothing like mine.

> "Address?"
>
> "P.O. Box 342, Colorado Boulevard, Santa Monica, California. 90401."
>
> "Item number, please?"
>
> "B614. It's for my new puppy. I'm trying to decide what to call him. Maybe you can help."
>
> "I will if I can."
>
> "Which do you like better: Barry, David or Lisa?"

"*Barry* Winslow, *David* Hunter, *Lisa* Montgomery," I said. "He's having this conversation for our benefit. He knew he was being recorded. Knew we'd track down the tape." On tape, a confused Chandra said:

> "But Barry and David are male names. Lisa's a female."
>
> "I think society worries too much about male/female labels. How about Gideon? You like that name?"
>
> "Isn't that your name?"
>
> "Yeah, I was thinking about naming the dog after me. No?"
>
> "It does seem a little ... self-absorbed."
>
> "You know, you're right. I think I'll scratch the names off my list. Kill all four of them."
>
> "Then what are you going to name your dog?"
>
> "How about ... Chandra?"
>
> A giggle. "One of my personal favorites."
>
> "So be it."

Mary Rocket's finger mashed the OFF button. "The FBI can run a voice print on Gideon and one on the tape, but I can tell you right now what they're going to say: That's not Gideon's voice."

Piccolo grasped for straws. "That doesn't mean he's not collaborating with him."

"No, but I'm going with my guts on this one," Mary Rocket said to Piccolo. "Gideon's clean. Goodbye, Detective Piccolo. And next time, when I tell you to check something before making an arrest, do it."

"Yes, ma'am." A humbled Piccolo started out, but not before shooting me an 'I'm not through with you yet' look.

"Oh, and one more thing, Detective. I was talking to Colleen over at Channel 4, asking her where she got her information about the Magic Land shooting, and your name came up."

"I never talked to her."

"She claims you did. Claims you were so upset about Gideon Kincaid blowing the ransom and getting you shot that you had to talk to someone."

Remember what I said earlier about being able to tell when people are lying? The different clues like sweat on the lip, halting answers, contraction of a pupil, picking a cuticle? Well, sweat sprouted on Piccolo's upper lip and his pupils disappeared.

"Well, I don't ... I mean, I hardly know ... Sure I've talked to her. But I don't think I mentioned Magic Land. At least not anything we weren't supposed to talk about."

"You weren't supposed to talk about *anything*."

"Right. Well, I won't talk to her again," he said picking a cuticle. "And I'll make sure no one else does, either." He scurried out of there.

"He's lying," I said.

"I know. I'll take care of it. Right now I'm more worried about you. You may not be working with the Gravesnatcher, but you're not very forthcoming. You were supposed to call me as soon as you left Lisa Montgomery's house."

"My cell phone was dead."

"Then when you got to your office."

"I tried. As soon as I walked in I reached for the phone to call you, but before I could dial, Piccolo popped out of the woodwork with his butterfly net."

She eyed me skeptically but bought it. "So, what happened with Lisa?"

"Tit for tat, Captain. First tell me about Jason Tucker."

She got mad just thinking about it. "Some bureaucrat got his red tape wrapped around his brain and released Jason Tucker instead of Jerry Turner."

"Three weeks ago and we're just finding out?"

"They claim they called us just after it happened."

"Who'd they talk to?"

"They don't remember."

"How convenient."

"You want my opinion?" she said. "They didn't talk to anybody. They've been keeping this quiet until they could figure out how to save their asses. Hell, if we hadn't called to make sure Tucker was still in jail we might never have found out."

"Are you sure Jason Tucker is the Gravesnatcher?"

"The stars are sure lining up. He's got a grudge against you and Lisa. And since he was an actor the connection to Winslow or Hunter seems natural. We're searching all their files looking for his name. This Doggieworld tape may help. I've asked for Jason Tucker's police interview tapes to be pulled from the archive. With any luck we can match the two voices."

The tape reminded me of something. "We may be able to do better than that."

"Really, what?"

"We may be able to actually see him in action."

The Stuff Frozen Dreams are Made Of

"Here he comes now."

Barak Obama stepped out of a corridor and walked down the row of liquid nitrogen storage tanks. He wore surgical gloves and carried a small cooler in his right hand.

"Still wearing the Obama mask," Mary Rocket said. "Just like Magic Land."

Mary Rocket and I were in Beverly Hills. In the Beverly Hills police station, to be exact. Sitting in a lush conference room—to be more exact—watching a copy of a CryoZy Laboratory surveillance tape. Beverly Hills has its own police department. With relatively little crime and enough money for all the new high tech toys, cops from all over California lined up twenty deep for every available opening on the BHPD. Judging by the detective standing in front of us, Peter Burke, they choose the tall, handsome guys with broad shoulders, square jaws and piercing blue eyes. Movie star looks. Nothing but the best for the BHPD. Burke walked us through his investigation.

"CryoZy Labs has an elaborate security system. Alarm tape on all the windows. Front door is reinforced steel, triple locked. Motion detectors crisscross the entryway. And, as you can see, a video camera guards the vault. Look at the time stamp: he first appeared at eleven twenty-three p.m., but the alarm didn't go off until eleven thirty-seven."

"He must've gotten in during business hours," I said.

"Hidden in a closet or something, and come out after everyone was gone."

"That's right. Then he stole the sperm, walked into the lobby, used a hammer to break the plate glass window, and disappeared into the night."

Mary Rocket shook her head. "All the security in the world won't help you if the perp's already inside."

"We think it was the computer room. There was a crushed box in a storage area behind the main frame. Looks like he was sitting on it while waiting for everyone to clear out. On the floor we found a cotton fiber, one that matches the cotton on disposable surgical boots. Check out his feet."

Mary Rocket nodded. "He's got surgical booties over his shoes."

"We also found a fiber in front of tank six."

On screen, Barak Obama stopped in front of tank six. "There are ten tanks total, each five feet high." He opened a wedge-shaped drawer on the side of the tank. After searching for a moment or two, his left hand reached in and started withdrawing thin, four inch long, white plastic vials. He took eight of them. "They're called cryovials," Burke said. "There are between eight and ten thousand cryovials in each tank. The tanks are kept at 193 degrees below zero."

"Why's he taking so many of them?" Mary Rocket asked.

"There's no guarantee that a woman will get pregnant the first time she uses the sperm, so she asks for extra donations. Hudson King made eight deposits."

I asked, "How'd he know where to find Lisa's cryovial?"

"He accessed a terminal in the computer room, left Lisa Montgomery's file on the screen."

Obama opened up the cooler, put the cryovials inside. Burke froze the frame. "As you can see, he wore gloves, so we got no prints. Aside from the cotton fibers, we found no forensic evidence. However … see his hair sticking out from behind the Obama mask? Long and brown, tied in a pony tail."

"That's how Jason Tucker wore his hair," I said.

The tape showed us something else, I was sure of it. I felt this tugging at my brain again, but I couldn't put my finger on it.

"It looks like Tucker is our man," Mary Rocket said. "Our best shot to catch him is the next ransom drop. When is it, Gideon?"

"Noon, tomorrow."

"Where?"

This is where it got tricky. Lying to the Captain could backfire big time and I could make Piccolo's day and wind up in jail. Plus, if someone in the police department was working with the Gravesnatcher, and I told Mary Rocket that the drop had been switched to the zoo, there was a chance the Gravesnatcher would hear about it and not show up. Besides, I really felt I had the best chance catching this SOB alone, so I said: "The Hollywood Bowl."

"The Hollywood Bowl? You're sure?"

Uh oh, did she know something I didn't think she knew? "Yeah, I'm sure, why?"

"Well, the Bowl's practically deserted at noon on a weekday. So it's not nearly as risky a place as Magic Land for us to plan an operation. This is good. Very good," Mary Rocket said. "Gideon, you go about your business, make sure the ransom is put together, act like you're doing everything the Gravesnatcher wants. I'm going to huddle up with SWAT and come up with a plan. Thanks for all your help, Detective Burke. Gideon, I'll call you later." And with that, an excited Mary Rocket limped out of the conference room.

I turned back to the TV monitor. "Detective Burke, would it be all right if I kept a copy of this DVD?"

"Sure, take this one. I've got the master locked up safe and sound."

"Thank you." I focused on the frozen image of Obama. There was a clue there; I knew it. What the hell was it?

A Promise is a Promise and it Must Be Kept

Roy stared at the bedroom TV. A cute blond reporter stood in front of City Hall, the microphone with an NBC logo gripped firmly in her manicured hand. "Police sources have just confirmed that they have new evidence tying escaped convict Jason Tucker to the Gravesnatcher investigation." A picture of Tucker flashed on the screen. The reporter continued, "If you see this man or know of his whereabouts, please contact the LAPD immediately. Police caution that he is to be considered armed and extremely dangerous."

Good, Roy thought. They must've looked at the surveillance tapes from the sperm bank. The wig was a great idea.

He was also conflicted. Happy the cops had taken the Jason Tucker bait. Sad he wasn't getting credit for the ingenious crimes. Oh, well, his day would come.

With a flick of the remote, Roy extinguished the broadcast, then went to work digging through the stack of magazines on the floor of his closet. He was looking for a particular issue, one of his favorites. He found it and hurried into the bathroom, closing the door behind him.

In the mirror's reflection, Roy saw the movie poster he'd tacked to the back of the bathroom door. Forgetting the magazine for a moment, his eyes caressed the poster. A waif lay curled among rumpled sheets. She was young, innocent-looking, and yet incredibly sexy. A bare leg stuck out the bottom, a languid arm draped out the side. She had long brown hair, a trusting look in her huge hazel eyes, and a provocative smile on her slightly parted lips. Her name was Tiffany Granger. She had actually been nineteen when she was cast in the movie but the character she played was sixteen. The title of the movie was *Jailbait.* On the top left of the poster her name was printed: Tiffany Granger. On the top right of the poster was the name of her co-star: Roy Cooper.

That's right. Our Roy Cooper. He'd starred in a movie. Well, *almost* starred in a movie. It was produced and directed by David Hunter. And it was the reason David Hunter had needed to die.

After the *Ramrod* debacle Roy had rededicated himself to the art of acting. More workshops, more classes, more plays. It was while acting in one these small plays that Roy noticed a guy sitting in the audience with a poodle on his lap. A famous dog in a famous lap. Jennifer the dog and David Hunter the producer.

Hunter's nephew was playing a part—a football player with a drug habit—and Hunter showed up as a favor to his sister. His nephew sucked, but Roy's performance as the best friend caught Hunter's attention. He was about to cast a new movie about a sixteen-year-old girl who falls in love with the high school football coach. Roy was perfect for the coach.

Hunter was being very selective with this role. More selective than usual.

It isn't unusual for co-stars to fall in love while making a movie, especially when a lot of love scenes are involved. Hunter wasn't about to let that happen, because Hunter was in love with Tiffany Granger.

Hunter had first seen Tiffany on a billboard. It was a Calvin Klein ad. Tiffany was wearing nothing but CK jeans. Tiffany had a fresh face that enchanted Hunter. He had his casting people track her down and fly her to Hollywood for a meeting.

Tiffany had just turned eighteen and had only been a model for six months after being discovered in a Bath and Body Shop in a Houston mall. In truth, she was eighteen going on thirty-eight. Her mother was a stripper at an exclusive Men's Club, and occasionally Mama would bring home a customer to make a few extra bucks. By the time Tiffany reached puberty, she had no illusions about the sanctity of sex. Her mother had taught her that it was a commodity, and that's how Tiffany used it.

At fifteen Tiffany lost her virginity to one of her mother's clients. He'd spotted her sitting in front of the TV wearing shorts and a tube top. Tiffany looked at the john with those big hazel eyes of hers and smiled. He offered Tiffany's mother two thousand dollars if he could make love to Tiffany. Tiffany's mom looked at her, and Tiffany looked him over. Businessman-type, maybe 35, cute enough.

"Five thousand," she said. "I'm a virgin."

"Deal," he said.

Afterwards, Tiffany's mother asked if she liked it. Tiffany just smiled. "What's not to like?"

Tiffany's mom was a meth head, which meant the money never lasted long. They sold her 'virginity' a few times over the years, once for ten grand.

Tiffany was ambitious. She didn't want to spend her life in Houston, waving her tits in a strip club, so when she was asked in that Bed and Bath if she'd like to model, she jumped at the chance.

New York was great. But she found the modeling work itself just another form of stripping. Posing for hours in scanty clothes looking sexy for the camera. She wanted more. When David Hunter's people contacted her, she knew she had a shot at the big time: Hollywood.

She drooled at the house in Holmby Hills. Saw the lust in Hunter's eyes when they talked in his massive living room. He was talking about all the careers he'd built, rattling off an impressive list of movie stars. Meanwhile she noticed the way his eyes probed the skin of her thigh, the freckled mounds of her breasts. He didn't want to make her a star so much as he wanted to bury his face in her sweet, young bush.

He loved her youth and presumed her innocence. She fed his fantasy. She flirted with him, but feigned shyness, naïveté. He took her out for dinner and dancing and, back at the hotel, Tiffany timidly let him seduce her. She moved into his Holmby Hills mansion two days later.

That had been six months before Hunter saw Roy in the play. During that time Hunter had developed *Jailbait* for Tiffany. He was sure it would make her a star. All Hunter needed now was a 'safe' co-star. Directors and stars sometimes hook up as well; Hunter eliminated that possibility by directing the movie himself.

He went backstage, introduced himself to Roy, told him about the movie, and promised to send him a script and set up an audition.

When Roy read the script he knew this could be his big break. It was a terrific story—provocative, sexy, yet still intelligent. Even though the coach sleeps with an underage girl, he ends up being the sympathetic one, the victim.

Roy was surprised when he walked into Hunter's office a few days later and was introduced to Tiffany. She looked so ... sweet. A wide-eyed kid. How could she ever pull off this Lolita-like vixen? But as they talked he sensed the sensuality simmering behind those hazel eyes. It turned him on.

Tiffany liked Roy's looks, too. Those sculpted cheekbones, the jutting jaw, the sea-green eyes. Even through his clothes, Tiffany knew his body would be hard—a welcome change after David's pudgy flesh. She also knew she'd have to be careful, not let David know how attracted she was to Roy. If David knew, he'd never cast him.

The audition went well. Tiffany was a natural, and all of Roy's work had paid off.

Roy gave the coach texture; you sensed a man being pulled apart at the seams, his desperate love for the forbidden fruit driving him to risk everything. The very real chemistry between them came through in their performance. When they finished Roy looked expectantly at Hunter.

"Excellent," the producer said, but he looked worried. "Tiffany, would you leave Roy and me alone for a few minutes?"

Tiffany didn't like being excluded from anything but she managed to shove a smile into place. "Of course, darling." Careful not to look at Roy—fearing Hunter might try to read attraction into it—she left.

Hunter got up, the poodle in his arms, and began to pace around the large office.

Now Roy looked worried. "Is something wrong, Mr. Hunter?"

"Yes. You were terrific, and I'm not going to cast you."

"What? Why? You just said—"

"Because I'll lose Tiffany if you co-star with her."

"I don't understand."

"You guys clicked together. I could feel the heat. And this script has plenty of heat. Total nudity for Tiffany, and if the actor playing the coach is up to it, maybe even a quick shot of his cock for the ladies in the audience."

"You could shoot a long shot of my cock if you cast me."

Hunter shook his head, continued his pacing. "No, it just won't work. You and Tiffany have three major love scenes. You have to kiss her, caress every inch of her body, pretend to make love to her while you're both naked in a shower. Naked on a desk. Naked in bed. There is no way you two could spend that much sexual time together and not fall in love. Or at least in lust. You're going to end up fucking her for real."

"No, I won't. I promise."

"You won't be able to help yourself. I can't tell you how many 'fake' love scenes have turned into the real thing. There are hundreds—hell, *thousands*—of actors who pretended to screw on screen, and got so worked up they couldn't wait to get off the set so they could fuck each other's brains out for real. In each case, marriages were ruined and relationships destroyed.

"No, I must've been nuts thinking I could stand by and watch some gorgeous hunk put his hands on my precious Tiffany. Look, I'm sorry to have wasted your time, Roy, but I can't cast you. I can't cast anybody. I just can't make this movie."

Roy couldn't believe it. He was this close again! He had to say something, find a way to change Hunter's mind. Then he realized a simple truth. "If you don't make *Jailbait* you'll lose her anyway."

"What're you talking about?"

"She wants to be an actress, right?"

"More than anything."

"So what's she going to say when you pull the plug on the movie? 'That's okay, honey, I'll just knit for the rest of my life?' No, she'll leave you and find someone else to put her in a movie."

"I'll develop another movie for her. A safer movie."

"Playing what, a nun? 'Course there would still be a few male actors in the cast, any one of which could seduce her away from you. Or maybe do a movie about a bunch of wild women, you know, Amazons. 'Course she could fall in love with one of the women in the cast. Hey, I know, how about a movie about a woman trapped alone on a deserted island?"

Hunter put up a pudgy hand. 'Enough. You made your point."

"David, Tiffany was born to play Suzie. *Jailbait* will make her a big star. But it will do something else. It will make *me* a big star. So I'll promise you this: I will keep the relationship between Tiffany and me completely professional. Nothing more. She'll be safe with me, I guarantee it."

Hunter looked deeply into Roy eyes, unyieldingly, as if trying to see the soul, judge the soul, decide if he could believe this man, turn over the love of his life to him and get her back whole. Finally, hesitantly: "Okay."

They rehearsed for two weeks prior to shooting. Always at Hunter's mansion, and always with at least the three of them in the room—Tiffany, Roy and Hunter. Four, if you counted the poodle on Hunter's lap.

Sometimes the writer joined them. Sometimes the script supervisor. Once a couch full of studio brass watched them rehearse. Everyone could see what Roy and Tiffany felt: a sizzling sexual tension.

It was all the more impressive because Hunter never allowed Roy and Tiffany to kiss during rehearsal. Not even to touch. Hunter's paranoia dictated the rule. Unbeknownst to him, his precautions were actually backfiring. Unable to let off any sexual steam, both Roy and Tiffany were getting horny as hell. Even though Roy was determined not to fall in love/lust with Tiffany, he couldn't help fantasizing about that first kiss. Tiffany, on the other hand, had no compunction about love or lust, and was fantasizing about sitting on Roy's face. No wonder their rehearsals were so hot.

On the last day of rehearsal David presented them each with a gift, a *Jailbait* movie poster. Roy stared at his name on the one sheet and an involuntary smile swept his face. He'd finally made it. He was going to be a star.

Hunter had planned the schedule to start with an innocuous scene on the football field when Suzie first saw the Coach and they flirted a little. Then to spend a couple days filming innocent scenes of Suzie with her parents and the Coach with the football team. Hunter said he wanted to build up to the sex scenes, but Roy and Tiffany knew that he was putting them off as long as he could.

Rain changed all that. A cold front attacked L.A. the first day of shooting and they had to start on the sound stage; the only set that was ready was the men's locker room. It was a critical scene, the first seduction. The Coach is taking a shower and Suzie sneaks into the locker room, takes off her clothes, and slips into the shower with him.

At six a.m. a nervous Roy sat next to a surprisingly calm Tiffany in the makeup trailer. He wore sweatpants and a tee shirt. She was in a robe. As hair and makeup people fussed over them Roy said, "Don't worry, you'll be fine."

"I'm not worried."

"Really? I am."

"You should be. I mean, *I* should be. Any normal person

would be. Maybe I'm too inexperienced to be nervous. Or too stupid."

He met her eyes in the reflection of the makeup mirror. "You're not stupid."

She held his look. "Thank you."

Jenny, Tiffany's makeup girl, said she was going to get a cappuccino and asked if anyone wanted anything. Roy and Tiffany said no, but Jorge, Roy's makeup man, said he wanted fruit from the craft service table and left with her. For the first time since they'd met, Roy and Tiffany were alone.

Without a word, Tiffany got out of the makeup chair and sat on Roy's lap. Roy looked into those huge hazel eyes, the deceptively innocent face. Then Tiffany leaned forward and kissed him. Tender at first, then lips opened to tongues, until the pent up passion of the last two weeks overwhelmed them both. His hands went under her robe to her breasts, her hands dug under his shirt for a feel of his hard stomach. She began to grind her hips into his, "Fuck me," she begged. "Oh, Jesus, fuck me."

Tiffany grabbed his sweatpants and pulled them down to his knees. She stared hungrily at his cock. "God, it's beautiful," she sighed then hurriedly pulled off her panties. "I want you inside me, now." After another smothering kiss she took his cock in her hand and lowered herself slowly, wanting to enjoy every millimeter of his penetration.

"No," he said suddenly. Roy twisted out from under Tiffany, climbing out of the chair. "I can't do this."

"Why not?"

"I promised David I wouldn't touch you."

She slithered out of the chair toward Roy. "Then let me touch you."

He backed away. "No, Tiffany. If David thinks for one minute we're having an affair he'll fire me."

"It'll be worth it."

"Tiffany, please. This is my big chance. I worked hard for it."

Her eyes focused on his crotch. "I can see how hard ..."

As much as Roy wanted her, he said, "No, I can't do it."

Tiffany suddenly dropped to her knees and took Roy in her mouth. He groaned in pleasure. Oh, God, she was good. Too good. Roy felt the first stirrings of an orgasm. He had to make her stop. Roy took his hands and placed them on the side of Tiffany's head.

And that's when David Hunter walked into the trailer. He had the dog in his arms and his assistant director at his side.

Roy, seeing Hunter, instinctively pulled away from Tiffany. Unfortunately, it was just as he was coming, and he sent a blast of sperm into Hunter's face.

Tiffany screamed, Hunter screamed, Roy screamed, the dog barked.

Hunter went nuts, grabbed a pair of scissors from the counter and charged Roy. Roy's sweatpants were still gathered at his feet, and as he backed away from Hunter he fell.

Hunter lunged at Roy, slashing away with the scissors. Roy ducked, avoiding the blades, then scrambled to his feet. Unfortunately his sweatpants were still on the floor.

Roy was naked from the waist down.

Hunter attacked again and Roy panicked. He had to get out of there. He burst out of the trailer door, Hunter right behind him.

It was a sight no one would soon forget: a very exposed Roy, his junk blowing in the wind, being chased across the Warner Brothers back lot by an enraged David Hunter.

Tiffany, the cast and crew watched, stunned, as Roy raced around the craft service table, putting a little distance between himself and the crazed Hunter. Then Roy tripped over the edge of a light stand and fell. So did the light, exploding as it hit the ground.

Hunter loomed over Roy. He swung the scissors, Roy rolled right, the scissors just missing him. Roy rolled left, but too late, and the blade caught him on the shoulder, ripping open the skin.

Roy screamed out in pain as Hunter swung again, only this

time a couple of grips finally got up the guts to grab Hunter and pull the scissors out of his hand.

Hunter glared at Roy. "I trusted you."

Those words sliced through Roy's soul. "I'm sorry," Roy said, ashamed. "I tried, David. I really did. I'm so sorry."

"Sorry my ass," Tiffany screamed at Roy. "You tried to rape me!" Then she turned to Hunter, threw herself into his arms. "He forced me to do it, darling. I swear."

You bitch, Roy thought. You fucking bitch.

David tilted Tiffany's face up to his, wiped the tears from her eyes. "You're a good actress, baby. But not that good." Hunter pushed her away and stalked off.

"David, wait!" Tiffany yelled and ran after him.

Roy just lay there, devastated.

They were both fired, of course. And the picture was shut down.

Roy never saw Tiffany again. Hunter threw her out of his mansion. That night she got drunk and drove her BMW off Mulholland Drive. She was decapitated as the car tumbled down the hillside.

Roy never thought it was an accident. There were rumors that Hunter had used Underworld connections to finance his early movies, and Roy was sure Hunter had contacted them again to get rid of the bitch who had betrayed him.

Roy figured he was next, that Hunter would arrange another 'accident.' But the industry rumor mill saved his life. Word spread about what had happened that morning on the Warner Brothers lot. And questions started to be asked about the timing of Tiffany's car accident. Another 'accident' would raise too much suspicion.

So Hunter did something even worse. He started spreading rumors that Roy was always late to rehearsal, would show up unprepared for work and had done drugs all day long. Before long word was out: Roy Cooper was bad news. Hunter made it his mission to ruin Roy's career. Roy would never work again.

Back in his bathroom, Roy stared longingly at the *Jailbait* poster. He had been so close to stardom.

Fuck.

But now back to the business at hand. Roy turned his attention to the magazine, an oldie but goodie, a 1984 issue of Playboy. The issue had come out the same time Roy reached puberty, and the centerfold, Terri Jackson, was the first playmate Roy ever masturbated to. Roy turned to Terri every so often, knowing he could always rely on her for a fabulous fantasy. Well, he needed her tonight. This Gravesnatcher bullshit had him totally stressed out.

He opened the centerfold and looked into those familiar blue eyes. "Hello, baby, I'm back ..."

The Road Too Often Traveled

I needed one important ingredient to start making my letter bomb—a pinch of explosive. Not an item you can easily pick up at the local market. Luckily, I happened to have a small cache of C-4 hidden in my apartment, partial payment from a Serbian gunrunner who hired me to find out if his brother was sleeping with his wife. He was, but so was his cousin Milos, his Uncle Stephan and his best friend, Ilija. My client was furious, but so was Milos, who didn't know she was also sleeping with Stephan and Ilija. So was Uncle Stephan, who didn't know she was sleeping Ilija and Milos, likewise Ilija, who didn't know about Uncle Stephan and Milos. The wife, not the least bit remorseful, left them all and moved to Las Vegas with an aerialist from Cirque du Soleil.

That's probably more than you wanted to know, but the point is, on my drive from the Beverly Hills Police Department to my apartment, I did the cell phone shuffle. First call, movie star Lisa Montgomery.

"How you coming with the ransom?"

"I've got the money, in used hundred dollar bills like he asked."

"Good. And don't worry about a backpack to put it in, I'll bring one."

"Okay ..." With a trace of fear in her voice, she added, "Look, Gideon, do I really have to come with you tomorrow? Can't you just take him the ransom and let me stay here?"

"If you want the sperm back he says you have to be there."

"Is it true what they said on TV? Do you really think it's Jason Tucker?"

"Looks that way."

"I told you this was all your fault, Kincaid," a voice screeched. It was Lisa's manager, Joan Hagler, on an extension.

There was real fear in Lisa's voice now. "He's going to kill me, isn't he?"

"No, he's not. I've got a plan, Lisa. I'm not going to let anything bad happen to you."

"You can't guarantee that," Joan Hagler said. "Don't listen to him, Lisa. Let's just leave town."

"We've been through this before," I reasoned. "If you leave, he'll find you. The only way to be safe is to let me handle it. You won't get hurt, I promise. Okay?"

A long pause, then a hesitant, "Okay."

I was in trouble. They were ready to bolt. I had to do something to keep them in town. In a perfect world I'd drive over there now and stay with her until the drop tomorrow. But the world's never perfect and I needed time to make my little Gravesnatcher surprise. "Tell you what, I'm going to send over one of my operatives, Hillary Bennett, to stay with you for a while. I'll come by later on tonight. Just to make sure nothing happens ..."

"I'm an operative now? That is so cool."

"Yeah, well, all you've got to do is keep Lisa's manager from talking Lisa into leaving town."

"Not a problem. I've always been a good debater."

"Debate if you want, but if you want my advice, lock the bitch in a closet."

"If you don't mind a little constructive criticism, Gideon, you are always a little too quick with a violent solution to every problem. I think you'd be pleasantly surprised what a quick wit and facile tongue can accomplish. According to ancient Hindu teachings and Maharajah—"

"Please, no New Age gibberish. Just do whatever it takes to keep Lisa home."

"You can count on me, chief. Oh, do you want your messages before I go bodyguard my little heart out?"

"Yeah."

"Okay, well, a bunch more reporters, more secretary wannabe's, a producer from *60 Minutes* and the Pope."

"The Pope?"

"Just kidding. You're not that famous yet. And Amy called from Pac Bell. She's pissed. Me, too, by the way."

"Why are you pissed?"

"I thought we were a team. Partners, with you being the most senior and only licensed member of the team, I'll admit. But partners shouldn't have secrets from each other."

"What kind of secrets?"

"Telephone secrets ..." She was using that 'only an idiot' tone again.

"Okay. Uncle. I give up. Please tell me what you're talking about."

"Amy said *you* paid for the cell phone. That *you're* paying the monthly bills. On your credit card."

That son of a bitch, I thought. Just like Doggieworld. "No," I said. "Somehow the Gravesnatcher got hold of my Visa number. He also used it to order the dog collar."

"Sneaky. Well, I'll call Amy and tell her you're not a scum sucking bastard for wasting her time."

"Her words or yours?"

"Hers. Oh, I almost forgot, your agent, Elliot, called. He said he knows you don't want to talk to him but, like, it was urgent. Then he spelled it: U-R-G-E-N-T. I think you should call him."

I did.

"This is the big one, Gid baby, the once in a lifetime moment that all dream about but few realize."

"I'm almost afraid to ask."

"Books Read2U. They want you, *Bubele*. They want to make a deal for *Death of a Gravesnatcher*. They plan to do a deluxe edition: a nice photo of you, then pictures of all the victims and with any luck a shot of Jason Tucker's dead body. They want a fold-out map illustrating all the ransom drop sites and murder locations. Plus, if you want, you can record it yourself. Since your voice is a little nasal, I suggested Robert Downey, Jr. I bet he can sound like a tough PI."

"If I remember right, *Death of a Gravesnatcher* is what you want to rename *Rear Entry,* if I somehow manage to live through all this."

"Keep breathing and I'm dealing!"

"And does Books Read2U have a plan if I'm killed?"

"As a matter of fact, we did talk about that. I mentioned my *Ultimate Sacrifice* idea and they flipped. Dig this: they'll shape the entire package like a coffin!"

"Brilliant."

"And that's why it was U-R-G-E-N-T that I talk to you. They want you to record a Preface, a brief capsule of your feelings and emotions before you face the greatest challenge of your career. Just in case you, you know ... And time is of the essence. Tragedy could strike at any minute. I was wondering if you could stop by the office right now, so we could lay down the track."

"Why don't you ask Robert Downey to drop by to do it for me?"

"Believe me, I've thought of that. He's in Hawaii until next week. I wonder how they'd feel about Mark Wahlberg?"

"Elliott, I think we've got a priorities problem here."

"Hey, if tonight's not good, I can book the studio first thing in the morning. But you have to promise me you won't do anything dangerous tonight."

"I have bigger things to worry about right now than the damn book."

"Really? Well, maybe that's because I haven't told you the really B-I-G news."

"What could be bigger than Books Read2U?"

"The latest sales figures on *Rear Entry.*"

"They're up?"

"These are just L.A. figures, but how's this sound? Barnes and Noble at the Westside Pavilion, sold out. Barnes and Noble at the Grove, sold out. The Barnes and Noble on Pico, do I even need to say it? Sold out! The trend's your friend, Gid baby, and it's up, up, up. Of course, most of the stores only stocked two or three copies, but still, it's amazing what a little publicity, murder and mayhem can do for a career."

"Elliott, if *Rear Entry* is selling so well, we don't have to rename it to take advantage of the press. It's happening already."

"That's what I've been trying to tell you. *Rear Entry* is fine. *Death of a Gravesnatcher* will be your *second* book. All you've got to do is write it, and I guarantee a *New York Times* bestseller. It all hinges on you living through this, of course. Use your literary future as inspiration. Now I've got to go, Gid-man. Lines two, three and four are blinking, and that can only mean one thing: money, money, money. Ciao."

Another Country Heard From

I hung my proverbial hat and the rest of my actual clothes in a one-bedroom apartment in Sherman Oaks. Decent enough building on a quiet enough street—Milbank, just two blocks from the never quiet Ventura Boulevard. The best thing about the apartment was Delany's, an ersatz Irish pub within walking distance. Walking distance was important for those all too frequent nights since the divorce when I drank myself into a weaving, wall-banging, only-a-fool-would-be-driving oblivion.

Stacy got all the furniture in the divorce. The lawyers got all the money. A quick trip to a used furniture store on Sepulveda got me the basics: a brown Naugahyde couch—its numerous rips patched with spray-painted duct tape—small dining room table with one short leg and only three matching chairs, a queen-size mattress and box spring that sat directly on the floor, and a laminated, four drawer bureau. I didn't realize until I got it home that someone had lined the inside of the drawers with *Winnie the Poo* wallpaper.

And that was it.

I remember the day I moved in. My clothes were piled in a pyramid on the bedroom floor. Cardboard boxes full of books and a lifetime of junk lined the living room. I sat amid the rubble, staring at the bare walls, and wondered what the hell I'd done to my life. I'd lost my job, my wife, and my passion.

Passion had driven me to police work. Passion had driven me to marriage. I had deprived myself of both. Without passion I had no direction.

When I was a kid I plastered my walls with pictures and posters: baseball players, rock stars, astronauts, movie stars. I'd sit on my bed staring at them, dreaming of all the things I could become.

When I was married to Stacy, travel became my obsession. I peppered the walls with pictures of all the places I wanted us to go together: scuba diving off Grand Cayman, photo safari in Kenya, fly fishing in Alaska. I'd look at those pictures cut out of the Sunday travel section and take thrilling imaginary adventures. But that's all we ever took—imaginary vacations. Besides our honeymoon in Maui, we never left southern California.

For years the walls of my Milbank apartment remained bare. I had no passion. No obsession. I'd even become a PI by accident. After I resigned under pressure, Mary Rocket felt sorry for me and suggested I become a private investigator. She sent me my first client, the father of a Chicago runaway who he thought may be hiding out in Hollywood. I found her before the vultures had done too much damage; she had a tattoo of a butterfly on her ass, a stud through her tongue, and a ring through her belly button, but she wasn't addicted to heroin yet and had only done two pornos. I was paid five hundred bucks by the grateful dad and had a new business. But it wasn't my passion.

For the next few years, I drifted. Working enough to pay the bills. Drinking enough to dull the pain. Waiting for something to happen. Waiting to find a new passion.

It came by accident, during a stakeout on an unusual corporate vandalism case. Every few weeks on a Monday morning, Mark Weller—the President of Weller, Bindleman and Schuster, an L.A. advertising agency—would walk into his office and find a pile of fecal matter in the middle of his desk. Fecal matter, as in human excrement. That's right; someone would take a shit on the middle of his desk and leave it there as a not-so-subtle message.

It had happened three times during the preceding six months. At first Weller thought it was a sick practical joke. The second time got him worried. The third time was my charm and he hired me to find out who was leaving the surprise package and catch the person in the act.

I planted a video camera in Weller's office and set up a weekend surveillance HQ in an unused corner of a file room. The file room was at the far end of the building, but at a full run I could get from the file room to Weller's office in forty-six seconds. Plenty of time to see the perp arrive on video and reach him before he finished his 'grunt' work.

If you think surveillance is boring, then imagine surveillance of an empty office on a weekend. It's torture. My partner on any surveillance was a book—usually a thriller or mystery. Over the years I'd read hundreds, and having been a cop, I always found them fun either because the writer got it so right, or so wrong.

Well, I got it wrong this Saturday morning. I'd brought the wrong book—the one I'd finished last night. I had nothing to read. By ten a.m. I was bored out of my gourd. After counting all the holes in the ceiling tiles I thought about running out to pick up a book at a 7-Eleven. But I was sure that the minute I left, the perp would show up, so I decided to stay.

And that's when it happened. From out of nowhere this thought wrapped itself around the right side of my brain. *If you can't read a book, then why not write one?* I found a yellow pad on one of the shelves, took out my pen and went to work. It was love at first scrawl.

Soon I was writing all the time. When I wasn't writing, I was reading about writing, thinking about writing, dreaming about writing. I went back to that Sepulveda furniture store and bought a desk. Went to the office supply next door and bought a Compaq computer and Microsoft Word.

Then one day I was in Barnes & Noble buying a dictionary

and thesaurus when I noticed they were throwing away a poster for *The Scarecrow*, a fabulous book by Michael Connelly. I asked for it. My wall finally had something on it. *The Scarecrow* soon had company—pictures of Dashiell Hammet, Raymond Chandler and Micky Spillane.

I found myself spending less time at Delany's and more time at the computer. The boxes lining the wall were finally unpacked. The pile of clothes began to shrink until everything was in the bureau or the closet. And I spent a lot of time looking at my wall and dreaming.

By the way, the shitter was one of the Creative Directors, Artie Palmer. Seems Palmer dreamed up this great campaign for Ford Motor Company, using famous Norman Rockwell paintings for all the new commercials but electronically replacing the old cars with new Fords. Weller loved the idea, taking credit himself during the big presentation. Artie didn't mind that so much, but when he asked Weller for a raise after the agency had landed the account, Weller said no. He said Artie was paid enough for his work. "Thinking up ideas is easy, fun even," Weller said. "I've got the tough job. All the shit comes across my desk."

Weller did the same thing a few months later. Stole Artie's idea for a new Cocoa Puffs campaign. They got another mega-buck account, and when Artie asked for a raise Weller told him, "I get the big bucks because all the shit comes across my desk."

"I was just proving *his* point," Artie said after I caught him squatting on Weller's desk. After listening to Artie's side of the story, I began to feel sorry for the guy. I mean, who among us hasn't been screwed over by a superior? And what's worse than taking credit for someone's work?

So I made a deal with Artie. He stops dumping on Weller's desk, and I'd tell Weller word had leaked out about the hidden camera in his office so there's no way the perp would ever reappear. Artie agreed and Weller bought it. Case closed, passion reignited.

Anyway, I got home, pulled into my underground parking garage and took a new backpack out of my trunk. I was in a hurry. I wanted to make the bomb and get to Lisa's house as soon as possible.

I burst through my front door and headed for the bedroom closet. I'd installed a safe in the closet wall to keep a little cash, guns and a few explosive goodies. As I turned into the corridor I heard: "You fuck her yet?" Stacy's unmistakable voice.

I backpedaled into the living room. Stacy was sitting on the battered couch, her legs tucked under her. She was wearing jeans and a black turtleneck. Her brown hair was pulled back in a ponytail. I loved that look on her and she knew it. She wanted something. "Who?"

"Who else? Little Miss Hollywood. Lisa frigging Montgomery."

"If I had it'd be none of your business, but just to keep the record straight, no. I don't intend to, either."

"Yeah, might as well wait until you're married again. Break some other woman's heart."

"What're you doing here?"

"I don't know. I was home, alone, with nothing to do. You see, I've got nothing to do because I've been taken off the biggest case to hit L.A. since O.J., because of you."

"Me? You got put on ice because you turned Magic Land into a battlefield. And how'd you get in here, anyway?"

"You forget who taught you to pick locks?"

She did. A few weeks after our wedding we'd gone to Santa Barbara for a weekend. We locked ourselves out of our room one night after one too many bottles of wine. I was going to the office for another key when Stacy told me to wait, and pulled a lock picking kit out of her purse. "Watch," she said. "Learn." Moments later we were inside. Then she waggled the picks in front of my face. "I bet these would work on your zipper, too." Then she slipped them into the pull-tab and slid it open. "Bingo."

"Let me try." I used them on her skirt's zipper. Then I used the picks to undo the buttons on her blouse. We were laughing by then, drunk and happy. Stacy fell into my arms and we made love right there on the floor.

I looked at her now, sitting on the couch. "You taught me to pick locks."

"I thought of that night in Santa Barbara when I came in tonight. We used to have some fun, didn't we?"

We did, and many times I'd lie here in bed, alone, remembering them.

Stacy got off the couch, drifted toward the pictures on the wall. "You've gotten really serious about this writing stuff, haven't you?"

"Yeah."

She pointed. "Dashiell Hammett, right?"

"Maltese Falcon and The Thin Man, right."

"Nick and Nora Charles. You used to say we were like them—the drinking, and the wisecracks. And you know, even though you said that all the time, I never read the books."

"Little late now."

"I read your book, though. And except for the unfortunate description of the woman who was stabbed thirty eight times, I thought it was surprisingly good."

"Okay, now I *know* you want something. What is it, Stacy? Spill."

"Why do I have to want something?" She stepped in closer. "What if I were to tell you that spending so much time with you the last few days made me remember how good we were together." Even closer. "And how I may have acted a little too emotionally, a little too hastily, to your little ... indiscretion. In fact, it was probably all *my* fault."

"Your fault?"

Closer still. "You were going through hell. You'd been kicked off the force and didn't know what you were going to do with the rest of your life. Instead of trying to understand you, help you, I only thought of myself. How your problems might hurt me. I disconnected from you, emotionally deserted you at your most desperate time." Her lips were millimeters from my lips.

Her brown eyes drilled a hole in my corneas. "How can I ever make it up to you?"

Okay, you've got to understand something. Back in my single days, long before I ever met Stacy, I used to have this dream. I was with this beautiful woman and we were laughing, and everything was perfect. It was a euphoric feeling. But then I'd wake up and realize it was just a dream, I hadn't met this wonderful woman. I was heartbroken, overcome with a feeling of deep loss. When I tried to remember what she looked like I could never put a face to her. Until I met Stacy. From the moment I first set eyes on her—cracking that poor SOB's kneecap—I knew she was the woman from my dreams. Of my dreams.

I tell you this now to explain what I did next. For, in spite of the fact that I knew everything she'd said was probably just a crock of shit, I leaned forward and kissed her. It was a long, loving kiss, familiar and comfortable.

As the kiss ended we folded naturally into a tender hug. She felt so good in my arms, I found myself squeezing her tightly, subconsciously willing her never to leave. "I've missed you," I whispered.

"You don't have to. Not anymore."

"What? You mean go out? Start dating again?"

"I was thinking more about working together."

I got this uncomfortable tickling at the base of my spine. "Working together, how?"

"On this case, the Gravesnatcher. I'm sure if we told Captain Rocket that we'd settled our personal problems, and that you insisted I be reinstated, she'd have to agree."

I felt like I'd just woken up from that dream. "You bitch."

"What?"

"What, what? Admit it, the only reason you're here, the only reason you gave me that soul-searching confession, was to get me to talk to Mary Rocket."

"I did come here hoping to enlist your help. But everything I said, I meant. And the kiss, I meant. Like this one ..." Another kiss, as sweet as the first, maybe a touch more urgent, from Stacy.

"Well," she said as our lips parted. "Will you talk to her?"

The last thing I needed right now was Stacy hanging around. First of all, she'd probably figure out I lied to Mary Rocket about the location of the drop. Second, she was too personally involved in the case. She was so embarrassed by the fiasco at Magic Land I wasn't sure she'd be able to make cool, rational decisions.

Her lips brushed my cheek. "Please ..."

"No."

I felt her go rigid. "No?"

"I can't, Stacy. Captain Rocket will never let you back on the case."

"Just tell her you need the best help available, someone who knows exactly how you work, how you think. Someone who's got a vested interest in your not getting hurt."

Then I realized I had nothing to lose. There was no way Mary Rocket would say yes. Why not be a gentleman, keep Stacy happy and tonight's prospects alive. "All right," I said, brushing my lips across her cheek. "I'll talk to her."

She brushed her lips across mine. "Thank you." Then she was out of my arms and heading for her purse on the couch. "I'll keep my cell phone on. Call me once you get hold of her."

"Wait a minute, where're you going?"

"I've got a date. I'm taking Irving to Spago's for dinner."

"You're leaving me for a date with Piccolo?"

"It's his birthday."

"But what about ... us?"

"There'll be an 'us' once you get Captain Rocket to say yes."

"Are you saying that if Captain Rocket says no, there is no us?"

"Let's just say I'll be much more motivated once I'm back on the task force."

"Forget it, Stacy. We're talking about our relationship here. It has to be bigger than a decision by Captain Rocket. Hell, it has to be bigger than the Gravesnatcher. Bigger than anything!"

"Relationship? Who said anything about a relationship?"

"You did. Or your lips did. If you didn't want to get back together, what was the big confession all about? The kisses?"

"I can be sorry about what led to the divorce without wanting to move back in with you, can't I? And I hope I can sleep with you without putting a ring back on."

"It feels like blackmail."

"It is." She crossed back to me, gave me a peck on the cheek. "You get a yes out of Captain Rocket and I'll be back with my lock picks." With that, she breezed out the door.

I tried to put Stacy out of my mind as I assembled the bomb. But it was tough. After all, she's the one who'd taught me how to make it.

A feeling of dread engulfed me as I rolled out a six–by-three inch rectangle of C-4, made a circuit out of the leg wires of an electric blasting cap, made a loop switch, and attached a nine-volt battery.

Dread because emotions I'd long since buried wrapped around the outside of my brain and began to peak over the top of my parietal lobe. Shame. Regret. Remorse. Guilt.

The same emotions that had bombarded me after the divorce. Emotions I dulled with booze and finally vanquished with a finely honed hate of Stacy. I made her the enemy. Stacy's disconnect during my emotional collapse after the disastrous frame of Ernie Wagner became my justification for jumping Lisa's bones. My justification for concluding the divorce was long overdue. My justification for wondering if I'd ever really loved Stacy in the first place.

I opened the backpack and slipped the bomb inside. It wasn't armed yet; I'd have to attach a string to the loop switch and connect it to the zipper. Once done, the bomb was ready. When the Gravesnatcher unzipped the backpack, the string would be pulled taut, the loop switch would be thrown, the circuit would close, the sudden jolt of electricity would fire the blasting cap and that would trigger the C-4. BOOM.

BOOM. That's what Stacy's visit had just done to my emotional equilibrium. Blown it up. When I realized how much I wanted to kiss her, how much I wanted to hold her, how much I wanted to be with her, I realized how much I still loved her.

Or, should I say, I finally admitted to myself that I still loved her. For, you see, I still had that dream about the perfect woman every so often, and yes, it was always Stacy.

As I folded the deadly backpack under my arm, I made a promise to myself. After the Gravesnatcher case was closed, I was going to win Stacy back.

The Best Laid Plans

It was magic hour as I reached Lisa's gate. A dazzling, iridescent sunset smeared itself across the sky thanks to a volcanic eruption half a world away in Papua, New Guinea. Sixty-three people had been killed when the Rabaul volcano blew, spewing ash and dust into the stratosphere. And thanks to the jet stream, the dust and ash residue from that killer volcano was treating the rest of the world to a month of fabulous sunsets. The irony that is life.

I buzzed the gate, no answer. I buzzed again. Nothing. Shit, this was not good.

I got out of the car. The wall around Lisa's property was eight feet high. I jumped, hoping to grab onto the edge of the wall and pull myself over. But it was too high.

Fuck. This was bad and getting worse.

I got back into my car, pulled up until the front bumper was touching the wall, then got back out of the car and carefully climbed onto the hood. My front end was still mashed, thanks to the Gravesnatcher's hit and run, but the hood itself was okay. I didn't want to dent the delicate metal, but two metallic groans and a loud POP told me the body shop was going to have even more work to do. It was worth it, however, because I could now easily reach the top of the wall. I pulled myself up and over, hit the ground hard but I stayed on my feet, and raced for the house.

Hillary's Prius was parked in front, along with the dark blue Lexus I assumed belonged to the bitch manager, but Lisa's ivory 280 was gone. *Shit. Fuck. Piss.*

I tried the front door. Locked. A side window, locked. I circled the house, trying all the windows. Nothing. The sliding glass doors leading from the pool to the living room were also locked. Then, looking through the glass doors, I noticed a body lying on the floor near the white couch. All I could see were two legs sticking out, one of them bent at a gruesomely unnatural angle. *Oh, my God, Hillary*, I thought.

In a move seen on innumerable TV shows, I grabbed an iron lawn chair and hurled it at the sliding glass door. But life is life, not a TV show, so the fucking chair just bounced off.

Now I was mad. I pulled my gun, aimed for the edge of the glass where the door handle and lock would be, and fired three times. Three small holes appeared as the glass spider webbed but didn't shatter. The three holes formed a pattern big enough to punch my hand through. I did, felt around for the lock mechanism, found it and unlocked it. I slid the door open and rushed to the body.

I'd expected to find Hillary. I didn't. It was the manager, Joan Hagler. She had a split lip, a black eye and—judging from the akimbo angle of her leg—a broken tibia. I pressed a finger to her carotid, got a strong pulse. I also got a shock when I saw all the blood on my hand. I'd shredded the skin punching through the glass.

I was looking around for something to wrap my hand in when I noticed the room. It was a wreck. A chair was turned over, the glass coffee table was shattered, and there was a gaping hole in the TV. With a start I realized I could smell gunpowder. That's when I saw the bullet holes in the wall leading up to the TV. I counted four of them. Number five must've hit the screen.

My thoughts reeled from Lisa running away to Lisa and Hillary dead, killed by the Gravesnatcher. I called out: "Lisa! Hillary!"

Silence. Damn it. "Lisa! Hillary!" I heard something, not a voice but a banging. Thump. Thump. Thump. I followed the sound into the huge kitchen and to a pantry door. THUMP. THUMP. I yanked it open to find Hillary on the floor, a gag in her mouth, her hands tied behind her.

"Where's Lisa?" I blurted.

She answered, but it came out, "mmmm mm mmmmm mmm," because of the gag. I pulled it off. "She got away. I am so fired, right?"

"Lisa locked you in the pantry?"

"Yes."

"Who beat up Hagler?"

"Mostly me."

"And who shot up the living room?"

"Me and Hagler, but Lisa helped a little."

"The overturned chair? The broken coffee table?"

"Ditto, all three of us. You know you're bleeding?"

I spotted a roll of paper towels, pulled off a few sheets and wrapped my hand. "The Gravesnatcher wasn't here? Just the three of you?"

"That's right, just a good old fashioned cat fight."

I undid Hillary's hands. "It was going great at first," Hillary explained, untying her feet. "Lisa was real sweet, like a normal human being. I had expected this movie goddess number but no, she was, like, so there. We talked about her career, poor dead Hudson King, and the very much alive Jake Gyllenhaal who she dated for a while and I think is so hot, but to be honest he's no Leonardo DiCaprio. But I should've been suspicious because the whole time Lisa is throwing these, like, really furtive glances at her manager. How is she, by the way?"

"Unconscious."

"She is such a bitch. This is all her fault if you ask me."

"I am asking you."

"Oh, right. Well, underline the *bitch* part. So about an hour ago Lisa and I were sitting in the living room watching a video of *Heartache*, that movie she did with Nicolas Cage last year.

Lisa and Joan exchange another one of those *looks* and Joan excuses herself. Says she's got to go to the bathroom. Like a total dunce, I let her. She comes back a few minutes later holding a gun, this giant .45 automatic.

"Joan says to Lisa, 'I called the airline, we're booked on the eight o'clock.' Then Joan says to me, 'Sorry, little miss bodyguard, but they only had two seats available. Now, stand up.' I did, never taking my eyes off that cannon.

" 'I'm sorry,' Lisa says to me. 'Tell Gideon I'm sorry, too.'

" 'Fuck Gideon,' the manager says. 'This is all his fault. You have any rope, Lisa?'

" 'In the garage.'

" 'Get it. And bring something to gag goldilocks.' Lisa runs out and Joan says to me, 'I've got a message for your boss. Tell that SOB that I'll get him for this. He is personally responsible for disrupting Lisa's career arc. And the longer she's forced to be in hiding, the more money I'm going to sue him for. In fact, I'll sue you, too, Blondie, right down to your black roots. You're going to regret the day you ever met Gideon Kincaid.'

"First of all," Hillary said, interrupting her story. "I'm a natural blond. I hate chemicals of any kind and would never soak those poisons into my hair. Second of all, I love working for you, especially now that I'm an operative. She can sue me for a hundred billion dollars and it won't change how I feel about you. So, in spite of this little setback, I hope you don't fire me."

"You're not fired," I said, picking up the phone and dialing 911. To my surprise they answered immediately. I reported an unconscious woman with a broken leg, gave the address and hung up. "You were saying ..."

"Right. So Lisa comes back with the rope and stuff. 'Tie her hands behind her back,' the manager says. I suddenly realize that to do that Lisa has to walk in front of me, between me and the manager, between me and the .45. And when she does I grab her, using her as a shield, and shove her, hard, into the manager. They both go down and the gun skitters over toward the bar. I dive for it, but so does the manager, and we both end up with our hands on it. We wrestle back and forth and she must have her finger on the trigger because BANG, it goes off. Lisa screams and BANG, BANG, BANG it goes off again. The TV blows up, more screams from Lisa, but I finally manage to get a leg behind the manager and I shove her back, over my leg. She goes down. Now I've got the gun, but just for a second because the manager's leg whips me and I go down. The gun goes flying again as the manager jumps on me and we go rolling around on the floor knocking over a chair, breaking the coffee table. I'd had fights before in my karate classes, but it's different when it's for real. It's hard to remember all those cool moves, and the ones I did remember didn't work too well. I'm going to have to talk to Chang about that. Anyway, I finally got the upper hand. I was sitting on her chest, ready to pop her one, when I feel this hard poke in my back and Lisa says, 'Stand up or I'll shoot.' I turn around and Lisa's got the gun and this terrified look in her eyes. Now I'm terrified that she's going to shoot me by accident. So I stand up.

"The manager grabs the rope and ties my hand behind my back, and she's so mad at me she pulls the rope really hard. She's ranting and raving, calling me, like, every name in the book. By the time she ties my feet and gags me, she's practically foaming at the mouth. Then she takes the gun from Lisa and aims it at my head.

" 'What're you doing?' Lisa asks her.

" 'I'm going to kill her,' the manager says. 'The cops'll blame the Gravesnatcher.'

" 'But you can't kill her,' Lisa says.

" 'Watch me,' the nutzoid manager says and cocks the gun.

"Lisa screams no, grabs the Golden Globe statue from the table and hits the manager in the face with it! The manager falls back over the couch, and there's this horrible CRACK sound as she lands. But she doesn't move. 'Oh my God, oh my God, oh my God,' Lisa keeps saying. She's totally freaked now. She picks up the gun, tells me to get in the kitchen. I hop down the hall, into the kitchen and she sticks me in the pantry. I figured she would've gone back and taken care of the manager, but I guess not. She must've panicked and run."

"Did she take the money?"

"I don't know. It was in the study."

"Show me."

Hillary led me down a hall, around a corner and into a wood paneled study. In the middle of the rosewood desk was a three-foot-high stack of hundred dollar bills.

"This case goes from one fucked up mess to another," Mary Rocket said, angrily limping around the study. I stood behind the desk, Hillary next to me.

Through the window I could see the paramedics load the now conscious and loudly complaining manager into the ambulance. Since the paramedics had revived her, Joan Hagler had threatened to sue me, Hillary, Lisa, the paramedics, the ambulance company, the police department and the Gravesnatcher.

One of the task force detectives, Gabriel Ruiz, poked his head into the room. "There are thirty-two flights scheduled to take off from LAX at eight o'clock. We'll have someone at every gate."

"You don't have much time," I said, glancing at my watch. It was seven forty-five.

"A lot of those flights have already boarded," Mary Rocket said. "Coordinate with airport security, search every aircraft. We've got to find her." Ruiz left.

When 911 got my call they alerted the closest fire department paramedic unit and police dispatch. Lisa's address was on the Watch List because of the Gravesnatcher case so the operator notified Captain Rocket. Because the Gravesnatcher might be watching the house, and since his note said 'No Cops,' Mary Rocket and Ruiz were smart enough to show up in a second ambulance, both dressed as paramedics.

"What do we do if we can't find her," Mary Rocket asked me.

"Will the Gravesnatcher still show up if Lisa's not there?"

"I don't know."

"I'll go with you," Hillary said. "I can wear a wig, some of her clothes."

I shook my head. "Good idea, but you're too short."

"I can wear heels."

"Seven inch heels? You're five two, Lisa's five nine."

"No problem," Mary Rocket said. "We'll find a five nine policewoman."

I knew a five-nine policewoman. A couple of hours ago I'd kissed her. This was almost too good to be true. "How about Stacy," I said. "She's five nine." Mary Rocket scowled but I plowed ahead. "She's perfect, Captain. She knows exactly how I work, how I think." I couldn't believe I was actually quoting Stacy's words to me. Fate had given me the opportunity, so why not?

Hillary looked at me like I was crazy, but not Mary Rocket. She actually said, "I have heard worse ideas."

Encouraged, I kept selling. "You can't put me with a stranger, Captain. Someone I don't know, can't trust. If it's not Stacy then it has to be someone I've worked with before."

"No," Mary Rockett said, "the more I think about it, the more I think Stacy would be the right partner. Okay, if Lisa's a no show at LAX, you've got a deal."

By nine-fifteen it was clear that Lisa had never gone to the airport. Joan Hagler had told us she'd booked two seats to Hawaii on United, and a call to the airline confirmed it. But Lisa didn't show up for the flight. She was MIA so, using the speakerphone on Lisa's desk, Mary Rocket called Stacy.

"Hello," Stacy said through a mouthful of food.

"Stacy, it's Captain Rocket."

"Yes, ma'am," she said, suddenly all business. "It's awfully noisy in here. Hold on while I step outside." We heard Stacy say, "I'll be right back," to someone I knew was Piccolo, and then we heard ambient restaurant sounds.

"Sounds like she's in a restaurant." Mary Rocket whispered to me.

"Spago's," I said, and instantly regretted it.

"How do you know that?"

"Just a guess."

"Okay, I'm back," Stacy said. The background was quieter now, just light street traffic.

"You're back on the case, Stacy. Lisa Montgomery has flown the coop and we need you to double her at the drop tomorrow."

"Do I have to work with that limp-dicked asshole, Gideon?"

I knew Stacy wanted to keep up the pretense that we still hated each other, but *limp-dicked asshole*?

"Careful, Detective, I'm on a speaker phone and he's here with me."

"Oh, in that case, do I have to work with that microscopically small, limp-dicked asshole?"

"Oh, this is going to work ..." Hillary muttered.

Mary Rocket said, "If you don't want to work with him, Stacy, just say so. I can always assign someone else."

"No, the case is bigger than my enmity for Gideon." Enmity? Stacy was definitely spending too much time with Piccolo. "Just out of curiosity," she continued, "whose idea was it to use me?"

She was testing, making sure I was keeping my end of the bargain. "It was mine," I said. "I've put my *enmity* on hold, too. But don't worry, as soon as we catch the Gravesnatcher I promise to hate you with all my heart."

"What heart?"

"Okay, I'm glad we've got that straightened out," Mary Rocket jumped in, trying to preempt further argument. "There's a chance the Gravesnatcher's watching Lisa's house, so Stacy, report to my office at seven a.m. I'll have Special Operations arrange for a wig and a makeup man who'll turn you into a Hollywood superstar."

"We better be careful who we tell about this," I said. "I think Piccolo's right about one thing. I think a cop is working with the Gravesnatcher."

Mary Rocket didn't buy it. "Just because Jason Tucker hasn't left any forensic evidence? He's been in jail for the last few years; that's like getting a PhD in crime."

"There's something else. He planted a cell phone in my office. Called me on it."

"He did? Why didn't you tell me? What did he want?"

I had to be careful here. Mold the truth to keep me out of trouble but still get the point across. "He warned me not to tell the cops about the Hollywood Bowl drop location, that's all. But I hit the SEND button, to see if he'd made any calls with the phone, and got Robbery Homicide."

Mary Rocket was floored. "Shit."

"Now, he may just be fucking with us," I said. "But maybe not. I don't think we should take any chances. I don't think Stacy should tell anybody about her taking Lisa's place. Not even Piccolo. We should keep this on a strict need-to-know with as few people dealt in as possible."

"I agree," Mary Rocket said. "I'll hand-pick everyone. Now, what kind of car did Lisa drive?"

"An ivory, 280 Mercedes."

"Nice wheels," Stacy sniped. "I guess waving your tits in front of a camera has its rewards."

"Depends on the tits," I said.

"So now something's wrong with my tits?"

"You have great tits, Stacy."

"Then why am I driving a Honda?"

"You used to drive a Lincoln. You traded it in for the Honda to get better mileage."

"I drive a Prius," Hillary said. "And I've been told I have, like, perfect breasts. So don't get caught in the self-image spiral, Stacy. It'll suck you down like a vortex from hell."

"I don't give a shit about anybody's tits," Mary Rocket snapped, losing it. "Or what kind of car you drive or spiraling vortexes from hell. All I care about is catching the Gravesnatcher. Anybody confused about that?"

"No."

"No."

"No."

"Good. I'll find us an ivory 280 and at ten o'clock tomorrow morning, after Stacy's been transformed into a Lisa Montgomery look-a-like, she'll drive back here to Lisa's house and meet up with Gideon. Then, as instructed, you two will get in Gideon's car with the backpack full of cash and proceed to the Hollywood Bowl. I'm going to meet with SWAT tonight to plan our strategy. I'll brief you both in the morning. Anybody confused yet?"

"No."

"No."

"No."

"Good. Get some sleep, children. Tomorrow's a big day."

Tomorrow's more than just a big day, I thought as I carried the backpack from Lisa's living room into Lisa's office. Tomorrow had become very complicated. Somehow I was going to have to tell Stacy about the Gravesnatcher's demand that I secretly switch the drop location from the Hollywood Bowl to the zoo and convince her to go along with it. I also had to decide whether to tell her about the letter bomb.

Hillary was standing at the office window as I walked in, watching Mary Rocket and Ruiz drive away in the ambulance. "I've got the greatest idea."

"What?"

"Sell your Taurus and buy an ambulance."

"Excuse me?"

"You know how you hate traffic. Well, if you drove an ambulance you could just put on the red lights and siren and everyone would, like, pull over."

"That is such a good idea, it can't be legal," I said, stuffing the first stack of hundreds into the backpack. This talk of ambulances and cars reminded me of something Hillary had said earlier, her crack about driving a Prius and having perfect breasts. I realized I'd never looked at her breasts in any qualitative way, and as stupid as this sounds, I decided I had to look now. I surreptitiously glanced at her standing at the window. She was still looking outside, so it was safe to drop my eyes to her breasts.

Though covered by a bra and yellow polo shirt, they did look pretty good—not too big, not too small. But what really were the criteria for *perfect* breasts? Was it just size? Did skin color matter? And firmness? What about the nipples? Nipples have their own size and color to consider. An ugly nipple could ruin an otherwise perfect breast, but a perfect nipple couldn't save a scarred, saggy mess.

What was I doing contemplating all this? I realized I must be under a lot more stress than I realized. I lifted my eyes from Hillary's breasts back to her face and found her looking right at me.

"So, what do you think?"

"About what?" I stammered, caught and embarrassed.

"The ambulance? Cool or uncool?"

Whew, she hadn't seen me looking. "Cool. Check around town, see if you can find us a used one."

"Okay. Here, let me help you with that." She crossed to the desk, picked up two stacks of money, handed them to me and I stuck them in the backpack. She handed me two more. I stuck them in the backpack. We had our own assembly line going. "I've never seen this much money before," she said. "It's almost too much money. It doesn't seem valuable when there's so much of it. Kind of like too much of the same word. You know, if you write a word, like say, LOVE, it seems special. But write it down ten times: LOVE LOVE LOVE LOVE LOVE LOVE LOVE LOVE LOVE LOVE, and it loses all meaning. Stare at it and it doesn't even look like a word anymore." Then her eyes shifted from the money to the battery, wires and six-by-three rectangles of gray C-4 I'd rested on the edge of the backpack. "What's that?"

"Nothing."

"No, really, what is it?"

"Better if you don't know."

She stopped passing me the money and leaned in closer to the letter bomb. "If I didn't know better, I'd say it looked like a bomb."

"If it looks like a duck, walks like a duck, and quacks like a duck ..."

"You're putting a bomb in the backpack? You can't do that!"

"Well, write the word BOMB ten times and it'll lose all meaning."

"Gideon, it's murder!"

"No, this is a small bomb. Hardly worthy of the name 'bomb.' It'll only blow off his hands, maybe part of his forearms. That's it."

"Seriously, throw it away."

"Seriously, no fucking way. This guy's killed two people and probably plans to kill Lisa and me. What am I supposed to do, wait for it to happen? Sorry, Hillary. He plays dirty, I play dirty."

"But something could go wrong. It could go off early, hurt you. Or Stacy. He might open it in a crowd and innocent people could be injured. Or he might lose it and some kid might find it and open it. No, Gideon, it's too dangerous. Get rid of it."

"The bomb stays."

"And if it does go off as you plan and blows off his hands, the police will arrest you for assault with a deadly weapon. If he bleeds to death, it'll be murder. You'll go to jail. Is that what you want? Please, Gideon, you've got the entire police force to help you catch him, SWAT and everything. Put another AJ-1800 tracer in the backpack, or indelible dye, or something, anything but a bomb."

"This discussion's over."

"You're doing it again."

"Doing what again?"

"Letting your dark side take over."

"Don't even start with the *Star Wars* analogies."

"It'll ruin your life, just like before."

"What're you talking about?"

"Ernie Wagner. Planting evidence on an innocent man. Getting kicked off the force. Any of this sound familiar?"

"How do you—"

"You got the blues about a year ago, put on that damn *Frank Sinatra Live* album and drank almost a full bottle of gin. Right after Sinatra sang "One For My Baby," you got all, like, teary-eyed and told me the whole, sad story."

"Remind me to drink alone from now on."

"Afterwards, I asked you the ultimate question. If you had it to do over again, would you still plant the knife? Remember what you said? Of course not, you were too drunk. Well, you said no, you wouldn't. You told me planting that knife ruined your life. If somehow you could stop time, take back one decision, turn one signpost on the road of life, that would be it."

"Yeah, well, now I think everything happens for the best."

"Do you really? If you hadn't planted that knife you'd still be on the police force. You never would have been a PI. You never would have met Lisa Montgomery. You never would have been involved in the Gravesnatcher case."

"I never would have met you."

"I'm beginning to wish you hadn't. Gideon, you're standing at that crossroads again. The signpost is right there, wrapped in wire and C-4. Turn that sign now, before it's too late."

"The bomb stays."

"Then I'm leaving. For good. I can't be part of this. Unless you take that bomb out of there, I quit."

There was a hardness to Hillary's eyes I'd never seen before, a determination that reached to her soul. If I'd been thinking clearer I might've listened to her, but my dark side had taken over, making me stubborn and stupid. "You want to quit? Fine, quit. I don't need you anyway. I don't need anybody."

"If you could just hear yourself ..."

"Hey, I heard you. You said you quit. So quit! Go on, get out of here!"

Tears sprung from her blue eyes. Her lips quivered, about to say something, but she realized it was useless. With a final plea on her face, Hillary turned and ran out of the room.

I stood there motionless, listening to her footsteps on the floor, the sound of the door opening and closing, her car starting and finally pulling away.

I stood there motionless with the backpack, the money, and the bomb, knowing she was right but realizing I didn't care.

My monster was out again.

Nick and Nora

With the backpack locked up in my apartment safe, I spent a fitful night in bed. I half expected Stacy to show up with her lock picks. I half expected Hillary to call and unquit. I half expected the Gravesnatcher to call, checking up on me. I even half expected to get a call from Lisa, apologizing. None of the above.

When I finally did fall asleep I dreamt about my parents. We were on our trip to California, checking into the Holiday Inn. Mom and I watched as Dad dropped his suitcase on the bed and unzipped it. Suddenly the suitcase exploded. Dad turned to me, his hands gone, his arms bloody stumps. My mother screamed, "What have you done, Gideon? What have you done?!"

The Gravesnatcher was the lead story on the morning news. Pictures of Jason Tucker were on every channel and the front page of the *L.A. Times.* I made coffee as Matt Lauer interviewed Mary Rocket about the LAPD's efforts to stop him. Captain Rocket was coy, giving no indication that she knew anything about the Gravesnatcher's next ransom demand.

I dropped the backpack in the trunk of the Taurus and stopped by the office on the way to Lisa's Brentwood estate. I hoped that Hillary would be there, a smile on her face, ready for a new day, sorry about the spat.

She wasn't. I picked up the phone and called her. It rang once, twice, three times. I pictured Hillary in her studio apartment, staring at the ringing phone, knowing it was me, trying to decide whether to answer. Four, five, six times. Clearly, she was just going to let it ring. With a sigh, I hung up.

I pulled out a Thomas Guide—a book of maps covering the entire L.A. area—and studied the possible routes between Lisa's house and the Hollywood Bowl. Also an escape from that route to the Griffith Park Zoo. Then I headed for Brentwood.

I knew I was in trouble as I pulled up to Lisa's estate. I'd spotted two unmarked cars parked on Mandeville Canyon. Shit. Mary Rocket planned to have us followed from Lisa's house to the Bowl. This complicated things and had me worried. If the Gravesnatcher was watching the house, maybe he'd spotted them, too.

I punched in the gate code, which Mary Rocket had gotten the night before from the alarm company, and let myself into the house. The message machine light was blinking. I didn't remember it blinking when I left last night. I hit the button, heard Lisa's voice.

"Don't hate me, Gideon. I did save Hillary's life. And I know that by running away I'm giving up a piece of my own life, giving up any chance of ever having Hudson's baby. I'm not as brave as you are. I'm not bad, just a coward. Catch him for me, please."

The message ended as I heard a car door open. I looked out the window to see Lisa climb out of her 280. My heart skipped a beat, thrilled she'd come back. Then I realized it wasn't Lisa but Stacy in disguise. My heart skipped another beat. She looked great.

I opened the door and took a closer look. Stacy wore a blond wig and sunglasses, both Lisa Montgomery trademarks. And the make-up artist had worked wonders, highlighting her cheekbones and softening her chin. She wore red nail polish. Stacy never wore nail polish, but Lisa did. Whoever had picked her wardrobe had also done a great job. She wore a yellow cashmere sweater over a simple green skirt and stiletto pumps.

"Well, what do you think?" she purred, walking past me into the foyer, then doing a pirouette, giving me a three-sixty of the transformation.

"Amazing."

"Mary Rocket hired Lisa's makeup man to do the face and her wardrobe designer to do the clothes. She wore this outfit in *Heartache*."

"You even walk like her."

"I'm surprised I can walk at all in these shoes." She leaned against me. "I'm even wearing her perfume, Obsession. Smell me."

I traced my nose down her long neck. "Delicious."

"Me or her?"

"You." Our eyes met and then our lips, a short but loving kiss. Then, impulsively, I said what I was thinking. "I was hoping you'd come by last night."

"I couldn't. Piccolo had me handcuffed to the headboard until almost two a.m."

"What?"

"Kidding. I'm kidding. I wanted to come over but I was afraid Captain Rocket would find out. If she did, she'd figure out we wanted to work together, and she might've been mad enough to pull me off the case again. But I'll make you a promise," she cooed. "Tonight I'm all yours ..." She kissed my chin, my nose and then my lips.

As we drove along Sunset Boulevard—past towering palms, sweeping lawns and my-dick-is-bigger-than-your-dick mansions—Stacy outlined Mary Rocket's plan for the Hollywood Bowl. "There'll be a construction crew building a set on stage. All cops. Three janitors will be sweeping the aisles. Cops, too. And in case the Gravesnatcher somehow gets past all those cops and tries to escape, there are two tree trimming trucks parked across the street from the exit. Only they're not tree trimmers, they're snipers. They'll take out his tires."

"Sounds good," I said. "Only one problem: the Gravesnatcher's not going to be there."

"What do you mean?"

"He called me yesterday, assumed the cops would have the drop covered and gave me an alternate location."

"And you didn't tell the Captain?"

"I want to catch this prick, Stacy, and I'm not going to do that if the LAPD's got men 'hidden in plain sight' as carpenters and gardeners. The Gravesnatcher's too smart for that. He'll figure out it's a trap and boogie. Our best chance is to meet him alone. Take care of him ourselves."

"Do you have any idea what Captain Rocket will do to you when you don't show up at the Bowl?"

"What can she do? Force me to quit again? I don't work for her. Besides, her business card's not the one attached to all the ransom notes. I'm the one with something to lose here. So I figure I've got a little leeway in how I deal with the Gravesnatcher."

"I'm going to need a little leeway, too, Gideon, since I'm the one in the blond wig and red nail polish. Since the Gravesnatcher won't show up unless 'Lisa' shows up, this party ain't going to happen without me."

"We'll never catch this guy playing by the rules. *He* doesn't play by the rules."

"Yeah, well, if I don't play by the rules, I'll get fired. I need my job."

"No, you don't. You can become a PI, too."

"No, thanks."

"You can work with me. Be my partner."

"I've got plans, Gideon. To make Captain, like Dad. That's not going to happen by disobeying a superior officer." She took a cell phone out of her purse, started punching in numbers.

"I hate to bust your bubble, Stace, but thanks to the Gravesnatcher, you are on a career path to nowhere. If you think my evidence planting hurt your career, that's nothing compared to your turning Magic Land into a shooting gallery and David Hunter into hamburger. That's going in your jacket. Think about it; you're never going to make Captain. Hell, when the dust settles from this case, you'll be lucky if they don't bust you back to patrolwoman."

Stacy had the number punched in, her finger poised over the SEND button. It stayed there, poised, as she digested what I'd said.

"The best chance you've got to save your career is to catch this creep. And that's not going to happen without our playing by *his* rules. You and I can do it, Stacy, I know we can."

"What's your plan?"

Okay, here's where it got tricky. I could lie to her, make up some bullshit about trying to get the drop on him at the zoo, or I could be honest and tell her about the C-4. If she reacted to the bomb the same as Hillary, she would pull out now and that would be that. No 'Lisa,' no Gravesnatcher.

But, I thought, if Stacy and I really had a chance to make it as a couple again, it shouldn't be built on a lie. Besides, she was bound to find out the truth when the Gravesnatcher did open the backpack and his hands did a disappearing act. So ...

"I've hidden a letter bomb in the backpack."

She looked at me, expressionless, like she was having trouble processing what I'd said. "A bomb ..." she finally repeated.

"Not very ethical, I know. Comparisons to my fuck-up with the Ernie Wagner evidence planting must spring to mind. But so does the old expression, 'fighting fire with fire.' "

An incredulous quality snuck into her voice. "A bomb ..."

"Look, if you have a better idea, I'd be happy to hear it."

"No. I just can't believe I didn't think of it first. It's brilliant, Gideon! Let the motherfucker take the backpack, and when the bomb goes off he's got two choices: call for help or bleed to death. I love it!"

"I love that you love it!"

"And it's foolproof. No cops for him to spot. No chance of another Magic Land. We just do what he says and boom de de boom boom."

"Boom de de boom boom."

"How'd you make it?"

"The way you taught me. Six-by-three strip of C-4, blasting cap, nine-volt battery, loop wire attached to the zipper."

"Oh, this is good."

"So, you're in?"

"I'm in. I must be nuts, but I'm in."

I was thrilled. No, *elated*. And the ferocity of my emotions surprised me. The thought of Stacy and me working together, *being* together, clearly meant more to me than even I realized.

"Ironic, isn't it?" she asked.

"What?"

"That we reunite while I'm dressed as Lisa Montgomery, the woman that broke us up in the first place."

"I've got more irony for you. Now that we've got a plan, we may never get to use it."

"Why not?"

"We're being followed." Instinctively, she started to turn around. "Don't," I said. "Use the makeup mirror."

She dropped the visor, opened the mirror compartment and angled the visor so she could see through the back window. I glanced in the rear-view mirror.

"See the black LTD?"

"Yeah. That's Bennie Hernandez driving. The bald guy next to him is Healy."

"And three cars back, the silver Crown Victoria—"

"Betty Rutledge and her partner, Pat something-or-other."

"Captain Rocket mention a tail when she briefed you?"

"No."

"So she doesn't trust us."

"Or doesn't trust the Gravesnatcher. She may be afraid he'll try to intercept us on the way to the drop and put the babysitters back there just in case."

"What about helicopters?"

"She nixed them. Said they were too easy to spot."

"That's a break. We'd never shake the tail if there was air support."

"I'm not sure we can shake them, chopper or no chopper.

The minute we do anything hinky, they'll call for backup."

"I know." I wracked my brain for options. I thought about the old Run and Hide: making a sudden, unexpected turn down a side street then quickly hiding the car in a parking lot, fast food drive-thru or a car wash. That way, when the cops gave chase they wouldn't see me and go roaring past. But we were in the middle of Beverly Hills on Sunset Boulevard, which offered zero parking lots, fast food joints, or car washes; these are usually built on less pricey real estate.

I kept wracking. There was a Suicide 180, but that was dangerous. I'd have to get in the right hand lane, then at an appropriate intersection throw the car into a 180, skid across the two left lanes—hopefully without hitting anybody—then slide into the oncoming traffic, again without inflating any air bags. Once I had the car going the opposite direction I'd duck into a side street, scoot up to Mulholland, take it to Coldwater, then slip on down to the 101. Dangerous, but effective, and at the moment, our best option. I was about to tell Stacy to tighten her seat belt when a cop stepped into the street, stopping traffic. That's when I spotted the UFO.

That's right, a UFO. It was at least seventy-five feet across. But it wasn't flying under its own power. It was attached to a thick cable suspended from a gigantic crane that dangled it 100 feet over Beverly Drive. Two tanks were parked on the street beneath it, their turrets aimed at the UFO. Cars were parked haphazardly on the street, creating the look of a panicked traffic jam.

They were shooting a movie. Traffic cones and police barricades blocked the street. I saw one camera on a big crane, another sitting on a dolly, a third on a tripod. Lights, equipment and crew were everywhere. Someone yelled into a bullhorn: "Okay, people, here we go. Quiet please and roll cameras!"

"Speed!" from someone on the crane.

"Speed!" from someone on the dolly.

"Speed!" from someone at the tripod.

A skinny girl ran between the tanks, held up a slate and

yelled: "Marker!" Then she clapped the slate and ran behind a bank of two TV monitors where a bunch of director's chairs were clustered.

Someone at the monitors called, "Action!" And all hell broke loose. The tanks fired, a fireball rocked the UFO, the UFO fired and an explosion obliterated one of the tanks. Terrified drivers leapt screaming out of their cars and raced for cover—and a light bulb went off in my head.

"Hang on," I said and floored it.

"Oh, shit," Stacy said when she realized what I had in mind.

"My thoughts exactly."

The traffic officer started waving his arms, trying to make me stop. I ignored him, plowing through the cones.

Since everyone on the film crew was watching the action on the street, no one saw my lowly Taurus heading straight for them. I glanced in the mirror to see the LTD and Crown Vic pull out of traffic and follow us.

As I roared past a few crew members at the outskirts of the set they starting screaming at us, and I heard someone yelling, "Cut! Cut!" But no one could hear him over all the pyrotechnics.

The tank fired again, another blast blistered the side of the UFO as I started weaving in and out of the cars abandoned on the set. Now the UFO fired again and flames engulfed the tank. The hatch opened and four men poured out, one of them rolling into the street directly in front of me. As he got to his feet I recognized him—the heartthrob of the moment, Jack Stone.

His face registered three entirely different emotional states. First, surprise that we were there at all. Second, anger over us ruining the take. Third, panic at the realization that I wasn't stopping. He dove out of the way as we zoomed past, giving us the finger.

Meanwhile, in my rear-view mirror I could see the LTD and Crown Vic trying to follow us, but their larger vehicles were having trouble inching between the parked cars.

Up ahead, a soldier had a SAM launcher on his shoulder, aimed at the alien invader. He fired. A huge explosion shook the UFO when we were only fifty feet away; to my horror I saw the cable holding the UFO release and the UFO begin to fall.

"It's going to land right on us!" Stacy screamed.

"Not if I can help it!" I stomped on the gas and prayed for a tail wind.

I could see the shadow of the thing getting bigger and bigger as it got closer and closer, swallowing us. A tremendous CRASH rocked the car—but the UFO had only clipped the rear bumper, ripping it off. The UFO landed with a metal-screeching, ground-shaking THUD. Not only did it miss us, but the twisted prop now blocked the road behind us, trapping the cops.

"Cut, print," I said as I headed into the hills for our rendezvous with the Gravesnatcher.

It's Showtime, Folks

The zoo parking lot was surprisingly full. Roy had expected the parked line of school buses. He remembered in the fifth grade taking an hour and a half bus ride from his home in Macon, Georgia, to the Atlanta zoo. The highlight was watching a bull elephant mount one of the females while the embarrassed zoo guy tried to break them up with a fire hose. They'd also seen two chimps doing it on the limb of a big fake tree. And two snakes all curled up together, either fucking or trying to choke each other to death. Nobody, including the teacher, was exactly sure how snakes 'did it.'

Nobody had come to the Atlanta Zoo in those days unless they had to. It was small and smelly and all the animals did was eat and screw.

Well, something special had to be happening at the L.A. Zoo because the place was packed: young couples with kids in strollers, old farts walking in slow motion, camera-toting tourists wearing logo-spackled tee shirts, and lots of lovers, all holding hands, all with that 'gee whiz life is so beautiful' look in their eyes.

Well, today would be a day none of them would ever forget. Today they would all witness a murder.

Roy hadn't felt guilty before killing Winslow. Maybe a little nervous. A little anxious. But never guilty. Snuffing out that life had been a justified act.

Roy hadn't felt guilty before killing Hunter. Another justified execution. The fucker had ruined his career. Roy just wished he could have been there to see the producer's face pulverized by the explosion.

But he felt guilty now.

Put it out of your mind, he told himself. Just focus on the plan.

The plan. A plan is just like a script, its execution like a performance. And the secret to any good performance is preparation. Roy had prepared well.

He looked at the paper bag next to him. The same size bag his mother had used to pack his egg salad sandwich in when he went to Minnie Burghard Elementary School. The very same size bag Roy brought with him to the Atlanta Zoo all those many years ago. There wasn't a sandwich in the bag today. Today there was just a two-pound chunk of Semtex.

Finally, Roy thought, as he watched Kincaid pull into the parking lot at eleven-thirty. Kincaid was still driving the piece of shit Taurus. Roy smiled as he saw the crumpled front end, courtesy of Roy's fender bender leaving Hollywood. There was new damage—the rear bumper was gone. Roy wondered what had happened as Kincaid parked at the back of the lot, next to a Jeep Grand Cherokee.

Roy had left the Mercedes at home today and rented a Lincoln Towncar. The SL 550's trunk was just too small. He was parked in the handicapped section, thanks to a stolen placard. The handicapped section afforded an unobstructed view of the parking lot. Roy watched Kincaid and the beautiful blond in the cashmere sweater as they got out of the car and headed into the zoo.

Roy's eyes searched the parking lot. *Excellent,* he thought. *No sign of cops. Kincaid's following instructions.* Now it was time for Roy to do the same thing.

He pulled a cell phone out of his pocket, punched in a number he knew by heart and hit SEND. After three unanswered rings an answering machine picked up.

"Hi, this is Detective Irving Piccolo. I'm not home right now, but at the sound of the tone, please leave a message."

Roy did.

Lions and Tigers and Bears

I'd never been to the L.A. Zoo. I guess the reason most people go to the zoo is for the kids' sake, and since Stacy and I never had them, we never went. I had gone to the zoo in Milwaukee with my folks. I remember standing in front of the gorilla cage staring into the big black eyes of one of those hulking beasts as he stared back at me. He looked thoughtful, intelligent even. I'd been about eight at the time, and I thought he looked smarter than me. *If he's so smart*, I wondered, *how come he can't talk? Or won't talk*. That was it, I realized. He could talk, all the apes could talk, but they wouldn't when we humans were around. I shared my revelation with my parents, but they never bought it.

And now, thirty years later, I found myself looking into the big black eyes of another gorilla and thinking the same thing.

"You ever notice how smart gorillas look?"

Stacy studied the gorillas for a beat. "You mean when they stick their fingers up their asses or when they jerk themselves off?"

"Okay, they don't have our social skills, but look in their eyes. They seem intelligent, don't they?"

"Yeah, but that doesn't mean anything. When I look in your eyes, *you* seem intelligent."

I laughed. We were actually having a good time. It was almost as if we were lovers out for an afternoon of fun, rather than a PI and a cop on a ransom drop to a cold-blooded killer.

I glanced at my watch, 11:55. We'd been out there for about twenty minutes, killing time until noon. The zoo was packed but the folks looked different than at Magic Land. People were much calmer here, no one rushing to get into the next long line.

A few of the folks stared at Stacy. A couple others took pictures. Obviously they thought she might be Lisa Montgomery so I knew the make-up was working.

I wondered how the Gravesnatcher would show up this time. A few people were floating around in costumes—a couple of clowns, a green dinosaur and a giant kangaroo. He could be any one of them. Or he could show up wearing just a fake beard and wig.

I moved to the bench, sat down. I'd had to lug the heavy backpack full of money from the back of the parking lot all the way to the gorilla cages. Two million bucks in one hundred dollar bills weighs about forty-two and a half pounds, so I was pooped. Stacy sat down next to me, rubbed a foot. "I don't know how Lisa walks in these things. My feet are killing me."

A young couple walked by pushing a baby carriage. Stacy watched them, wistfully. "I never thought I wanted children," she said.

"I remember. I think your exact words when I first asked you were, 'No fucking way.' "

"But now here I sit, thirty-five, divorced, about to be fired, and alone."

"It's not too late to have children."

"Is that hope I hear in your voice, Kincaid?"

"I wouldn't go that far."

"Oh, come on. You always wanted to recreate that apple pie Milwaukee boyhood of yours. But it's not possible anymore. The world's changed."

"It changed when I was still a kid, remember? At least for me."

She took my hand. "Oh, God, Gideon, I forgot about your parents, I'm sorry. I didn't mean—"

"I know. Don't worry about it." I squeezed her hand and our eyes met. We smiled at each other.

BRRRING.

That oh so familiar old-fashioned ringtone.

"It's him," I said. "He's hidden a cell phone somewhere."

BRRRING.

I dug through a nearby trashcan. Stacy searched through some bushes. My nose reacted to a vaguely familiar smell, but I placed it too late, right after I stuck my hand into a discarded, and very full, baby diaper.

"Got it," Stacy called, pulling a cheap Motorola out of the scrubs. She held it out to me, and I took it with my left hand. "What's all over your right hand?" she asked. Then the smell hit her. "Never mind."

I flipped open the phone. "You buy these phones by the case?"

"As a matter of fact, I bought them on the Internet. With your credit card."

Stacy grabbed a handful of napkins from a guy selling pretzels and handed them to me. "I know," I said. "Just like you charged the dog collar. Thanks a lot. I got hauled in by the cops."

"Good. They finally made the Doggieworld connection. They figure you and I were working together?"

"For a few minutes. How'd you get my credit card number?"

"Your office trash. You really ought to shred those credit card bills."

"Thanks for the tip."

"Where's Lisa?"

"Right here."

"Put her on."

Oh, shit. Stacy didn't sound anything like Lisa. I turned to Stacy. "He wants to talk to you, *Lisa,*" I said pointedly.

Stacy took the phone, holding it between us so we could both hear him. Closing her eyes for a moment—trying to recall Lisa's voice, I imagined—she said, "Hello."

"Tell me you love me, bitch."

"I have great affection for you, sir," Stacy said in a breathy Southern accent. "And I'll have even more if you return my precious property."

"Beg me for it. Beg me, baby."

Stacy shot me a 'man, is he a nut case' look, then: "Please, oh, please, give it to me."

"Tell me you love me."

"I love you. I've always loved you."

"That's good. Remember that the next time I come see you."

I wanted to grab the phone, threaten to kill him if he came anywhere near Lisa, but I didn't. I couldn't. I had to make sure he took the backpack. So I throttled back my anger and said, "Okay, can we get on with this? We've got your money; let's trade."

"Patience is a virtue, Gideon. You really ought to work on that."

"So now you're a hyphenate: Kidnapper/Murderer/ Shrink."

"Hey, you've got this all wrong. *I'm* the good guy."

"Look, I'm not here to judge you. I'm just here to deliver a couple million bucks. Interested?"

"Absolutely. Oh, and just so you know, after I collect this ransom, I'll have all the money I need. You won't be hearing from me again."

"Good, I guess."

"And I couldn't have done it without you, thanks."

"You're welcome."

"Now leave the backpack under the bench. Then get back in your car and drive to the Greyhound Bus Station in Hollywood, on Cahuenga."

"I know where it is."

"The ticket agent's holding an envelope with your name on it. Inside the envelope is a locker key. Locker number 345. And you better hurry. There's only enough ice in the cooler for a couple of hours." He hung up.

"That means he's here somewhere," Stacy said, looking

around. "If he wanted us to leave the backpack under the bench, he must be close by."

"Forget about it, Stace. We *want* him to get the backpack, remember. Let's not do anything to scare him off." I slid the ransom under the bench. "We better hurry. It could take almost an hour to get to Hollywood this time of the day."

We half-walked, half-ran toward the exit. "Let me ask you this," Stacy said. "If Lisa bailed on us, why do we give a shit about her sperm?"

"She left us the two million bucks. I figure getting it back is the least we can do."

When we reached the edge of the parking lot Stacy suddenly stopped. "Shit."

"What?"

"I forgot my purse. I put it down next to the bench, by the bushes. I've got to go back." As she turned around she caught a heel and almost fell. "God damn shoes," she muttered.

"Wait," I said. "Tell you what, I'll go back." I handed her the car keys. "You bring up the car."

"You sure?"

"Yeah, don't worry about it."

"Thanks, Gideon," she said, kissing my cheek. "I'll meet you right here." She hobbled into the parking lot and I jogged back toward the bench.

It probably only took me four or five minutes to get there, but when I got to the bench, the backpack was gone. The Gravesnatcher had been close by. I did a quick 360, but didn't see anyone lugging the backpack. I did see Stacy's purse, though, right where she said she left it—next to the bench, almost hidden by the bushes. I picked it up and started back toward the parking lot.

That's when I heard the explosion. Not the small BOOM setting off the letter bomb would have made, but a loud, ear-rattling **BOOM,** like a car bomb makes. Then I saw the plume of black smoke coming from the direction of the parking lot.

I sprinted to the exit, dodging and weaving through the

swarm of people. I hurtled into the parking lot. Car alarms blared. Car windows were shattered. I raced toward the smoke and flames that I knew had to be my car.

And it was. A huge explosion had ripped through the Taurus leaving it a twisted, molten mess. The flames were so hot, so fierce that I couldn't get closer than fifty feet. But inside the car I could see the burnt remains of Stacy.

And I stood there, helpless, watching her funeral pyre.

Midnight in the Garden of Anguish and Guilt

It took only six minutes for the fire department to arrive. But for those six minutes the voracious flames fed on every molecule of combustible material—leather, fabric, plastic, gasoline, skin and bone. The car cried out in agony, the metal groaning as the superheated flames twisted the chassis into a fetal position.

The firefighters poured water on the car from two pumpers. The fire resisted, rearing up like a primordial beast, fighting back stubbornly, unwilling to give up its death grip on the Ford. Finally the black roiling cloud of smoke turned to white, the first sign of a fire's surrender. The car cried out again, as the cooling began and the metal tried unsuccessfully to regain its original shape.

It was finally safe enough to get close to the car. I splashed through the puddles of water to look in the driver's side window. There was almost nothing left of Stacy. Her body had melted into and become part of the charred seat. As I turned away horrified, I saw one of her scorched stiletto pumps lying next to the car.

"You want to talk about it?"

"No."

"Try."

"The Gravesnatcher knew you'd have the Bowl staked out,

Captain. He moved the drop to the zoo, made me swear not to tell you."

Mary Rocket and I stood in the middle of the parking lot turned crime scene. The coroner's assistants had removed what they could of Stacy's corpse, putting no more than fifty pounds of remains in a body bag. Hector Ruiz and his crime scene technicians were now at work. They'd do a preliminary investigation here, then move the car to a city garage for a more detailed analysis.

"That's why you ditched your tail."

"I figured my best shot at catching the Gravesnatcher was to make sure he'd show up. He wouldn't have if I had a parade of cops following me into the parking lot."

"Of course, then he wouldn't have had a chance to plant a bomb in your car and Stacy would still be alive."

"Good, just what I need, more guilt."

"Get used to it, Gideon. You'll probably be crucified for this."

"I know."

"And just what, may I ask, was your great plan to catch him without backup?"

My plan was actually still in effect. Hell, our maniac might already be on his knees screaming in agony, his mangled fingers stuck to a ceiling somewhere. But should I tell the Captain? There's an old saying when dealing with the police: *When in doubt, say nothing*. So I said, "It doesn't matter what my plan was anymore." Then something occurred to me. "The bus station! The Gravesnatcher left the sperm at Greyhound Station in Hollywood."

"Another locker?"

I nodded. "Ticket agent's holding an envelope in my name with a key in it. And since the last locker we opened had a dog collar made of C-4 in it, I'll bet the cyrovial's not the only thing he left us."

"I'll send the bomb squad to check it out."

Suddenly a tortured voice screamed out: "Why didn't someone tell me? Why didn't someone tell me Stacy was decoying Lisa Montgomery?" I turned to find an enraged Piccolo charging through the police tape. He bulled past a couple of uniforms, grabbed Mary Rocket's arm. "I'm her partner! Someone should have told me!" He turned to me. "This is all your fault. You killed her! You killed her, you son of a bitch!" He launched himself at me, hitting me full in the chest, slamming me to the wet ground. "Murderer!" he screamed, his fists smashing into my face, landing punch after punch as I did nothing to protect myself.

I looked into his wild eyes, saw my blood smeared on his knuckles, and knew that I deserved this beating. Two more punches landed, dazing me, before two cops grabbed him under the arms and pulled him off. But Piccolo wasn't finished. In desperation he gave a mighty kick, catching me in the temple, knocking me out.

I spent the rest of the day in agony. The outside of my head hurt from the beating, the inside ached from grief. Once the paramedics pulled me out of my all too brief respite from with consciousness, they put a butterfly stitch on the cut over my left eye, rubbed antiseptic over my split lip and told me to see my dentist about a couple of loose molars. Mary Rocket decided I'd suffered enough for one day and told me to come see her for a debriefing in the morning.

A black and white dropped me at the office. I walked in, ignored the ringing phone—though I did notice the answering machine was stuck on fifty-three again—and pulled the bottle of Tanqueray gin out of my desk drawer. By nightfall, sitting in my darkened office, I was drunk enough to feel real sorry for myself.

I had blamed myself for my parents' murder. They'd asked me to work in the store that morning and I'd talked my way out of it. After I found out they'd been killed I did a major Woulda Shoulda Coulda. Everyone told me I was nuts to blame myself. I had survivor's guilt, or some such shit. If I'd been in the shop the only difference would have been that I'd have been killed, too, they said. They kept telling me it wasn't my fault, and finally, I believed them.

Well, Stacy's death *was* my fault. I was the one who had decided to lie to Mary Rocket about the drop location. I was the one who'd talked Stacy into coming to the zoo. I was the one who'd told her to get the car. I was the one stupid enough not to realize the Gravesnatcher's plan. In fact, he'd all but told me when he said this would be the last ransom. That was why he'd wanted Lisa there. He was planning to get his money and kill us both with the car bomb.

Now knee deep in melancholy, I took another swig of the sweet sauce. What hurt the most was, I'd finally realized how much I still loved Stacy. So what happens? She's taken from me.

Irony. That most awful of words. God is, when all is said and done, nothing but a sadistic practical joker.

I was about to get up and put a Sinatra CD on the stereo when I heard the front door of the office open, and a voice call out, "Gideon?" Hillary's voice. "Gideon?" I'm not sure I've ever heard a sweeter sound than Hillary's voice at that moment. "Gideon, are you here?"

I opened my office door. Hillary stood in the middle of the reception room. "I heard about Stacy on the news. I'm so sorry. I've been trying to call you, here, at your apartment. I left message after message you didn't call back. I know we're supposed to be in the middle of a huge feud, but under the circumstances ..." She ran across the room into my arms. I hugged her, hard. She was the first person to show me any real sympathy. The only one left in the world who offered unconditional love. Holding her close, I realized how much I needed it. The hug ended, and Hillary pulled back, studying me in the sketchy lighting. Wincing, she reached up to caress my pulped face. "What happened? Were you hurt in the explosion?"

"Yeah. The emotional detonation of a grieving boyfriend."

"Piccolo."

"I did nothing to defend myself. Let him wail away, hoping he'd kill me."

"Don't even talk like that. I don't want to sound cynical or anything, but, like, you and Stacy weren't exactly Romeo and Juliet. I mean, nobody should die like that, and I'm sure deep down in that shriveled heart of yours there's probably an itty bitty pilot light of affection, but ..." She trailed off as she finally whiffed the despair in the air. "Or I'm completely off base and you had a real heart-on for Stacy."

"Door number two."

"I am such a jerk. Okay, I'm sorry, Gideon. I really am. But suicidal obsession doesn't look good on you and I'm not going to allow you wallow in this cesspool of misery. I'll make sure we schedule plenty of time for you to grieve, but first things first. We've got a murdering SOB to catch, and we can't do that emptying bottles of vodka and boxes of Kleenex."

"With any luck he's already maimed or dead. Remember my much debated letter bomb?"

"I sure do." Hillary marched back to the front door of the office and threw it open. "Ta da!" She waved her arms like Vanna White, indicating a lump on the floor just outside my office door.

"What is it?"

"You tell me."

Knowing I wasn't going to like this, I crossed to the threshold. I was right. The lump was the backpack I'd left at the zoo. The zipper was still zipped. The back of the canvas bag had been slashed open. The money was gone, and the letter bomb was still inside, still rigged to the zipper.

"Goddamn it," I said. "How'd he know?"

"Maybe he's got one of those bomb-sniffing dogs or an X-ray machine. Or maybe he's just smarter than the average bear. Point is, he's still out there, unmolested, and you are, like, in here, your face looking like something out of a horror movie."

I picked up the backpack, hurled it into the office. "Goddamn it!"

"That's not very safe, is it?"

"Er, no."

"Is there a way to defuse the thing?"

"Yeah." I reached through the gash in the canvas, disconnected the battery.

"Thank you. So, what's next?"

It was a little tough thinking clearly through the alcohol and the anger, but I gave it a shot. "By leaving the backpack here he was giving me a message."

"Something like, and I'm just guessing here: screw you."

My eyes went to the blinking 53 on the answering machine. "So maybe he left something a little more specific." I hit the play button. There was a high-speed whir as the machine rewound; then the first message started to play.

Hillary's voice: "Gideon, it's Hillary. I just heard what happened. I'm sorry, for everything. Call me." BEEP.

Unknown voice: "Mr. Kincaid, this is Foster Stern, CBS News—" I hit fast forward until I heard the BEEP.

Elliot's voice: "Talk about your plot twists! Beautiful woman struck down in the prime of life. Bereaved ex-husband left to pick up the pieces. Shakespeare, eat your heart out. Ring my bell." BEEP.

Elliot's voice: "P.S., if you can live through this, you'll be up there with Grisham and Lee Child. For God's sake, be careful!" BEEP.

Unknown voice: "Mr. Kincaid, I'm calling for Bill O'Reilly at FOX News—" Fast forward, BEEP.

Hillary's voice: "Me again. Are you there …? Pick up, please … Gideon …?" BEEP.

Joan Hagler's voice: "Well, are you happy now? The TV said an undercover cop was burnt to a crisp this afternoon. Undercover, as in dressed up like Lisa? As in, if Lisa *had* been with you, she'd be dead now?! I'm never wrong about people, and I knew you were a dangerous psychopath the minute I laid eyes on you." BEEP.

Alex Snyder's voice: "Mr. Kincaid, this is Alex Snyder from the Westwood Mortuary. Sorry to hear about your ex-wife. If there is anything I can do, professionally speaking—I mean, casket, plot, you know—please don't hesitate to call. Oh, and we are very anxious for the safe return of Christine's remains. *Very* anxious. Please encourage the police department to return her as soon as possible." BEEP.

The Gravesnatcher's voice: "Nice try, PI. Smart. But I've got a 143 IQ, and that makes me smarter. Sorry about the lady cop. Ex-wife, huh? Don't say I never did anything for you. Of course, that means Lisa's still alive. You're still alive. Guess I'm not done, after all." BEEP.

We listened to the rest of the messages, just in case he'd called back. There were lots of reporters, vultures from the all the tabloids, two more panicked calls from Hillary, a few more women applying for the secretary job, a bunch of potential clients who'd heard about me on TV and wanted to hire the suddenly famous Gideon Kincaid, and a call from Mary Rocket. I started dialing. Even though it was nine-fifteen, I figured she might still be at work.

"Captain Rocket's office."

"Gideon Kincaid returning her call."

I was put on hold for a few moments, then: "Nothing but spermatozoa."

"Excuse me."

"In the locker," Mary Rocket said. "Just eight cryovials of sperm. No bomb, which is the good news. No fingerprints, other than the ticket agent's, or any other trace evidence, which is the bad news."

"What about the ticket agent? Could he describe whoever left the envelope?"

"He was a she, Larisa Baumgartner, and no, she never saw him. She turned around to answer a phone, and when she turned back the envelope was sitting there, with 'Hold for Gideon Kincaid,' written on the flap. By the way, the D.A. is thinking about filing obstruction charges against you."

"What do you think about that?"

"I told him to wait and see if the Gravesnatcher kills you first."

"Thanks, I guess."

"I wasn't doing you a favor, Gideon. I was serious. This Jason Tucker is smarter than I remember. More dangerous than I remember. More ruthless than I remember. And we don't have any idea where the hell he is. Watch your back."

"I will." She hung up and I starting thinking. Jason Tucker was awful fucking smart. I mean, he'd tricked me with the collar, had been clever with the hidden cell phones, had done that number with my credit card, planted a bomb in my car, figured out I'd planted a letter bomb. How? "Hillary, you know where my file on Jason Tucker is?"

"Sure, I pulled it as soon as I heard he'd escaped from prison." She dug through a pile on her desk and handed me a file. On the inside cover was a copy of his mug shot, supplied by the LAPD. I looked into those arrogant, unapologetic gray eyes, observed the lean, hard face and the dishwater blond ponytail. I read through the basics: height, 5'9", weight 165. There was a brief summary of how I'd spotted his shadow on the wall while dropping Lisa off five years ago, his shooting at me inside the house, my chasing him through the window and my beating the shit out of him on the street.

There was also a copy of the psychological profile one of the department shrinks wrote after interviewing him. There was the usual psycho babble about why Jason Tucker became a stalker: frustration over his career, his adoration of young beautiful starlets—women he felt he would be able to date if his career had been more successful—speculation that Tucker's adoration had turned to obsession … If I hadn't spotted him that night, his obsession might have turned deadly. Considering the murder spree Tucker had been on since his inadvertent release from jail, I'd say the deadly speculation had been right on.

And yes, there it was on page three of the report: "One of the reasons Mr. Tucker has become so dissatisfied with his life was that an IQ test, taken when he was 12, showed he had extraordinary intelligence—143, according to Mr. Tucker. As a result, his mother spent his entire adolescent years filling his head with lofty expectations, preparing him for the rich, successful, pampered life of a genius. A life that never materialized." All right, so he was a genius. A short, ponytailed, perverted, failed genius.

And then it hit me. That niggling I'd had ever since I'd seen the videotape taken by the surveillance camera at CryoZy Laboratory. The clue I knew I was missing.

’Til Death Do Us Part

“Cancer? I’m so sorry, Mr. Kincaid.”

“The doctor thinks we’ve caught it early enough, but before he doses me with the radiation, he asked if we ever wanted children. And we do, right, honey?”

“I’d hoped for three children,” Hillary said. “I come from a big family, seven if you must know, but in this overpopulated world I think it’s irresponsible to have more than three kids, don’t you, Mr. Oyster?”

It was ten o’clock the next morning. Ken Oyster was executive vice president of CryoZy Labs. Hillary and I were sitting in his office posing as man and wife. Why? Because I didn’t want the police to know what I was up to. At least, not yet.

“Please, call me Ken,” Oyster said, a nice enough man, tall, skinny, about forty, with a hawk-like nose and ears a little too small for his long face. Speaking of faces, he’d reacted to mine. I explained away the cuts and bruises as the result of a car accident. “I happen to have two children myself,” Oyster told us. “A boy and a girl. And I’m searching the files for a third.”

“Excuse me?” I asked.

He lowered his voice, leaned forward, confidentially. “The fact is, I’m sterile. Not impotent, mind you,” he added quickly, “there’s nothing wrong with the rocket ship; let’s just say the payload bay is empty.”

“Is that why you work here,” Hillary asked. “Because you’re sterile?”

"No. I got this job because my best friend was a fertility doctor and started the company. He needed someone to run it, so he lured me out of the furniture business and we started CryoZy. A few years later I met Melissa. We got married and tried to start a family. No luck. I went to see Alex and he did the tests and gave me the bad news: Mission Control, we have a problem.

"Ironic, isn't it? I work here and turn out to be sterile. Anyway, we've got thousands of clients. Some deposits are earmarked for personal use, but the majority of our deposits are for sale to the public. Tell us the physical attributes you want, we'll find it for you. Short, tall, blond, brunette, we got it. Black, white, brown, yellow, we got it. Want a donor who was a doctor, lawyer, actor, artist, we got it. Nobel prize winning scientist, Rhodes scholar, Cy Young award winner, look no further. We've even got star sperm."

I had to ask. "Star sperm?"

"Sure. One 'A' list movie star and three TV series leads. Of course, the donations were made before their careers took off, when they'd do anything to make a few bucks, but the sperm is as good as new. Now I'm not allowed to give out names, but if I drop a few titles and you happen to guess, well, who can blame you for being smart?"

"If it's all the same to you, Mr. Oyster," Hillary said, "I'll stick with Gideon's seed."

"Of course, I was just listing the options."

"Any chance we could have a tour of the facility?"

He stood up. "Of course. If you'll follow me, please."

Finally we'd got to the good part. The part I came there for in the first place—a tour of the storage facility. He walked us down the rows of liquid nitrogen tanks, explaining about the cryovials, the -193 degree temperature, all the stuff I'd already heard from the Beverly Hills detective.

"Fascinating," I said, starting to walk on my own, stopping in the exact same spot the Gravesnatcher had stopped on the tape—next to tank six. There was a knob on the top of the tank, right in front of me. It came up to my chest. Since I'm six feet tall, that would make the tank, as the detective had told me, five feet high.

I caught Hillary's eye and almost imperceptibly nodded. She pulled out her cell phone, activated the camera app. "Gideon, let me take a picture of you. For the family album. We can show the kids where they were kept on ice."

"Ken, stand here next to me," I said. He drifted over and I draped an arm around his shoulder.

"Say cheese ..."

"Cheese."

FLASH.

"What do you think?"

"He looks taller. Though not by much."

"Maybe an inch, two at the most, right?"

"Right."

We were in Hillary's car, still parked in CryoZy Laboratory's parking lot. We were comparing my height from the picture on Hillary's cell phone not to Ken's height, but to someone's in a second picture. A picture of the Gravesnatcher I'd made on the computer last night from the CryoZy Laboratory surveillance tape.

The detail that had been subconsciously nibbling at my temporal lobe was the Gravesnatcher's height. Detective Burke had mentioned the tanks were five feet high. Jason Tucker was five foot nine, so he should only reach ten inches above the tank. 'Obama' seemed to taller by more than a foot.

The two photos confirmed it. I was six feet tall, but 'Obama' was even taller. At least six two.

"Wait a minute," Hillary said. "This doesn't make sense. If you're six feet tall and Jason Tucker is five nine, Obama should be shorter, not taller."

"That's right."

"So ... oh, shit. Does this mean what I think it means?"

"Afraid so. Jason Tucker isn't the Gravesnatcher."

Rule number one: Never assume. And I had, the cops had. We all had. We'd assumed because Jason Tucker was out of jail he had to be the Gravesnatcher. And since he was the Gravesnatcher, nobody had continued the search to find the connection between Winslow, Hunter, Lisa and me. But there was one, there *had* to be one, and now I was determined to find it.

"What do we do?" Hillary asked.

I stared at the picture of Obama. "Start at the beginning. Try to find the common denominator. The 'number one on the call sheet' remark still makes me think he's an actor and ..." I trailed off as something on the picture caught my attention. Obama was picking up the cryovial with his *left* hand. Could he be left-handed? I'd only seen him once. Disguised as Merlin at Magic Land. Think ...

A memory: Merlin at Magic Land. Sweeping the backpack off the bench with his *left* arm.

A memory: Merlin shooting with his *left* hand.

Yes, he could be left-handed. Who did I know who was left-handed? Left-handed and connected to Winslow, Hunter and Lisa?

A memory—a hunky actor lunging for Lisa at the Universal audition. Me punching the shit out of him. Him fighting as a southpaw.

The realization rocked me. "I know who the Gravesnatcher is."

"You do?"

"Look," I said, pointing to the picture. "He's using his left hand. At Magic Land, he used his left hand to pick up the backpack and fire his gun. And when I was protecting Lisa from the stalker there was this guy, this actor. They were auditioning guys to be Lisa's co-star. He was one of them. He came out of a crowd to say hello to her, and I mistook him for the stalker, lumped him up pretty good."

"So he'd hate you."

"Wait, there's more. Afterwards he auditioned and did great.

He was the best, actually. They wanted to cast him but Lisa said if they did, she'd walk off the picture."

"Why?"

"There were in college together. He'd pulled a Casanova number on her when she was a freshman then dumped her as soon as he'd slept with her. Broke her cherry and her heart."

"Keeping him off the movie was her revenge."

"Exactly."

"I know the expression 'genius' is like, overused, but in this case I think it applies. Brilliant, Gideon."

"Thank you."

"So, what's his name?"

"I don't know."

"Excuse me."

"I only met him once. Five years ago. How am I supposed to remember his name?"

"Guess I was a little too hasty with that genius thing."

"Give me a minute to think about it ... oh, I almost had it."

"Long name? Short name?"

"Short, I think."

"Foreign or domestic?"

"What?"

"Igor or Ike? Tony or Tom?"

"Oh, domestic. I think."

"Okay, go through the alphabet; A, B, C, until the name comes to you."

"That's crazy."

"No, it works. I took a mnemonic class in college. I can still name all the state capitals: Albany, Annapolis, Atlanta—"

"Okay, okay. Abe, Allan, Bert, Bob, Carl ..." And so it went as I made my way through the alphabet, certain I was wasting my time, until I got to the R's. "Ralph, Rick, Ray ... Ray. That's it, Ray!"

"You're sure?"

"I'm sure. Ray!" I grabbed her, hugged her. Then ... "No wait, it was Roy. Not Ray, Roy."

"You're positive?"

"Absolutely. Roy!"

"Roy what?"

That stopped me. "I have no idea. And I'll never remember. I only heard his full name once or twice."

"You're the professional here, so correct me if I'm, like totally off base, but don't we need a first *and* a last name to have any chance of finding this guy?"

"Yeah."

"So what do we do?"

"Ask Lisa what his last name was."

"We don't know where Lisa is."

"Maybe not. But I know somebody who does."

Joan Hagler was in Cedar Sinai's special wing, reserved for L.A.'s rich and famous. The hospital rooms look more like four star hotel suites, with original artwork and pricy antiques tastefully arranged around the standard medical paraphernalia. Guests are usually registered under aliases, to keep fans and the press away.

I knew the floor well, thanks to a three-day job guarding the door of a movie star who, because of a confidentiality agreement I signed, must remain anonymous (but if you used Hillary's alphabet system and you concentrated on N for the first name and P for the second you could probably figure it out).

While there I noticed that Isabella, the pretty but frazzled head nurse, seemed to be fighting back tears. I befriended her, and she told me she'd been the victim of identity theft. Her bank account had been emptied and her credit cards maxed out. She was so overwhelmed with her work at the hospital she didn't know what to do. So I told her I'd take care of it. I called the bank, the credit card companies, all three credit report bureaus and I filed a police report. By the time N.P. left the hospital with her six-pound seven-ounce baby boy, Isabella's credit cards had been replaced and her bank account restored.

I didn't charge Isabella. I told her that since she spent her life taking care of strangers, it was my pleasure to take care of her.

Deep down, of course, I knew that a friend on the VIP floor of Cedar Sinai could come in handy one day.

And I was right. A phone call to Isabella got me Hagler's room number, 812, and a visitor's pass to the eighth floor.

Hillary and I quietly stepped into Joan Hagler's room.

Her shattered leg was in traction, entombed in a thick cast. We couldn't see her face because it was turned away from the door, glued to a TV where what looked like movie dailies were playing. There was a shot of Jack Stone on screen, sitting on a tank, talking to a handful of soldiers.

JACK STONE

Don't you understand? If we don't stop them in Beverly Hills, the next thing you know, the aliens will be having bagels in the White House.

She was watching dailies of that UFO movie! I asked, "You come to the part where the Taurus almost runs him over, yet?"

The sound of my voice startled her. The sight of me standing in the doorway terrified her. "You!" She reached for the call button, but I was faster, ripping it out of her hand.

"Now, now, Joan, I think we better have this conversation in private."

Her face looked horrible. A bloodstained bandage covered her nose, her left eye was blue green and swollen shut, and when she spoke I could see the caps had been knocked off her two front teeth.

"She actually looks worse than you do, Gideon," Hillary said, closing the door. "Remember me, Joan? The one you were going to shoot down in cold blood?"

"What do you want?"

"Information," I said. "A name, that's all. But I don't think you can give it to me."

"Then what're you doing here?"

"Lisa knows the name. Where is she?"

"Go fuck yourself."

"That's so rude," Hillary said, crossing to the bed.

"If I'd let Lisa go through with his cockamamie plan, she'd be dead now. That would've been pretty fucking rude, too, don't you think?"

Hillary sat on the side of the bed and rested her hand on the cast. "We only want to talk to Lisa. Ask her one question."

She ignored Hillary, turned to me. "I hope you have liability insurance, because I'm suing you for millions!"

Hillary pulled down on the cast. Joan screamed. "I was talking to you, Joan."

"I'll sue you, too."

"That doesn't frighten me as much as looking down the barrel of that .45 did." Hillary pulled on the cast again. Another scream. "Gideon told me that they thought of everything when they designed these fancy schmancy hospital rooms," Hillary said. "State of the art beds and top notch electronic monitoring equipment. Why they even installed extra sound proofing so the patients wouldn't have to listen to anyone else's suffering. Which is good. Because unless you tell us what we want to know, you are going to suffer."

I'd never seen this sadistic side of Hillary before. I never even suspected she had one. Amazing what almost getting executed can do for you.

"Do you have any idea what happens to your psyche when you think you're facing imminent death?" Hillary continued. "I always imagined I'd see my life flashing before my eyes; bassinet to bicycle to first prom—I went with Carl Fisher, by the way, a geek by some standards but his mom taught him to swing dance and he was, like, totally awesome. Anyway, none of that happened. No reruns of my generally happy middle-class life, no great insights into the ultimate truths of the universe, no memorable last words for humanity. All I could think about was how unfair it was that I'd be killed by a skinny, self-centered bitch. Well, Joan, payback's a bitch." Hillary pulled on the cast. Joan screamed. Then, nice as can be, Hillary asked, "Where's Lisa?"

"I don't know."

Hillary looked at me. "You believe her?"

"No."

"Me, either." Another pull on the cast.

Joan screamed, and then whimpered, "Stop, please, no more."

I picked up the phone. "You don't even have to tell me where she is. Just give me the number. I'll call her from right here."

Joan's eyes went from me, to Hillary, to Hillary's hand on her cast. Hillary said, "I almost hope you say no."

A resigned sigh, then: "All right."

"Cooper. Roy Cooper. You think he's the Gravesnatcher?" Lisa asked from her suite in the Santa Barbara Biltmore.

"I think there's a good chance. You have any idea where he lives?"

"No. I haven't heard about him in a long time. His name would pop up every once in a while in the trades. There was a TV pilot a few years ago. And a movie, but I don't think it was ever released."

"Well, don't worry. I'll find him."

"That would have been me. In the car, I mean. If I hadn't run away I'd be dead, right?"

"Yes."

"Jesus. I don't feel like such a low life coward now."

"The Gravesnatcher knows you're alive, Lisa. You're still in danger."

"You won't tell him where I am, will you?"

"No. But if I thought of going through Joan, so could he. Move again and don't tell anybody where you are."

"You're scaring me."

"I'm trying to."

"Okay. If the Gravesnatcher is Roy, will you do something for me?"

"Sure."

"Kill him."

Nice Work if You Can Get It

Hillary was thrilled. “This is so cool! Would you believe I’ve lived in Southern California my whole life and this is, like, my first time on a movie studio back lot?”

Paramount, to be exact. We were on our way to Barry Winslow’s office. I wanted to know if Roy Cooper had ever worked for him, and if he had, whether they had his address.

“Oh, look,” Hillary said, pointing at the New York Street. The *Payback* crew was shooting another scene. “There’s Tornado Marshall.” The ex-boxer stood in the middle of the street; last week’s five black ninjas had been replaced by six hulking bikers toting bats and chains. One guy even had a fire axe. “Must be the final action scene,” Hillary said. “His shirt’s ripped.”

Someone called “Action,” and the six stuntmen closed in on Tornado. Punching, kicking, leaping, rolling, he took them out one by one, until he was left facing one lone survivor, a giant wielding the fire axe.

“Here it comes,” Hillary whispered.

“What?”

Hillary lowered her voice in a rough impression of Tornado. “You’ve just made a big mistake.”

Tornado put up his dukes in a classic fight stance and snarled, “You’ve just made a big mistake.”

Tornado sounded better than Hillary, but the line sounded stupid, nonetheless. The giant charged, swinging the axe.

Tornado ducked, landed a punch to the kidney, another to the belly, then—in one of his patented moves—he boxed the giant's ears with the palms of his hands. In another patented move, he finished him off with his RAT-A-TAT-TAT: a quick right, left, right, left to the chin. The biker's knees buckled and, like a giant oak tree, he went down.

"Cut, print!" the director called.

"They really say it," Hillary gushed. "*Action, cut, print.* Just like the movies!"

"This is the movies."

"TV, actually, but who's counting?"

A mixed metaphor worthy of my agent, Elliot, but I didn't say anything. Instead I scanned the dispersing crowd for a dreadlock-topped, overly pierced, 200-pound, surly black woman. I found her, just finishing a hug with one of the crewmembers. As she turned to go I called out, "Maggie!"

She saw me, almost smiled, and came forward. "Hey, shamus, how you doing?"

"Good, Maggie. The office told me I could find you on the set. Meet my secretary, Hillary Bennett."

"Former secretary," Hillary said, shaking her hand. "I'm a field operative now."

"Then we have something in common. I'm a former secretary, too."

"Of course," Hillary said. "Your boss is dead. They must be planning to shut down the show now that Barry Winslow is out of the picture."

Maggie snorted a laugh. "Shut down a top ten show? Are you kidding? Honey, this is television. Nothing shuts down the show. Not that they're heartless or anything. Tornado led a minute of silence for Barry the morning after his murder, and there'll be a special card at the end of the show dedicating the episode to him. Oh, and the crew all chipped in for a flower arrangement for the funeral. However, by ten o'clock that day the studio announced that Tornado would be taking over Executive Producer duties on the show, and that his first official act was to fire all the writers. A new writing staff starts next week, and they all have their own secretaries, so, as they say in Hollywood, I'm 'at liberty.' "

Hillary elbowed me in the side. I shot her a 'what?' look. She nodded her head toward Maggie but I still didn't know what the hell she was trying to say. Finally she just said, "Gideon and I are looking for a new secretary."

"Really? Would I get to carry a gun?"

"Absolutely not." I said.

"I don't even carry a gun," Hillary said. "But now that I think about it, I'd like to. I'm checked out on the range and everything, Gideon. What do you think?"

"No. You might shoot someone."

"Duh. Like the Gravesnatcher."

"The only one shooting the Gravesnatcher will be me. And in case you forgot, that's why we're here. So before we find ourselves a secretary, let's find him. Tell me something, Maggie, does the name Roy Cooper mean anything to you?"

"Sure. He starred in *Ramrod*, a pilot we made a few years ago. Pilot sucked, but Roy wasn't too bad." Then, amazed, she asked, "You think he's the Gravesnatcher?"

"Maybe. How'd he get along with Winslow?"

"Fine, as far as I know." Then she thought about that for a beat and added, "Though, their relationship was a little more strained than most. What I mean is, Barry would always blow a lot of smoke up the ass of any actor starring in a pilot. He wanted the actor to think he was his new best friend, so that if the pilot sold, the actor wouldn't even consider replacing him with another Executive Producer. That's how it was with these two—at first. Just before the shooting something must've happened. They were still civil and all, but none of that back slapping, best-pal-of-mine kind of shit I was used to seeing."

"You have an address on Roy?"

"Back in the office, but it's old; he may not live there anymore."

"Could you give it to me?"

"That depends."

"On what?"

"How's your dental plan?"

Meet John Doe

Nobody was more surprised than Roy. Or happier. The plan had actually worked. Three ransoms, six million dollars. Barry Winslow and David Hunter dead. Lisa shivering in her Gucci boots, Gideon and the cops chasing their tails looking for Jason Tucker.

Of course, for Roy's revenge to be complete he'd have to kill Lisa and Gideon. But no one said that had to happen now. Better to take the money and run. Kick back for a while, let the heat cool down, and let them spend night after sleepless night wondering when the Gravesnatcher would return. Wondering when it would be their turn to die.

Roy was driving North on the 405, coming from Inglewood, on the way to his apartment. He was back in his SL 550 and was listening to Jasmine sing her new hit song, "Dumped."

> See me, smile me, talk me, touch me
> Manipulate
> Prevaricate

The lyrics sucked but the song had a great beat, incredible bluesy piano riffs, and ever since Roy had seen a naked picture of the twenty-year-old redhead on the Internet, he always imagined she was standing naked in his bedroom, singing to him only.

Roy had just spent an interesting hour with a guy named

Rafe. Rafe owned a stamp and coin shop in a crappy strip mall in an even crappier part of town. But location didn't really matter to Rafe. He didn't get much walk-in traffic. In fact, he didn't get much stamp and coin traffic at all. The store was a front for his real business, fake documents. Green cards, driver's licenses, social security cards, passports. You name it. For the right price, Rafe would make it for you.

Roy knew the Jason Tucker ploy wouldn't work forever. They'd eventually tumble to him. Hell, for his plan to work, they had to. So Roy needed a new name. He worked with Rafe, trying to come up with just the right one. Truth be told, he'd never been crazy about the name Roy. Sounded soft. He'd always wanted to be a Maximilian or a Duncan or a Preston. Something with more than one syllable. He finally decided on Zachary because in the ninth grade, a kid named Zachary had the biggest dick in the locker room.

Rafe said Roy should really change his look, too. Grow a moustache or beard, dye his hair, wear tinted contacts to get rid of his distinctive green eyes. Maybe even plastic surgery. This was tougher for Roy. Like a lot of actors, he'd spent thousands of hours staring at himself in the mirror. Practicing expressions, running dialogue. And he liked how he looked. Maybe he'd try a moustache, or darker hair. But the eyes stayed. Roy couldn't even count the number of times his sexy, bedroom eyes had gotten him laid.

The new passport and driver's license cost Roy fifteen hundred dollars. A week ago, a fortune, chicken feed now. So was the first class ticket Roy booked on his cell phone as he drove away from Rafe's shop. He was flying to Hong Kong tomorrow, the first stop in his round-the-world exploration. Roy pulled off the 405 at Wilshire, headed east.

The idea of giving up acting bothered Roy. All he'd ever wanted was to be an actor. He had enough money to last a while, but he knew it couldn't last forever. He'd have to find some sort of work. Or marry someone with lots of money.

Of course, that was it! Do the round-the-world tour looking for a rich wife. And not the old, widowed type, nipped and tucked until the face looked like it was sheathed in Saran Wrap. He was thinking the forty- to fifty-year-old divorcee, the fading beauty whose husband had turned her in for a trophy wife. Hell, for enough money, Roy could close his eyes and pretend he was fucking anybody—even Jasmine.

On the radio she was singing:

> But fire turns my skin to steel
> I'm armorized
> Sanitized

Yeah, Jasmine was definitely pissed off at some poor dude. Roy usually hated the "my heart's been broken, woe is me" song. But "Dumped" had a great beat and Jasmine was so hot, he didn't mind listening to her musical whining.

Roy turned south on Veteran.

Or he could stick with acting, he thought. Using his new name and face, he could take up acting in the new country of his choice. He'd never been good with languages, so it would probably have to be somewhere they spoke English—London or Dublin or maybe Sidney, Australia. Australia wasn't that far from Hong Kong. Maybe Sidney should be stop number two.

Roy turned left onto Kelton, then braked to a sudden, surprised stop. Half a block ahead he saw Gideon Kincaid and that cute, blond secretary of his sneaking into the building's underground parking lot. There was a security gate, but someone could sneak in by waiting for a tenant to open the gate with a key card by running inside before the gate had a chance to close.

Shit! Kincaid had found him. He'd known it was inevitable, but hadn't expected it so soon. He hadn't dropped the final clues.

Roy spun his head looking for police cars. None. He cocked his ears, listening for a siren. Silence. Good. True to form, Kincaid was cowboying it. He hadn't told the cops that Roy was the Gravesnatcher.

That little mistake was going to cost him his life.

Getting To Know You

Maggie had given us not only an address for Roy Cooper, but a phone number, too. I called immediately and got a recording, "Who, what, where, when, why, how?" BEEP. Roy didn't give his name but I recognized the voice: the Gravesnatcher.

Just because he hadn't changed his number didn't mean Roy hadn't moved to a new address in the same neighborhood. So Hillary and I drove to Westwood in her Prius. I used the time to call David Hunter's office, to ask if they knew if Hunter had ever worked with Roy Cooper. The receptionist I spoke to was new and didn't know. She transferred me to Hunter's line producer, a guy named Toby. He hadn't been with Hunter too long, either, but the name rang a bell.

"Roy Cooper? I think I saw his name on this old poster for a movie called *Jailbait*. David never talked about it though. His fiancée was killed during production, a car accident, I think, so the movie was never finished."

"You know of any reason Roy Cooper would want to kill Mr. Hunter?"

"I've heard rumors about Mr. Cooper and David's fiancée at the time. And there was a confrontation between David and Roy Cooper on the back lot. I honestly don't know all the details. I'll ask around and get back to you."

"That would be great, thanks."

I gave him my cell phone number and hung up, satisfied. I'd now connected Cooper to all the victims. I had no doubt he was the Gravesnatcher.

We pulled up to the apartment building, got out and checked the names on the building's directory. There it was next to Apartment 308: R. Cooper.

Now what? I couldn't buzz his apartment, ask if he wanted to come out and play. Actually, I was hoping he wasn't home. I wanted to search his apartment for proof he was the Gravesnatcher. You know, that incontrovertible kind that got me in so much trouble in the Ernie Wagner case.

I called his number on my cell phone and got his machine again. Good, he was still out. Now we had to find a way to get in. Pushing all the buttons on the directory until someone buzzed me inside was one option—a device first used by Dashiell Hammet in *The Maltese Falcon,* by the way. Only it doesn't really work anymore; people in L.A. have become much too wary to let anyone in unless they know or expect them.

That left my favorite mode of entry, sneaking into the parking garage. The trick was not to run under the gate until the car you followed in has turned, so the driver doesn't spot you in his rear-view mirror. You stay hidden behind a car until the driver is safely in the elevator. That's what we did.

"Hillary, you wait here," I said, as we crouched behind a Ford Edge. "Call me on the cell if you see Roy Cooper pull into the garage."

"Oh that sounds like a lot of fun. Doesn't an operative, like, 'operate'? I want to sneak, skulk and search with you."

"Too dangerous."

"And keeping an eye on Lisa Montgomery wasn't? I almost had a bullet sandwich."

"Exactly my point. They overpowered you."

"There were two of them. Now there are two of us. Besides, you're going in there to find evidence, right?"

"Right."

"Well, who's going to believe old evidence-planting you? The D.A. may want a more reliable witness. Like, moi."

She had a point, and once we were in the apartment I could have her keep an eye on the corridor in case Roy showed up. Worried I was making a mistake, but not really having a choice, I said okay.

Riding up in the elevator I remembered something Maggie had said the morning I went to her house with the latte—that even though she'd worked for Winslow for years, he'd never asked her about her personal life.

How often had I asked Hillary about her personal life? Never, I realized. "This may sound like a stupid question, Hillary, but do you have a boyfriend?"

"No."

"Have you ever had one while you've worked for me?"

"I had one when I first started working for you. But we broke up about a year ago."

The elevator door opened. The corridor was empty. We started walking.

"What's with the 411, Gideon?"

"Oh, it was something Maggie said about Winslow. That he only dealt with her as an employee. That he showed no interest in her outside of work. It hurt her. She even said, 'I'm sorry he's dead but I'm not about to shed any tears.'"

"You're worried that if you die I won't, like, cry buckets?"

"No. Well, yes, kind of. I mean, we've been together two years and I'm realizing I don't know very much about you."

"You're sounding seriously sentimental. This could ruin your whole image."

We reached 308. A Baldwin deadbolt guarded the door. I knocked just to make sure he really wasn't home. No answer. I knocked again. Nothing.

A quick glance told me the hallway was still empty so I took out my picks and went to work. Fifteen seconds later, the lock clicked opened.

"You are so going to have to teach me that." Hillary said.

"Stay here in the hall until I give the all clear." I pulled out my Glock, pushed open the door with my shoulder, then spin into the room in crouched combat stance. I was in a small entryway. A living room was directly in front of me, a doorway to what I assumed to be the kitchen to the right. Quickly, I moved through each room—kitchen, living room, bedroom, both bathrooms, the two closets. Roy Cooper wasn't home.

"All clear," I called, quietly.

Hillary gingerly stepped inside. "This may be the first really illegal thing I've ever done."

"You never smoked grass? Drank booze as a minor? Rolled a stop sign or ignored a speed limit?"

"Yes to some of the above, but they are a far cry from, like, breaking and entering."

"We didn't break and enter. The door was unlocked."

"Oh, the cops'll believe that."

"It doesn't matter what the cops believe. It's what they can prove. That's why there are a hell of a lot more crooks on the streets than in the jails." Then I switched subjects. "You have a compact mirror in your purse?"

"Is this another of your getting-to-know-me-better questions?"

"No. Do you?"

"Yes."

"Take it out and prop it open in the doorway—that way you can stay inside the apartment and still keep an eye on the hall."

"Very clever," she said, putting the mirror in place. "Now what?"

"Stay there while I search."

The apartment was small, cramped and depressing. It had the ugliest couch and love seat I'd ever seen. Red plaid. What had he been thinking?

"What if he's already left town?" Hillary asked. "Taken the money and run?"

"Then I'll find out where he's gone and track him down."

"I hope he's gone to Maui. I've always wanted to see Hawaii."

That didn't even deserve an answer. I searched the living room first.

"What exactly are we looking for?"

"Proof that he's the Gravesnatcher. The ransom money, the magazines he cut up to make the ransom notes, evidence that'll link him to the two bombs, the Obama mask, the wig to make him look like Jason Tucker. Anything that can conclusively tie him to the case. I'd also like to find out if he really has a partner. And if it's a cop, who the hell it is."

I looked under the couch, under the cushions, under the chair, under the chair's cushion. I looked in the cheesy fake fireplace. Glowing electric logs? Please. The walls were filled with pictures of Roy. I figured I'd study them later. There was a DVD on top of the DVD player, the title was typed on the label, *Ramrod.* I picked it up. "This is the pilot he made with Barry Winslow. In fact, it looks like some of the DVDs I saw at Winslow's condo. I bet Roy took this when he shoved Winslow out the window."

"Want to watch it?"

"Later."

There was a huge pile of unpaid bills on the kitchen counter. I checked all the kitchen cabinets, the almost barren refrigerator and freezer, oven and microwave. Nothing.

A search of the guest bathroom and hall closet showed more bad taste but yielded no clues. The bedroom was a mess—bed unmade, clothes piled on the floor. A familiar sight in a bachelor's apartment. So was the stack of old *Playboys* on the closet floor.

Like a lot of actors Roy had expensive clothing: Polo sport coat, white Versace suit, Armani shirts. In L.A. it's not only how good you act, it's how good you look. Even if you're destitute, you've got to dress like you make twenty million a picture.

The only item of interest in the bathroom was a poster hanging on the back of the door for the movie *Jailbait*. Just as Hunter's producer had told me, there was Roy's name as star and David Hunter as producer/director. The centerpiece of the one sheet was a picture of a sexy waif wrapped in a sheet. Her smoldering eyes promised forbidden carnal delights. I vaguely remembered reading about a car crash and this young actress dying, but the details eluded me.

Then I heard it. A scream. Hillary's scream. I whirled, raced out of the bedroom as I pulled my gun and thumbed back the hammer. I followed my Glock into the entryway and saw Hillary on the ground, facing the wall, her body twisted grotesquely.

Dear God, not Hillary, too! My eyes searched wildly for Roy Cooper, but I didn't see him. Was he hiding in the kitchen? Outside in the hall?

I saw movement out of the corner of my eye. I spun back to Hillary. Had she moved? She groaned. I leapt for her, rolled her over.

"Hey, what're you doing," she cried. "I almost had it."

"Had what?"

"The bag."

"What bag?"

"Ta da ..." She pointed to the wall. There was a small air vent at the bottom of the wall. The grate was off, lying on the floor. "There's something stuck in the back of the vent. I was reaching for it, but my arm's not long enough." Then she saw the stricken expression on my face and it hit her. "You saw me on the floor like that, all twisted up ... You thought I was dead."

"I heard a scream."

"A yelp. A delighted burst of emotion when I realized I'd found his hiding place."

I got down on my hands and knees and, sure enough, I could see something stuffed in the back of the vent. It looked like a black plastic bag. I reached in, stretched out, caught the end of the backpack with my fingers and pulled. It was heavy, and jammed tightly in the wall, but inch-by-inch I worked it until I got the edge of the bag to the vent. Then Hillary grabbed hold and together we pulled it out of the wall.

It dropped to the floor like a gargantuan afterbirth. I ripped open the plastic to find stacks and stacks of used one hundred dollar bills. And there was something else sticking out from under a pile of bills. I yanked it out—the Barak Obama mask.

A very pleased Hillary said, "So that's what six million dollars looks like."

"Actually, having just packed three backpacks with two million dollars each, this looks like a lot less than six million. More like half that. He must have another hiding place."

Hillary poked her head back into the vent. "Not here. Let's see if there are any other vents in the apartment."

As she went to look I sat with the money, thinking. Now I was sure. I had proof. Roy Cooper was the Gravesnatcher. Question was, what should I do about it? The smart move would be to call Mary Rocket right now, let the cops take it from here. Since Roy Cooper still thought we were after Jason Tucker, his guard would be down. And since the money was still in the apartment, Roy Cooper was sure to return. Soon.

It would be a simple matter for the cops to stake the place out, take him when he comes back. Simple and proper.

It would also be a simple matter for me to hide out in his apartment and shoot him through the heart when he came back. I could claim self-defense and probably get away with it. But that would be wrong and immoral.

Hillary returned. "I found two other vents but didn't see anything hidden inside."

"He's probably hidden the rest of the money elsewhere."

"So what's the plan?"

"I stay here, you leave."

"Leave? Leave and go where?"

"Back to the office. I'll call you when it's over."

" 'Over' as in the cops arrive and arrest him or 'over' as in you're about to do something really stupid?"

"Hillary, I don't want to fight. I don't want to talk about signposts on the road of life. The less you know, the better off you'll be. Go back to the office. Wait for my call."

Hillary's sweet face hardened. "Oh, this is good. Living proof of Darwinism. You've evolved from wanting to maim him with a bomb to killing him with a bullet."

"Goodbye, Hillary."

"Oh, I could leave all right. But what's to, like, stop me from calling the cops? Just because I'm not here doesn't mean I don't have blood on my hands. I know you're planning to execute him. If I don't stop you, doesn't that make me a murderer, too?"

"No. Because you don't know what I'm going to do. Hell, *I* don't know what I'm going to do. I feel like killing him, but mostly I want to talk to him. Find out why he had to kill Winslow, Hunter, Lisa and me. I mean, really, Lisa kept him from getting *one* role. I took a couple of swings at him. *That's* motive for murder?"

"It is if he's nuts."

"Fine, but then I want to hear him explain his warped thinking myself. He killed Stacy. I've got to know why."

"And then you'll kill him."

"And then I'll probably kill him."

Hillary shook her head, confused. "This is all my fault. If I'd, like, stayed a secretary I wouldn't be faced with moral dilemma after moral dilemma."

"Then go back to being a secretary. At least for the rest of the day. Please."

Hillary paced, pondering. "Real life is hard. Here I've only been in the field for two days, and I'm about to turn my back on every philosophical principle and moral touchstone I believe in."

"Let me tell you about real life, my philosophical principles and moral touchstones: my passion for justice blinded me. I framed an innocent man and lost my badge. *That's* real life. I realized I loved someone I thought I hated, only to lose her forever. *That's* real life. A frustrated actor turns into a homicidal maniac. *That's* real life."

"Will killing Roy Cooper fix any of that?"

"No. But it'll make the world a safer place. It'll give him what he deserves. It'll save the taxpayers millions of dollars for his trial, appeals, and execution. And, it'll make me feel a lot better."

Hillary sagged, defeated. "I hate this but all right, I'm going back to the office."

"I'll call you when it's over."

Hillary started out the door, and then turned back to me. "You know, life really sucks sometimes."

"Tell me about it."

Plan B

"I hate this but all right, I'm going back to the office."
"I'll call you when it's over."
A pause, then: "You know, life really sucks sometimes."
"Tell me about it."

Listen to them, Roy thought, taking off the headphones, thanking his lucky stars that he had the presence of mind to plant the bug in his apartment. Those two are feeling so sorry for each other. Poor babies.

Roy started his SL 550, slipped it into gear and squealed away from the curb. It would take a few minutes for the blond to get out of the building and back to her Prius, plenty of time for Roy to get to Kincaid's office ahead of her.

Goddamn Kincaid. Roy had no idea how the PI figured out he was the Gravesnatcher. But he had, and now Kincaid sat in Roy's apartment, with all his money and most of his weapons. All Roy had with him was a couple of guns, and with Gideon waiting in ambush, Roy didn't like the odds of trying to storm his own apartment.

So it was time to improvise.

The first time Roy broke into Kincaid's office to plant the cell phone he'd been lucky. He found an unlocked bathroom window just big enough for him to slip through.

While inside he'd searched Kincaid's desk and found an extra key to the front door. It was loose in one of the drawers, with a white tag identifying it. *Probably been there for years,* Roy thought. *Kincaid will never miss it.* So Roy pocketed it.

Good thing, Roy thought to himself now, as he parked in the strip mall, pulled a gun out of the glove box, a plastic bag out of the trunk, and walked past the pet store and up the stairs to Kincaid's office. He slipped the key into the lock, unlocked the door, entered, and then re-locked the door behind him.

Now all he had to do was wait for the blonde to return. He opened the bag he'd taken from the trunk, took out a bottle of chloroform and a handkerchief. *It's an amazing drug,* he thought, as he poured the liquid onto his handkerchief. He'd only needed a little bit for that goddamn dog, but the blonde would require more. He soaked the handkerchief through and through, and then sealed it in the plastic bag.

The blonde was cute. Girl-next-door cute. Maybe he'd have a little fun with her before he killed her. He'd never been into bondage, but the thought of the blonde, stripped naked, bound and gagged, turned Roy on. *Why not,* he thought. *Hey, you only live once.*

BRRRING.

The phone startled Roy.

BRRRING.

Roy glanced at the message machine. He wondered how many times it had to ring before the machine picked up.

BRRRING.

"Hi, you've reached Imperial Investigations." The blonde's voice. "Sorry we missed your call, please leave a message. BEEP."

"Gid, baby, it's me again, Elliott. I just checked CNN Headline News, and unless they've missed the story of the decade, I assume you're still alive. Well, I've got B-I-G news. And I can summarize it in one word: Dreamworks. I know it sounds like two words, but it's only one. And what a one! Dreamworks is the hottest studio in Hollywood. And you know what makes them hot? Taste. They've got it. And do you know how I know?

Because they've made an offer for *Death of a Gravesnatcher*. I'm not sure we should take our first offer, but we're talking real money, Gidman. The kind with lots of zeros and commas. Call me!"

Who the fuck was that freak? Roy wondered. Oh yeah, Gideon Kincaid thinks he's a writer. Well *Death of a Gravesnatcher* would have to be renamed. Maybe *Death of a Two-Bit Detective* or *Death of a Washed-up Cop Turned Detective*, but there wouldn't be a book titled *Death of a Gravesnatcher*. Roy planned to live forever.

Roy heard a key in the lock. He quickly slipped behind the door, pulled out the chloroform soaked handkerchief.

The door swung open and the blonde entered. She shoved the door closed with her hip and started for her desk. Roy's plan was to sneak up behind her, wrap his left arm around her chest, and immobilize her arms while he slapped his right hand—the one holding the chloroform soaked handkerchief—over her nose and mouth. Before he could move, the blonde stopped, as if sensing Roy's presence. She turned. Her pale blue eyes went wide when she saw Roy.

Without the advantage of surprise Roy didn't think he could chloroform her. So he dropped the handkerchief, stuck his hand in his jacket pocket and pulled out a gun.

Hillary's eyes went wider as he pointed it at her.

Wider still as he shot her in the chest.

Dead and Not Yet Buried

I'd thought a lot about Stacy as I did a detailed search of Roy Cooper's apartment. It was the first chance I'd really had to reminisce, or mourn, or whatever the hell I was doing.

First of all, I told myself, she was dead and there was nothing I could do about it. I just hoped the explosion had killed Stacy instantly. I couldn't imagine being burned alive, a truly horrific way to die.

I didn't even consider the irony that Stacy wanted to be cremated. She always thought the whole idea of cemeteries and burial plots to be a colossal waste of space.

I tried to hold on to the good memories. Like the time Stacy cooked our first meal. Live Maine lobsters, but they got away, started skittering all over the kitchen, our laughing as we tried to catch them... wait a minute, that was the movie *Annie Hall*. But in my memory it was Stacy. Weird, I don't even think we saw it together.

I was sure of the memory of our honeymoon. It was our only trip out of California together, in spite of my wall full of travel fantasies. Maui. The Grand Wailea, to be more exact. Room 514 to be even more exact. Way too expensive, even on two cops' salaries, something like 700 bucks a day not counting the incredibly expensive food or ridiculously expensive tropical drinks. But it was our honeymoon, a once-in-a-lifetime opportunity, and we'd wanted to splurge.

We sunbathed, snorkeled, sailed, stuffed our faces, sipped umbrella-draped drinks and made love.

"This is my favorite place on earth," Stacy told me one night as we sat in a hammock drinking champagne, gently buffeted by the trade winds. A crescent moon dappled enough light on her face to make her appear to be the most beautiful woman in the universe. "When I die I want this to be heaven."

"Let's just make this our heaven on earth," I said in the grip of the wildly romantic tropical night. "We'll come back here every year, get the same room even, and renew our love for each other."

"Every year," Stacy said, and we kissed on it. One of those long, sweet, loving kisses you remember for a lifetime.

We'd never gone back. Our work schedules never meshed, though we kept promising we'd find a way to work it out. Down deep I think we both felt the same way about our honeymoon. We were both embarrassed by how sickeningly romantic and sentimental we'd been. The behavior was out of character for both of us, and very uncoplike. And that idiotic passion had faded. If we'd tried to recreate it, we would have failed miserably.

And there were other memories. When I found a cache of guns hidden in Roy Cooper's mattress, I thought of the time Stacy and I tied for first place in the LAPD Sharpshooter Competition. We settled the matter by driving to the desert and shooting apples off each other's heads at fifty feet. We were drunk at the time. Drunk enough to make it a *really* stupid idea. But drunken cops do stupid things all the time, just read any of the early books of the aforementioned Mr. Wambaugh. We determined the winner by whose shot was closest to dead center. Stacy won. My shot was high. Another sign of my devotion.

Funny what you remember. Like when I examined the stack of *Playboys* in Roy Cooper's closet and noticed the many words that had been cut out from various pages, cannibalized to write his ransom notes. It reminded me of our first real fight.

We'd just moved into the North Hollywood house and were unpacking Stacy's dishes, these old china abominations, with a purple and yellow flower pattern, that had been handed down by her grandmother. After we'd run out of Mayflower standard issue wrapping paper, we'd wrapped them in magazine pages, and I'd bitched the whole time about how ugly they were and that we should just throw them out.

Well, as I was unwrapping them I went into the same spiel, bitching about how hideous they were, when I accidently dropped one of the dinner plates. It shattered on the peg and grove floors.

"You did that on purpose!" she said.

"No, it was an accident. I swear."

"Bullshit. You've been bitching for two days about Grandma's plates."

"You mean *atrocities*, don't you? Grandma's atrocities!"

"What I hate is your lack of honesty. You've admitted you hate them. Now admit you broke it on purpose."

"All right, you want me to admit I broke it on purpose?" I picked up another plate and hurled it into the kitchen wall. CRASH. "*That* plate I broke on purpose."

"You cocksucker!" she screamed, picking up a stack of Grandma's salad plates and throwing one at me, underhand, like a Frisbee. I ducked and it smashed into the cupboard behind me. Then she started chasing me, and I was ducking and she was screaming, punctuating each word with another thrown dish. "I. Am. Going. To. Kill. You!" CRASH. CRASH. CRASH. CRASH. CRASH.

The last one hit me in the back of the head and actually stunned me. My knees buckled and I sank to the floor. She stood over me, reveling in my pain, and then she saw the thousands of shards that used to be her precious china. Sanity staged a comeback as she surveyed the destruction. When she realized that all the china was ruined she burst into tears and ran into the backyard.

It was pouring rain. She'd just run into a deluge. I groaned as I stood up. My head hurt like hell. I looked out through the kitchen window and saw her standing in the rain, sobbing.

To see someone I loved in so much pain broke my heart. I walked out in the rain to talk to her.

"I know they were ugly, Gideon. That's not the point. They were Grandma's. That's all I have left of her. The only thing of hers that's left."

I put my arms around her, but she didn't return the embrace. "I'm sorry," I said. "I'll find you another set. Identical. If I have to scour every flea market in Southern California."

"And Nevada?"

"And Nevada."

"Might have to check Arizona, too."

"Done and done."

She looked into my rain-soaked face. "I love you, even if you're insane."

"I love you because you're insane."

She smiled, kissed me, and then finally returned the hug.

I could almost see us standing there, like the end of some sappy movie. Standing in the rain, drenching wet, arms around each other, blissfully happy. If this had been a movie, the camera would then BOOM UP and a few seconds later the image would FADE TO BLACK.

Fade In

Roy looked at the blonde's body. She lay where she'd fallen, in the middle of the floor, arms splayed above her head, legs spread. Roy could see a hint of her white panties. He closed her legs, positioned each arm at her side. *Better,* Roy thought. *Much more dignified.*

Then Roy took the tranquilizer dart out of her chest. He checked her pulse, strong. Checked her breathing, slow and steady. Good, she'd be fine.

That was the only good thing to come out of that TV movie where he'd played a cop trying to capture an escaped lion with the help of a beautiful zoo vet. The technical consultant on the movie was a stringy, slightly horse-faced brunette, Dr. Betty Yablans. She was in her mid-thirties and had one of those smart/funny personalities that made her more attractive than she actually looked. So Roy had banged her a couple of times.

He had to use a dart gun in the movie to capture the lion. Betty brought a real one to the set for everyone to see, along with two real darts filled with Ketamine Hydrochlozide. One day, when no one was looking, Roy stole the gun and darts. But he told himself he wasn't really stealing them, he was taking them for services rendered. Dr. Betty had multiple orgasms both times he jumped her. The lousy dart gun was the least he deserved.

Roy picked the blonde up and carried her from the reception

area into Kincaid's office. He deposited her gently on the large leather couch, sat down next to her, and gazed into the angelic face. Normally, the sweet young things weren't his type. He preferred the 'slut-next-door' to the 'girl-next-door.' They were usually better in bed. Understood that sport fucking was just that, not a commitment to cuddle or read poetry to each other.

Sex had always been important to Roy, but even more so lately. The successful seduction of a woman was an ego boost. A validation. Something he'd needed more and more as his acting career had gotten worse and worse. Every time he parted the naked thighs of another willing woman Roy felt a triumphant rush. It was his own personal Academy Award ceremony and she was handing him the Oscar for Best Actor.

He'd needed the boost a lot lately. At the Viper Room and Sky Bar, where he was a regular, there was never a shortage of actress/model wannabes to take home. Roy hadn't had time for sex since the Gravesnatcher thing had started and he was horny as hell.

Roy stroked the blonde's cheek. He'd looked up Ketamine Hydrochlozide after he stole the dart gun. It was a powerful tranquilizer, sometimes sold on the street as a recreational drug called 'Special K.' It was a muscle relaxant, slowed the psychomotor responses and even caused hallucinations. Not exactly a Roofie, but damn close.

Hmmmm. He leaned down and kissed her on the lips, no response. Like kissing a corpse. He shook her a little and gently slapped her face. "Hey, wake up ..." Her eyes fluttered open, and she looked at him dully, not really conscious.

He tried another kiss, pushed opened her lips with his tongue. Nothing at first, then almost instinctively her tongue responded, softly, moving back and forth against his.

Interesting, Roy thought as he pulled away. Not exactly, mad passionate love, but it was a beginning.

His eyes traveled the length of her body, down the striped blouse, the light blue skirt to the off-white pumps. About five foot two or three he guessed, fit and trim, all the bumps and curves where they were supposed to be. It was time to see her naked.

Roy slipped off her shoes. Her toes were painted a delicate pink. He took a foot in each hand. They were soft and warm. He ran his fingers up her feet, past her ankles to her calves, felt the supple skin, the firm muscle tone. He kissed the inside of her left knee. She must've liked it; she stirred pleasantly beneath him.

Now it was time to get rid of the skirt. He rolled her toward him, undid the hook in back and pulled down the zipper. With one hand he elevated her hips, with the other he pulled off the skirt.

She had long, lovely legs with a generous spray of freckles. As Roy's fingers brushed against her thighs, goose bumps erupted in their wake. He put his face between her thighs, kissed each one, drinking up her sweet, clean smell. Then he brought his face to her panties and pressed against them. She even smelled good there, just a whiff of musk. He playfully took a little of the fabric in his teeth, pulled on it. Then lifted her hips again and slid off the panties.

Her pubic hair formed a perfect dark blond triangle. He looked closely and saw she shaved to keep it tidy. Who was she was doing the housekeeping for? Irrationally, he even felt a twang of jealousy.

Next, the blouse. He unbuttoned it slowly, pulled her arms through the sleeves one by one, and dropped the blouse to the floor. His fingers traced along her forearms and more goose bumps appeared.

The bra hooked in front. He unhooked it, then after waiting a moment for the drama to build, he pulled off the bra to reveal her breasts.

Lovely, he thought. Real, to start with. And big. Not so big they'd droop as she got older. Or would stretch with children. Big enough to overflow the hand. Big enough to hold together and bury your face in. Round pink nipples crowned the milky white skin, and no tan lines marred the visual flow.

They were perfect. This girl had perfect breasts.

Hillary's eyelids fluttered open. The world was a blur, and her body felt cold, like there was a draft in the room. Then the air stirred. The blur in front of her suddenly changed. She heard a voice, soft, friendly. "You're awake, good." The blur slowly came a little more into focus. She could tell it was a man. "How you feeling?" She tried to answer but nothing came out.

"Oh, you don't have to say anything," The voice cooed, nice as could be. "It was a rhetorical question."

The man stood and started doing something she couldn't figure out. Moving his arms a lot, reaching down like he was ... yes, that was it ... he was taking off his clothes. Why would he be taking off his clothes? Then she looked at herself and realized she was naked.

Why am I naked?

Thoughts came at Hillary like bright headlights sweeping across a windshield. There for an instant, then gone. She thought of the first man she'd ever seen nude. Carl Fisher, her high school sweetheart. She'd made him wait two years, until graduation day, to finally have sex with her. She was amazed how big his penis got, and how sensitive it was. She accidentally scratched the shaft with her fingernails while trying to put on a condom. The way he screamed, you'd have thought she'd slit his throat.

The sex was only okay. The first time he came in about ten seconds. They reloaded another condom—this time Carl put it on himself—but thirty seconds later it was over. It didn't hurt as much as she'd feared, but there weren't any fireworks either.

Hillary knew all about climaxes. She'd been masturbating since she was fourteen. Her favorite spot was in the bathtub. She slide to the end of the tub, put her vagina under the faucet, and let the water run onto her clitoris. Sometimes, that would be enough, other times she'd help a little with her finger. She was a screamer. She'd clamp a hand over her mouth so no one else in the house would hear her come.

She dated Carl through sophomore year in college. Never came once with him, but got real good at faking it.

Then there was Nick Miller, the only other man she'd had sex with. She met him junior year; he was pre-med. Until a year ago, Hillary had lived with him.

She was working for Gideon by then. Nick was in UCLA Medical School. The relationship had always been a little one-sided. Nick's passion was medicine, which left little time or emotion for Hillary. She thought her love would be enough for the both of them. She took the job in Gideon's office thinking it would just be temporary. Once Nick finished his residency and set up his own practice, she planned to quit, get pregnant, and raise a family.

Hillary never had an orgasm with Nick, either. She'd been honest with him from the start. Told him Carl had never made her come. So Nick guaranteed her that he would. Easier said than done. They tried Missionary position, doggy style, Hillary on top, side by side. They bought a Kama Sutra and twisted themselves into all sorts of shapes. His tried his fingers, his tongue, vibrators, Ben Wa balls, pornos. Nothing. "Don't worry, baby," Nick said. "I'll never give up."

But of course he did give up. What man wants to make love to a woman again and again, knowing he can't get her off? Soon the calls started coming, "Honey, I've still got a lot of work to do at the library; don't wait up." Then the credit cards charges to fancy restaurants like Bouchon Bistro and Crustacean. "Just business, sweetie, you know, dinner with my pal Jack Huston." Then Hillary found a smear of lipstick on his collar. Picked up the aroma of strange perfume on his jacket.

He was having an affair. It was her own fault, she realized. If she'd just faked her orgasms like every other woman in the world Nick never would've strayed. She was still trying to decide what to do when he came home one day, told her he was in love with another woman. Jack Huston turned out to be Janet Huston, and he asked Hillary to move out.

Hillary had decided that being Nick's wife and mother of his children was going to be her occupation. So when he dumped her she lost more than a lover, she lost a career.

That's when she started thinking seriously about becoming a PI. She spent a lot of time studying Gideon, watching what he did, how he worked. And she felt sorry for him. He had more ghosts than *Poltergeist I, II*, and *III* put together. He was also good, not just at what he did but also as a person.

She wasn't exactly sure when it was she fell in love with him, but in love she was. And she knew he never thought of her that way. Hell, he probably thought she was nothing but a kid. But the age difference wasn't that bad. He was forty, she was twenty-five. Not May-December, more like May-October. Perfectly acceptable. And that's why she wanted to be a real PI, not a secretary. She wanted to be in the field with him so he would realize she wasn't just a kid. So he would realize they belonged together.

But there was another problem. Stacy. Hillary knew long before Gideon realized it that he was still in love with her. She could tell by the diatribes he'd go into. The horrible stories he'd relate. He might have been complaining, but there was always a hint of affection coming through. And now she was dead. A martyr. How could she ever compete with that?

She was so confused. Where was she and how'd she get there? Couldn't remember. What was the last thing she remembered? Couldn't remember the last thing she remembered. That struck her as funny.

The smell of the couch was familiar. Gideon's couch, she realized. She'd napped there a few times, always found it very comfortable. She felt the couch sink, fought her eyes open, and saw the out-of-focus man sitting next to her. Her eyelids, which seemed to weigh a hundred pounds, banged shut again.

If this was Gideon's couch, could the man be Gideon? The man kissed her lips. Yes! It must be Gideon. At last, he's realized I love him. She tried to kiss back but her body wasn't taking orders. His lips left her lips, moved to her chin, her neck. She felt his tongue dart into her ear. It tickled, felt good.

Don't worry, Gideon, I'll fake an orgasm for you. You'll never feel inferior.

His hands were on her breasts, kneading, a little harder than she liked. Then his mouth was around her right breast, sucking, his tongue nibbling on her nipple. She felt it harden. A lovely tingling, then ouch! He was biting her.

Gently, darling Gideon, gently.

He climbed on her now, spreading her legs with his knees. She'd hoped for more foreplay, wanted this moment to last.

What's the hurry, Gideon?

She wanted to see his face, watch the ecstasy as they made love. She concentrated all her energy into her eyelids, willing them to open. They did. But Gideon was still out of focus. She concentrated her energy again.

Focus, damn it, focus!

She did. Hillary found herself looking into the fiendish face of Roy Cooper. And Hillary screamed.

Shit, Roy thought, clamping his hand over the blonde's mouth, stifling the scream. She'd been so wonderfully compliant just a second ago. She must've been hallucinating early and had finally returned to earth.

No matter. The rest of her body was still slack. Her mind may be back but her muscle control wasn't. She couldn't fight back. Her legs were spread, and he was rock hard. Just a quick thrust and he'd be home.

But then he looked into her eyes. Saw the terror. The horror. The plea: *Don't rape me, dear God, please, don't rape me.*

And he remembered how he felt when he'd been raped. The humiliation. The shame.

And that's when he knew he couldn't do it.

His sank back on his haunches, signaling the end of the attack.

Roy saw the relief in the blonde's eyes. The look of gratitude.

But if she thought she was out of danger, she was woefully wrong. Because as insane as it sounded, even though Roy couldn't rape her, he was still going to kill her.

Demons and Dragons

A close-up of Roy Cooper filled the television screen. Sweat glistened on his tanned face, blood oozed from a cut above his hazel eyes.

RAMROD

I'm no saint. Sure I risk my life every day for God and country. Spill my blood for people I don't know. But that comes with the territory.

I was watching the TV pilot, *Ramrod*. The angle switched to a gorgeous Island girl. The trade winds played in her silky, black hair, and her big brown eyes stared adoringly at Ramrod.

ISLAND GIRL

But you saved my life. Can't I do something to thank you?

RAMROD

That look in your eyes says it all. That look that says, 'my hero.'

The music swelled and Ramrod walked into the sunset.

Oh, please, I thought, snapping off the TV. Another corny TV hero. No wonder it never got on the air.

Why did TV heroes always have to be hunks who looked like

Roy Cooper? There are tens of thousands of real life heroes, brave men and women who risk life and limb every day as cops, soldiers and firefighters. Folks who are too short, too tall, too skinny, too fat, too ugly, too ethnic, too this and too that to ever get cast by Hollywood. But these real life heroes look death in the eye every day to save total strangers.

It takes guts. And a few loose screws.

I know. I used to be one.

When I was a cop I saved eight lives I knew about. Each time I did it, I hoped that I'd spared someone the crippling grief I felt as a ten-year-old boy.

I never came right out and said I was a hero. But I knew it inside. And yes, as bad as that scene from *Ramrod* was, I could often see it in other people's eyes. And it felt good.

I miss that. Strapping on a gun every day to fight evil. And that's what cops do, make no mistake about it. There is evil in the world. It carries knives and guns and bombs. It wants to kill and maim. Rape. Steal. Plunder. It's real. And it is a thin blue line indeed between us and them.

Which side was I on now? Prowling around an apartment trying to decide how to kill a man. I thought about the other men I'd killed. Not counting Roy Cooper, the number was ... zero.

I'd shot at a few and missed—a bank robber fleeing a Chase branch on a Harley, a carjacker who tried to run me over in a stolen Lexus, a gangbanger taking pot shots with an M16 on a Compton street corner. I'd also shot at and wounded a few: I hit a hot prowl burglar in the thigh as he held a woman hostage in a Holiday Inn lobby, I hit a junkie in the shoulder as he threatened a terrified pedestrian with a syringe filled with AIDS-tainted blood, I hit a rapist in the knee as he tried to slash me with a butcher's knife.

In each case I was trying to kill them. And I'm a good shot. Moral: it's a lot harder than it looks to actually shoot someone in high stress situations. However, I thought, this was more like an ambush than a shootout, so I didn't anticipate having too much trouble hitting him.

I was still bothered by the cold-blooded murder part of it, though. Not very heroic. But whenever my resolve weakened, I thought of Stacy's scorched, mutilated body.

I prowled some more, stopped in front of the collection of pictures on the living room wall. Roy's life, arranged in chronological order from left to right. Baby pictures to Little League team photo, along with a newspaper article announcing Roy Cooper as the team's MVP, to a grammar school play, *Grease*. He'd starred as Danny Zuko, of course. To high school productions—*Man of La Mancha, Oklahoma, West Side Story*—always starring, always at the center of the cast picture with his arm around the prettiest girl. To his college triumphs—*Othello, Amadeus, Jesus Christ Superstar*. Just a quick glance at these early years showed the transformation from a cute kid to an attractive adolescent to really handsome man.

But great looks and a dime still leave you two dollars and fifty cents short of a cup of coffee at Starbucks in Hollywood. There are thousands of high schools in this country and each one does a production of *Grease;* the hunky kid who played Danny Zuko invariably comes to Hollywood figuring he's going to be the next Matt Damon. So it takes more than great bones to make a living acting. The chronology on Roy's wall showed that his high hopes had crashed and burned.

Roy had a promising beginning, with guest shots on *CSI: Miami, Grey's Anatomy, Lost, Nip/Tuck,* and there was a picture of him with a lion from something called *Claws of Death.*

Then there was a shot from *Ramrod*—Roy in scuba gear, standing next to a smiling Barry Winslow. I wondered what could have happened on that shoot for Roy to sentence Winslow to death.

Next were a few more television shows—*Cold Case, Dexter, V* and *Castle*. Then came an 8x10 from the movie, *Jailbait*. That nymphet from the poster stood between Roy and David Hunter. Hunter had his poodle, Jennifer, tucked under his left arm and his right arm wrapped possessively around the nymphet's shoulder. Roy and Hunter were looking into the camera, smiling. But the girl was looking adoringly at Roy. Interesting. Hunter's arm is around her but she's only got eyes for Roy. I didn't know what put Hunter on Roy's hit list, but I was willing to bet this doe-eyed waif had something to do with it.

That's where the pictures ended. It looked like he never worked again after *Jailbait*.

A career gone awry. So far off course that Roy decided that four people had to pay for his failure with their lives. It was a good thing all failed actors didn't go postal when their careers went bust or this town would be corpse city.

I heard a sound from the hallway. I spun to the door, my Glock aimed at the door.

I heard a key dig into a lock. I cocked my gun. Then I heard a door squeak open—not Roy's door, the door across the hall. "Jill, honey, it's me, I'm home," the voice called, then I heard the door close.

My heart was hammering in my chest. Adrenaline scorched my veins. I lowered the gun, collecting myself.

This cold-blooded murder stuff was harder than I thought. I began to wonder if I could actually do it. Put a bullet in an unarmed man.

I wasn't worried about going to jail for his murder. I fully intended to put a gun in his dead hand and claim self-defense. So why were my hands shaking?

Because I'm not a murderer, I realized. If I executed Roy Cooper I would be no different than the Gravesnatcher. No different than Ted Bundy, John Wayne Gacy, Jeffrey Dahmer—all those sick, perverted serial killers. No different than the gangbangers who shot complete strangers as an initiation. No different than the predators who roam the streets looking for children to slaughter. No different than the SOB who had shot Mom and Dad.

Epiphany. I still wanted to be a hero. Heroes didn't murder people.

I was glad I got it before I pulled the trigger. There's nothing worse than a bolt of enlightenment a second *after* you've changed your life forever.

Hillary would be happy. I'd stood in front of that signpost on her infernal Road of Life and made the right decision.

Okay, so now what? I was in Roy Cooper's apartment, surrounded by incontrovertible evidence that he was the Gravesnatcher. If I wasn't going to blow him away, I might as well call Mary Rocket and let the cops arrest him.

I started for the phone on the kitchen counter when I noticed something. A trash can in the corner of the room. I realized I never checked the trash, always fertile ground for clues. Hell, just ask Roy, that's where he got my credit card number.

I had all the proof I needed that he was the Gravesnatcher. But I still hadn't nailed down anything to point to a partner. So I dumped out the small living room trashcan. A couple cans of beer, a month old *Maxim* magazine, some junk mail. The kitchen trash was just trash. Same went for the trash in Roy's bedroom. But I hit gold in the bathroom. Hidden at the bottom, wrapped in an old tee shirt, was a small cassette tape. An answering machine tape. What the hell was it doing in there, I wondered. I hurried back to the answering machine, swapped tapes and hit PLAY.

> You were right. Kincaid's an imbecile. You should've seen his face when I hauled him in. Later, partner.

Holy shit! I'd recognize that whiny fucking voice anywhere: Piccolo!

If I had my choice of two-timing backstabbing traitors, it would've been Piccolo.

He must've called Roy after he dragged me into the station and we listened to the Doggieworld tape. He dragged me in even though he knew I wasn't guilty. It was certainly a great way to draw suspicion away from himself.

Then it hit me. The greatest irony of all. I had warned Stacy and Mary Rocket about the leak in the department. I had told them to tell nobody, not even Piccolo, that Stacy would be doubling Lisa.

If Piccolo had known, they never would have planted that bomb.

If Piccolo had known, Stacy would still be alive.

BRRRING.

The phone rang. I could pick it up, but what if it was Roy Cooper calling his machine to check for messages?

BRRRING.

I tried to remember how many times it rang before the machine picked up.

BRRRING.

Four, I thought.

BRRRING. "Who, what, where, when, why, how?" BEEP. "Kincaid, it's Roy Cooper. I know you're in there."

Oh shit, I thought, picking up the phone. "Hello."

"We've got to stop meeting like this."

"It's over, Roy. I found the money, all the evidence. The only smart choice you've got left is to turn yourself in."

"You're the one with only one smart choice. Bring my money to the Hollywood sign at midnight tonight or I'll kill the little blonde."

"Hillary?"

"I've got her, Kincaid. Or should I say I've had her. Kissed her sweet lips. Sucked her milky white tits. And unless you're there at midnight, with all my money, I'll cut her fucking throat." CLICK. He hung up.

That son of a bitch!

Fuck. I had to do something. I wrapped up the plastic bag full of money thinking that it I never should have let Hillary go back to the office alone. I should've anticipated Roy Cooper might've seen us as we entered the building. I should've kept Hillary with me, where she'd be safe.

I ran down the hallway, the sixty pounds or so of the money pounding me on the back.

Irony again. If I hadn't planned to kill Roy Cooper I wouldn't have sent Hillary away. If I'd just called the cops, Hillary would be safe now.

I took the fire stairs to the first floor. The exit opened onto Kelton. I ran for the street, then stopped when I realized I didn't have a car. My Taurus was toast, and Hillary had driven us here.

Shit.

It was almost six o'clock. The sun was making a beeline for the horizon. And I wanted to make a beeline for the office. Not that I thought Roy Cooper and Hillary were still there. But if they were, if there was any chance I could rescue her now, I had to try.

But I couldn't walk there.

Then, I saw a possible solution. A young couple walked out of an apartment building across the street. They were blond, athletic and attractive, probably actors, or models. They were dressed for tennis and carried rackets. They tossed the rackets in the back of an old red Fiat convertible.

"Excuse me," I called running to them, the black plastic bag slung over my shoulder like some bizarre Santa Claus. "I need to borrow you car. Police business."

The guy looked at me skeptically. "Let me see your badge."

"It's in my other pants."

"Then forget about it." They quickly got into the convertible.

"Wait," I pleaded. "It's an emergency."

The girl was freaked. She pulled out a cell phone. "Get away from us before I call the police."

"Tell you what," I said. "I'll buy the car from you." I reached into the plastic bag, pulled out a stack of hundreds. "Here's ten grand. This piece of shit's not worth half that." He stared at the money, turning it over, checking to see if it was real. "It's genuine, trust me." I threw him three more stacks. "Here's thirty grand more. Go buy yourself a Mercedes."

He must've liked that idea because he flashed a perfect smile. "Mister, you just bought yourself a car. Come on, Pam." They climbed out. I climbed in, dumping the plastic bag in the passenger seat. I started the car.

"Wait!" he screamed.

"Okay, whatever. How much more do you want?"

"No, the money's fine. I want our rackets. They're still in the back seat." He grabbed them. I jammed the car into first gear and peeled out.

I broke them all. Traffic laws, I mean. Speeding. Failing to signal. Illegal passing on the right. Reckless driving. Failure to stop at a stop sign. Failure to stop at a traffic light.

Failure to protect the only person left on earth who still cares about you.

I called the LAPD trying to find Piccolo but was told that Captain Rocket had given him a leave of absence to mourn.

This was bad and getting worse.

I squealed into my parking lot at 6:28 and hurdled the steps two at a time. My knees ached with the added weight of the money. My office door was open. I barreled through the door, dropping the money and pulling my gun. A quick sweep of the office told me what I already feared; they were gone.

Questions bombarded me. How could this have happened? Where were they now? Where would he hole up until midnight? What would he do to her until then? What had he done to her already? Had he really raped Hillary or was he just torturing me?

Something caught my eye, a pair of white panties sitting in the middle of my couch. Hillary's panties.

That son of a bitch.

Now what? What was I supposed to do until midnight? The question was answered for me by a voice at the door. "Hello, Gideon."

I turned and found myself staring at Jason Tucker. The former stalker, current escaped convict was holding a .44 magnum and pointing it at my heart.

I'd actually forgotten all about him. Once I'd eliminated Jason Tucker as the Gravesnatcher, I'd never given him another thought.

In the words of Rick "Tornado" Marshall: Big mistake.

"I'm not the Gravesnatcher."

"I know."

"Good." He gestured with the gun. "Turn around."

I did. Then I felt the barrel of the gun smash into the back of my skull.

Then I felt nothing.

Afternoon Delights

"How you feeling?"

Hillary said nothing.

"Can I get you anything? Soda? Taco? There's a Jack in the Box next door."

Hillary shook her head. It was the only part of her body she could really move. Muscle control had returned as the effects of the Ketamine Hydrochlozide had worn off. But her arms were tied to her side and her ankles were taped together.

Roy stood by the window of the small room in the La Siesta Motel on Ventura Boulevard. It was a weather-beaten '50's remnant, with individual cottages, XXX movies and a primarily short-term-stay business. Like an hour, or less. Luxurious it wasn't, but it was close to a Hollywood Freeway on ramp and a convenient place to hang out until it was time to head for the Hollywood sign.

After calling Kincaid, Roy had put the blonde's clothes back on. Some muscle control had returned so he slung her left arm over his shoulder and walked her to his car as if she was drunk. The drive to the motel had been short, uneventful, and punctuated only by an occasional sob.

Roy looked at the blonde on the bed. She was pretty even when disconsolate. He knew she was afraid of him. Probably hated him. But he wanted her to understand him. If she knew what he'd been through, how Hollywood had raped him, she'd realize he wasn't a soulless monster. He crossed the room, sat on the bed. She recoiled, squeezing herself against the wall to get as far away from him as possible.

I repulse her, he thought, saddened. But if she only knew the truth. "I'm an actor, you know."

Her pale blue eyes ignored him.

"You ever see me on TV?"

Hillary shook her head.

"I've acted here, at this motel in an episode of *Quicksilver*. I was holding this girl, Izzie, hostage in this very room, and after a lot of back and forth with a hostage negotiator, I dragged Izzie to the parking lot at gunpoint. Cops were everywhere and SWAT sharpshooters were on the roof.

"And that's where I had this fabulous death scene. A SWAT guy shoots me. Mortally wounded, blood gushing from my chest, I dropped to my knees and looked at Izzie, plaintively. That's the word the script used, *plaintively*. Don't you love that word? *Plaintive?* It sums up that miserable, forlorn feeling so perfectly. You've probably never felt that way, but let me tell you, I have. Well, I was plaintive and then some.

"Anyway, we shot the show three years ago but I still remember my final speech. Every plaintive word. Every plaintive inflection."

Roy dropped to his knees in the middle of the motel room, recreating the blocking for his climatic scene.

"I'm sorry, Izzie. Sorry I stole your heart, only to break it. Sorry I made promises I couldn't keep." Roy broke character and said, "Next the director asked me if I could cry. I said, 'Left or right eye?' 'Left eye,' he said, sure I was full of shit. So, exactly on cue, a tear dropped from my left eye and I said, 'Sorry we'll never share another sunrise.' "

Roy slumped to the floor of the motel room, and with a tiny shudder, went still. Then he looked up at Hillary. "The whole crew applauded my death scene. Can you imagine? Battle-scarred veterans, applauding."

Hillary watched Roy's performance, dumbfounded. First

he'd tried to rape her; now he was trying to impress her. What was with this guy? Actors, they were all alike. Emotional children always crying out, "Look at me!"

What the hell does he want? For me to tell him what a good actor he is? After he almost rapes me! After he kidnaps me!

Easy now, she thought. Focus. *We've got to survive. Figure a way out of here.* She'd heard his call to Gideon. Knew they'd be meeting him at the Hollywood Sign. She also knew that Roy Cooper would kill them after he got his money. He'd killed Winslow and Hunter. Killed Stacy.

She was fighting for her life now. Gideon's life. Let the rage come later. She had to focus. Find a way to get untied. Find a way out of this room. And the first step was to give this sick bastard what he wanted. A compliment. Tell him how good an actor he was, but make it believable. So she said, "I'm not a battle-scarred veteran, but I thought you were good, too."

Roy looked at the blonde, trying to read her face. "You really think so?"

"Yes."

Simple, direct. Roy decided to believe her. "I really thought that guest shot would lead to my big break. I mean, I've got the chops to be a star. I could be Brad Pitt, Ben Affleck, Johnny Depp. I'm that good. I can cry from either eye!"

"How come?"

"How come what?"

"How come you don't get those roles?"

"Because everyone's out to get me. This nerdy director told me that the first week I came to town. 'Guys like me love to get even with guys like you.' That's what he said to me. Why? Because I was handsome. Why? Because I was popular. Why? Because I got all the girls. 'Well, tough shit, nerd boy,' I thought. 'I've got the goods and I'm going to be a star.'

"He did give me some decent advice, though. He said to train, study, work. And I did work. Got some decent gigs. Then I got my first real break, a TV pilot. *Ramrod* ..."

He trailed off as he remembered his rape by Jerry Marshall. Roy looked at Hillary, suddenly filled with compassion. He knew how she must feel. He'd felt that way. Violated. Humiliated. Shamed.

Hillary sensed the sudden empathy, was confused by it. But decided to use it. "Something happened while you were making *Ramrod*?"

"What? Oh, no." Roy shut his eyes tightly. "No. I was great but the show wasn't. Story of my life."

"Something must've happened. You killed Winslow."

"Oh, yeah, well, when the pilot didn't get picked up Winslow blamed me, not his dumb script." Hillary could tell Roy Cooper was lying but let it go.

Roy continued. "So, more acting classes, more workshops, more guest shots, then a big break. Starring in a feature film."

"*Jailbait*."

"How'd you know?"

"I saw the poster in your apartment."

"Of course. Great, isn't it? I love that look in Tiffany's eyes. So innocently wicked, just like she was."

"What happened to her?"

"Killed in a car crash. The police called it an accident. I know it was murder."

"Murder?"

"You know the saying, 'You're not paranoid if everyone is out to get you'? Well, listen to this. *Jailbait* was a great script. Tiffany and I were great together. It was going to be a big hit and make me a big star. But David Hunter loved Tiffany. Was engaged to her. Tiffany and I had this chemistry, it was combustible, and … well, let's just say we had a thing. Hunter found out, shut down the movie, probably killed Tiffany and spread rumors all over town that I had a drug problem."

"Trying to ruin your career."

"He did ruin my career. After that, no one would touch me. My career was over. What was I supposed to do, become a professional waiter? Clean swimming pools? Stock shelves at Ralph's? I've got the chops. I'm as good as Pitt, Affleck and Depp. I can cry from either eye! But my career was over. It wasn't fair!"

Hillary figured it was time to use a little psychology. "David Hunter deserved to die."

"You really think so?"

"Absolutely. He killed Tiffany. Killed your career. He had it coming. And Lisa Montgomery is a total bitch. Gideon told me what she did to you, keeping you off that movie. No wonder you wanted to dust her."

"Spiteful shrew."

"Tell me about it," Hillary said. "You know what she did to me? How's putting a gun in my face and tying me up ..."

Hillary trailed off as her eyes went to her bound hands and feet. Then she looked at Roy, who was also looking at her hands and feet. Chagrined, he met her eyes.

"Sorry about that, but I can't have you running away now, can I?"

"If you untie me, I won't run away."

"You won't?"

"No. Not if you promise that after Gideon gives you the money you'll let us both go."

"I will let you go. Promise."

She searched his face. "I believe you. And if you untie me, I won't run away. Promise."

He searched her face. "I believe you." Roy's face softened. His fingers went to work on the ropes.

Hillary smiled gratefully. She tried to gaze into his green eyes with the naïve devotion of all the captivated women who must have been bedazzled by his looks and charm. But behind Hillary's pale blue eyes a plan of attack was forming. A kick to the balls to disable him, fingernails into the eyeballs to blind him, the palm of her hand smashed into the bridge of his nose to kill him. Her karate teacher, Chang, had taught her these moves. She hoped they worked better than the ones she'd tried in her fight with Joan Hagler. Of course, if she could get Roy's gun, she could just fire a warning shot between his eyes and be done with it. But where had he put it? Hillary's eyes searched the room.

Meanwhile, Roy was busy with the ropes. The knot on her left wrist was stuck. As Roy twisted a fingernail between the tightly tied strands to get it started, he thought about her hands. Long and slender, well-manicured nails painted the same pale pink as her toes. Pretty. He wondered what they'd feel like caressing his chest. The knot finally gave, he pulled the rope through the loop and the ropes dropped from her hands.

"Thank you," Hillary said rubbing them together.

Roy took her hands in his, looked at the deep rope burns. "Sorry, I didn't realize they were so tight."

She met his gaze evenly. "That's all right. But my ankles, they're taped very tightly, too."

"Sorry." Roy bent over, digging into the tape. She could tell he was getting excited again.

Hillary spotted butt of a gun sticking out the windbreaker Roy had draped over the chair. If she could get off the bed she could reach it in two, maybe three steps. Two, maybe three seconds. No time at all. She just needed a little diversion.

"There," Roy said, pulling the tape off Hillary's feet.

She rubbed her ankles. "Ah ... Much better, thanks."

Roy brushed a few strands of blond hair away from Hillary's face. "You are a beautiful woman."

Does this freak actually think I would sleep with him right now? I know actors are self-absorbed, Hillary thought, but please ... "Thank you," she said.

He continued to stare into her eyes. It was a practiced stare, honed by years of successful seductions, as focused as a laser. It said, *You are the most desirable woman in the world. I want you with all my heart and soul. I'll fulfill all your fantasies.*

Okay, she thought. He does have remarkable eyes, and oozes sex appeal. But what twit would fall for this shit? It makes me want to puke.

He leaned forward for a kiss. *Uh oh, now what?* Their lips

met, his mouth opened, his tongue searched for hers. Gross! The tongue tango began. Hillary wanted to bite down, put her incisors through the tip of his tongue, but she fought back the urge. She needed that gun. Patience. The opportunity would present itself.

She felt his hands slide up her side, cup her breasts. Her instinct was to stiffen, but she fought it. He'd know this was all a ruse. She had to act like she was enjoying it. She tried to pretend he was someone else. Carl? No, he was never that good a kisser, stiff lips. Nick? No, he dribbled. Gideon? She felt herself instantly relax. *Yes, Gideon. Dear, sweet, Gideon.* When he starting asking all those personal questions back at Roy's apartment she almost said what she'd wanted to say to him for months now. *I love you.* But she didn't have the nerve. *Well, when this is over I'm going to do it. I'm going to tell him how much I love him.*

Roy Cooper's hand slipped under Hillary's blouse, and he fingered her nipples through the bra. *Shit,* Hillary thought. *I better think of something, fast.* Then she did. "Wait," she said, finishing the kiss. "Wouldn't this be more fun like, naked?"

He gave her a rakish smile. "Naked. I like naked." He stood up, slowly unbuttoned his shirt, putting on a strip show for her.

Jeeeesus! He is such a cliché.

He dropped the shirt to the floor. His chest was hard and tan, and he had a great six pack. On anyone but a homicidal maniac she might find it attractive.

He bent over to untie his Nikes. The bow on the left sneaker became a knot. He had to use both hands to undo it. Hillary knew this was her chance.

Springing from the bed, she reached the windbreaker in two swift steps. She pulled out the gun, whirled back toward Roy Cooper, and centered the cross hairs over his breastbone.

That's when she knew she was in trouble. There were no cross hairs. It wasn't a real gun. It was the dart gun. And it was empty.

Roy looked at her like a disappointed teacher. "You promised you wouldn't try to escape."

Hillary wasn't going to stand there and discuss it. She threw the gun at his head and bolted for the door. Ducking the weapon with ease, Roy launched himself at Hillary's back and grabbed her shoulder just as her fingers reached the doorknob. They slipped off as he slammed her into the ground.

Hillary tried to scream but Roy cut it off by wrapping both hands around her neck and choking. He squeezed so hard Hillary was afraid he'd break her neck.

She kicked her feet and pounded on his back, but as the oxygen left Hillary's brain her blows became weak, ineffective.

My self-defense classes really suck, she thought. I'm going to fire Chang.

Then she passed out.

Deadman's Curve on the Road of Life

I woke up in the trunk of a car. It was pitch black. My head hurt. My hands and feet were hogtied. A gag was stuffed in my mouth. The road was bumpy and a cannonade of rocks and pebbles battered the undercarriage. We were on an unpaved road somewhere. Going fast. I twisted my arm to get a look at my watch: 9:25.

This was bad. Every rotation of the tires brought me farther from the Hollywood sign. I had no doubt that Roy Cooper would kill Hillary if I didn't show up. I had no doubt he'd probably try to kill Hillary even when I did. Her only chance was for me to be there, not on this dirt road to oblivion. So this was really bad.

What I didn't understand is why Jason Tucker hadn't already killed me. What did he want? Where was he taking me?

Well, with any luck I'd never find out. If I could just get this gag off I might be able to gnaw through the ropes. I had good teeth. The rope felt very thick, however, so it might take a while. Did I have any other choice?

Once my hands were free, then what? How would I get out of the trunk? They never covered that in private eye school. How hard could it be? All I had to do was find an old tool in the coal black trunk, grope blindly for the trunk's latch mechanism and somehow pry it open. After that I would just leap out of a speeding car onto the rock-strewn road. If not killed or maimed by the fall, I'd crawl off into the night, borrow or steal a few million dollars and limp up to the Hollywood Sign in time to save the day.

Piece of cake.

Fortunately, I never got to implement my brilliant plan, because at that moment the car rocked to a stop. I heard a car door open, gravel ground under foot, a key engage the trunk lock, and the lid pop open.

Jason Tucker stood there, a grin on his face. "Have a nice ride?"

I tried to say "fuck you" but the gag reduced my words to an incomprehensible garble.

Another man joined us. He was taller than Jason Tucker, six one or two, but twice as wide. *Huge* to be more specific. Fat as a pig to be even more specific. With a pug nose and pock-marked face. A tattoo of a skull adorned his bald head.

"Here he is, Rhino," Tucker said, proudly. "The scum bag who sent me to prison."

"Thith is going to be fun." Rhino lisped as he pulled me from the trunk and tossed me to the ground. A cloud of dust swirled as I hit and felt the breath knocked out of me. As I struggled for air I noticed we were parked in front of a dilapidated cabin surrounded by pine trees and scrub oak. Not a bad spot to spend a weekend getaway, but a shitty place to die.

"We got a bonus," Tucker announced, opening the passenger door and pulling out the plastic bag full of cash. "Money. Lots of it." Tucker dumped the bag over my head. Stacks of hundreds rained down.

Rhino circled me. "You've been a bad boy, thaying all thoth thingth about Jason being the Gravethnacher. All thoth lieth. I'm afraid we're going to punith you." A buck knife flashed in his hand. The blade caught the moonlight as he slashed at me. I flinched, closing my eyes, waiting for the pain to come. None did. Then I looked down to see he'd only cut the ropes. "Thtand up."

I did. Tucker pulled the gag from my mouth. "You know why you're here?"

"You wanted me to meet Rhino before you turned yourself in?"

"He'th funny, Jason."

"Yeah, I remember that from the trial. A real smart ass. Well, when we finish with you Kincaid, you won't have much of a sense of humor left."

"Look, Jason," I said, as reasonably as possible. "Let's not overreact here. *I* never said you were the Gravesnatcher. The police leaked that story. And you have to admit, the timing of your escape couldn't have been worse."

"I didn't escape. I was released."

"By mistake. When you don't turn yourself back in, they call it escaping."

"Semantics."

"Fine, whatever, but the point is, you are not the Gravesnatcher. If you turn yourself in you'll finish your term and be out in a couple of years. Stay MIA, they'll tack on five more."

"He'th not going back. Ever."

"If you know I'm not the Gravesnatcher, how come my picture's still on TV and all the newspapers?"

"I haven't had a chance to tell anyone else."

"How long have you known I'm not the Gravesnatcher?"

"Since this morning."

"And you haven't told anyone?"

"I've been busy."

"Jathon'th life'th on the line and you've been buthy?"

I looked at Tucker. "Who exactly is he?"

"Rhino saved my life in the joint."

"He was being gang-raped by some athholth. I thet them thtraight."

"Rhino got out six months ago. When they set me free, I called him."

"We're betht buddieth. And we're going to thkin you alive."

"If you kill me, who's going to tell the police you're not the Gravesnatcher?"

"Who says I want anyone to know? I'm famous now." He kicked some of the money. "And, thanks to you, rich. Rhino and I can filet your ass, then skip the country and live like kings."

"Wait a minute. You're saying you *want* people to think you're a cold-blooded murderer?"

"It beats being a stalker. And I like having my picture in the paper."

"It'th Jathon'th fifteen minuteth of fame."

"Technically it's Roy Cooper's fifteen minutes of fame," I said. "But the hell with it. I give up."

"Oh, pleath, thtruggle a little or it'll be no fun."

There was a rustling in the trees. A voice called out from the darkness. "Well now, isn't this a pretty picture?" The three of us spun in the direction of the voice, which sounded familiar. "Put your hands on your head and get down on your knees."

"Fuck you," Rhino said, pulling out a Baretta and snapping off three quick shots into the trees.

"Hard to hit what you can't see, isn't it, fatso?" The voice called back. Then a shot rang out, hitting Rhino in the right shoulder. The Baretta tumbled to the ground as he dropped to his knees, groaning in pain.

Jason Tucker reached for the gun. A bullet ricocheted off the Baretta. Tucker pulled his hand back. The voice again: "Put your hands on your head and get down on your knees." We did. A moment later the shooter stepped out of the forest. Piccolo.

"Lucky thing I was headed for your office, Kincaid. I happened to see Jason here driving away, so I followed."

"You scumbag," I said, trying to get to my feet. Piccolo kicked me in the face. I went down.

Piccolo surveyed the three of us on the ground. "This is almost too good to be true. I've caught the Gravesnatcher and his two cohorts red-handed."

So Piccolo had it all figured out. We'd take the fall and he and Roy would get the money. "It'll never work," I said, spitting out a mouthful of blood. "I know the truth. I've got proof."

"Proof? What proof?"

Rhino spoke before I could answer. "Excuthe me, but I think I may be bleeding to death.

Piccolo looked at him. "What's that, Bluto?"

"I need to get to a hothpital."

Piccolo mocked him, sing-songing, "I need to get to a hothpital. Here, let me see that wound." Piccolo reached out with a finger, tenderly inspecting the gunshot, then suddenly jammed his finger into Rhino's wound. The man screamed.

Rhino's agony must've been too much for Tucker because he suddenly leapt to his feet and charged Piccolo. Piccolo spun toward him, leveled the barrel at Tucker's chest and fired.

A hole the size of a fist blew out of the center of Tucker's back. A mist of blood, flesh and bone filled the night. And, like a puppet whose strings had been severed, Tucker toppled to the ground.

"Holy thit," Rhino mumbled. Now he launched himself at Piccolo. Piccolo fired as Rhino charged, hitting him in the hip, but the big man just wrapped his arms around Piccolo and slammed him to the ground.

As they wrestled, I scooped up Rhino's discarded Baretta and leveled it at the ball of bodies rolling over and over in the stack of hundreds. They were having a tug of war over Piccolo's Glock. Piccolo's finger was still in the trigger guard, but Rhino had forced the barrel toward the cop; the muzzle was pointed at his face, so Piccolo couldn't fire. Meanwhile, Piccolo was trying to aim the gun back at Rhino, but Rhino was too strong.

They rolled toward me and the gun went off again. The bullet whizzed by, just missing me but blowing out the window of Jason Tucker's car.

So much for standing around and waiting for them to kill each other. I had to do something. What? I could shoot them both, but that seemed a little cold-blooded. I could shoot the gun out of their hands, but that only worked in old, bad westerns. I could jump in the car and hightail it to the Hollywood sign, but I needed the cash and they were still wallowing in it.

Another gunshot made the decision for me. They were facing in the opposite direction, so I didn't know who got shot. I knew someone had, because all the wresting had stopped. No one moved for a long beat; then Rhino rolled off Piccolo, eyes wide open, dead.

I aimed at the back of Piccolo's prone body, waiting for him to come after me. But he didn't move. *Maybe he's dead, too,* I thought. Maybe Rhino had gotten control of the gun and shot Piccolo with the last vestiges of his strength, then died of blood loss. Or maybe Piccolo was playing possum, waiting to get the drop on me.

I aimed at the ground a foot from Piccolo's head and fired. ZZZING. He didn't move. I aimed two inches from his head, fired. ZZZING. Nothing. With the back of his head in my sights I inched up to his body. His eyes were open, staring lifelessly into the night. Blood covered his chest. *Thank God,* I thought, lowering my weapon, *he's dead.*

And that's when he shot me.

He'd hidden the gun in the folds of his jacket. The blood was Rhino's, rubbed onto Piccolo during their fight.

I realized this as the force of the bullet spun me around and knocked me on my ass. *My left arm,* I thought dully, not really feeling any pain yet.

Piccolo leapt to his feet and fired at me again before he was really ready, missing high. That gave me one chance and I took it. I snapped off a shot, hitting him in the face. He was dead before he hit the ground.

The Price of Fame

Well, I'd finally killed someone.

It was a righteous shooting, as they say. Self-defense and all that. I wouldn't have to wrestle with the guilt of a first-degree murder. But it still felt a little weird. And to be honest, as much as I hated Piccolo, I would much rather have captured him alive and turned him over to Mary Rocket.

As I climbed to my feet my arm began to throb. I looked at it. Not bad, little more than a nick really, but it was bleeding profusely. I pulled out my shirttail, ripped off a strip at the end and wrapped it around the wound. I was tempted to hunt around inside the cabin for a first-aid kit but I didn't want to take the time. A glance at my watch told me it was ten-fifteen. I only had an hour and forty-five minutes to get to the Hollywood Sign. But first I had to collect all the money, much of it now soaked in the blood of three dead lunatics.

Incredible, I thought as I hurriedly tossed the stacks of hundreds back into the plastic bag. If Piccolo hadn't driven by my office just as Jason Tucker was putting me in his trunk, I'd be dead. Tortured and murdered by Tucker and Rhino.

Had some greater power sent Piccolo to my office at just the right moment? Was there a script we were all following and didn't know it? Was life just a giant *Perils of Pauline* with God standing behind the megaphone? Would I get Hillary off the tracks in time?

Stop it, I thought, still throwing money into the plastic bag. There is no Fate. We make our own Fate. God didn't make me plant that evidence against Ernie Wagner. That was my own stupidity. God didn't make me sleep with Lisa Montgomery. I did that on my own, thank you very much. If there were such a thing as Fate then you'd have to go back to Mom and Dad's murder to trace the depths of the plot. And to what end? What possible good would the hardening of my soul have to do with the Fate of the World?

Stop it, I thought, the plastic bag now more than half full. The loss of blood and the adrenaline hangover were making me nuts. What happens to me has nothing to do with what happens to anyone else. And who says there's a God in the first place? What kind of God would allow the death and destruction that plagues our world?

Unless ... Unless I had been put on this earth for one specific purpose. To save Hillary. Why? Who the hell knows? Maybe she was destined to give birth to a kid who would cure cancer, or make contact with extraterrestrial beings, or find the missing link. If there was a Fate, maybe the Hollywood Sign was my destiny. My Holy Grail.

My Holy Grail? *Now I know what a nervous breakdown feels like,* I thought, tossing the last of the money into the bag. I've managed to take a typical spiral of everyday, albeit tragic fuck-ups and turn them into Celestial conspiracy. I dropped the bag into the trunk of Tucker's car and climbed behind the wheel. Thank God, the keys were still in the ignition.

As I drove down the dirt road I kept an eye out for Piccolo's car. If he'd driven his unmarked police car I would've been able to stick his bubble on the roof and hit the siren. No such luck. I couldn't find it.

Wind blew through the shattered rear window, but it was scented with pine trees and reminded me of Christmas. Three miles later I reached a highway, but which one? Where the hell was I? How far from Hollywood? And more to the point, which way should I turn, right or left?

Left was uphill. Right was downhill. I turned right. Two miles later I saw a sign telling me I was on Route 2, the Angeles Crest Highway. Half a mile later another sign told me I was sixty-eight miles from L.A. It was almost ten-thirty. Shit, getting to the Hollywood Sign by midnight was going to be tough. I barely had time to make it. I pushed the speedometer past eighty and prayed for no cops.

I heard the first siren as I transitioned from the 210 to the 5. The blue and red flashing lights reflected in my rear-view mirror. If I stopped for the ticket I'd have to explain the blown out window, the bullet hole in my arm, the recently fired gun in my pocket and the millions of dollars of bloodstained money in the trunk. I'd be thrown in jail and Hillary would be thrown to the wolves. So I did the only thing I could, I floored it.

A second Highway Patrol car joined the pursuit a couple miles later. Then a third. I realized I was about to become L.A.'s latest high-speed chase, televised live to the Southland's salivating millions. Soon the TV helicopters would be overhead and the parade would follow me all the way to the Hollywood Sign. I had to do something. I dug the cell phone out of my pocket, dialed quickly and hit SEND.

BRRRING.

Please be there, I prayed.

BRRRING.

I know it's late, but the shit's flying and a good cop would still be at her desk.

BRRRING.

"Captain Rocket."

"Mary, thank God, it's Gideon."

"I'm not talking to you."

"You've got to talk to me."

"I've been trying to talk to you. All day. I must've called ten times but kept getting your goddamn machine."

"I've been busy."

"Doing what … Is that a siren I'm hearing?"

"Three, actually. I'm the subject of a high speed chase, but if I stop Hillary will die."

"Is she with you?"

"No. The Gravesnatcher's got her."

"How'd Jason Tucker get her?"

"Not Jason Tucker. Roy Cooper. Jason Tucker is dead. "

"Who the fuck is Roy Cooper?"

"Look, I'll be happy to explain as I drive, but can you make a call to the Highway Patrol and tell them to call off the chase?"

"I can't do that."

"You've got to do that. If I pull up to Roy Cooper with a police escort he'll kill Hillary. Her kid is going to cure cancer. We've got to save her."

"Want to run that one by me again?"

"Forget about the curing cancer part. I've been shot and I'm not really thinking clearly."

"Shot? Who shot you, Jason Tucker?"

"No. Piccolo. But—"

"Piccolo? Is he with you now?"

"No, he's dead, too."

"What?"

"And a guy named Rhino that Piccolo called Bluto is dead, too."

"Gideon, are you all right?"

"No! Mary, please, I'll tell you everything, but call the Highway Patrol!"

"I hope I don't regret this. Andrea," she called. "Get me the Highway Patrol Tactical Ops line. Now, Gideon, start at the beginning."

"Would that be when my Mom and Dad were murdered or when I realized the Gravesnatcher was too tall?"

"How would your Mom and Dad's murder have anything to do with any of this?"

"That depends. Do you believe in Fate ...?"

Hurray for Hollywood

"Stars above and below us. Where do you think there are more? The sky or Hollywood below?"

Roy and Hillary were at the base of the Hollywood Sign. They were above the city lights and had a spectacular view of a star-studded sky. There was only a sliver of a moon, but it cast ample light on this crystal clear night.

"I know, I know, there are billions and billions of stars in the sky, far more than Hollywood's churned out. And both kinds have a lot in common. They're fun to watch. They're hot. They'll eventually burn out. Hey, that's almost profound. What do you think?"

He didn't expect an answer. After all, the blonde was unconscious. Had been since he'd almost choked her to death. He had to admit he'd gotten a little carried away. There was an unexpected thrill from having his hands around a woman's throat, especially when she passed out and he knew that he had her life literally in his hands. He'd continued choking her until she'd started to turn blue. Then he'd released enough pressure for her to breathe. He watched as her color came back, and then choked her again. Amazing. Blue, pink. Blue, pink.

Finally he began to worry he might be doing permanent damage and stopped. He didn't feel any pity, though. She deserved it. She'd broken her word. Tried to escape. Tried to kill him, for Christ's sake.

But he figured he better get to the Hollywood Sign before she tried any more mischief. Once again he pretended to walk a "drunk" Hillary to the car and put her in the front seat with him, her head on his shoulder. In case she woke, he re-soaked the handkerchief in chloroform.

She did, once, as they were driving up Mount Lee on the way to the parking area above the Sign. He pressed her face into the handkerchief and seconds later she was back in dreamland.

As Roy stood on the dirt trail in front of the Hollywood Sign he remembered the first time he'd come here. He'd just moved to town and was so excited. He was taking what he was sure were his first steps to fame and fortune. Standing at the foot of the sign, he said a little prayer. *Please, God, make all my dreams come true.*

Over the years the sign became a touchstone for him. He came to celebrate when he got his first guest shot, when he was cast in *Ramrod* and *Jailbait*. He also came to mourn. When *Ramrod* wasn't picked up. When Tiffany was killed.

The years had turned his excitement to cynicism. The view that had once exhilarated him now mocked him. The dream had become a nightmare. His prayer had remained unanswered.

Soon he'd have a new view. Hong Kong, Sidney, London, Paris.

A new beginning.

Roy heard the sound of an approaching car, the engine straining to come up the final steep grade on top of Mount Lee. Roy looked at his watch: 11:58. Kincaid was right on time.

The Beginning of the End

Mary Rocket had driven a hard bargain. In exchange for pulling the Highway Patrol off my ass, I had to tell her where I was meeting Roy Cooper. I told her he'd kill Hillary if the cops showed up, and she understood that. So she promised not to have the police helicopters arrive until twelve-fifteen. By then, either the Gravesnatcher or I would be dead.

"So, where are you meeting him?"

"The Hollywood Bowl," I said. "Center stage at midnight." Okay, I know what you're thinking. Dummy. Why lie to her? You might need the help by twelve-fifteen. True. But I might still be talking to Roy Cooper and the sight of the choppers could be all he needed to freak out and kill Hillary.

"The Hollywood Bowl," she repeated, skeptically. "Gideon, we've danced that dance before."

"Exactly why you should know I'm telling you the truth. Only an imbecile would lie to you twice." Guilty, as charged.

"All right. We'll be there at twelve-fifteen. And Gideon, good luck."

"Thanks." Even if I survived Roy Cooper I was going to have an irate LAPD Captain to deal with. I couldn't worry about that right now. Right now the task at hand was to rescue Hillary.

The Hollywood sign stretches 450 feet across the side of Mount Lee. The letters are made of corrugated steel and are fifty feet tall. Originally built in 1923, the sign used to read:

HOLLYWOODLAND. It was a promotional gimmick for a housing development. But the sign fell into disrepair until the Hollywood Chamber of Commerce came to the rescue and had it rebuilt in 1978.

The sign is not easy to get to. You have to take Beachwood Canyon to Ledgewood and then snake around the winding streets to Deronda. More twisting and turning until Deronda dead ends at a gate. The gate is chained and locked by the Griffith Park Rangers. Nothing a pair of good bolt cutters couldn't handle. That's apparently what Roy Cooper had used, because when I got there the gate was wide open.

I followed the cracked, pothole-ridden asphalt road through a series of switchbacks until I got to the top of Mount Lee. The city has an array of communications equipment on the peak, and the view from there is a breathtaking, unobstructed view of both the city and the valley.

I'd only been here once before, when I was in Homicide. A gay couple who'd discovered they had AIDS had made a suicide pact, hanging themselves from the letter Y and W. The Chamber of Commerce did a remarkable job of keeping it out of the papers.

I pulled into the parking area on top of Mount Lee and parked next to an SL550. Roy Cooper's, I presumed.

Taking the plastic bag out of the trunk, I carried it along the cyclone fence to the path leading the hundred or so feet down to the Hollywood sign. "Hello," I called.

"Right on time," Roy Cooper's disembodied voice called back from the sign. "Come on down."

There wasn't much light and the path down was steep. I took a few careful steps, then slipped on some loose gravel and started to slide. For a panicked second I was afraid I was going to slip right off the mountain, but I managed to grab onto the letter H and come to a stop. I turned to find Roy Cooper standing in the middle of the path in front of the sign. He held two guns, a Colt .9mm pointed at me and a Sig Sauer .38 pointed at Hillary. She was next to him, eyes closed, curled up at the base of the letter W. She looked asleep, or dead. I was enraged to see her looking so vulnerable. "If she's hurt I'll kill you."

"You do realize how pitiful that sounds under the circumstances."

"Is she all right?"

"A little groggy, a little worse for the wear, but she'll be all right—unless I have to shoot her." His eyes went to the plastic bag. "Is that my money?"

"Yeah. All of it."

"Good." He noticed my bloodstained jacket. "What happened to your shoulder?"

"I ran into a little trouble getting here. Nothing I couldn't handle." I know, that sounds like a lame line from a Bruce Willis action movie, but it's the kind of things tough guys say in life and death situations. "So, are you going to keep your word? The money for Hillary?"

"Absolutely. I've had all the fun I want with her. But not with you." He cocked the. 9mm. "Throw me your gun."

"I didn't bring one."

He pressed the barrel of the Sig into Hillary's forehead. With the pressure of the muzzle, her eyes blinked open, and she looked around, disoriented. "One more lie and I blow her brains out. Now throw me your gun."

I knew he was serious. I dug the Baretta out of my jacket pocket and tossed it to his feet.

"Now the other gun. And don't even try lying. You wouldn't have come here without a second gun."

I sighed. So much for surprises. I lifted my pants leg, unholstered the .38 I had hidden there, and tossed it next to the Baretta.

Hillary was starting to regain her senses. Seeing me, she visibly brightened. "Gideon ..." As she took in the situation her expression clouded. "Oh, God ..."

"Good," Roy said. "You're back from the dead. I wanted you to see this." He turned back to me. "Now kneel down."

This was not good. I saw his expression: stone-cold-killer eyes. He was going to execute me. Just like I'd been planning to execute him. What would Hillary call it, karma?

He cocked the gun and pressed it into Hillary's forehead. "I said, kneel!"

"Gideon, no," she whimpered.

I knelt.

Roy yanked the Sig away from Hillary's head and in five long strides was standing in front of me. He placed both guns against my forehead.

"You know who got the role opposite Lisa in *Heaven Sent*? Jack Stone. You know who became a star instead of me? Jack Stone. Every time Jack Stone stars in another movie, I think of you. Every time the gossip columns talk about Jack Stone's latest girlfriend, I think of you. You humiliated me in front of Lisa. In front of all those other actors. No wonder she didn't cast me in the movie. I should have starred in *Heaven Sent*, not Jack Stone. I should be a big star. I should be in the gossip columns. But I'm not, because of you."

Behind Roy, unseen by Roy, Hillary had pulled herself up on her hands and knees. During his tirade she had inched slowly toward my discarded guns. But she was still too far away; I had to keep Roy talking. "I had nothing to do with Lisa's torpedoing you," I said. "She was getting even with you for college. For the way you dumped her."

"I didn't dump her. You have to be going out to get dumped. Be in a relationship. We only went out once."

"You seduced her, Roy. Popped her cherry. Broke her heart."

"Hey, it was just a fling, a one night stand."

Hillary's fingers were only inches from the Baretta. I said, "Isn't it amazing how two people can share the same event? For one, it's momentous, for the other, inconsequential."

"It's not my fault she got obsessed."

"Maybe not, but it cost you *Heaven Sent*, and that may have been the final straw on this descent into hell of yours. Think of it, your pathetic career may have its roots in that one selfish act of seduction." Christ, now I was even dealing him into my Celestial conspiracy theory.

"Kind of a strange time to get philosophical, isn't it, Kincaid?"

Tell me about it. Must be the stress or blood loss. Maybe both. But it had bought Hillary enough time. She wrapped her fingers around the Baretta's pistol grip. Just one final bit of distraction ... "Don't you believe that some Master Plan's at work? That everything's predestined? That we are at the mercy of Fate?"

Hillary lifted the gun, swung the barrel toward Roy. Having caught the movement out of the corner of his eye, he wheeled and kicked the gun out of Hillary's hand. It flew over the ledge and into the night. Next he picked up Hillary by the blouse and hurled her into the letter W. Her head smacked into the corrugated steel and she crumpled to the ground like a rag doll.

I went for the second gun. Just as my hand made contact, Roy kicked it away. I looked up into his craggy face, the demented green eyes. Putting both gun barrels against my forehead, he said, "Say goodbye, asswipe." I closed my eyes.

BANG. BANG.

I felt nothing. No searing pain. No heavenly choir. *That's weird*, I thought. I opened my eyes.

Roy had this funny expression on his face, and two holes in his chest. His eyes rolled into the back of his head and he collapsed, dead.

Someone had shot him, someone behind me. I turned around to find his killer standing there, holding a smoking gun.

Stacy!

The Middle of the End

"You're alive?"

"You always were perceptive, Gideon. That's what made you such a good cop." Stacy kept the pistol pointed at me as she picked up Roy's two guns and tossed them over the ledge.

"But I saw you blown up in the car."

"No, you *heard* me blown up. I sent you back to get my purse, remember?" She grabbed hold of the plastic bag full of money and pulled it towards her, possessively.

"Then who ...?"

"A five foot nine homeless woman who haunted the 101 exit ramp at Van Nuys with a sign that said: Won't You Help a Starving Christian?"

"Both you *and* Piccolo were working with Roy?"

"Just me."

"That's impossible. I found a tape in Roy's apartment. Piccolo called him."

"Piccolo called *me*. At home. Left the message on *my* machine. I brought the tape to Roy's. We planted it in the bathroom, knowing the cops would eventually find it. Roy also called Piccolo from the Zoo parking lot and left a message on Piccolo's home answering machine, just in case we needed more evidence to frame him."

"Piccolo was just a patsy ..."

"That's right. We knew you or the cops would eventually realize Roy, not Tucker, was the Gravesnatcher. It wouldn't take a genius to figure out Roy had to be working with someone, so we needed a fall guy."

Son of a bitch. I'd thought Piccolo was in on it. I assumed he admitted it at the cabin. But as I thought back I realized that all he'd said was, 'I've caught the Gravesnatcher and his two cohorts.' I just assumed he was going to frame and kill us. When I told him it'd never work, that I had proof, I never got to explain, because that's when the shit had hit the fan.

That's when the pieces starting coming together, the little inconsistencies that had been bothering me.

Why had half the money been missing from Roy Cooper's apartment?

Stacy had the other half.

How had Roy Cooper, an actor without any military training, fashioned the dog collar bomb and the car bomb?

He hadn't. Stacy, with three years in Army demolitions, had done the job.

How had Roy Cooper known Jason Tucker's IQ?

Stacy had pulled his file and Roy Cooper had read it.

How had Roy Cooper known to cut the back out of the backpack and avoid the letter bomb?

Stacy had warned him.

Why had Stacy left her purse by the bench?

To lure me away from the car so they could blow up the double.

Just then Hillary moaned. Groggy, she sat up and looked around. Her eyes saucered open when she saw Stacy standing over Roy Cooper's dead body. "Aren't you supposed to be dead?"

I was so relieved to see Hillary conscious that I started to crawl toward her. Stacy shoved the gun in my face. "Don't move," she scolded.

Hillary frowned. "I have this horrible feeling you're not here to rescue us."

"No," I said. "She came to kill her partner. Why scrape by on three million when you can have all six, eh, Stace?"

"How about a little gratitude? He was about to aerate your skull. I saved your life."

"It wasn't exactly a humanitarian gesture, now, was it? You weren't saving my life; you were only delaying my execution. You wanted to make sure I knew you'd made a fool of me first. You wanted to make sure I knew you were Roy's partner."

"That's right. I wanted you to know just how big a schmuck you really are."

"Fine. I'm all ears. Let me have it."

"I was in the Sugar Shack three months ago feeling sorry for myself. I'd been passed over for promotion, again. As I had been ever since you got kicked off the force for planting that knife. So I'm sucking on a Cosmopolitan, wishing I were rich enough to quit and move to Maui, when the bartender turns on the TV and a Lisa Montgomery movie comes on. That one where she plays a race car driver."

"*Bittersweet Agony*," Hillary said.

"Whatever. There's this big close-up of Lisa and I mutter, 'Bitch,' just as the guy next to me mutters, 'Bitch.' We look at each other, surprised. So we start talking."

"He tells you how Lisa ruined his career, you tell him how Lisa ruined our marriage, and you both decide to get even," I said.

"When he mentions Winslow and David Hunter," Lisa went on, "I start seeing dollar signs. Figure we can raise six million in ransoms, divided by two is three million—reason to retire from deadendsville."

"Then you did a little checking and found out Winslow was broke."

"That's right. Roy solved that problem. While he was making *Ramrod*, Winslow made him read the three books he'd written. Roy remembered *Eternal Love* and came up with the idea of kidnapping Christine."

"You knew I'd follow that trail to Winslow. "

"Yep."

"Roy snatches Hunter's dog, you make the dog collar, and everything's going according to plan until Piccolo starts shooting up Magic Land."

"He can be such a jerk sometimes."

"But you were dating him."

"It beat hanging out in single bars. And he was in love with me. Took care of me."

"You do know he's dead."

That surprised her. "He is?"

"It's a long story, but suffice it to say Jason Tucker made a belated, unexpected entry into the proceedings. Piccolo died in a bloody shoot out."

Her eyes dropped to my wounded arm. "He shoot you?"

"Yep."

"You kill him?"

"Yep."

She shrugged. "C'est la vie." But she couldn't hide the flash of regret behind her eyes.

"Speaking of Jason Tucker, how'd he fit into the picture?"

"A lucky accident. Three weeks ago Folsom called with a FYI about his accidental release. I just happen to be the one to answer the phone. With Jason Tucker on the loose, I realized I could set him up as the logical suspect and keep anyone from looking too closely at Roy's connection to all the victims."

"You leaked his name to the press and everyone assumed he was the Gravesnatcher."

"Exactly."

"But why'd you fake your own death?" Hillary asked.

"It wasn't part of the original plan. The original plan was simple: Gideon and Lisa go to the zoo, Roy plants the bomb, Gideon and Lisa are blown to kingdom Come. Roy and I split up the money, he disappears. I wait six months or so, then quit and retire to Hawaii with my safe deposit box full of cash. But I was afraid the spoiled bitch would chicken out. So I paid Gideon a visit, just in case."

"And softened me up so I'd push to get you back on the case."

She quoted herself. " 'What if I were to tell you that spending so much time with you the last few days made me remember how good we were together.' God, I can't believe you bought that line. And Roy thought *he* was a good actor. I don't know how I kept from throwing up when I had to kiss you."

Humiliation, good. I knew there was an emotion that had been missing from this evening. Stacy continued. "So when Lisa did bolt, I saw it as an opportunity. If I was dead I could start my vacation six months early."

"But you needed a body."

"Five dollars and the promise of a hot meal got the homeless woman into my car. Chloroform kept her there. Special Operations did my hair and make-up for the Lisa Montgomery transformation, but I'd brought my own dress. One of two that had been purchased the night before."

"The homeless woman was dressed in the other."

"Roy was parked in the lot when you and I drove into the zoo. While we walked up to the gorilla cage he put the starving Christian in your passenger seat. When you went back for the purse, Roy made sure she'd never go hungry again."

"You killed Barry Winslow, David Hunter, and an innocent homeless woman."

"Don't forget Roy Cooper," Hillary added.

"And Roy Cooper. How could you have traded every moral value you ever had for money?"

"Don't lecture me about morals, you hypocritical bastard. You traded your morals to frame an innocent man."

"But I thought he was guilty. I thought I was doing the right thing."

"You weren't. He wasn't guilty! And even if he had been, would planting evidence have been moral?"

"Yes. Legal, no. Moral, yes. Unlike your murders. Legal, no. Moral, no."

"Don't get self righteous with me. This is all your fault to begin with."

"My fault?!"

"You knocked over the first domino, Gideon. When you planted that knife in Ernie Wagner's closet. That was the start of the chain reaction. Ernie gets killed. You're forced to resign. My career is ruined by association. I get disillusioned. I meet Roy Cooper. Your fingerprints are all over his soul, too. We bond and plot our revenge. Don't you see, Gideon? If you'd never planted that knife, Ernie Wagner, Barry Winslow, David Hunter, Piccolo, the homeless woman and Roy would still be alive. It was your one goddamn *moral* act that started this Greek tragedy."

Wow. Now even Stacy was hooked into my Celestial conspiracy theory. Even scarier, it was starting to make sense.

Unexpectedly, Hillary chimed in: "If you're an advocate of Predestination, Stacy, I should warn you that its philosophical validity is a hotly debated topic. I mean, it, like, completely eliminates free will and the laws of natural science as mitigating circumstances. Let's take your domino analogy—"

"Let's not," Stacy snapped. "I don't give a shit about Predestination, fate, karma or destiny. My life sucked, and now it's going to be great. I've got six million dollars and—"

"Three million," I interrupted.

"Six million." She tugged on the bag. "This three million and the three million I've got stashed in a car equals six million."

"You didn't really think I'd give Roy the money until I was sure Hillary was all right? The plastic bag is full of newspaper. Not money."

Stacy looked dumbfounded, then her face cleared, a canny smile playing on her lips. "Oh, I get it. This is a trick to buy time. Forget it, Gideon," she said, untying the plastic knot on top of the bag. "I'm not falling for it." Stacy pulled open the bag.

The explosion was bigger than I expected. Stacy was catapulted back, screaming. Her hands were gone, pulped by the explosion. Blood gushed out of the ragged stumps that had been her wrists. Her face was bleeding, shredded by shrapnel, and her hair was singed and smoking.

My other surprise of the evening. The letter bomb I had made for the backpack that Roy had so thoughtfully returned. I had swung by the office on my way to the zoo and put it in the plastic bag.

I clambered over Roy's body to Hillary. She was dazed; her face had a couple of cuts, nicked by flying debris. Like a child waking from a nightmare, she threw her arms around me, desperately clinging. "You okay?" She nodded, her face buried deep in my shoulder.

And as I held Hillary, rocking her gently, I watched the life ebb out of Stacy. She lay in a pool of her own blood, but the writhing had stopped. The blood just seeped out of the stumps at the end of her arms, her heart too exhausted to pump any harder.

Then she died.

THE END OF THE END

"There's something I have to tell you. I love you."

"Cut it out."

"No, I really do."

"Stop it, Ernie, or I'm going to find another agent."

"But this is better than I ever hoped for. We've got sex, kidnapping, murder, betrayal, double-crossing, triple-crossing, gunfights, bombs, bodies ... Gid baby, you are so hot that your fame's been extended to a full thirty minutes. Now start writing."

"Yes, sir," I said and hung up. I was at my desk in my office. Hillary sat on the couch, sifting through a mountain of phone messages.

It had been only three days since "The Great Hollywood Massacre," as the *L.A. Times* had dubbed it, and a lot had happened.

After Stacy died I dug out my cell phone and called Mary Rocket. "This better be good, Gideon," she said, "because I'm in a helicopter circling the Hollywood Bowl, along with two other choppers full of SWAT team members, not to mention the twenty-five black and whites I've got on tactical alert, and I don't see anybody. Now, I can't believe you'd be stupid enough to lie to me again, so I am hoping, I am praying, I am counting on all my lucky stars that you are hiding backstage, or under a seat or in the goddamn bathroom, but that you are, for a fact, here at the Hollywood Bowl."

"Hollywood Bowl? I told you the Hollywood *Sign*."

"You son of a bitch."

"No, I'm sure I told you the Hollywood *Sign*. You must've misunderstood me."

"All calls to my office are recorded. Shall we check the tape?"

Oops. "You know, it doesn't really matter whose fault it was. Bowl, *Sign*, the important thing is, it's over. I've got the Gravesnatcher. I mean, Gravesnatchers."

"Gravesnatchers? As in, more than one?"

"As in *two*. You'd better bring some PR people. You're going to need some spin control." *Big time spin control.* Think about it. Stacy, one of the lead detectives in the Gravesnatcher Task Force, turned out to be a Gravesnatcher.

We stood around on Mount Lee all night trying to find a way to spin it. There wasn't one. Mary Rocket also spent a lot of time ranting and raving, threatening to lock me up forever. If you added together all the traffic laws I'd broken, threw in Obstruction, Collusion, Aiding and Abetting, Reckless Endangerment ... well, you get the idea. I was in serious trouble.

Until Hillary solved everyone's problems: "What if Stacy died a hero, killed by Roy Cooper while she was trying to save Gideon and me? No one has to know she was a Gravesnatcher."

"What about her 'death' at the zoo?" Mary Rocket asked.

"A clever police ploy to trick the Gravesnatcher."

You could see the light bulbs go off on all the LAPD spin-doctors. There were encouraging mumbles of:

"Good."

"I like it."

"Could work."

Hillary wasn't finished. "Of course, for Gideon and me to live such a huge lie, we'd need to have some sort of accommodation."

"What sort of accommodation?" a wary Mary Rocket asked.

"You drop all charges against Gideon. He's hailed as a hero, too. Which he is, by the way." She turned to me. "Thanks for saving my life."

"Thanks for being worth saving."

"Hold it, Kincaid." Mary Rocket said. "There is no way I'm letting you walk!"

"Hey, don't yell at me, Captain. This is all Hillary's idea. If you want to send me to jail as your last official act before you are humiliated before the entire world and forced to resign by an embarrassed department, fine by me."

Mary Rocket thought about it for a few beats, then grumbled: "All right. Stacy died a hero." Sticking a finger in my face, she added, "But you are officially on my shit list."

I may have been on Mary Rocket's shit list but I was on a lot of other people's *hit* list. When we got back to the office the phones went crazy. We got calls from TV reporters, newspaper writers, magazine journalists, and movie studios, wanting to buy rights to our stories.

Also a ton of calls from potential clients. As Elliot said, nothing like a little 'publicity, murder and mayhem' to boost business. The phones were so crazy, in fact, that Hillary and I couldn't handle them. We had to hire Barry Winslow's former secretary, Maggie, to help us.

Hillary and I have been spending a lot of time together. Work at the office. Dinner afterwards. Always platonic. We'd been through so much lately that just being together has been helping us both to heal.

I've often wondered what happened when she was with Roy Cooper—if he had raped or abused her in any way. She hasn't mentioned it. I haven't asked. She is in pain, though, I can tell.

And there's something else on her mind. More than once she's come into my office and said, "There's something I want to tell you." When I ask her what it is, she hesitates and says, "Never mind."

I'm not going to push her. I figure she'll tell me when she's ready.

"Gideon," Maggie said, sticking her dreadlocks into my doorway. "Lisa Montgomery is on line one."

From the couch, Hillary shot me a surprised look.

I hit a button, putting the call on speakerphone.

"Hello, Lisa. I'm here with Hillary."

"Hi," Hillary said.

"Hi, guys. I just called to let you know how happy I am that you're okay."

"Thank you," I said.

"And Hillary, I owe you *such* an apology. Can you ever forgive me?"

Hillary frowned, no doubt still angry. But she took a breath and said, "No worries, Lisa. I know you were totally freaked out."

"If it makes you feel any better, I fired Joan Hagler."

"How'd she take it?" Hillary asked.

"She's suing me."

"Figures," I said. "By the way, a lot of studios are calling. They want to make this whole thing into a movie."

"I know. I've been talking to a couple people at Fox."

"Hillary's been playing this game, trying to figure out who should play us."

"Robert Downey, Jr., or Bradley Cooper for Gideon," Hillary said. "And I'm thinking Rachel McAdams or Amanda Seyfried for the pretty secretary with the heart of gold."

"But I guess we all know who'll play Lisa Montgomery," I said.

"Actually," Lisa said. "My part was too small. All I did was run away. I was hoping to play Stacy."

We laughed.

"Seriously. Gideon, Hillary," Lisa said. "I'm glad you two are okay and I'm so relieved this nightmare is finally over. You guys are my heroes." With that she hung up.

Heroes. Funny, I didn't feel much like a hero. Too many innocent and not-so-innocent people were dead.

But Lisa was alive. And now she could have Hudson King's baby whenever she wanted. Hey, maybe her baby would cure cancer …

"Gideon," Hillary said, pulling me out of another insane reverie. She was pointing at her watch. "Time to go."

"Right," I said, getting up. "We can't keep the lady waiting."

The lady was Christine Cole. Hillary and I picked up her remains and returned them to Alex Snyder.

Hillary and I watched as Alex and Bernice placed Christine's remains back in her crypt. There was no ceremony. It was just the four of us. But, standing there, I imagined what it must have been like in 1967. Hundreds of reporters, photographers, police and fans mobbed outside the gates as Alex played "Yesterday," and thirty-five grief-stricken mourners said farewell to one of the biggest stars in the world.

She's an even bigger star today. An icon. She is an inspiration to thousands of actors and actresses—like Roy Cooper—who flood Hollywood every year.

And she is a poster child for the terrible price that some must pay.

"On behalf of Christine Cole fans everywhere," Alex said, "thank you."

"You're welcome," I said.

"So what happens now?" Alex asked.

And as I stood there, at the very spot where this crazy case had begun, a thought occurred to me. A lot of the emotional loose ends from my life had finally been buried, too. In a lot of ways I'd be starting over.

Judging by the phone calls, I'd have plenty of work as a detective. And, if you can believe Elliot, I might actually be able to sell a book or two.

To be perfectly honest, I can't wait to see what happens next.

James L. Conway has enjoyed a long and distinguished career in Hollywood as a writer, producer, director and studio executive. James lives in Los Angeles with his wife and two daughters. *Dead and Not So Buried* is his first novel.

You can find James online at www.jameslconway.com.